THE LIGHT BEHIND
THE WINDOW

THE LIGHT BEHIND THE WINDOW

Lucinda Riley

WINDSOR
PARAGON

First published 2012
by Pan Books
This Large Print edition published 2013
by AudioGO Ltd
by arrangement with
Pan Macmillan Ltd

Hardcover   ISBN: 978 1 4713 2021 7
Softcover   ISBN: 978 1 4713 2022 4

British Library Cataloguing in Publication Data available

Printed and bound in Great Britain by
MPG Books Group Limited

For Olivia

'What you are, you are by accident of birth; what I am, I am by myself.'

Ludwig Van Beethoven

The Light Behind the Window

Unbroken night;
Darkness is the world I know.
Heavy burden;
No lights behind the window glow.

Softer day;
A hand reached out amidst the gloom.
Touching gently;
Spreading warmth across the room.

Twilight hours;
Shadows ebb and flow from you.
Secret longing;
Heart grows tender, beats anew.

Unbroken light;
Darkness was the world I knew
Burning brightly;
Glowing with my love for you.

Sophia de la Martinières,
July 1943

1

Gassin, South of France, Spring 1998

Emilie felt the pressure on her hand relax and looked down at her mother. As she watched, it seemed that, whilst Valérie's soul departed her body, the pain which had contorted her features was disappearing too, enabling Emilie to look past the emaciated face and remember the beauty her mother had once possessed.

'She has left us,' murmured Phillipe, the doctor, pointlessly.

'Yes.'

Behind her, she heard the doctor muttering a prayer, but had no thought to join him in it. Instead, she stared down in morbid wonder at the sack of slowly greying flesh which was all that remained of the presence that had dominated her life for thirty years. Emilie instinctively wanted to prod her mother awake, because the transition from life to death—given the force of nature Valérie de la Martinières had been—was too much for her senses to accept.

She wasn't sure how she should feel. After all, she had played this moment over in her head on many occasions in the past few weeks. Emilie turned away from her dead mother's face and gazed out of the window at the wisps of cloud suspended like uncooked meringues in the blue sky. Through the open window, she could hear the faint cry of a lark come to herald the spring.

Rising slowly, her legs stiff from the long night-time hours she had been sitting vigil, she walked over to the window. The early-morning vista had none of the heaviness that the passing of the hours would eventually bring. Nature had painted a fresh picture as it did every dawn, the soft Provençal palette of umber, green and azure gently ushering in the new day. Emilie gazed across the terrace and the formal gardens to the undulating vineyards that surrounded the house and spread across the earth for as far as her eye could see. The view was simply magnificent and had remained unchanged for centuries. Château de la Martinières had been her sanctuary as a child, a place of peace and safety; its tranquillity was indelibly printed into every synapse of her brain.

And now it was hers—though whether her mother had left anything behind from her financial excesses to continue to fund its upkeep, Emilie did not know.

'Mademoiselle Emilie, I'll leave you alone so you may say goodbye.' The doctor's voice broke into her thoughts. 'I'll take myself downstairs to fill out the necessary form. I am so very sorry,' he added as he gave her a small bow and left the room.

Am I sorry . . . ?

The question flashed unbidden through Emilie's mind. She walked back to the chair and sat down once more, trying to find answers to the many questions her mother's death posed, wanting a resolution, to add and subtract the conflicting emotional columns to produce a definitive feeling. This was, of course, impossible. The woman who lay so pathetically still—so harmless to her now, yet such a confusing influence whilst she had lived—would always bring the discomfort of complexity.

Valérie had given her daughter life, she had fed and clothed her and provided a substantial roof over Emilie's head. She had never beaten or abused her.

She simply had not noticed her.

Valérie had been—Emilie searched for the word—*disinterested.* Which had rendered her, as her daughter, invisible.

Emilie reached out her hand and put it on top of her mother's.

'You didn't see me, Maman . . . you didn't see . . .'

Emilie was painfully aware that her birth had been a reluctant nod to the need to produce an heir for the de la Martinières line; a requirement contrived out of duty, not maternal desire for a child. And faced with an 'heiress' rather than the requisite male, Valérie had been further disinterested. Too old to conceive again—Emilie had been born in the very last flush of her mother's fertility at forty-three—Valérie had continued her life as one of Paris's most charming, generous and beautiful hostesses. Emilie's birth and subsequent presence had seemed to hold as much importance for her as the acquisition of a further chihuahua to add to the three she already owned. Like the dogs, Emilie was produced from the nursery and petted in company when it suited Maman to do so. At least the dogs had the comfort of each other, Emilie mused, whereas she had spent vast tracts of her childhood alone.

Nor had it helped that she'd inherited the de la Martinières features rather than the delicate,

3

petite blondness of her mother's Slavic ancestors. She had been a stocky child, her olive skin and thick mahogany hair—trimmed every six weeks into a bob, the fringe forming a heavy line above her dark eyebrows—a genetic gift from her father, Édouard.

'I look at you sometimes, my dear, and can hardly believe you are the child I gave birth to!' her mother would comment on one of her rare visits to the nursery on her way out to the opera. 'But at least you have my eyes.'

Emilie wished sometimes she could tear the deep-blue orbs out of their sockets and replace them with her father's beautiful hazel eyes. She didn't think they fitted in her face and, besides, every time she looked through them into the mirror, she saw her mother.

It had often seemed to Emilie that she had been born without any gift her mother might value. Taken to ballet lessons at the age of three, Emilie found that her body refused to contort itself into the required positions. As the other little girls fluttered around the studio like butterflies, she struggled to find physical grace. Her small, wide feet enjoyed being planted firmly on the earth and any attempt to separate them from it resulted in failure. Piano lessons had been equally unsuccessful and as for singing, she was tone deaf.

Neither did her body accommodate well the feminine dresses her mother insisted she wore if a soirée was taking place in the exquisite, rose-filled garden at the back of the Paris house—the setting for Valérie's famous parties. Tucked away on a seat in the corner, Emilie would marvel at the elegant, charming and beautiful woman floating

4

between her guests with such gracious professionalism. During the many social occasions at the Paris house and then in the summer at the château in Gassin, Emilie would feel tongue-tied and uncomfortable. On top of everything else, it seemed she had not inherited her mother's social ease.

And yet, to the outsider, it would have seemed she'd had everything. A fairy-tale childhood—living in a beautiful house in Paris, her family from a long line of French nobility stretching back centuries *and* with the inherited wealth still intact after the war years—it was a scenario that many other young French girls could only dream of.

At least she'd had her beloved Papa. Although no more attentive to her than Maman, due to his obsession with his ever-growing collection of rare books which he kept at the château, when Emilie did manage to catch his attention he gave her the love and affection she craved.

Papa had been sixty when she was born and died when she was fourteen. Time spent together had been rare, but Emilie had understood that much of her personality was derived from him. Édouard was quiet and thoughtful, preferring his books and the peace of the château to the constant flow of acquaintances Maman brought into their homes. Emilie had often pondered just how two such polar opposites had fallen in love in the first place. Yet Édouard seemed to adore his younger wife, made no complaint at her lavish lifestyle, even though he lived more frugally himself, and was proud of her beauty and popularity on the Paris social scene.

Often, when summer had come to an end and it

was time for Valérie and Emilie to return to Paris, Emilie would beg her father to let her stay.

'Papa, I love it here in the countryside with you. There is a school in the village . . . I could go there and look after you, because you must be so lonely here at the château by yourself.'

Édouard would chuck her chin affectionately, but shake his head. 'No, little one. As much as I love you, you must return to Paris to learn both your lessons and how to become a lady like your mother.'

'But, Papa, I don't want to go back with Maman, I want to stay here, with you . . .'

And then, when she was thirteen . . . Emilie blinked away sudden tears, still unable to return to the moment when her mother's disinterest had turned to neglect. She would suffer the consequences of it for the rest of her life.

'How *could* you not see or care what was happening to me, Maman? I was your daughter!'

A sudden flicker of one of Valérie's eyes caused Emilie to jump in fear that, in fact, Maman was still alive after all and had heard the words she had just spoken. Trained to know the signs, Emilie checked Valérie's wrist for a pulse and found none. It was, of course, the last physical vestige of life as her muscles relaxed into death.

'Maman, I will try to forgive you. I will try to understand, but just now I cannot say whether I'm happy or sad that you are dead.' Emilie could feel her own breathing stiffening, a defence mechanism against the pain of speaking the words out loud. 'I loved you so much, tried so hard to please you, to gain your love and attention, to feel . . . *worthy* as your daughter. My God! I did everything!' Emilie

6

balled her hands into fists. 'You were my *mother*!'

The sound of her own voice echoing across the vast bedroom shocked her into silence. She stared at the de la Martinières family crest, painted two hundred and fifty years ago onto the majestic headboard. Fading now, the two wild boars locked in combat with the ubiquitous fleur-de-lis and the motto, 'Victory Is All', emblazoned below, were barely legible.

She shivered suddenly, although the room was warm. The silence in the château was deafening. A house once filled with life was now an empty husk, housing only the past. She glanced down at the signet ring on the smallest finger of her right hand, depicting the family crest in miniature. She was the last surviving de la Martinières.

Emilie felt the sudden weight of centuries of ancestors upon her shoulders, and the sadness of a great and noble lineage reduced to one unmarried and childless thirty-year-old woman. The family had borne the ravages of hundreds of years of brutality but, in the space of fifty years, the First and Second World Wars had seen only her father survive.

At least there would be none of the usual scrapping over the inheritance. Due to an outdated Napoleonic law, all brothers and sisters directly inherited their parents' property equally. Many was the family who had been brought to near ruin by one child who refused to agree to sell. Sadly, in this case, *les héritiers en ligne directe* amounted simply to her.

Emilie sighed. Sell she might have to, but those were thoughts for another day. Now it was time to say goodbye.

7

'Rest in peace, Maman.' She placed a light kiss on top of the greying forehead then crossed herself. Rising wearily from the chair, Emilie left the room, closing the door firmly behind her.

2

Two Weeks Later

Emilie took her café au lait and croissant out through the kitchen door and into the lavender-filled courtyard at the back of the house. The château faced due south, so this spot was the best place to catch the morning sun. It was a beautiful, balmy spring day, mild enough to be outside in a T-shirt.

On the afternoon of her mother's funeral in Paris, forty-eight hours ago, the rain had fallen relentlessly as Valérie was interred. At the wake afterwards—held at the Ritz as per Valérie's request—Emilie had accepted condolences from the great and the good. The women, mostly of a similar age to her mother, were all in black and had reminded Emilie of a coven of elderly crows. A variety of ancient hats disguised their thinning hair as they'd tottered around sipping champagne, bodies emaciated by age, make-up plastered mask-like to their sagging skin.

In their heyday, they had been regarded as the most beautiful and powerful women in Paris. Yet the circle of life had moved them on and they'd been replaced by a whole new raft of young movers and shakers. Each one of the women was simply waiting to die, Emilie had thought, feeling maudlin as she'd left the Ritz and hailed a taxi to take her home to her apartment. Utterly miserable, she had drunk far more wine than usual and woken the next morning with a hangover.

But at least the worst was over, Emilie comforted herself, as she took a sip of her coffee. In the past two weeks, there'd been little time to concentrate on anything other than the funeral arrangements. She'd known that at least she owed her mother the kind of send-off that Valérie herself would have organised perfectly. Emilie had found herself agonising over whether to provide cupcakes or petits fours with the coffee, and if the creamy, overblown roses her mother had so loved were dramatic enough for the table decorations. These were the kind of subtle decisions Valérie had taken every week and Emilie had a new-found grudging respect for the ease with which she'd handled it.

And now—Emilie turned her face up towards the sun and basked in its comforting warmth—she must think about the future.

Gerard Flavier, the family *notaire*, who looked after the de la Martinières's legal and property affairs, was on his way from Paris to meet her here at the château. Until he divulged where the estate stood financially, there wasn't much point in making plans. Emilie had taken a month's leave from work to deal with what she knew would be a complex and time-consuming process. She wished she had siblings to share the burden with; legalities and finances were not her strong point. The responsibility terrified her.

Emilie felt the softness of fur against her bare

9

ankle, glanced down and saw Frou-Frou, her mother's last remaining chihuahua, gazing up at her mournfully. She picked up the elderly dog and sat her on her knee, stroking her ears.

'It seems there is only you and me left, Frou,' she murmured. 'So we'll have to look after each other, won't we?'

The earnest expression in Frou-Frou's half-blind eyes made Emilie smile. She had no idea how she was to care for the dog in the future. Even though she dreamed of one day surrounding herself with animals, her tiny apartment in the Marais Quarter and the long hours she worked were not conducive to looking after a dog who had been brought up in the emotional and physical lap of luxury.

Yet animals and the care of them were her day job. Emilie lived for her vulnerable clients, none of whom could express to her how they felt or where it hurt.

'It is sad that my daughter seems to prefer the company of animals to human beings . . .'

The words epitomised Valérie's feelings towards the way Emilie lived her life. When she had originally announced she wished to go to university and take a degree in veterinary science, Valérie had shaped her lips into a moue of distaste. 'I cannot understand why you would wish to spend your life cutting open poor little animals and gazing at their insides.'

'Maman, that's the process, not the reason. I love animals, I want to help them,' she had answered defensively.

'If you must have a career, then why not think about fashion? I have a friend at *Marie Claire* magazine who I'm sure could find you a little job.

10

Of course, when you marry, you will not wish to continue working. You will become a wife and that will be your life.'

Although Emilie did not blame Valérie for being stuck in her time warp, she couldn't help wishing her mother had taken some pride in her daughter's achievements. She'd come out of university top of her year and been taken on immediately as a trainee vet by a well-known Paris practice.

'Maybe Maman was right, Frou,' she said with a sigh, 'maybe I do prefer animals to people.'

Emilie heard the crunch of gravel under tyres, put Frou-Frou on the ground and walked round to the front of the house to greet Gerard.

'Emilie, how are you?' Gerard Flavier kissed her on both cheeks.

'I'm all right, thank you,' Emilie replied. 'How was your journey?'

'I took a plane to Nice and then hired a car to bring me down here,' Gerard said as he walked past her through the front door and stood in the vast hall, the closed shutters shrouding it in shadow. 'I was happy to escape from Paris and visit one of my favourite places in France. Spring in the Var is always exquisite.'

'I thought it was better we meet here at the château,' agreed Emilie. 'My parents' papers are in the desk in the library and I presumed you would need access to them.'

'Yes.' Gerard walked across the worn marble-tiled floor and surveyed a damp patch on the ceiling above them. 'The château is in need of some tender loving care, is it not?' He sighed. 'It's ageing, like us all.'

'Shall we go through to the kitchen?' Emilie

11

suggested. 'I have some coffee ready.'

'That's just what I need,' said Gerard with a smile as he followed her along the corridor which led to the back of the house.

'Please, sit down,' she said, indicating a chair at the long oak table and walking over to the range to reboil some water.

'There aren't many luxuries in here, are there?' said Gerard, studying the sparsely furnished, utilitarian space.

'No,' agreed Emilie. 'But then, this was only used by the servants to provide food for our family and their guests. I'd doubt my mother ever put her hands in the sink.'

'Who takes care of the château and its domestic needs now?' asked Gerard.

'Margaux Duvall, the housekeeper, who's been here for over fifteen years. She comes in from the village every afternoon. Maman dismissed the other staff after my father died and she stopped coming down to the house regularly each summer. I think she preferred to holiday on the yacht she rented.'

'Your mother certainly liked to spend money,' said Gerard as Emilie put a cup of coffee down in front of him. 'On the things that mattered to her,' he added.

'Which was not this château,' Emilie stated bluntly.

'No,' he agreed. 'From what I've seen of her finances so far, it seemed she preferred the delights of the house of Chanel.'

'Maman was fond of her haute couture, I know.' Emilie sat down opposite him with her coffee. 'Even last year when she was so ill, she still attended the fashion shows.'

'Valérie was indeed quite a character—and famous too. Her passing engendered many column inches in our newspapers,' he said. 'Although it's hardly surprising. The de la Martinières are one of the most noted families in France.'

'I know,' Emilie grimaced, 'I saw the newspapers as well. Apparently I'm to inherit a fortune.'

'It's true that your family were once fabulously rich. Unfortunately, Emilie, times have moved on. The noble name of your family still exists, but the fortune does not.'

'I thought as much.' Emilie was unsurprised.

'You may have been aware that your papa was not a businessman,' Gerard continued. 'He was an intellectual, an academic who had little interest in money. Even though many times I talked to him of investments, tried to persuade him to plan a little for the future, he was uninterested. Twenty years ago, it hardly mattered—there was plenty. But between your father's lack of attention and your mother's penchant for the finer things in life, the fortune has diminished substantially.' Gerard sighed. 'I'm sorry to be the bearer of bad tidings.'

'I was very much expecting this and it doesn't matter to me,' Emilie confirmed. 'I simply wish to organise what I need to and return to my work in Paris.'

'I'm afraid, Emilie, that the situation is not as straightforward as that. As I said at the start, I've not yet had time to peruse the details, but what I can tell you is that the estate has creditors, many of them. And these creditors must be paid as soon as possible,' he explained. 'Your mother managed to accrue an overdraft of almost twenty million francs against the Paris house. She had many other debts too, which will need to be paid off.'

'Twenty million francs?' Emilie was horrified. 'How could this have happened?'

'Easily. As the funds ran out, Valérie did not temper her lifestyle accordingly. She has been living on borrowed money for many, many years now. Please, Emilie—' Gerard saw the expression in her eyes—'do not panic. These are debts that can easily be paid, not only with the sale of the Paris house itself, which I believe should raise around seventy million francs, but also its contents. For example, your mother's magnificent collection of jewellery, which is held in a vault at her bank, and the many paintings and valuable objets d'art in the house. You are by no means poor, Emilie, believe me, but action must be taken swiftly to stop the rot and decisions for the future made.'

'I see,' Emilie answered slowly. 'Forgive me, Gerard. I take after my father and have little interest or experience in managing finances.'

'I understand completely. Your parents have left you with a heavy burden that rests purely on your shoulders. Although—' Gerard raised his eyebrows—'it's amazing how many relatives you suddenly seem to have acquired.'

'What do you mean?'

'Oh, you mustn't worry, it's usual for the vultures to descend at this time. I've had over twenty letters so far, from those who claim they are related in some way to the de la Martinières. Four hitherto unknown illegitimate brothers and sisters, apparently sired by your father out of wedlock, two cousins, an uncle and a member of

14

staff from your parents' Paris household in the Sixties, who swears she was promised by your mother to be the recipient of a Picasso on her death.' Gerard smiled. 'It's all to be expected but, unfortunately, every claim must be investigated under French law.'

'You don't think any of them are valid?' Emilie's eyes were wide.

'I highly doubt it. And if it's any comfort to you, this has happened with every well-publicised death I have ever dealt with.' He shrugged. 'Leave it to me, and don't worry. I would prefer you, Emilie, to concentrate your thoughts on what you wish to do with the château. As I said, your mother's debts can easily be paid off with the sale of the Paris house and its contents. But that still leaves you with this magnificent property, which, from what I've seen so far, is in a bad state of repair. Whatever you decide, you will still be a wealthy woman, but do you want to sell this château or not?'

Emilie stared into the distance and sighed heavily. 'To be honest, Gerard, I wish the whole thing would go away. That someone else could make the decision. And what about the vineyards here? Is the *cave* producing any profit?' she asked.

'Again, that's something I must investigate for you,' said Gerard. 'If you decide to sell the château, the wine business can be included as a going concern.'

'Sell the château . . .' Emilie repeated Gerard's words. Hearing them spoken out loud underlined the enormity of the responsibilities she had to face. 'This house has been in our family for two hundred and fifty years. And now it's down to me to make the decision. And the truth is,' she sighed, 'I have no idea what to do for the best.'

'I'm sure you don't. As I said earlier, it's difficult that you are all alone.' Gerard shook his head in sympathy. 'What can I say? We cannot always choose the situation we find ourselves in. I'll try to help you as much as I can, Emilie, I know it's what your father would have wanted from me under these circumstances. Now, I'll go and freshen up, and then maybe later we should take a walk down to the vineyard and speak to the manager there?'

'OK,' Emilie replied wearily. 'I've opened the shutters in the bedroom to the left of the main staircase. It has one of the best views in the house. Would you like me to show you?'

'No, thank you. I've stayed here many times before, as you know. I can find my own way.'

Gerard rose, nodded at Emilie and walked out of the kitchen to climb the main staircase to his bedroom. He paused halfway up, staring at the dusty, faded face of a de la Martinières ancestor. So many of the noble French families, and the history attached to them, were dying out, leaving a barely visible line in the sand to mark their passing. He wondered how the great Giles de la Martinières in the portrait—warrior, nobleman and, some said, lover of Marie Antoinette—would feel if he could see the future of his lineage resting on the slight shoulders of one young woman. And a woman who had always struck Gerard as odd.

During his many visits to the de la Martinières households in the past, Gerard had beheld a plain child, whose self-containment did not allow her to respond to affection from him or others. A child who seemed removed, distant, almost surly in her

16

reticence to his friendly approaches. As a *notaire*, Gerard felt his work not only encompassed the technical process of working on columns of figures, but also the ability to read the emotions of his clients.

Emilie de la Martinières was an enigma.

He had watched her at her mother's funeral and her face had betrayed nothing. Granted, she had become far more attractive in adulthood than she had been as a child. Yet even now, downstairs, faced with the loss of her one remaining parent and the responsibility of terrible decisions, Gerard had not found her vulnerable. The existence she led in Paris could not be further removed from that of her ancestors. She lived an unremarkable life. And yet, everything about her parents and the history of her family *was* remarkable.

Gerard continued up the stairs, irritated by her muted responses. There was something missing . . . something about her that was unreachable. And he had no idea how to find it.

*   *   *

As Emilie stood up and put the coffee cups in the sink, the kitchen door opened and Margaux, the château housekeeper, stepped through the door. Her face lit up as she saw Emilie.

'Mademoiselle Emilie!' Margaux moved to embrace her. 'I didn't know you were coming! You should have told me. I would have prepared everything for you.'

'I arrived from Paris late last night,' explained Emilie. 'It's good to see you, Margaux.'

Margaux drew back and studied Emilie,

sympathy in her eyes. 'How are you?'

'I am . . . coping,' Emilie answered honestly, the sight of Margaux, who had cared for her when she was a young girl staying at the château in the summer, bringing a lump to her throat.

'You look skinny. Are you not eating?' Margaux appraised her.

'Of course I'm eating, Margaux! Besides, it's unlikely that I'll ever fade away.' Emilie smiled wanly, sweeping her hands down her body.

'You have a lovely shape—wait until you're like me!' Margaux indicated her own plump figure and chuckled.

Emilie looked at the fading blue eyes and blonde hair, now streaked with grey. She remembered Margaux fifteen years ago as a beautiful woman, and felt further depressed at how time destroyed all in its ever-hungry path.

The kitchen door opened again. Through it appeared a young boy, slight of figure, with his mother's huge blue eyes dominating his elfin face. He looked in surprise at Emilie and then turned to his mother nervously.

'Maman? Is it all right for me to be here?' he asked Margaux.

'Do you mind if Anton is here in the château with me while I work, Mademoiselle Emilie? It's the Easter holidays and I don't like to leave him at home by himself. He normally sits quietly with a book.'

'Of course it's not a problem,' Emilie replied, smiling at the young boy reassuringly. Margaux had lost her husband eight years ago in a car crash. Since then, she had struggled to bring up her son alone. 'I think there's just enough room here for all of us, don't you?'

'Yes, Mademoiselle Emilie. Thank you,' Anton said gratefully, walking towards his mother.

'Gerard Flavier, our *notaire*, is upstairs. He'll be staying overnight, Margaux,' Emilie added. 'We're going down to the vineyard to see Jean and Jacques.'

'Then I'll prepare his bedroom whilst you're gone. Should I get some food ready for your supper?'

'No, thank you, we'll go up to the village to eat later,' Emilie replied.

'There are some bills that have arrived for the house, Mademoiselle. Should I give them to you?' Margaux asked, embarrassed.

'Yes, of course.' Emilie sighed. 'There's no one else to pay them.'

'No. I'm so sorry, Mademoiselle. It's hard for you to be left alone. I know so well how it feels,' Margaux sympathised.

'Yes, thank you. I'll see you later, Margaux.' Emilie nodded at mother and son and left the kitchen to find Gerard.

*   *   *

That afternoon, Emilie accompanied Gerard to the *cave*. The vineyard on the de la Martinières domaine was a small operation on ten hectares, producing twelve thousand bottles of the palest rosé, red and white a year, mostly sold to local shops, restaurants and hotels.

Inside, the *cave* was dark and cool, the smell of fermenting wine permeating the air from the huge Russian oak barrels lined up along its sides.

Jean Benoit, the *cave* manager, stood up from behind his desk as they entered.

'Mademoiselle Emilie! It's a pleasure to see you.' Jean kissed her warmly on both cheeks. 'Papa, look who's here!'

Jacques Benoit, now in his late eighties and stiff with rheumatism, but who still sat at a table in the *cave* every day, painstakingly wrapping each bottle of wine in purple tissue paper, looked up and smiled. 'Mademoiselle Emilie, how are you?'

'I'm well, thank you, Jacques. And you?'

'Ah, no longer up to hunting the wild boar your papa and I used to catch on the hills.' He chuckled. 'But I still manage to find myself breathing each sunrise.'

Emilie felt a surge of pleasure at both the warmth of their greeting and their familiarity. Her father had been great friends with Jacques, and Emilie had often cycled off to the nearby beach at Gigaro for a swim with Jean, who, being eight years older than her, had seemed very grown up. Emilie had sometimes fantasised that he was her older brother. Jean had always been so protective and kind towards her. He had lost his mother, Francesca, when he was young and Jacques had done his best to bring him up alone.

Both father and son, and their ancestors before them, had grown up in the small cottage attached to the *cave*. Jean now managed the vineyard, taking over from his father once Jacques was satisfied Jean had learned his special methods of mixing, then fermenting the grapes from the vines that surrounded them.

Emilie realised that Gerard was hovering behind them, looking uncomfortable. Pulling herself from her reverie, she said, 'This is Gerard Flavier, our family *notaire*.'

'I believe we've met before, Monsieur, many years ago,' said Jacques, holding out a trembling hand to him.

'Yes, and I still taste the subtlety of the wine you make here when I'm back in Paris,' remarked Gerard, smiling.

'You are most kind, Monsieur,' said Jacques, 'but I believe my son is even more of an artist when it comes to producing the perfect Provençal rosé.'

'I presume, Monsieur Flavier, that you're here to check the financial facts and figures of our *cave*, rather than the quality of our produce?' Jean was looking uneasy.

'I would certainly like some idea of whether the business is financially productive for my analysis,' confirmed Gerard. 'I'm afraid that Mademoiselle Emilie must make some decisions.'

'Well,' said Emilie, 'I think I'm of little use here for now, so I'll take a walk through the vineyards.' She nodded at the three men and immediately left the *cave*.

As she walked outside, she realised her own discomfort was heightened by the fact that the decisions she must make would endanger the Benoit family's livelihood. Their way of life had remained unchanged for hundreds of years. She could tell that Jean, in particular, was very concerned, understanding the ramifications if she did sell. A new owner might install a manager of his own, and Jean and Jacques would be forced to leave their home. She could hardly imagine such a change, for the Benoits seemed to grow out of the very soil she was standing on.

The sun was already on its descent as Emilie walked over the stony ground between the rows of fragile vines. In the following few weeks, they would grow like weeds to produce the fat, sweet fruit that would be picked in the *vendange* of late summer to produce next year's vintage.

She turned to look at the château, three hundred metres in the distance, and sighed despairingly. Its pale, blush-covered walls, the shutters painted a traditional light blue and framed by tall cypress trees on either side, melted into the softness of the approaching sunset. Simply yet elegantly designed to fit in with its rural surroundings, the house reflected perfectly the understated yet noble lineage both of them had been born from.

And we are all that is left . . .

Emilie felt a sudden tenderness for the building. It had been orphaned too. Recognised, but ignored in terms of its basic needs, yet maintaining an air of graceful dignity under duress—she felt an odd camaraderie with it.

'How can I give you what you need?' she whispered to the château. 'What do I do with you? I have a life elsewhere, I . . .' Emilie sighed and then heard her name being called.

Gerard was walking towards her. He came to stand next to her and followed her eyeline towards the château.

'It is beautiful, isn't it?' he said.

'Yes, it is. But I have no idea what I should do with it.'

'Why don't we walk back and I'll give you my thoughts on the matter, which may or may not be of help to you,' Gerard suggested.

'Thank you.'

*   *   *

Twenty minutes later, as the sun made its final departure behind the hill which accommodated the medieval village of Gassin, Emilie sat with Gerard and listened to what he had to say.

'The vineyard is under-producing what it could, in terms of both yield and profit. There has been an international surge in sales of rosé in the past few years. It's no longer thought of as the poor relation to its white and red sister and brother. Jean is expecting, as long as the weather conditions remain stable in the next few weeks, to produce a bumper crop. The point is, Emilie,' Gerard explained, 'the *cave* has always been run very much as a hobby by the de la Martinières.'

'Yes, I realise that,' Emilie agreed.

'Jean—who I was extremely impressed with, by the way—said no investment funds have been provided for the vineyard since your father died sixteen years ago. It was, of course, originally established to provide the château itself with a home-grown supply of wine. In its heyday, when your ancestors were entertaining here in the old, grand style, much of the wine would have been consumed by them and their guests. Now, of course, everything's different, yet the vineyard is still running as it did a hundred years ago.'

Gerard looked at Emilie for a reaction, but received none, so he continued.

'What the *cave* needs is an injection of cash to fulfil its potential. Jean tells me, for example, that

23

there's enough land to double the size of the vineyards. It also needs some modern equipment to be brought up to date and produce, Jean believes, a healthy profit. The question is,' summarised Gerard, 'whether you wish to carry the vineyard and the château into the future. They are both renovation projects and would take up much of your time.'

Emilie listened to the stillness. Not a breath of wind blew. The calm atmosphere wrapped a warm shawl of tranquillity around her. For the first time since her mother had died, Emilie felt at peace. And, therefore, disinclined to come to a conclusion.

'Thank you for your help so far, Gerard. But I don't think it's possible to give you an answer right now,' she explained. 'If you'd asked me two weeks ago, I would have categorically told you my inclination was to sell. But now . . .'

'I understand,' Gerard said with a nod. 'I can't advise you emotionally, Emilie, only financially. Perhaps it would be a comfort for you to know that, when you sell the Paris house, its contents and your mother's jewellery, I believe it would not only cover the cost of restoring the château but also leave you with a large income for the rest of your life. And, of course, there is the library here,' he added. 'Your papa may not have spent his energies on the fabric of either of his homes, but his legacy is housed inside. He built on what was already a fine collection of rare books. Having glanced earlier at the ledgers he kept, he seems to have doubled it. Antiquarian books are not my field of expertise, but I can only imagine the collection is very valuable.'

'I would never part with it,' replied Emilie firmly, surprising herself with her sudden defensiveness. 'It was my father's life's work. I spent many hours here in the library with him as a child.'

'Of course, and there's no reason why you should. Although, if you decide not to keep the château, you may have to find somewhere larger than your Paris apartment to house the collection.' Gerard smiled wryly. 'Now, I must eat. Will you accompany me to the village for supper? I leave early tomorrow, and I must, with your permission, investigate the contents of your father's desk to acquire any further financial papers.'

'Of course,' Emilie agreed.

'First, I must make a couple of calls,' he said apologetically, 'but I'll see you down here in half an hour.'

Emilie watched Gerard as he left the table and walked into the house. She felt awkward in his company, even though he had been present throughout her life. She had treated him then as any child would a distant adult. Now, with a third party no longer present, having a direct conversation with him was a new and uncomfortable experience.

As she wandered inside, Emilie realised she felt patronised, although she understood that Gerard was merely trying to help. But, sometimes, she saw in his eyes what she could only read as resentment. Perhaps he felt—and who could blame him—that she was not in any way accomplished enough to receive the mantle of the last surviving de la Martinières, with all its weight of history. Emilie was painfully aware that she had none of the glamour of her predecessors. Born into an extraordinary family, her only wish was to appear ordinary.

3

Emilie heard Gerard's car making its way along the drive and away from the château early the next morning. She lay in the narrow bed she had slept in since childhood, the room's windows facing north-west so there was little early-morning sun. Of course, she mused, there was no reason why she could not now inhabit any one of the vast and beautiful bedrooms at the front of the house, with their huge windows facing out over the garden and vineyards.

Frou-Frou, who had whined so much last night that Emilie had relented and let her in to sleep on her bed, barked at the door to signal it was time for her morning ablutions.

Downstairs in the kitchen, Emilie made herself some coffee then wandered along the passage to the library. The high-ceilinged room, which her father had always kept shrouded from light to protect the books, smelt comfortingly fusty and familiar. Placing her coffee on her father's worn, leather-topped desk, she walked to a window and drew back one of the shutters. A million dust motes left their hiding places at the sudden and unusual breeze, and danced frenziedly in the soft shafts of light.

Emilie sat down on the window seat and studied the floor-to-ceiling bookshelves. She had no idea how many books the library contained. Her father had spent most of his latter years cataloguing and adding to the collection. She stood up and walked slowly around the sides of the room, the books stretching up to four times her height. Sentinel and stoic, she felt as if they were surveying her—their new mistress—and wondering what fate would befall them.

Emilie remembered sitting with her father and playing the Alphabet Game, which entailed her choosing two letters from the alphabet of any combination. When she had chosen them, her father would move around the library searching for an author whose book held those initials. Only very rarely had he failed to produce a book from the two letters Emilie had given him. Even when she tried to be clever with Xs and Zs, her father would manage to procure a fading, battered copy of Chinese philosophy, or a slim anthology by a long-forgotten Russian poet.

Though she'd watched Édouard do this for years, Emilie now wished she'd paid more attention to the eclectic methods her father had of cataloguing and filing the books. As she glanced at the shelves, she knew it was not as simple as alphabetical order. On the shelf in front of her, the books ranged from Dickens to Plato to Guy de Maupassant.

She also knew the collection was so extensive that any cataloguing her father had completed in the ledgers stacked on the desk would have barely scratched the surface. Even though *he* had known where to place his hands on a book almost immediately, it was a skill and a secret Édouard had taken with him to his grave.

'If I'm to sell this house, what would I do with you?' she whispered to the books.

They gazed back at her silently; thousands of forlorn children who knew their future lay in her hands. Emilie shook herself from her reverie of the past. She could not let emotion sway her. If she decided to sell the château, then the books must be found another home. Closing the shutter and returning the books to their shrouded slumber, she left the library.

*   *   *

Emilie spent the rest of the morning exploring the endless nooks and crannies of the château, suddenly appreciating a wonderful 200-year-old frieze that adorned the ceiling in the magnificent drawing room, the elegant but now shabby French furniture and the many paintings that hung on every wall.

At lunchtime, Emilie made her way into the kitchen to pour herself a glass of water. She drank it thirstily, realising she felt breathless and exhilarated, as if she'd woken up from a bad dream. The beauty she'd seen so clearly for the first time this morning had been around her for the whole of her life, yet she had never thought to appreciate it or give it credence. And now, rather than seeing her inheritance and her family lineage as a rope around her neck from which she wished to be free, she was experiencing the first traces of excitement.

This wonderful house, with its wealth of exquisite objects, was *hers*.

Feeling suddenly hungry, Emilie rooted around

in the fridge and the kitchen cupboards, but to no avail. Taking Frou-Frou under her arm, she put the little dog in the car next to her and drove towards Gassin. Having parked the car, she walked up the ancient steep steps through the village to the hilltop boulevard that housed the bars and restaurants, and took a table at the edge of the terrace in order to admire the spectacular coastal view below her. Ordering a small jug of rosé and a house salad, she basked in the strong lunchtime sun, thoughts circling in no particular order around her head.

'Excuse me, Mademoiselle, but are you Emilie de la Martinières?'

Shading her eyes from the strong sunlight, Emilie looked up at the man standing by her table.

'Yes?' She looked askance at him.

'Then I'm pleased to make your acquaintance.' The man held out his hand. 'My name is Sebastian Carruthers.'

Emilie reached out a tentative hand to his in return. 'Do I know you?'

'No, you don't.'

Emilie noticed he spoke excellent French, but with an English accent. 'Then may I ask how you know me?' she said, imperious out of nerves.

'It's a long story, and one I would like to share with you at some point. Are you expecting company?' he asked, indicating the empty chair opposite her.

'I . . . no.' Emilie shook her head.

'Then may I sit down and explain?'

Before Emilie had a chance to demur, Sebastian had pulled out the chair opposite her. Without the sunlight blinding her eyes, she studied him and saw that he was probably of a similar age to her, his good quality, casual clothes worn easily on a slim body. He had a smattering of freckles across his nose, chestnut hair and attractive hazel-coloured eyes.

'I'm sorry to hear of your mother's death,' he offered.

'Thank you.' Emilie took a sip of her wine and then, her engrained good manners surfacing, said, 'Can I offer you a glass of rosé?'

'That would be very kind.' Sebastian signalled for the waiter and caught his attention. A glass was placed in front of him and Emilie poured the wine into it from the jug.

'How did you hear of my mother's death?' she asked.

'It's hardly a secret in France, is it?' Sebastian answered, his eyes filling with empathy. 'She was rather well known. May I offer my condolences? It must be a difficult time for you.'

'Yes, it is,' she replied stiffly. 'So, you're English?'

'You guessed!' Sebastian rolled his eyes in mock horror. 'And I've worked so hard to lose my accent. Yes, I am, for my sins. But I spent a year in Paris studying Fine Art. And I admit to being a fully paid-up Francophile.'

'I see,' murmured Emilie. 'But . . .'

'Yes,' he agreed, 'that still doesn't explain how I knew you were Emilie de la Martinières. Well now—' Sebastian raised his eyes mysteriously— 'the connection between you and me goes back into the deep and distant past.'

'Are you a relation?' Emilie was reminded suddenly of the warning Gerard had given her only yesterday.

'No, most definitely not,' he said with a smile, 'but my grandmother was half French. I discovered recently that she worked closely with Édouard de la Martinières, who I believe was your father, during the Second World War.'

'I see.' Emilie knew almost nothing about her father's past. Only that he had never discussed it. And she was still nervous of what this Englishman wanted from her. 'I know little about that time of my father's life.'

'I didn't know much either until my grandmother told me, just before she died, that she was over here during the Occupation. She also said what a brave man Édouard was,' Sebastian added.

This revelation brought a sudden lump to Emilie's throat. 'I didn't know . . . You must understand that I was born when my father was sixty, more than twenty years after the war ended.'

'Right,' said Sebastian, nodding.

'Besides,' Emilie took a healthy gulp of wine, 'he was not the kind of man to ever boast about his triumphs.'

'Well, Constance, my grandmother, certainly seemed to hold him in high esteem,' Sebastian said. 'She also told me about the beautiful château in Gassin that she'd stayed in whilst she was in France. The house is very close to this village, isn't it?'

'Yes,' said Emilie as her salad arrived. 'Will you eat?' she asked, again out of politeness.

'If you're happy to have my company, yes.'

'Of course.'

Sebastian ordered and the waiter retreated.

'So, what brings you to Gassin?' Emilie queried.

'That's a very good question,' Sebastian said. 'After my degree in Fine Art in Paris, I went on to make the art business my career. I show from a small gallery in London, but spend much of my time searching for the rare paintings that my wealthy clients desire. I came to France to try to persuade the owner of a Chagall to sell it to me. The chap lives up in Grasse, which, as you know, isn't far from here,' he explained. 'I happened to read in the newspaper about your mother and that prodded my memory of my grandmother's association with your family. So I thought I'd stop off and take a look for myself at the château I'd heard so much about. This really is the most beautiful village.'

'Yes, it is,' she answered, nonplussed by this strange conversation.

'So, Emilie, do you live at the château?' Sebastian asked.

'No,' she replied, uncomfortable with his direct line of questioning. 'I currently live in Paris.'

'Where I have many friends,' Sebastian enthused. 'One day, I hope to spend more time in France, but for now I'm still establishing my reputation in the UK. Not being able to get my hands on the Chagall for my client is very disappointing. It would have been my first negotiation in the big league.'

'I'm sorry,' she offered.

'Thank you. I'll get over it. You wouldn't have any priceless paintings which you wanted to shift hanging around in that château of yours, would you?' Sebastian's eyes were full of humour.

'I'm not sure,' she replied truthfully. 'Valuing the

art in the château is on my list of things to do.'

'I'm sure you'll be using one of the top Paris experts to authenticate and value the collection. But if you needed a knowledgeable and very much on-the-spot eye to guide you in the interim, I would be happy to oblige.' As Sebastian's croque-monsieur arrived, he drew out his wallet and passed Emilie a card. 'Promise I'm kosher,' he emphasised. 'I can provide references from my clients if necessary.'

'It's very kind of you, but our family *notaire* is dealing with all that kind of thing.' Emilie could hear the hauteur in her voice.

'Of course,' he said, pouring them both some more rosé and tackling his croque-monsieur. 'So,' he swiftly changed the subject, 'what do you do with yourself in Paris?'

'I work as a vet in a large practice in the Marais Quarter. The money is not very good, but I love it,' she answered.

'Really?' Sebastian raised an eyebrow. 'I'm surprised. I'd have thought, coming from the family you do, that you'd be involved in something very glamorous, if you even needed to work at all.'

'Yes, that's what everyone assumes . . . I am sorry, but I really must go.' Emilie signalled hurriedly for the bill.

'I do apologise, Emilie, that sounded trite,' Sebastian said immediately. 'What I meant to say is, good on you! I really didn't mean to insult you.'

An urge to get away from this man and his persistent questions suddenly assailed her. Emilie reached for her bag, took some francs out of her purse and put them on the table. 'It was nice to meet you,' she said as she picked up Frou-Frou and walked smartly away from the table. She descended the steep stone steps towards her car as hurriedly as she could, feeling ridiculously shaken and tearful.

'Emilie! Please, wait!'

Taking no notice of the voice behind her, she continued walking down the steps determinedly until Sebastian caught up with her.

'Look,' he panted, 'I'm really sorry if I offended you. I seem to have a knack of doing that . . .' Sebastian kept pace with her as she continued walking. 'If it's any consolation, I was born with endless baggage too. Including a crumbling mansion on the Yorkshire moors that I'm meant to somehow restore and save, when there's not a bean to pay for it.'

They had reached the car and Emilie had no choice but to stand still. 'Then why don't you sell it?' she asked him.

'Because it's part of my heritage and—' he shrugged—'it's complicated. Anyway, I'm not throwing you a sob story, just trying to explain that I know how it is to be defined by your past. I'm there too.'

Emilie searched silently for the car key in her bag.

'I'm not trying to compete with you,' Sebastian continued, 'merely trying to say I empathise.'

'Thank you.' She'd found her car key. 'I must go now.'

'Am I forgiven?'

She turned and looked at him, despairing of her own sensitivity, yet unable to control it. 'I just . . .' She stared out across the verdant landscape below her, trying to find the words to explain. 'I want to

34

be judged for myself.'

'I understand, I really do. Look, I'm not going to hold you up any more, but it was a pleasure to meet you.' Sebastian held out his hand. 'Good luck with it all.'

'Thank you. Goodbye.' Emilie unlocked her car and released an irritated Frou-Frou onto the passenger seat. She climbed inside, started the engine and drove off slowly down the hill, trying to understand why she had reacted so violently. Perhaps, used as she was to the formal French protocol of a first meeting, Sebastian's openness had startled her. But, Emilie told herself, he had simply tried to be friendly. It was *she* who had the problem. Sebastian had pressed her most sensitive button and she'd reacted accordingly. Emilie watched him strolling down the hill a few metres ahead of her and felt guilty and embarrassed.

She was thirty years old, Emilie chastised herself. The de la Martinières estate was hers to do with as she wished. Perhaps it was time she began to behave like an adult, not a temperamental child.

As she drew the car adjacent with Sebastian, taking a deep breath, she wound down the window.

'As you've come all the way here to see the château, Sebastian, it would be disappointing if you didn't fulfil your goal. Why don't you let me drive you there?'

'If you're sure . . .' Sebastian's expression echoed the surprise in his voice. 'I mean, of course I'd love to see it, especially with someone who knows the house intimately.'

'Then, please, climb in.' She leant over and unlocked the passenger door for him.

'Thank you,' he said as he closed it behind him and they set off once more down the hill. 'I feel dreadful for upsetting you. Are you sure I'm forgiven?'

'Sebastian,' she sighed, 'it's not you who's at fault, it's me. Any mention of my family in that context is what I think a psychologist would call a "trigger". And I must learn to deal with it.'

'Well, we all have plenty of those, especially when we've had successful, powerful relatives who've gone before us.'

'My mother was certainly a strong character,' Emilie agreed. 'There's a space in many people's lives now she has passed away. As you said, it's a lot to live up to. And I've always known I couldn't.'

Emilie wondered whether the two glasses of wine at lunch had loosened her tongue. But she suddenly didn't feel uncomfortable telling him this. It thrilled and unnerved her at the same time.

'Well, I can hardly say the same of my mum, or "Victoria" as she insisted we called her,' said Sebastian. 'I can't even remember her. She gave birth to my brother and me at a hippy commune in the States. When I was three and my brother two, she arrived with us in England and dumped us both on my grandparents in Yorkshire. A few weeks later she took off again, leaving us behind. And she hasn't been seen or heard of since.'

'Oh, Sebastian!' Emilie responded, shocked. 'You don't even know if your mother is still alive?'

'No,' he confirmed, 'but our grandmother more than made up for it. Because we were so young when we were left with her, to all intents and purposes Constance *was* our mother. And I can honestly say that if my real mother ever appeared

36

in a crowded room in front of me, I wouldn't be able to spot her.'

'You were lucky to have your grandmother, but it's still very sad for you,' Emilie sympathised. 'And you don't even know who your father is?'

'No. Or, in fact, whether my brother and I share the same one. We're certainly very different. Anyway . . .' Sebastian stared into the distance.

'Did you know your grandfather?' she asked.

'He died when I was five. He was a fine man, but he'd been out in North Africa during the war and the injuries he sustained there made him very frail. My grandparents were devoted to each other. So my poor old granny not only lost her adored husband, but her daughter too. I think having us grandsons kept her going, actually,' said Sebastian. 'She was the most amazing woman, still drystone-walling at the age of seventy-five and hale and hearty until a week before she fell ill. I'm not sure they make them like her any more,' he mused, a timbre of sadness entering his voice. 'Sorry,' he said suddenly, 'I'm talking too much.'

'Not at all. It's comforting for me to know there are other people who have grown up in difficult circumstances. Sometimes—' Emilie sighed—'I think that having too much of a past is just as bad as having none at all.'

'I totally agree.' Sebastian nodded then grinned. 'Dearie me, if other people heard this conversation, they might think we were a couple of spoilt, privileged kids feeling sorry for ourselves. Let's face it, neither of us are on the streets, are we?'

'No. And of course it's what people would think. Especially of me,' she agreed. 'Why should they

not? They don't see what lies beneath. Look—'
she pointed—'the château is just down there.'

Sebastian gazed into the distance at the elegant,
pale-pink building nestling in the valley beneath
them. He let out a whistle. 'It's absolutely
beautiful, and just how my grandmother described
it to me. And rather a contrast to our family home
on the bleak moors of Yorkshire. Although the
rawness of the surroundings make Blackmoor Hall
spectacular in a different way,' he added.

Emilie turned into the long drive that led to the
château then steered along the side of the house to
park at the back. She pulled the car to a halt and
they climbed out.

'Are you sure you have time to show me
around?' Sebastian looked at her. 'I can always
come back another day.'

'No, it's fine,' Emilie assured him as she walked
with Frou-Frou towards the château and Sebastian
followed her through the lobby and into the
kitchen.

She took Sebastian from room to room,
watching as he paused continually, studying the
paintings, the furniture and the vast collection of
objets d'art that lay dusty and unvalued on the tops
of mantelpieces, bureaux and tables. She led him
into the morning room and, straight away,
Sebastian walked over to examine a painting.

'This reminds me of *Luxe, Calme et Volupté*,
which Matisse painted in 1904 when he was staying
in St Tropez. The stippled effect is similar.'
Sebastian traced his fingers just above the oil.
'Although this is a pure landscape of rocks and sea,
without the figures.'

'*Luxury, Peace and Pleasure*,' Emilie repeated in

38

English. 'I remember my father reading me Baudelaire's poem.'

'Yes.' Sebastian turned, his eyes bright with enthusiasm that she knew it. 'Matisse took *L'Invitation au Voyage* as his inspiration for the painting. It now hangs in the Musée National d'Art Moderne in Paris.' He turned his attention back to the painting in front of him. 'It isn't signed from what I can see, unless the name's hidden under the frame. But it may be that this was some form of a practice run for the actual painting itself. Especially given that Matisse was in St Tropez at the time when his style was so similar to this. And that's a stone's throw away from here, isn't it?'

'My father knew Matisse in Paris,' offered Emilie. 'Apparently he used to come to the salons Papa gave for the creative intelligentsia in the city. I know he liked Matisse very much and spoke of him often, but I don't know if he ever came down to the château.'

'Well, like so many other artists and writers, Matisse spent the Second World War years down here in the south, out of harm's way. Matisse is my absolute passion.' Sebastian was quivering with excitement. 'May I remove it from the wall to see if there's any dedication on the back? Often pictures would be given by artists to generous benefactors. Such as your father, perhaps.'

'Yes, of course.' Emilie went to stand next to Sebastian as he tentatively gripped the frame and lifted it carefully from the wall, revealing a square of darker wallpaper behind it. He turned the painting round to study the back with Emilie, but there was nothing to be seen.

'Never mind, it's not the end of the world,'

Sebastian reassured her. 'If Matisse had signed it, it would simply be a less complex process to prove that it is his work.'

'You really think it is?'

'With the provenance you've just described, and the trademark stippling, which Matisse was experimenting with around the period he painted *Luxe, Calme et Volupté*, I'd say there's every chance it is. Obviously, it would have to go to the experts for authentication.'

'And if it *is* a Matisse, how valuable would it be?' she asked.

'Given there's no signature, I wouldn't be experienced enough to judge. Matisse was extremely prolific and lived a very long life. Would you want to sell the painting?'

'That, again, is another query to put on my list.' Emilie gave an exhausted shrug.

'Well,' he said as he hung the painting carefully back in its rightful place, 'I certainly have some contacts who would be able to establish its authenticity, but I'm sure your *notaire* will wish to use his own. Thank you, though, for showing it to me, and the rest of this wonderful château.'

'My pleasure,' said Emilie, leading him out of the morning room.

'You know—' Sebastian scratched his head as they stood in the entrance hall—'I'm sure my grandmother mentioned the amazing collection of rare books that she'd once seen here, or am I imagining things?'

'No.' Emilie realised she'd managed to overlook the library on her tour. 'It's just along here. I'll show you.'

'Thank you, as long as you have time,' he

countered.

'I do.'

Sebastian was suitably awed on entering the library. 'My goodness,' he said as he made his way slowly around the shelves, 'this is a simply outstanding collection. God knows how many books there are in here—do you know? Fifteen, twenty thousand?'

'I really have no idea.'

'Are they catalogued? In any kind of order?' he questioned.

'They're in the order my father chose to put them, and his father before that. The collection was begun over two hundred years ago. The newer acquisitions are catalogued, yes.' Emilie indicated the leather ledgers sitting on her father's desk.

Sebastian opened one, turned the pages and saw the hundreds of entries made in Édouard's immaculate handwriting. 'I know this isn't any of my business, Emilie, but really, this is an extraordinary collection. I can see from this that your father purchased many rare first editions, not to mention the books already here. This must be one of the finest collections of rare books in France. They should be professionally catalogued on a database.'

Emilie sat down in her father's leather armchair, feeling overwhelmed. 'My God,' she murmured, 'there seems to be more and more to do. I'm realising that organising my parents' affairs is going to be a full-time job.'

'A worthwhile one, surely?' Sebastian said encouragingly.

'But I have another life, a life that I like. That is quiet and—' Emilie wanted to say 'safe', but knew that sounded strange—'organised.'

Sebastian strolled over to her then knelt down next to her, leaning his arm on her chair for support. 'I do understand, Emilie. And if you want to return to that life, then you must simply find people you trust to sort all this out for you.'

'Who *can* I trust?' she asked the air.

'Well, you mentioned your *notaire*, for a start,' Sebastian suggested. 'Maybe you could place everything in his hands?'

'But . . .' Tears pricked the back of her eyes. 'Surely I owe it to my family and its history? I cannot simply run away.'

'Emilie,' Sebastian said gently, 'it's very early days, of course you're feeling overwhelmed. Your mother has only been gone for a couple of weeks. You're still in shock, still grieving. Why not give yourself some time to make the right decisions?' He patted her hand then stood up. 'I must be off, but you have my card, and it goes without saying I'd be happy to help you in any way I can. This château is manna from heaven for me, especially the paintings, of course.' He smiled. 'Anyway, I'm almost certainly going to stay in Gassin for a while, so if you decide you'd like me to set about the process of having the possible Matisse authenticated, just call me on the mobile number on my card.'

'Thank you,' said Emilie, checking that she still had his card in her jean pocket.

'I'd also be happy to find out the names of the best rare books and antique furniture dealers through my contacts in Paris. At the very least,' added Sebastian, 'whatever you decide to do with the château, it's probably a good idea to know the value of what you own. Presumably your parents must have had some form of insurance?'

'I have no idea.' She shrugged, inwardly doubting it knowing her father and making a mental note to ask Gerard. 'I appreciate your advice,' she said gratefully as she stood up. She gave Sebastian a weak smile as she led him through the house to the back door and out towards her car. 'I'm sorry I seem . . . emotional. It's unlike me. Perhaps, another time, we can talk about what your grandmother told you of my father during the war.'

'I'd like that—and please don't apologise,' he added as they climbed into the car. 'You're not only bereaved, but it seems you've been left with one hell of a task on your hands.'

'I will cope. I must,' said Emilie, starting the engine and setting off down the drive.

'And I'm sure you will. As I said, if there's anything I can do to help, you know how to contact me.'

'Thank you.'

'My gîte is just to the left down there—' Sebastian indicated a turning—'so if you drop me here, I can walk the rest of the way. It's such a beautiful afternoon.'

'OK.' She brought the car to a halt. 'Thank you again.'

'Take care, Emilie,' he said as he climbed out. Then, with a wave of his hand, Sebastian ambled off down the road.

Emilie reversed the car and drove back to the château. Unsettled, she walked aimlessly from room to room, feeling the sharp emptiness of the lack of human presence.

As night fell and the temperature dropped, Emilie sequestered herself in the kitchen by the range, eating the cassoulet Margaux had left for her. Her appetite had deserted her and Frou-Frou happily reaped the benefit.

After supper, she bolted the back door and turned the key in the lock. Taking herself upstairs, she ran a slow stream of tepid water into the ancient, limescale-covered bath. She lay in it, musing morbidly how it fitted her length exactly, making it a perfect prototype for her coffin. Climbing out of the bath, she towelled herself dry then, unusually, let the towel drop to the floor in front of the full-length mirror.

With effort, Emilie forced herself to survey her naked body. She'd always regarded it as a piece of substandard equipment, given out at random in the genetic lottery. Stocky as a child, in her teenage years she'd become plump. Despite her mother's pleas to eat healthily and less, somewhere around seventeen Emilie had given up the endless round of cucumber and melon diets prescribed, covered her imperfect torso in loose-fitting and comfortable clothes and let nature take its course.

At the same time, she had also refused to attend further parties, designed to introduce her to the crème de la crème of young men and women her age. *Le Rallye* was organised by a group of mothers to make sure their progeny would meet suitable friends and possible future partners of similar class. The competition to be part of an élite *rallye* for the most socially aware French teenagers was intense. Valérie, with her de la Martinières name, could attract anyone who she wished to become a member of her own group. She had despaired when Emilie had announced she would no longer be a part of the cocktail parties in grand private homes which formed the heart of the event.

'How can you turn your back on your birthright?' Valérie had asked, outraged.

'I hate them, Maman. I am more than a surname and a bank account. I'm sorry, but no more.'

As Emilie looked in the mirror at her full breasts, rounded hips and shapely legs, she realised she must have lost weight in the last few weeks. What she saw, even to her critical eye, surprised her. Although her bone structure would never allow her to be sylph-like, she was not, by any stretch of the imagination, fat.

Before she began, as she inevitably would, to pick fault, Emilie removed herself from her reflection, donned her nightshirt and climbed into bed. Switching off the light and listening to the perfect silence around her, she wondered what had prompted her uncharacteristic naked revelation.

It had been six years since she'd last had what could loosely be termed as a boyfriend. Olivier, an attractive new vet at her Paris practice, had not lasted much longer than a few weeks. She hadn't even particularly liked him, but at least a warm body beside her at night, someone to talk to occasionally over dinner, had eased the loneliness of her existence. Olivier had eventually disappeared, she knew, through lack of effort on her part.

Emilie didn't really know what love was comprised of—a mixture of physical attraction, a meeting of minds . . . a *fascination*, perhaps. But she knew she had never fallen in love. Besides, who would ever love *her*?

That night, Emilie tossed and turned, feeling her mind might burst with the decisions she must make and the responsibility she couldn't shirk. But, more than that, her sleep was disturbed by the picture in her mind's eye of Sebastian.

Even for the short time he'd been in the château, she'd felt a security in his presence. He seemed capable, solid and . . . yes, he was very attractive. When his hand had touched hers for an instant in the library, she hadn't flinched as she normally did when somebody invaded her personal space.

Emilie chastised herself. How sad and lonely she must be that a man she'd met by chance for no longer than a couple of hours had affected her like this. Besides, why on earth would a man as seemingly accomplished and handsome as Sebastian look at her twice? He was out of her league and the chances were she'd never come across him again. Unless, of course, she called the number on the card he'd given her and asked for his help with valuing of the Matisse . . .

Emilie shook her head grimly, knowing she'd never gather the courage to do that.

It was a road to nowhere. She'd decided years ago that life was best lived alone. Then no one could hurt her or let her down again. And with that thought lodged firmly in her brain, Emilie finally drifted off to sleep.

4

Due to her disturbed night, Emilie woke late the next morning, and over coffee wrote down a never-ending list of things 'to do'. Then she started a fresh sheet of paper with the questions she needed to ask of herself. At the beginning of this process, all she had wanted was to sell both houses as quickly as possible, sort out the complexities of her family estate and return to her safe life in Paris. But now . . .

Emilie rubbed her nose with the pencil and stared around the kitchen for guidance. The house in Paris she would sell—it did not hold good memories for her. However, the past few days had altered her thoughts about the château. Not only was it the original family 'seat'—built by Comte Louis de la Martinières in 1750—but it had an atmosphere she'd always loved. It calmed her, reminded her of happy days here with her father.

Should she consider keeping it?

Emilie stood up and wandered about the kitchen, mulling the thought over in her mind. Wasn't it ridiculous, not to mention obscene, for one single woman to maintain a home on such a scale?

Obviously her mother hadn't thought so, but then the social set Valérie mixed with were in a rare league of their own. Emilie had stepped out of that league years before and knew how ordinary people lived. Yet the thought of being able to live here, amidst its peace and tranquillity, was appealing to her more and more. Having felt like

47

an outsider to her family all her life, ironically she felt for the first time that she'd arrived home. It shocked her how much she suddenly wanted to stay here.

Emilie sat back down at the kitchen table and continued the list of questions she would need to ask Gerard. If she could restore the château to its former glory, it would not only be for her own benefit, for surely it was a part of French history too? She would be performing a service to the nation. With this thought comforting her, she picked up her mobile and dialled Gerard's number.

After a long conversation with him, Emilie looked at the notes she had made. Gerard had reiterated that there would easily be enough to restore the château. The one thing he'd made clear was the lack of actual hard cash—anything she wished to do would have to be funded by what was sold in the immediate future.

He had seemed taken aback at her sudden change of heart. 'Emilie, it's certainly commendable that you wish to maintain your family's heritage, but restoring a house of that size is an enormous undertaking. I would go as far as to say a full-time job for the next two years. And it will be all down to you. You're alone.'

Emilie had almost expected him to add 'and a woman', but thankfully he had refrained. Gerard was probably wondering how much of the work would land on his own shoulders, as it was patently obvious to him she couldn't cope by herself. Irritated by his condescension, but aware she had done little to alter his attitude otherwise, Emilie pulled her laptop out of its pouch and switched it on. Then, chuckling to herself for expecting an Internet signal in a house that probably hadn't been rewired since the 1940s, she drove with Frou-Frou up to Gassin village. Climbing the steep hill, she asked Damien, the friendly proprietor of Le Pescadou Brasserie, whether she could log on to their Internet access.

'Mademoiselle de la Martinières, of course you may,' he said, leading her into the small office at the back of the restaurant. 'I apologise for not being here to greet you before, but I've been away in Paris. Everyone in the village was sad to hear of your maman's passing. Like your family, mine has been in the village for many hundreds of years. Will you sell the château now she is gone?' he asked.

Emilie knew this was the question Damien wanted the answer to. His bar and restaurant were the high altar of village gossip.

'I really don't know at the moment,' Emilie replied. 'I have many things to look into.'

'Of course. I hope you don't decide to sell, but if you do, I know many a developer who would be willing to pay a fortune to turn your beautiful château into a hotel. I've had many enquiries here over the years.' Out of the window, Damien indicated the château far below in the valley, its greying terracotta rooftops glinting in the sunshine.

'As I said, Damien,' Emilie repeated, 'I still have to make up my mind.'

'Well, Mademoiselle, if there's anything you need, please call us. We were all very fond of your father here. He was a good man. After the war, we in the village were so poor,' Damien explained.

49

'The Comte helped to push the government for proper roads to be built up to us here on the hill and encourage the tourists to visit from St Tropez. My family opened this restaurant in the 1950s and the village began to grow prosperous. Your father also promoted the planting of vineyards to grow the grapes for the wonderful wine we now make here.' Damien swept his arms across the vine-covered valley below them. 'When I was a child, all we had around us was farmland, fields of corn and grazing cows. Now our Provençal rosé is world famous.'

'It's comforting to hear my father helped the area he loved,' Emilie answered.

'The de la Martinières are part of Gassin, Mademoiselle. I hope you will decide to stay here with us.'

Damien continued to fuss around her, bringing her a jug of water, bread and a *plat au fromage*. Once Emilie had connected her laptop successfully, Damien left her alone. She checked her emails, then took out Sebastian's card and looked up his gallery on the Internet.

'Arté' was on the Fulham Road in London and mainly dealt in modern paintings. Emilie was comforted to see it existed. Making up her mind, she dialled Sebastian's number. His voicemail answered, so she left her number and a short message, asking him to contact her about their conversation yesterday.

When she'd finished, Emilie thanked Damien for the use of the Internet and lunch, then drove back to the château. She felt energised, more motivated than she had in years. There was no doubt that if she decided to renovate the house, she would almost certainly have to give up her veterinary career in Paris and move down here to oversee the project. Perhaps this was just what she needed—and, ironically, the last thing she would have considered a few days ago. It would give new purpose to her life.

However, her excitement gave way to fear as she drew nearer to the house and saw a police car sitting outside. Hastily bringing her car to a halt, Emilie grabbed Frou-Frou and climbed out. She stepped into the hall to find Margaux talking to the gendarme.

'Mademoiselle Emilie—' Margaux's eyes were wide with shock—'I believe we've had a break-in. I arrived here as usual at two and the front door was wide open. Oh, Mademoiselle, I'm so very sorry.'

With a sinking feeling in her stomach, Emilie realised that in her excitement over her decision to renovate the château she hadn't locked the back door before she'd driven up to the village.

'Margaux, this is not your fault. I think I left the back door open. Has anything been taken?' Emilie thought of the potentially valuable painting in the morning room.

'I have looked carefully in every room and I can't find a thing missing. But perhaps you can look too,' said Margaux.

'Often these kinds of crimes are opportunist,' offered the gendarme. 'There are many gypsies who see what they believe is a deserted house, break in and are simply looking for jewellery or cash.'

'Well, they won't have found any of that here,' Emilie replied grimly.

'Mademoiselle Emilie, do you by any chance

51

have the front-door key in your possession?' asked Margaux. 'It seems to be missing. I wondered if you had placed it somewhere safe for extra security, rather than it standing as it normally does in the lock.'

'No, I haven't.' Emilie surveyed the oversized, empty keyhole, looking bare without its rusting mate inserted into it. She blinked, trying to remember if the key had been in the lock this morning. But it was not the kind of detail she would have noticed on her way to the kitchen through the hall.

'If the key cannot be found, it's important that you call a locksmith who can fit a new one immediately,' said the gendarme. 'You will not be able to lock the door and it's possible that the thieves have taken it with them and are preparing to return at a later date.'

'Yes, of course.' Emilie's earlier vision of a secure paradise was fast evaporating as her heart beat unsteadily in her chest.

Margaux looked at her watch. 'I apologise, Mademoiselle Emilie, but I must go home. Anton is alone at our house. Am I free to leave?' she asked the gendarme.

'Yes. If I need any further information, I'll be in contact,' he answered.

'Thank you.' Margaux turned to Emilie. 'Mademoiselle, I'm worried about you being here by yourself. Perhaps it would be better to move out to a hotel for the next couple of nights?'

'Don't worry, Margaux, I'll contact a locksmith and I can always lock my bedroom door, for tonight, anyway.'

'Well, please call me if you're at all concerned.

And remember to secure the back door in future.' With a harassed wave, Margaux scurried off to collect her bicycle.

'Please search the château in case your housekeeper or myself have missed something.' The gendarme pulled a pad out of his top pocket and scribbled down a number. 'Contact me if you discover anything has been stolen and we'll take the matter further. Otherwise—' he sighed— 'there's not much more I can do.'

'Thank you for coming,' said Emilie, feeling guilty for her stupidity. 'As I said, it is my fault.'

'It's no problem, but I would suggest that you tighten security here as soon as you can and—as this château is so often empty—invest in an alarm system.' The gendarme nodded at her and walked towards his car through the open front door.

As soon as he'd left, Emilie mounted the stairs to begin checking nothing had been taken. Halfway up, she noticed a car snaking down the drive towards the house and saw it disappear around the back. Heart beating, Emilie scurried into the kitchen to lock it against unknown intruders. But it was Sebastian's face peering through the glass pane. Emilie unbolted the door and re-opened it.

'Hello!' Sebastian looked at her questioningly. 'Are you sure you want me to come in?'

'Yes. Sorry, I've just had a break-in and didn't recognise your car.'

'Oh God, Emilie, how awful!' he said, stepping over the threshold. 'Did they take anything?'

'Margaux thinks not, but I was just going upstairs to check.'

'Do you want me to help you?'

53

'I . . .' Her legs suddenly turned to jelly and she sat down abruptly on a kitchen chair.

'Emilie, you're very pale,' said Sebastian. 'Look, before you go dashing off round the house, why don't you let me make you the Englishman's version of the "cure-all"—a nice cup of tea? You've had a shock. Sit where you are, calm down and I'll put the kettle on.'

'Thank you,' she said, feeling dazed and shaky as Frou-Frou whined for a cuddle. She pulled the dog up onto her knee and stroked her, the motion comforting her.

'How did they get in?' Sebastian asked.

'We think through the back door, but they left through the front and the key is missing,' explained Emilie. 'I must get a locksmith out as soon as possible to replace it.'

'Do you have a telephone directory here?' Sebastian put down a mug on the table in front of her. 'Whilst you drink your tea, I could contact a locksmith for you.' He pulled out his mobile phone.

'Yes, in the drawer over there.' Emilie indicated a large dresser. 'Really, Sebastian, this is not your problem. I'll sort it out . . .'

But Sebastian had already opened the drawer and pulled out the directory.

'Right,' he said after a few minutes of browsing the numbers. 'There are three listed in St Tropez and one in La Croix Valmer. Why don't I call them now and see who's available?' He picked up the receiver and dialled the first number. 'Hello, yes, I'm calling from Château de la Martinières and I was just wondering if . . .'

Emilie didn't listen to the conversation, simply

sipped her tea and basked gratefully in the comfort of someone else taking charge.

'Right,' Sebastian said as he ended the call, 'unfortunately the locksmith can't come out until first thing tomorrow. But he told me he's used to replacing old locks on doors around here.' Sebastian glanced at her. 'You seem to have a little more colour. Before the light fades, are you up to double-checking the house? You really should. I'll come with you if you like.'

'Surely, Sebastian, you must have other things to do?' Emilie entreated. 'I don't wish to hold you up.'

'Don't be silly. An English gentleman would never abandon a damsel in distress.' He offered his hand to help her up from the chair. 'Come on, let's get this over with.'

'Thank you. I'm concerned they're still here, hiding somewhere.' Emilie bit her lip. 'Margaux didn't see the intruders leave.'

All the rooms were as Emilie remembered them, and although it was impossible to be sure that absolutely nothing had been taken, given her unfamiliarity with the detail of the individual objects in the house, she arrived back with Sebastian in the hall reassured.

'Well, that's the entire house checked,' he confirmed. 'Anywhere else they could be hiding?'

'The cellars perhaps? But I've never been down there,' Emilie admitted.

'Maybe you should then,' he suggested. 'Do you know how to access them?'

'I believe the door is in the lobby just off the kitchen.'

'Come on then, let's go and take a look.'

'Do you think it's really necessary?' Emilie said reluctantly. Dark, enclosed spaces terrified her.

'Would you prefer me to go down alone?'

'No, you're right. I should see the cellars for myself.'

'Don't worry, I'll keep you safe,' he said, grinning as they walked into the lobby. 'This door?'

'Yes, I think so.'

Sebastian pulled back the rusting bolts and turned the key with difficulty. 'This hasn't been opened for years, so I'd doubt anyone is lurking down there.' Managing to drag the door open, he searched for a switch and found a crude piece of string hanging above his head. Pulling it, a straggle of light appeared from below. 'Right, I'll go first.'

Tentatively taking the steps downwards behind Sebastian, Emilie followed him into a cold, low-ceilinged room, the air stagnant and damp.

'Wow!' Sebastian exclaimed at the lines of wine racks, filled to the brim with dust-covered bottles. Pulling one out at random, he dusted off the label and read it. '*Château Lafite Rothschild 1949*. I'm no wine expert, but this lot could be a vintner's dream come true. On the other hand—' he shrugged as he replaced the bottle—'they may all be undrinkable.'

They both wandered around the room, pulling out bottles and inspecting them.

'I can't find a single bottle after 1969, can you?' asked Sebastian. 'It looks like no one bothered to add to the collection after that date. Wait a minute—'

Sebastian put the two bottles he was holding onto the floor, then pulled out four more, making six, then twelve. 'There's something behind this rack. It's a door, can you see?'

Emilie peered through the rack and saw what he meant. 'It probably leads to another cellar which no one used,' she offered hopefully, eager to remove herself back upstairs as soon as possible.

'Yes, surely a house like this would have extensive cellars running underneath. Aha—' Sebastian removed the last bottle, then took hold of the rotting wooden wine rack and eased it out into the centre of the room—'I was right, it is a door.' He brushed the cobwebs from the lock and tried the handle. It opened grudgingly, the wood no longer fitting its frame comfortably, having warped in the damp atmosphere. 'Shall we see what's inside?'

'I . . .' Emilie was nervous of going further. 'It's probably empty.'

'Well, we shall see,' said Sebastian, using all his strength to drag the door fully open along the cellar floor. His hands groped again for a light switch, but none appeared within his grasp.

'Wait there a moment,' he instructed Emilie as he stepped forward into the blackness. 'There does seem to be some natural light coming from somewhere . . .' Sebastian disappeared completely into the gloom. 'Yes, there's a small window in here—ouch! Sorry, just banged my shin on something.' He reappeared at the entrance. 'Do you by any chance know where there might be a torch?'

'I can check upstairs in the kitchen.' Emilie turned and headed for the stairs, grateful for an excuse to escape.

'If you can't find a torch, bring a candle or two,'

he called after her.

The torch she eventually found was inconveniently out of batteries, so she collected an old box of wax candles and some matches from the pantry, took a deep breath and returned down the cellar stairs.

'Here,' she called into the room. Sebastian took two of the candles out of the box and held them as Emilie lit both. He offered her one then turned back inside, with Emilie reluctantly following behind him.

They stood in the centre of the small room, casting the eerie glow of their candles around it. Neither of them spoke as they took in what they saw.

'Correct me if I'm imagining things, but this looks to me like a room someone once occupied,' said Sebastian eventually. 'The bed over there, with the small table beside it, the chair by the window, presumably placed so as to catch what little light comes in, the chest of drawers . . .' He wafted his candle towards it. 'There's even a blanket still on the mattress.'

'Yes,' agreed Emilie as her eyes adjusted to the dim light, 'and a mat placed on the floor. But who would live down here?'

'A servant perhaps?' Sebastian suggested.

'Our servants had attic rooms on the top floor. My family would never be so cruel as to place their staff in a room such as this.'

'No, of course not,' said Sebastian, suitably chastised. 'And, look, there's another small door over there.'

He strode towards the door and opened it. 'I'd say this was used as a washing area. There's a tap

58

on the wall and a large enamel sink on the floor beneath it. And a commode.' He bent his head carefully as he stepped out. 'This was definitely used by someone once, but who?' He walked towards Emilie, his eyes alight with interest. 'Let's go upstairs, pour ourselves a glass of wine from one of the bottles next door and mull over the possibilities.'

5

Upstairs in the kitchen, Emilie suddenly started to shiver violently, whether from the cold cellar or delayed shock, she didn't know.

'You run upstairs and find a jumper, and I'm going to try and light a fire. It's turned chilly this evening,' Sebastian commented. 'Can you hear that wind blowing outside?'

'Yes. It's the Mistral,' she acknowledged. 'The temperature always falls, but I don't think we have the ingredients for such a thing as a fire.'

'What! In a house surrounded by trees? Of course you do.' Sebastian winked. 'Be back in a moment.'

Upstairs, Emilie collected a cardigan and, pulling a blanket off her bed, walked around making sure all the shutters were secure against the escalating wind. There were many residents in the area who dreaded the Mistral, which blew with relentless force along the Rhône Valley, often arriving unheralded and blowing up within minutes. There were old wives' tales that told of everything from the wind summoning witchery, to

59

affecting female hormonal rhythm and animal behaviour. Yet Emilie had always admired its power and majesty, and the freshness of the air once it had blown itself out.

Sebastian appeared ten minutes later in the kitchen with a wheelbarrow full of broken branches collected from the garden and a few ancient logs he'd found in a shed. 'Right,' he said, 'let's get this started. Show me where to light it.'

Emilie led him into the morning room and soon a fire was burning merrily in the grate.

'This is a fantastic fireplace,' Sebastian said approvingly, wiping his hands on his chinos. 'They really knew how to make a decent chimney in those days.'

'I wouldn't know where to begin to build a fire,' admitted Emilie. 'The servants lit them in our houses and I don't have one in my apartment.'

'Well, my little princess,' Sebastian grinned, 'where I come from, they're an everyday fact of life. Now, I'll go and open that bottle of wine we brought up from the cellar and see if it's drinkable. And, if I may, I'll also have a root around in the kitchen to see if there's something I could knock up to eat. I've had nothing all day and I'm sure you could do with something in your stomach too.'

'Oh, but . . .' Emilie made to stand up, but Sebastian pushed her back down onto the sofa.

'No, you stay there and get warm. I'll go and see what I can find.'

Emilie pulled the blanket closer around her body and stared into the leaping flames, feeling warm and comforted. Not since she'd been a little girl and looked after by her favourite nanny could she remember being cared for like this. Tucking her legs underneath her, she laid her head on the ageing damask silk of the sofa arm and closed her eyes.

*   *   *

'Emilie!' She felt a hand shaking her gently. 'Time to wake up, sweetheart.' She opened her eyes and saw Sebastian's hazel ones staring down at her.

'It's almost nine o'clock. You've been asleep for the past two hours. And dinner is served.'

Emilie sat upright, sleepy and embarrassed. 'Sebastian, I'm so sorry.'

'No apology necessary. You're obviously exhausted. Right, I've brought our supper in here as it's very cold in that kitchen. The Mistral was really blowing as I came back from the Spar. Dig in,' he said, indicating the steaming plate of spaghetti Bolognese on the low table in front of her. 'This wine we brought up from the cellar smells all right; let's see if it's drinkable.' Sebastian put his glass to his mouth, sipped and swallowed. He nodded in pleasure. 'That is spectacular. I hope I haven't opened a few hundred francs' worth of red to accompany our spaghetti Bolognese!'

'There are so many bottles down there, I'm sure it's fine to drink one.' Emilie reached for her glass and tried it. 'Yes, it's lovely.' She took a mouthful of the spaghetti, suddenly realising how hungry she was. 'This is very kind of you. And you're a good cook.'

'I wouldn't go that far, but I know how to put a few basic ingredients together. Now, whilst you were asleep I took some time to think of the best way forward for the possible Matisse. I called a

61

friend of mine at Sotheby's in London, and he recommended a chap he knows in Paris. I have his number, so if you'd like to give him a call tomorrow, you can get the ball rolling.'

'I will certainly contact him, thank you, Sebastian.'

'He's one of the top Paris auctioneers and comes with a glowing reference from my friend. I must say, I'd love to be a fly on the wall when he sees it, to know whether I'm right,' said Sebastian, smiling.

'Of course you can be here,' Emilie nodded. 'When do you return to England?'

'At the end of next week, so I'm available until then to help you if you need me to,' he replied. 'You have so much to think about just now. The main priority really has to be making sure that this house and you are safe. If you'd like me to, I could speak to the chap who's coming to change the front-door lock tomorrow and ask him who he would recommend locally to fit an alarm system.'

'If you're sure, then yes, that would be helpful,' she said gratefully. 'I wouldn't know where to start with that.'

'Good. Now,' said Sebastian, in between forkfuls of spaghetti, 'on to the more interesting subject of why there seems to be a secret hiding place in your cellar. Have you come up with any ideas?'

'No.' Emilie shook her head. 'I'm afraid I know very little about my family history.'

'What I've been wondering, of course, is whether that room downstairs was used as a hiding place during the war. God, a few minutes down there would be enough to send you mad.' Sebastian raised his eyebrows. 'Can you imagine how it would have been for days, weeks or even months on end?'

'No, I can't,' agreed Emilie. 'And I wish my father was still alive so I could ask him. I'm ashamed I know so little of the past. Maybe through the process of sorting out the estate, I'll learn much more.'

'I'm sure you will.' Sebastian stood up and began collecting the empty plates.

'Please, you've done enough, let me,' Emilie urged. 'It must be time for you to be going.'

'What?' Sebastian looked horrified. 'You honestly think I'm going to leave you here alone tonight with a front door we can't lock? I wouldn't sleep a wink. No, Emilie, let me stay. I can bed down here on the sofa in front of the fire, no problem.'

'Sebastian, I'll be fine, really. Lightning rarely strikes twice in one day, does it? As I told the gendarme, I can lock my bedroom door. And I feel I've already put you to too much trouble. Please, go home,' she begged.

'Well, if you're uncomfortable having me here, then of course I will.'

'It isn't that, I just feel guilty for taking up your time,' Emilie replied hastily. 'After all, we hardly know each other.'

'Please don't feel guilty. The bed at my gîte is as hard as a board anyway.'

'Well, if you're sure, then yes, thank you,' Emilie surrendered. 'And, of course, you must take one of the bedrooms. It's silly for you to sleep down here.'

'Deal.' Sebastian reached for the poker by the fire. 'And I'll have this by my bed, just in case.'

Having shared the washing-up, Emilie locked the back door, then guided Sebastian along the upstairs corridor and led him to a bedroom. 'Margaux always keeps this made up for unexpected guests. I hope you'll find it comfortable,' she said.

'Just a little.' Sebastian surveyed the spacious room with its exquisite antique French furniture. 'Thanks, Emilie, and I hope you sleep well.'

'And you. Goodnight then.'

Sebastian took a step towards her. On a gut reaction, Emilie swiftly closed the bedroom door before he could reach her and scurried along the corridor to her own room, shutting the door and locking it firmly behind her. She lay down on her bed, feeling strangely breathless.

Why had she done that? Sebastian had probably just wanted to give her a chaste kiss goodnight. She thumped the bed in frustration. Now she would never know.

*   *   *

After a disturbed night, every nerve-ending alert to the fact that Sebastian was sleeping only a few metres away from her—it somehow felt so intimate—Emilie made her way downstairs the following morning to make some coffee. Presuming Sebastian was still in bed, she was surprised when she heard a car approaching and he appeared through the back door.

'Morning,' he said. 'I went up to the bakery to get breakfast. Wasn't sure what you wanted, so I got baguettes, croissants and pains au chocolat. Oh, and some of my favourite French jam.' He laid his shopping out on the kitchen table.

'Thank you,' Emilie said, feeling she was using

the word repeatedly to him. 'I've made some coffee.'

'Collecting the fresh bread in the morning is actually one of the most pleasurable things about being in France. A tradition that has long gone in England,' he commented. 'Oh, and the locksmith called me to say he'd be here in an hour.'

'I feel so stupid.' She sighed. 'Of course I should have locked the back door when I left yesterday.'

'Emilie,' Sebastian said gently, placing a hand on her shoulder. 'You really have been under the most enormous pressure in the last two weeks. Grief and shock can affect you on all sorts of levels.' The hand on her shoulder began to move, massaging it. 'Don't be too hard on yourself. Thankfully, there's no real harm done. Just take it as a warning for the future. Now, what's your breakfast preference?'

'Baguette, croissant . . . I don't mind.' She walked away from Sebastian to pour the coffee then sat at the table silently, chewing through her breakfast and listening to Sebastian call the various alarm-system companies the locksmith had suggested.

'OK,' he said, putting down the receiver and jotting a couple of things on a sheet of paper. 'They're all saying they can provide a suitable system for the house, but would need to come and survey it before they can give you a quote. Want to book them in for tomorrow?'

'Yes, thank you.' She looked up at him suddenly. 'Why are you helping me?'

'What a strange question,' said Sebastian. 'I suppose it's because I like you and I can see you're having a hard time. Besides, I'm sure

Grandmother Constance would expect nothing less of me for her friend Édouard's daughter. Now, do you want to speak to the chap in Paris who's been suggested to come and value the Matisse, or shall I?'

Emilie was feeling sick after a breakfast she hadn't wanted. 'Perhaps it's best if you do it, as you can talk the language he'll understand.'

'Right. I'd also suggest he values the other paintings in the château whilst he's here. It's never a bad idea to get two or three estimates anyway.'

'Yes. And then there's the art in the Paris house, which I must also have valued.'

'When will you return to Paris?' Sebastian asked.

'Soon,' she sighed. 'But you're right, whilst I'm here it's good to do as many things as I can. If I decide to keep the château, it will be only the beginning.'

'You think you might keep it?'

'Yes. Although if I can forget to lock the back door, perhaps it's stupid of me to consider taking on a project which would be a challenge for anyone.'

'Well,' said Sebastian, 'just know I'll be happy to do anything I can.'

'It's very kind of you and I am grateful,' said Emilie. Frou-Frou whined at the kitchen door to be let out. She stood up and opened it for her. 'Surely you must have your own life to lead?'

'I do,' he agreed, 'but as beautiful paintings happen to be my passion, it's not exactly a hardship. Now, what about the library? Would you like me to investigate a good rare books' expert to come and take a look at the collection?'

'No, thanks,' said Emilie quickly, her head spinning, 'there's no urgency as I'll never sell the books. I must call Gerard, my *notaire*. He left me three messages yesterday afternoon, but I didn't get back to him.'

'Whilst you do that, I'm going to nip back to my gîte for a change of clothes and a shower. I'll see you later. And don't forget,' he reminded her, 'the locksmith will be here any minute.'

'Thank you, Sebastian.'

* * *

Having shown the locksmith to the front door and left him to it, Emilie did at least manage to get a shiver of satisfaction as she called Gerard and told him she had things under control at the château. She arranged to meet him in Paris next week at her parents' house, checked the locksmith's progress and walked into the library, needing to feel the calmness of its atmosphere. Wandering around the shelves, Emilie ruminated on what a huge job it would be to put the thousands of books into storage if she decided to either sell or renovate the château.

She noticed two of the books were standing proud of the others on the shelf. She pulled them out and saw that they were books on the cultivation of trees. Pushing them neatly back into line, she walked into the kitchen as she heard Sebastian's car approaching across the gravel.

He burst through the back door, panting. 'Emilie! I tried to call you!' He ran a hand through his hair. 'I'm afraid I just found your little dog lying on the side of the road. She's very badly injured and we need to get her to a vet immediately. I've got her on the back seat of the car. Come on, let's go.'

Horrified, Emilie ran out with Sebastian to the car, climbing in beside a bleeding and barely breathing Frou-Frou. Sebastian drove at speed, heading for the vet she'd told him had a practice in La Croix Valmer, ten minutes' drive away. Tears dripped down Emilie's cheeks as she stroked the lifeless Frou-Frou on her knee.

'I let her out this morning,' she sobbed, 'then the locksmith arrived and I forgot to call her back in. She doesn't usually stray, but maybe she was following your car . . . and once she was on the road, she's blind and wouldn't have been able to see anything coming . . . Oh God! How could I have forgotten!'

'Emilie, Emilie, try and keep calm. The vet may be able to save her,' Sebastian said, doing his best to comfort her.

One look at the vet's grave face was enough to tell Emilie what her professional eye already knew.

'I am very sorry, Mademoiselle, but she has sustained serious internal injuries. We could try operating, but she is old and very weak. Perhaps it's simply best for us to help her pass away comfortably. It's what you would advise a client of yours, is it not?' he suggested gently.

'Yes.' Emilie nodded miserably. 'Of course.'

Twenty minutes later, having kissed Frou-Frou a last goodbye as the vet injected her and her small body gave a final twitch of surrender, a devastated Emilie emerged and walked shakily up the steps from the practice, holding on to Sebastian's arm for support.

'My mother adored her and I promised I would take care of her and—'

'Come on, sweetheart, let's get you home,' Sebastian said as he led her towards the car.

Emilie sat next to him as he drove, catatonic with guilt and emotion. They walked through the kitchen door and she sat down at the table, resting her head on her forearms in despair.

'I can't even take care of one small dog! I'm hopeless, just as my mother always told me! I can't get anything right, nothing. And I'm the last in the line of such a great noble family! So many heroes, including my father, and look at me—I'm useless!'

As all the pain of her mother's disappointment in her poured out, Emilie sobbed like a child, her head buried in her own arms for comfort.

When she eventually looked up, she saw Sebastian was sitting quietly at the table, watching her.

'Please,' she exclaimed, immediately embarrassed at her outburst, 'forgive me, I'm . . . a mess! And I always have been,' she choked out.

Sebastian stood up slowly, walked around the table, then bent down on his haunches and offered her a handkerchief to wipe her dripping nose. 'Emilie, I promise you, the picture that you have of yourself, which is obviously taken from your mother's point of view, is completely inaccurate. For what it's worth—' he smiled as he moved a lock of hair away from her face and tucked it behind her ear—'having only just met you, I think that you're a brave, strong and intelligent woman. Not to mention beautiful.'

'Beautiful!' Emilie looked at him with ridicule in her eyes. 'Really, Sebastian, I appreciate you're trying to make me feel better, but barefaced lies only patronise me. I am not "beautiful"!'

'And I suppose that, too, is something your mother told you?'

'Yes, but it's true,' she said with force.

'Well, forgive me for voicing my own opinion, but I thought it the day I first set eyes on you. And as for being a "failure", well, I've never heard such rot in my life. From what I've seen so far, you've handled what would have sent other people into total despair with amazing strength. And you've done it virtually alone. Emilie, listen to me,' Sebastian pleaded, 'whatever your mother's attitude towards you was, you really must not see yourself through her eyes. Because, my darling, she was wrong. Very wrong. And now she's gone and it's your turn. She can't hurt you any more, she really can't. Come here.'

Sebastian reached for her and pulled her into his arms. He held her tightly against him and she continued to sob into his shoulder. 'I promise you, everything is going to be fine. And I'm here if you need me to be.'

She looked up. 'But you hardly know me! How can you say all these things?'

'Well—' Sebastian chuckled—'I suppose it's been a pretty dramatic couple of days. And I'm sure that if I'd met you in Paris and we'd just gone out for a few dinners, I wouldn't feel as qualified to have an opinion. But adversity can sometimes reap positive rewards. Barriers that normally take weeks are broken through much faster. And I think I understand you. And I would like to spend lots more time with you if you'd let me.' He pushed her shoulders away from him and tipped her chin up so she was looking directly at him. 'Emilie, I know this is all happening very fast, and you're scared and frightened, so the last thing I want to do is to push you. And I won't, I promise. But I must admit that, just at this moment, I'd like to kiss you.'

Emilie looked at him and gave a small smile. 'Kiss *me*?'

'Yes. Is that so shocking?' Sebastian mocked her gently. 'But don't worry, I'm not going to pounce on you. I just wanted to be honest.'

'Thank you.' Emilie stared at him and came to her own decision. She reached her head forward and tentatively touched his lips with her own. 'Thank you, Sebastian, for everything. You have been so kind, I . . .'

He took her face in his hands and kissed her back, then broke away suddenly, checking himself. 'Look,' he said, taking her fingers and entwining them with his, 'please tell me if you're comfortable with this. I don't want you to think I'm taking advantage of you in any way. You're confused, I'm sure you can't possibly know how you feel just now, and—'

'Sebastian, it's OK.' It was Emilie's turn to comfort him. 'I know exactly what I'm doing. I'm a big girl, as you said. So, please, don't worry.'

'Well then, I won't,' he replied softly.

As Sebastian drew her back into his arms, Emilie felt the pain being slowly washed away by his tenderness. And surrendered to it.

6

Paris, January 1999—Nine Months Later

Emilie sat at the back of the auction room watching the gaggle of effortlessly chic Parisian women raising delicately manicured hands to bid for an exquisite canary diamond necklace and matching earrings. She glanced down at the catalogue on which she had scribbled figures in the margin and realised that, by her reckoning, the sale had so far raised almost twelve million francs.

Over the next few weeks, apart from a few paintings and choice pieces of furniture that she had decided to keep and eventually ship down to the château, the entire contents of the Paris house would be auctioned too. The house itself was already sold and its new owners would be taking up residence shortly.

She felt a slight pressure on her left hand and turned. 'Are you OK?' Sebastian whispered.

She nodded, grateful for his empathy as she watched her mother's precious jewellery collection go under the hammer. The money raised would pay off a big chunk of the overdraft Valérie had accrued, leaving Emilie the funds from the sale of the Paris house to finally begin renovations on the château. And the Matisse had been authenticated, thanks to Sebastian's help. He had immediately found a private client for it, and had proudly handed her a cheque for five million francs.

'Such a shame Matisse didn't sign the canvas. It would have been worth at least triple that amount,'

72

he'd sighed.

Emilie glanced sideways at Sebastian, who was watching the feverish bidding for the necklace and earrings with amused interest. She often found herself staring at him in wonder and amazement that he'd walked into her life and changed it so irrevocably.

He had saved her. Everything was different now; she felt a little as though she'd woken up from a long and painful dream and stepped out into the sun. Reticent in the first few weeks to believe in his feelings for her, frightened that at any minute he might disappear and leave her, his stoic warmth had eventually broken down all her barriers. And now, nine months on, she was basking in his love, blossoming like a wilted flower suddenly given water. She no longer looked in the mirror and saw a reflection full of hopelessness; now she could see that her eyes sparkled and her skin glowed with a new luminescence . . . there were even some days when Emilie thought she might be considered pretty.

Not only that, but Sebastian had been wonderful in helping her organise the enormous job of sorting out the de la Martinières's estate. Even though they'd spent time apart, with Sebastian having to commute between France and his business in England, he'd joined her as much as he could to support her through the process of valuing, then emptying the Paris house. Then through the rigmarole of surveyors, architects and builders who came to the château to help Emilie form a picture of exactly what was needed to restore it and provide an idea of costs.

Emilie knew she was becoming more and more

reliant on Sebastian, not only emotionally but in terms of the practical, financial maze she was having to cope with. It wasn't that she couldn't deal with the endless paperwork sent through from Gerard, and his suggestions of how to invest the money once it materialised; it was more to do with the fact that, like her father, she simply wasn't interested. As long as she had enough to complete the renovations on the château, and some future funds to live on, where and how the money was looked after was irrelevant. Emilie was far too happy to care.

As she heard the bidding topping the 1,200,000 francs that was expected for the necklace and earrings, Emilie swore to herself that once the Paris house was out of her possession she'd sit down and go through the financial details with Sebastian. It was important she remained in control, she knew, but Sebastian was far better at all that kind of thing than she was. And she had learned to trust him implicitly. So far, he had never let her down.

The gavel smashed onto the auctioneer's rostrum. Sebastian smiled at her.

'Wow, three hundred thousand francs more than we'd anticipated. Congratulations, sweetheart.' He kissed her affectionately on the cheek.

'Thank you.' Then she saw the auctioneer showing a simple string of creamy pearls and matching earrings and a sudden taste of bile came to Emilie's throat. She bent her head, unable to watch.

Sebastian noticed immediately. 'Emilie, what's wrong?'

'My mother wore those pearls almost every day

of her life. I . . . excuse me.' Emilie stood up and headed for the exit, then went in search of the powder room. Slumping onto the closed toilet seat, she rested her head in her hands, feeling dizzy and sick, and surprised at the way the sight of the pearls had affected her. So far, disposing of her mother's possessions had not touched her emotionally. There had been little grieving; if anything, only a sense of relief that she was finally free of her past.

Emilie looked up at the carved oak of the toilet door. Had she judged Maman too harshly? After all, Valérie had never been physically cruel to her. The fact she had felt irrelevant to her mother's world—an appendage at best, and nowhere near the centre—did not mean that her mother was an intrinsically bad person. Valérie was the centre of Valérie's world, and there was simply no room for anyone else.

And . . . when she'd been so ill and the awful thing had happened to her at thirteen, it had not been out of cruelty. It had simply been because her mother had once more failed to notice.

She stood up, left the cabinet and splashed her face with water.

'She did the best that she could. You have to forgive her,' Emilie told her reflection in the mirror. 'You have to move on.'

Taking a few deep breaths, Emilie left the cloakroom and found Sebastian hovering in the corridor outside.

'Are you all right?' he asked anxiously, taking her in his arms.

'Yes. I felt faint, but I'm better now.'

'Sweetheart, that would be enough to upset

anyone,' he said, indicating the saleroom, 'watching the vultures picking over the remnants of your mother's life. Why don't I take you out for lunch? There's no reason for you to stay here and upset yourself further.'

'Yes, I'd like that,' Emilie replied gratefully.

A brisk January wind blew as Sebastian walked her along the Paris street to a restaurant he said he knew.

'It's a bit rough and ready, but their bouillabaisse is superb, especially on a cold day like this.'

The two of them sat down at a rustic table, Emilie feeling chilled to the bone and grateful for the fire that burned in the grate next to them. Sebastian ordered the fish stew and took Emilie's hands in his, rubbing them to warm her.

'The good news is that this process is nearly over and hopefully you can begin to concentrate on the future, not the past.'

'And I couldn't have done it without you, Sebastian. Thank you, thank you so much for everything.' Emilie's eyes glistened with tears.

'My pleasure, really,' he said firmly. 'And maybe this is a salient moment to talk about *our* future.'

At his words, Emilie's heart began to beat in her chest. Being so busy sorting out the past, she had simply lived from day to day in the present. Besides, she'd hardly dared to project into the future, having no real idea how Sebastian saw their relationship progressing and being too uncertain to ask. She sat quietly, waiting for him to continue.

'You know that my business is based in England, Emilie. And for the past few months whilst I've been here, I've done my best to run it, but I admit

76

to having taken my eye off the ball.'

'Oh, that's my fault,' Emilie interrupted guiltily. 'You've done so much for me whilst your business has been suffering.'

'Well, it's not that awful,' he assured her, 'but I certainly need to be thinking about getting back and concentrating on it more fully, in terms of time, headspace and proximity.'

'I see . . .' Her voice tailed off as what Sebastian was hinting at sank in. He'd helped her through a very difficult period of her life. Did he feel that the worst was over now and she didn't need him any more? Emilie's stomach turned over.

All her thoughts must have betrayed themselves in her eyes, for Sebastian took her hand and kissed it. 'Silly girl. I know what you're thinking. Yes, I do have to return to England, certainly for now, but I'm not thinking of leaving you behind.'

'Then . . . what are you thinking?'

'That you would come with me, Emilie.'

'To England?'

'Yes, to England. Do you speak much English, by the way? I've no idea, given we've always spoken in French.' He grinned.

'Of course,' she nodded. 'My mother insisted I learned and I had some clients at the Paris practice that were English.'

'Good, that will help a lot. So maybe you could come with me, at least for a while. Your Paris apartment can easily be rented out, and you can come and sample the delights of beer and Yorkshire pudding with me.'

'But what about the château? Surely I should be there to oversee the work?' she questioned.

'Well, once the renovations begin, the house will

77

be a building site for the next few months. The whole place has got to be rewired and replumbed, let alone the re-roofing. You can't live there whilst the work is being carried out, especially not through the winter months. It simply won't be habitable. You could stay at your Paris apartment and commute down to Gassin, but you can fly in to Nice almost as quickly from a British airport. And it would mean we could be together. If—' he looked at her—'that's what you want.'

'I—'

'Well, why don't you think about it?' Sebastian interjected. 'Obviously, from my point of view, it would be a hell of a lot easier to have you in situ in England rather than me flying back here all the time. But really, Emilie, it's up to you. And I'd understand if you decide to stay put here in France.'

'But . . .' Emilie didn't know quite how to voice the words. Did he want her move to England to be permanent? Or was it simply until the château was renovated?

'Emilie,' Sebastian sighed, watching her, 'I can read you like a book. What I'm suggesting is less a practical scenario and much more of an emotional one. I love you. I want to be with you for the rest of my life. Where and how that life takes place are all questions we can answer together in the fullness of time. But I would like to ask you one more question . . .'

Emilie watched as Sebastian felt inside his jacket pocket and produced a box. He opened it to reveal a small sapphire ring. 'I want to ask you if you'll marry me.'

'What?'

'Please don't look so horrified,' said Sebastian, rolling his eyes. 'This is meant to be a romantic moment and you're meant to respond accordingly.'

'I'm sorry, I'm just shocked, that's all. I didn't expect it.' Emilie's eyes filled with sudden tears. 'Are you sure?' she asked as she looked at him.

'Honestly!' Sebastian sighed. 'Of course I'm sure! Asking a woman to marry me and producing a ring is not the kind of thing I do every day, you know.'

'But we hardly know each other.'

'Emilie, we've lived in each other's pockets for the past nine months. We've worked, slept, eaten and talked together. Although—' Sebastian's eyes darkened—'if you feel uncertain about me, then of course I'd understand.'

'No! No.' Emilie tried to pull herself together from the shock. 'Sebastian, you're wonderful and I . . . love you. If you really do mean this, then . . . yes.'

'Are you sure?' The ring still hovered in Sebastian's fingers.

'I am,' Emilie replied.

'Then I,' said Sebastian, placing the ring on Emilie's finger, 'am a very happy man.'

Emilie looked down at the ring. 'It's beautiful,' she breathed.

'It was my grandmother's engagement ring. I think it's rather lovely too, but undoubtedly far less extravagant than the rocks your mother favoured. And, by the way, I wouldn't be at all insulted if you wished to keep your maiden name,' he added, taking a sip of wine. 'You are the last of the de la Martinières, after all.'

This was a thought Emilie had never

contemplated. 'I really don't know,' she said, the gravity of what had just happened sinking in and turning slowly to amazement and delight.

'Of course you don't,' Sebastian comforted her as their fish stew arrived. 'I'm sorry if I'm bombarding you, I've just been planning this for rather a long time. So, any thoughts of where and when you'd like to tie the knot?'

'Not yet, but somewhere in France, if you wouldn't mind,' she added hastily, 'and very small.'

'Yes, that was what I thought you'd say. And how about when?'

Emilie shrugged. 'I don't have a preference, do you?'

'The sooner the better, in my book,' commented Sebastian. 'I was thinking how wonderful it would be to arrive back in England with my new wife in tow. And if you'd prefer France and something very quiet, how about in a couple of weeks, right here in Paris?'

*   *   *

A few days later, Emilie arrived at the château to oversee the furniture being put into storage. After her marriage and subsequent move to Yorkshire, she would return to organise the library being packed away before the renovations began. Sebastian had flown home to England to retrieve his birth certificate in order to complete the documentation needed for them to be married in France.

She'd managed to rent out her Paris apartment for six months, then gritted her teeth to call Leon, her boss at the vet's practice, to tell him that she would not be returning after all.

'We'll be very sorry to lose you,' Leon had said. 'And your patients will miss you too. If you ever want to return, please let me know. Good luck with the marriage and the new life in England. I'm so glad you've found happiness—you deserve it, Emilie.'

Emilie was aware that the few friends she'd told about her decision to throw everything up and follow her heart to England had been surprised.

'It's very out of character for you to make such a rash decision,' Sabrina, her friend from university, had commented. 'Hope I get to come to the wedding, so I can finally meet the Knight in Shining Armour who's whisking you off with him.'

'We're not having anyone, just Sebastian and me and our witnesses. I prefer it that way.'

'You are funny, Emilie,' Sabrina had sighed in disappointment. 'I was expecting a big party. Oh well, keep in touch and good luck.'

As Emilie walked towards the château, Margaux was there to greet her at the front door, visibly flustered by the removal men lugging Louis XIV armoires and fragile gilt mirrors out past her to the removal van.

'I've asked them to take care, but they've already damaged a corner on a valuable chest of drawers,' she huffed as she put a cup of coffee in front of Emilie in the kitchen.

'Of course we must expect some breakage,' Emilie shrugged. 'Margaux, I have something to tell you.' Smiling, she held out her hand to indicate her engagement ring. 'I'm getting married.'

'Married?' Surprise registered on Margaux's face. 'Who to?'

'Sebastian, of course.'

'Of course.' Margaux nodded. 'But, Mademoiselle, it's so fast. You've only known him for a few months. Are you sure?'

'Yes. I love him, Margaux, and he's been so good to me.'

'Yes, he has.' Margaux came to Emilie and kissed her on both cheeks. 'Then I'm delighted for you. It's good you will have someone to take care of you.'

'Thank you.'

'Now, you must excuse me. We have a dust explosion taking place upstairs as the furniture is moved out. I will see you later, Mademoiselle.'

After lunch, realising there was little she could do to help the removal process and feeling she'd prefer not to see the operation anyway, Emilie wandered down to the cottage to see Jean and Jacques and tell them the news of her marriage. As she walked the short distance to the vineyard, she knew she must also reassure them that she would not lose interest in either the *cave* or the château renovation programme once she began her new life far away.

Jean insisted on breaking out a bottle of champagne one of his vintner friends had given him.

'I needed an excuse to open it,' he said, smiling as they walked into the warm sitting room, where Jacques was dozing in the chair by the fire. 'Papa, Emilie has good news! She's going to be married.'

Jacques opened one eye and gazed dazedly at Emilie.

'Did you hear that, Papa? Emilie is getting married.' Under his breath, Jean added to Emilie,

'He's had another bout of bad bronchitis. It always hits him in the winter.'

'Yes.' Jacques opened his other eye. 'Who to?'

'The young Englishman we've met when Emilie has brought him down here to the vineyard. His name is Sebastian—?' Jean looked to her for a surname.

'Carruthers,' finished Emilie. 'He comes from a county called Yorkshire, in England. I'll be moving there after I marry. Just for a while, during the renovations here, but I'll be back often,' she added firmly.

'"Carruthers", you say?' Jacques's expression was suddenly alert. 'Yorkshire?'

'Yes, Papa,' Jean confirmed.

Jacques shook his head as if to clear it. 'I'm sure it's coincidence, but I knew a Carruthers from Yorkshire many, many years ago.'

'Really, Papa, how?' asked Jean.

'Constance Carruthers was here with me during the war,' said Jacques.

'That was his grandmother's name! And Sebastian told me she was over here in France at that time.' Feeling a tingle of excitement running through her, she added, 'I'm wearing her engagement ring.' She held out her hand to Jacques, who studied it intently.

'Yes, that is her ring.' Jacques stared up at Emilie, a mixture of shock and emotion registering in his eyes. 'You are to marry Constance's grandson?'

'Yes.'

'My God!' Jacques fumbled for a hanky in his trouser pocket. 'I can hardly believe it. Constance . . .'

83

'You knew her well, Papa?' Jean was as surprised as Emilie.

'Very well. She lived with me here in the cottage for many months. She was—' Jacques swallowed with effort—'a compassionate and brave woman. Is she still alive?' His teary blue eyes burned with a flicker of hope.

'I'm afraid not, no. She died about two years ago,' said Emilie. 'Jacques, how did Constance Carruthers end up living here with you? Can you tell me?'

For a long time, Jacques stared into the distance, then closed his eyes, deep in thought.

'Papa, some champagne?' encouraged Jean, passing his father a glass.

Jacques took it with a shaking hand and sipped it, obviously gathering his thoughts. 'How did you meet this man, Constance's grandson, Emilie?' he asked.

'Constance told Sebastian just before she died about her time here in Occupied France. He tracked down the château owned by our family and came to find out more,' Emilie explained. 'But, like me, he knows very little about why she was here. We would both love to know what happened.'

Jacques sighed. 'It is a long story. And one which I never thought I would tell.'

'Please, Jacques,' begged Emilie, 'I would be fascinated to hear it. I'm realising every day how little I know, especially of my father.'

'Édouard was a wonderful man. He was awarded with an Ordre de la Libération for his bravery and services to France but—' Jacques shrugged sadly—'he refused to accept it. He felt there were others who deserved it more.'

'Please, Jacques, could you at least begin?' Emilie urged him. 'After all, I'm about to marry Constance's grandson, and I feel it's important I understand the past connection between us.'

'Yes, you're right. You should know. It is your family history, after all. But where to start . . . ?' Jacques looked off into the distance for guidance. 'So,' he said eventually, 'I shall begin with Constance. There is little I do not know of her.' He smiled. 'During the long evenings here in the cottage, she talked of her life in England many times. And how she came to be in France . . .'

I'd Like To See

I'd like to see the red
Of the roses in full bloom.
I'd like to see the silver
Of sun's reflection on the moon.

I'd like to see the blue
Of the ocean when it's roaring.
I'd like to see the brown
Of the eagle when it's soaring.

I'd like to see the purple
Of grapes hanging on the vine.
I'd like to see the yellow
Of the sun in summertime.

I'd like to see the russet
Of the chestnuts on the tree.
I'd like to see the faces
Of those that smile at me.

                    Sophia de la Martinières,
                              1927, age 9

7

London, March 1943

Constance Carruthers opened the plain brown envelope she'd found sitting on her desk when she'd arrived at work, and read its contents. The letter was requesting her to attend an interview that afternoon in Room 505a at the War Office. As she removed her coat, she wondered if they had managed to mix her up with someone else. Connie was quite happy in her current position as filing clerk—a 'snagger', as the clerks were affectionately known at MI5—and had no interest in working elsewhere. Walking across the busy room, she tapped on the door of her boss's office.

'Come in.'

'I'm sorry to disturb you, Miss Cavendish, but I've had a letter requesting me to go for an interview at the War Office today. I wondered if you knew what it could be about.'

'Ours is not to question why,' barked Miss Cavendish, glancing up briefly from her desk piled high with files. 'I'm sure they will explain everything when you attend the interview.'

'But . . .' Connie bit her lip. 'I hope you're happy with my work here.'

'Yes, Mrs Carruthers, I am. I suggest you leave all your questions until this afternoon.'

'So I must go?'

'Of course. Will that be all?'

'Yes, thank you.' Connie closed the door behind her, walked back to her desk and sat down, realising it was a fait accompli.

That afternoon as she was led through the maze of subterranean passages that comprised the basement of the War Office, housing the heart of the British government's war operations, Connie was aware that this would be no ordinary interview. She was led into a small, bare room, furnished with a table and two chairs.

'Good afternoon, Mrs Carruthers. I am Mr Potter.' A portly, middle-aged man stood up from behind the table and reached across it to shake her hand. 'Please, kindly sit down.'

'Thank you.'

'I'm told you speak fluent French. Is this true?'

'Yes, Sir.'

'Then you will not mind if we conduct the rest of our little chat in French?'

'I . . . *non*,' Connie agreed, switching languages.

'Now, tell me how you came to speak French so well?' Mr Potter enquired.

'My mother is French, and her sister, my aunt, has a house in St Raphaël, where I've spent every summer of my life.'

'So you are passionate about France?'

'Of course. I feel I'm as much French as I'm British, even though I was born here in England,' she explained.

Mr Potter's gimlet eyes appraised Connie's thick chestnut hair, brown eyes and strong, Gallic bone structure. 'Yes, you certainly look like a Frenchwoman. I see from your file that you also studied French culture at the Sorbonne?'

'Yes, I lived in Paris for three years. And adored every second of it,' added Connie with a smile.

'Why did you choose to return to England once

you had completed your studies?'

'I came back here to marry my childhood sweetheart.'

'Quite,' said Mr Potter. 'And you currently reside up in Yorkshire?'

'Yes, my husband's family estate is up on the North Yorkshire moors. Although, for now, I'm staying at our flat in town whilst I work at Whitehall. My husband is abroad, in North Africa.'

'He is a captain in the Scots Guards?'

'Yes,' Connie confirmed. 'But currently missing in action.'

'So I heard. My sympathy is with you. No children yet?' Mr Potter asked.

'No. The war rather put paid to all that.' Connie sighed grimly. 'We'd barely been married a few weeks before Lawrence was called up. So rather than sitting knitting socks in Yorkshire, I thought I would come down south and find something useful to occupy me.'

'Are you a passionate patriot, Mrs Carruthers?'

'I am, Mr Potter.' Connie raised an eyebrow at the direct line of questioning.

'Prepared to give your life for the countries you love?'

'If it came to it, yes.'

'I hear you are also something of a crack shot,' Mr Potter continued.

Connie looked at him in surprise. 'I'd hardly say that, although I've certainly shot on my husband's estate since I was young.'

'Would you say you are a tomboy?'

'I've never thought about it,' Connie stuttered, struggling to give lucid responses to these most unusual questions, 'but I certainly love outdoor pursuits.'

'And you enjoy robust health?'

'I do, I'm very lucky.'

'Thank you, Mrs Carruthers.' Mr Potter snapped the file closed. He stood up. 'We'll be in contact. Good day.'

He held out his hand and Connie shook it.

'Thank you. Goodbye,' she replied, surprised at the way the interview had come to such an abrupt end and having no idea how she had acquitted herself.

Connie emerged from the stuffy basement into the spring air of the busy London street. As she walked back towards her office, she gazed upwards at the barrage balloons that hung menacingly on the London skyline. And began to ponder why she had been called in to meet the man named Mr Potter.

Three days later, Connie found herself summoned again to sit beneath the harsh artificial lighting of Room 505a. Another grilling ensued: was she carsick, airsick, how were her sleep patterns, would she know how to navigate the French railway system, was she familiar with the layout of Paris . . . ?

Even though nothing had been said about the task they had in mind for her, Connie had begun to formulate a definite inkling. She went back to her flat just off Sloane Square that night knowing that if she had been successful today, her life could be about to change forever.

*   *   *

'So, Mrs Carruthers, we meet again. Please, sit

down.'

Connie read that Mr Potter was visibly more relaxed with her today. For a start, he smiled at her.

'I am sure, Mrs Carruthers, that you may by now have an idea of why you are here.'

'Yes,' she replied, 'I believe you're thinking I may be suitable for some form of work in France?'

'Correct. You will have heard of F Section and the Special Operations Executive through your work at MI5?' he asked.

'Files have passed through my hands, yes,' Connie agreed. 'But only to vet the girls concerned.'

'As we have vetted you in the past few days,' said Mr Potter. 'And nothing of concern has emerged. We now believe that you are suitable to become one of our band of SOE agents. However, Mrs Carruthers, so far we have skirted around the gravity of not only the trust that we in Britain and France would place in you, but also the very real threat of death.' Mr Potter's face was serious. 'How do you feel about that?'

Connie, already aware of what was going to be asked of her, had suffered a week of sleepless nights pondering this very thought and her response to it. 'Mr Potter, I believe passionately in the cause the Allies are fighting for. And I would do my best to never let you down. However, I also understand that I have not, so far in my life, been tested sufficiently to answer that question. I am twenty-five years of age, with no experience in such matters, and I have a lot to learn about both myself and life.'

'I appreciate your thoughtful personal appraisal,

Mrs Carruthers, but I wish to reassure you now that your inexperience presents no problem. Most of the women we employ in this highly sensitive role have no more experience than you. Currently, we have a shop assistant, an actress, a wife and mother, and a hotel receptionist. On a positive note, we will do all we can to help and support you before you leave. You will be sent on an intensive training course, which will equip you as far as possible to handle the many dangerous situations you may find yourself in. And I can assure you, Mrs Carruthers, at the end of that process, both you and the heads of SOE will know whether you are capable of carrying out the tasks you will be set. So,' Mr Potter repeated the question, 'I must ask you again now, are you prepared to take up a role which may subsequently lead to your death?'

Connie stared straight back at him. 'I am.'

'Excellent, then that is settled. As you are employed at MI5, you have already signed the Official Secrets Act, so I need not trouble you further. You will be hearing from F Section directly in the next few days. Congratulations, Mrs Carruthers.' Mr Potter stood up, and this time walked round the table to shake her hand, then led her to the door. 'Both Britain and France are grateful for any sacrifices you might make.'

'Thank you, Mr Potter. May I ask—'

'No more questions, Mrs Carruthers. All you will need to know will be answered shortly. It goes without saying that our meetings here and your future are to remain of the utmost secrecy.'

'Yes.'

'Good luck, Mrs Carruthers.' Mr Potter shook her hand again and opened the door for her.

'Thank you.'

*　　　*　　　*

Arriving at the office the following morning, it was clear that Miss Cavendish, her boss, had already been informed of her departure.

'I hear you're moving to pastures new,' she said, her harassed eyes managing the ghost of a smile when Connie came into her office. 'Here.' Miss Cavendish handed her an envelope. 'You're to report to that address tomorrow morning at nine o'clock. Thank you for your commitment here. I'll be sorry to lose you.'

'And I'll be sorry to go.'

'I'm sure you will cope with whatever lies ahead of you, Mrs Carruthers.'

'I'll do my best,' Connie replied.

'Jolly good. Don't let me down,' Miss Cavendish added as Connie walked towards the door. 'It was I who recommended you.'

*　　　*　　　*

At nine o'clock the following morning, Connie reported, as ordered, to Orchard Court, just off Baker Street. She gave her name to the doorman, who nodded and opened the gilded gates of the lift. He escorted her up to the second floor, unlocked a door along the corridor and ushered her inside.

'Right, Miss, wait in here, please.'

Rather than finding herself in an office, Connie saw she was in a bathroom.

'They won't be long, Miss,' nodded the doorman

as he closed the door behind him. Connie sat down on the side of the jet-black bath, choosing that over the onyx bidet, and wondered what on earth would happen next. Eventually, the door re-opened.

'Follow me, Miss,' said the doorman, leading her out of the bathroom and along the corridor into a room, where a tall, fair-haired man was sitting atop his desk waiting for her.

He held out his hand and smiled at Connie as the doorman withdrew.

'Mrs Carruthers, I'm Maurice Buckmaster, head of F Section. It's a pleasure to meet you. I've heard many positive things about you.'

'And you, Sir.' Connie returned the firm handshake, trying to hide her nerves. This was a man whose name she'd heard mentioned many times at MI5. Reputedly, Hitler had commented of him recently: 'When I get to London, I am not sure who I will hang first—Churchill or that man Buckmaster.'

'Would you prefer to converse in French or in English?' Buckmaster asked.

'Either is fine,' Connie confirmed.

'That's the ticket,' he said with a smile. 'So, French it is. Now, I'm sure you're eager to find out more about what we here at F Section are up to, so I'm going to pass you over to Miss Atkins, who will be looking after you from now on.' Buckmaster swung his long legs down from his desk and moved towards the door. Following him, Connie caught his energy and purpose as he strode off along the corridor and into another room, thick with cigarette smoke. 'Now then, Vera—' he smiled at a middle-aged woman sitting behind a desk—'this is

Constance Carruthers. And I shall leave her in your capable hands. Constance, meet Miss Atkins, the power behind the whole of F Section. See you shortly.' Buckmaster nodded at both of them and left the room.

'Please, sit down, dear,' said Miss Atkins, fixing her piercing blue eyes on Connie. 'We are pleased you're joining us for your special employment. I'm here to answer any questions you may have and to explain what will happen next. What have you told your family so far?'

'Nothing, Miss Atkins. My husband is missing in action in Africa and I telephone my parents once a week on a Sunday. It's only Friday today.' She smiled.

'Your parents are up in Yorkshire and you have no siblings,' Miss Atkins read from a file in front of her. 'That makes it easier. You will tell your parents and any friends who enquire that you've been transferred to the FANY, which as you know, Constance, is the First Aid Nursing Yeomanry. You will say you've been enlisted for driving services in France. You are not under any circumstances to tell them the truth.'

'No, Miss Atkins.'

'You'll be leaving shortly for training at a location outside London. You'll be there for a number of weeks, and your progress in all aspects of your forthcoming tasks will be monitored closely by me on a day-to-day level.'

'What will the training programme consist of?' Connie enquired.

'You will learn all the skills you will require, Mrs Carruthers. Smoke?' She offered Connie a cigarette.

'Thank you.' She took one from the packet and Miss Atkins did the same.

'You live alone in your flat in London?' she asked.

'I do.'

'Then there's no need to change your address. How-ever, having discussed your name with Mr Buckmaster, we've decided you should use your mother's maiden name from now on, which I believe was Chapelle. And your maternal aunt, who lives in St Raphaël, is the Baroness du Montaine?'

'Yes,' Connie nodded.

'Then you will be as you are in France: your aunt's niece. It's a good idea, we find, to get used to your new name as soon as possible,' Miss Atkins explained. 'So, are you happy with Constance Chapelle?'

'Perfectly,' agreed Connie. 'How long will it be before I leave for France?'

'We like to give our agents at least eight weeks' training, but, with things as they are in France and the need to deploy our girls there urgently, it may not be that long,' sighed Miss Atkins. 'We are all indebted to you and your fellow agents for being prepared to carry out such dangerous work. Any further questions, dear?'

'May I ask exactly what my duties will be once I arrive in France?'

'Excellent question,' agreed Miss Atkins. 'Many of the girls who come here seem to think they're being deployed as spies, but that isn't what F Section does. Our agents are there for both communication and sabotage purposes. Our only objective is to frustrate and handicap the Nazi regime in France. The SOE work alongside the Maquis and the French Resistance, supporting them in any way we can.'

'I see. I would have thought there were better qualified people than me for this role?' Connie frowned.

'I'd doubt it, Constance,' Miss Atkins reassured her. 'Your impeccable French and knowledge of both Paris and the south of the country, combined with your Gallic looks, make you perfect for purpose.'

'But surely men are more suited to this task?' she asked.

'Interestingly, that isn't true. Any French male can now be routinely pulled in for questioning to their local Milice, or Gestapo headquarters. They can also be strip-searched. Whereas a woman travelling through France, whether by rail or bus or bicycle, is far less likely to attract attention.' Miss Atkins raised her eyebrows and gave a grim smile. 'And I'm sure that with your attractive looks, Constance, you would know how to charm your way out of trouble. Right then—' she looked at her watch—'if you have no more questions for now, I suggest you return to your flat, write a letter to your parents telling them what we have discussed, and then enjoy what may be your last weekend on Civvy Street for some considerable time.' Miss Atkins's blue eyes appraised her. 'I think that you will do very well, Constance. And you should be proud of your achievement: we only take the best at F Section.'

8

On Monday morning, Connie found herself deposited on the steps of Wanborough Manor, a large country house on the outskirts of Guildford, Surrey. She was ushered upstairs to a room containing four single beds. It seemed that, so far, only one was occupied. Connie unpacked the contents of her small suitcase and hung her clothes in the spacious mahogany wardrobe, noting that, whoever her room-mate was, she had a far more bohemian approach to clothes. A gold sheath evening dress hung haphazardly next to silk smoking pants and a long, colourful scarf.

'You must be Constance,' drawled a voice from behind her. 'So glad you're here—didn't fancy going through the next few weeks being the only girl. I'm Venetia Burroughs, or should I say, Claudette Dessally!'

Constance turned round to greet the girl and was struck by her dramatic appearance. She had shiny, jet-black hair which fell almost to her waist, skin the colour of ivory and huge green eyes, the latter rimmed with kohl to complement a pair of painted red lips. The contrast between the girl's wild looks and her regulation FANY uniform could not have been more marked. Connie was surprised this woman had been deemed suitable; she would naturally stand out in any crowd.

'Constance Carruthers, or should I say, Chapelle.' Connie smiled and moved towards Venetia to shake her outstretched hand. 'Do you know if there are any other women coming?'

'No, when I enquired I was told there would only be the two of us. We're training alongside the chaps,' Venetia said, dropping onto her bed and lighting a cigarette. 'At least this job does have some perks.' She raised her eyebrows as she inhaled. 'You know, we both must be completely mad!'

'Perhaps,' agreed Connie, walking to the mirror and checking her hair was still tidily clipped into a neat bun.

'So where did they find you from?' asked Venetia.

'I was working as a filing clerk at MI5. I was told it was because of my fluent French and knowledge of the country that I was deemed suitable.'

'The only knowledge I have of France is drinking cocktails on the terrace in Cap Ferrat,' Venetia laughed. 'Well, that and the fact that I have a German granny, so I'm rather good at their language, at least. My French, so I'm told, isn't bad either. I came from Bletchley Park . . . I'm sure you know of it, if you were working at MI5?'

'Of course,' agreed Connie. 'We heard all about the Enigma Code.'

'Yes, that was rather a triumph.' Venetia wandered over to a plant pot on the window sill and tapped her ash into it. 'Apparently they need wireless operators desperately out in France. Due to my decoding skills, I'm their girl. Did you know,' she added, walking back to her bed and throwing herself lengthways onto it, 'that the current life expectancy of a wireless operator is approximately six weeks?'

'Surely not!'

'Well, it's hardly surprising, is it?' Venetia

drawled. 'I mean, one can hardly hide a wireless set in one's undies, can one?'

Connie could hardly believe the casual way Venetia was talking about her own possible death. 'Aren't you frightened?'

'I've no idea,' Venetia answered. 'All I do know is that the Nazis have to be stopped. My father managed to get Granny out of Berlin just before the war started, but the rest of his family in Germany have disappeared. They're Jewish, you see,' she said, 'and our family's suspicion is that they've been herded off to one of these Death Camps we've heard about. So—' Venetia sighed— 'whatever I can do to stop them, I will. The way I see it, life won't be worth living for any of us unless Hitler and his merry gang are buried six feet under. And the sooner the better, in my book. Only bugger is, they've told me I have to cut off my hair. Now that,' she said, sitting up as she shook her lustrous ebony mane around her shoulders, '*is* a problem.'

'Your hair is beautiful,' Connie said, thinking that if anyone was likely to outwit and defeat the Nazis single-handedly, it was this extraordinary woman.

'How life changes,' said Venetia, lying back down on the bed, resting her head on her palms. 'Only four years ago, I was coming out as a debutante in London. Life was simply one big party. And now—' she turned to Connie and sighed conspiratorially—'look where we are.'

'Yes,' agreed Connie. 'Are you married?' she asked.

'No fear!' Venetia smiled. 'I decided years ago I wanted to live life first before I settled down.

Looks like I'm doing just that. You?'

'Yes, I am. My husband, Lawrence, is a captain in the Scots Guards. He's out in Africa at the moment. But he's missing in action.'

'I'm sorry,' said Venetia, her eyes full of sympathy. 'Bloody awful, this damned war. Sure your hubby will tip up, though.'

'I have to believe he will,' replied Connie with more stoicism than she felt.

'Do you miss him?'

'Dreadfully, but I've learned to live my life without him,' Connie answered, 'like so many other women with men away fighting.'

'Any *amour* since?' Venetia gave a knowing smile.

'Gosh, no! I would never . . . I mean . . .' Connie could feel herself blushing. 'No,' she answered abruptly.

'Of course not,' agreed Venetia. 'You look like the faithful type.'

Connie wasn't sure whether this was meant as a compliment or an insult.

'Anyway,' Venetia continued, 'I'm jolly glad I've been single for the last four years. I've had enormous fun. And in these difficult times, my motto is seize the day, because you have no idea whether it will be your last. And with what you and I have lying ahead of us—' she stubbed her cigarette out in the plant pot—'that may well be the case.'

*   *   *

Later that afternoon, the two women were called downstairs into the grand drawing room, offered

103

tea and cakes and introduced to their fellow trainees.

'You know what SOE stands for, don't you, darling?' whispered Venetia to Connie. 'The Stately 'Omes of England!' She dissolved into silent giggles. 'Wonder who lived here before it was requisitioned?'

'Yes, it's beautiful,' said Connie, taking in the high ceilings, the grand marble fireplace and long Georgian windows that led to an elegant terrace.

'And so is *he*.'

Connie followed Venetia's eyeline to a young man leaning against the fireplace, deep in conversation with one of the instructors. 'Yes, he is rather,' she agreed.

'Why don't we go and introduce ourselves? Come on.'

Connie trailed behind as Venetia walked over to the man and introduced them both.

'A pleasure to meet you, girls. I'm Henry du Barry,' he replied in perfect French.

Connie could only watch in awe as Venetia went into action—charm and sexuality personified. Feeling left out as Henry and Venetia engaged in conversation, she moved tentatively backwards.

'Well now, that's the Mata Hari of the group,' whispered a teasing voice behind her. 'James Frobisher, AKA Martin Coste. And you are?'

Connie turned round and focused on a man no taller than her, with thinning hair and a pair of horn-rimmed glasses. 'Constance Carruthers—I mean, Chapelle.' She held out her hand and he shook it.

'How's your French?' James asked her companionably.

'My mother is a native, so I've grown up fluent.'

'Sadly, I don't have that advantage,' James sighed. 'I'm progressing after my intensive course, but forget being arrested by the Gestapo. I'm more concerned that I won't remember on which occasion to say *vous* or *tu*!'

'Well, I'm sure they wouldn't be sending you out there if they weren't confident with your language skills,' comforted Connie.

'No, although France is in such a mess, they're bloody desperate for agents. Being arrested like wildfire at the moment, so I hear.' James raised his eyebrows. 'Never mind, we're all on board for our different skills, and I seem to have proved myself rather good at blowing things up. And one doesn't have to converse much with a stick of dynamite.' He grinned. 'I must say, I admire the women who volunteer for the SOE. It's a dangerous job.'

'Well, I wouldn't quite say that I "volunteered", but I'm glad to be able to do my bit for my country,' Connie replied staunchly.

*   *   *

Over dinner in the elegant dining room that evening, Connie got to know the four male agents who would be training with her. Plucked from different walks of life due to their particular suitability for the job in hand, she chatted to Francis Mont-Clare and Hugo Sorocki, both, like herself, half French, James, and of course, Henry the fighter pilot, the heart-throb of the group. As the wine flowed, Constance experienced a sense of the surreal; looking at the people gathered around the table, it could easily have been a dinner-party scene being played out at many similar tables across Britain.

After pudding, Captain Bevan, the instructor in charge, clapped his hands for silence.

'Ladies and gentlemen, I hope this evening has given you all a chance to get to know each other better. You will be working very closely alongside each other in the next few weeks. But I'm afraid the fun stops here. Breakfast is at six o'clock tomorrow morning, after which you will each receive an assessment of your general health and fitness. From the following morning, you will be obliged to take a five-mile run before breakfast every day.'

There were groans from the assembled company.

'Much of the work you do here will be about building up your physical stamina. I cannot underline how imperative it is that each of you departs for France as fit as we can possibly get you. That strength alone may well save your life.'

'Sir, I'm sure a Nazi with a gun right behind me will make me run very fast indeed, if needs be,' joked James.

Venetia giggled and the Captain smiled.

'A number of you have already been through army training, so you'll be used to the rigours of physical exercise. For some of you, especially the ladies—' he glanced at Venetia and Connie—'you may find it tougher. The next few weeks will be some of the hardest of your life. But if you *value* your life, you will give the skills we will teach you every ounce of the concentration and energy you possess. I will post the day's schedule on the board in the entrance hall at six o'clock every evening.

During the weeks that you are here, you will learn to shoot, detonate dynamite, learn basic Morse code, survival skills and how to parachute. What you learn will ready you for the challenges that you face. You are all aware that SOE agents perhaps face the greatest danger of any of your fellow countrymen who are fighting against the Nazis in France for our human right to freedom.'

The room was hushed now, sober suddenly. All eyes were on the Captain.

'But may I also add that without the calibre of men and women like yourselves, who know and understand the grave danger and yet are prepared to take up the challenge, this war and our victory could never be achieved. So, on behalf of the British and French governments, I thank you all. Now, there's coffee and brandy in the drawing room for those who wish it. For those who don't, I will say goodnight.'

James and Connie were the only two who declined the offer of coffee, finding themselves standing in the entrance hall together as the others disappeared into the drawing room.

'Not joining them?' James asked her.

'No, I'm a little tired.' Connie wanted to say 'overwhelmed', but refrained.

'Same here.'

They both took a couple of paces towards the stairs. James stopped on the bottom step and turned to her.

'Are you frightened?' he asked her.

'I'm really not sure,' said Connie.

'I am,' James admitted. 'But I suppose one must do one's bit. Goodnight, Constance.' He sighed as he walked up the stairs.

'Goodnight.' Connie watched him disappear out of sight. Shivering suddenly, she folded her arms about her and walked over to one of the huge windows, gazing up at the full moon. *Was* she frightened? She didn't know. But perhaps the war, which had raged for over four years of her young life, had blunted her emotions. Ever since Lawrence had left to fight within weeks of their marriage, Connie had felt as though her life was in a holding bay, at a moment when everything should have begun. At first, she'd missed him so dreadfully she'd hardly been able to bear it. Living in his huge, draughty house in Yorkshire, with only his brusque mother and her two ageing black Labradors for company, she'd had far too much time to think. Her mother-in-law hadn't approved when she'd decided to go to London to take up the offer of a job at MI5, gleaned through a contact of her father, who could see she was wasting away alone up on the bleak moors.

Many of the girls who had worked with her at MI5 had enjoyed the oddly gay atmosphere of wartime London; they were constantly being asked out by officers on leave who took them for dinner and on to a club. And a number of those women were already either engaged or, even worse, married. Like her, their young men were fighting somewhere abroad, but that didn't seem to stop them.

For Connie, it was different. Lawrence was and always had been, since she'd met him at a tennis party in Yorkshire at the age of six, the only man she had ever loved. Even though she'd been bright enough to pursue a career after her course at the Sorbonne *and* preferred France to the grimness of

North Yorkshire, she had willingly signed up for a lifetime of being no more than the eventual chatelaine of Blackmoor Hall and wife to her beloved Lawrence.

And then, after the happiest day of her life, when she'd walked into the small Catholic chapel on the Blackmoor estate and said her vows, the man she'd loved for fourteen years had been abruptly removed from her just a few weeks later.

Connie sighed. For four years, she'd lived every day in fear of receiving the telegram that would tell her that her husband was missing in action. And subsequently it had arrived. Working at MI5, she knew all too well that the chances of Lawrence still being alive after two months of not being accounted for were receding by the day.

She turned and walked back across the hall towards the stairs. She'd faced the greatest fear of her life when she'd opened that telegram a few weeks ago. And with Lawrence still missing, she no longer particularly cared whether she lived or died.

She settled herself into bed, leaving the night light on for Venetia. It was almost dawn before Connie heard her enter the room, emitting a small giggle as she stumbled over something on the floor.

'You awake, Con?' came a whisper.

'Yes,' she answered sleepily as she heard Venetia's bed creak.

'My goodness, that was a fun night! Henry is completely dreamy, don't you think?'

'He's very handsome, yes.'

Venetia yawned and said, 'I'm thinking the next few weeks may be far more pleasurable than I thought they were going to be. Night, Con.'

*   *   *

Contrary to Venetia's initial assessment, the following weeks tested every one of the trainee agents to their limits. Each day was packed with rigorous physical and mental exertion; if they were not in a trench learning to detonate dynamite, they were shimmying up trees and hiding themselves amongst the branches. Edible nuts, berries, mushrooms and plant leaves were identified, as well as endless shooting practice and the ubiquitous early-morning five-mile run. Venetia, engaged as much in her rip-roaring affair with Henry as she was with her daily activities, and often rolling into bed past four, groaned at the back of the pack.

Connie surprised herself by coping far better than she'd expected with the demands of the course. Always athletic due to her outdoor life on the moors, she could feel her physical strength growing daily. She was the best shooter in the class and had become a dab hand with dynamite, which was more than could be said for Venetia, who had almost managed to blow them all up by detonating a grenade in the trench itself.

'Well, at least it shows I can do it,' she'd said as she'd stomped back to Wanborough Manor afterwards.

'Do you really think that our Venetia is suited to the job ahead of her?' asked James one evening as Connie and he sat over coffee and brandy in the drawing room. 'She's hardly the discreet type, is she?' He laughed as they watched her and Henry in a full-blown embrace on the terrace outside.

'I think Venetia will do very well indeed,' Connie defended her friend. 'She lives on her wits and, as we keep being reminded, ninety per cent of the reality when we get there will be down to that.'

'She's jolly attractive, certainly,' agreed James, 'and I'm sure she'll be able to charm herself out of most situations. Far better than I will,' he added morosely. 'This really is the lull before the storm, isn't it, Con? And, frankly, I'm dreading it, especially the parachute jump in. My knees give me hell as it is.'

'Never mind,' said Connie, patting his hand, 'you may get the luxury of being flown onto terra firma in a Lizzy.'

'Hope so,' said James. 'Extricating myself from a tree, which is where I'm bound to end up knowing my luck, is sure to attract attention.'

Out of all the trainees, James was the only one to express his nerves at the task ahead. Connie and he were the quieter, more cerebral members of the pack and had formed a supportive friendship.

'Isn't it strange, the path that life can take you?' James continued, sipping his brandy. 'If I'd had the choice, I'd have opted for a very different life to this.'

'I think that goes for most of the human race just now,' replied Connie. 'If it wasn't for the war, I'd be sitting on the North Yorkshire moors, probably getting fat and producing a sprog a year.'

'Any news?' James knew about Lawrence.

'No, nothing.' She sighed.

'Don't give up hope, Con.' It was his turn to pat her hand. 'It's such a bloody mess out there. There's as much chance your husband's alive as the other alternative.'

'I try not to,' said Connie, but every day that passed felt like another spade of soil on Lawrence's grave. 'If this damned war ever ends,' she said, changing the subject to a less maudlin topic, 'what will you do?'

'Golly!' James chuckled. 'That seems such a bizarre thought at the moment. My life is similar to yours, in that I will simply return home and take over the family heap. Get married, produce the next generation . . .' He shrugged. 'You know how it is.'

'Well—' Connie smiled—'at least you'll be able to teach your children French. Really, you've improved so much in the past few weeks,' she said encouragingly.

'That's kind of you, Con. But I must tell you that I overheard the Captain discussing all of us over the telephone in his office earlier with Buckmaster. Yes, I lurked.' James grinned. 'Haven't we been told to always use our ears to glean information? Anyway, the Captain was waxing lyrical about you, saying you were the surprise star of the pack. An "A Grade" student, it seems. F Section is expecting great things of you now, my dear,' he concluded.

'Thank you for that; I was always rather a swot at school,' Connie said with a laugh. 'The trouble is, I've never had the opportunity to test myself at life.'

'No fear, Con,' James replied, 'I think your chance may be upon you.'

*　　　*　　　*

A month later, the preliminary training was over.

112

Each agent was called in for a long, gruelling session with the Captain, who bluntly pointed out their strengths and weaknesses.

'You've done extremely well, Constance. And we're all satisfied with your progress here,' the Captain confirmed. 'The only critical comment that has been made by your training officers is on your somewhat ponderous decision-making. Out in the field of operations, your fate can be decided by your immediate reaction to a situation. Do you understand?'

'Yes, Sir.'

'You've proved you have good instincts. Trust them and I doubt they'll see you wrong. We're sending you off now to Scotland with the other agents who have passed muster here,' the Captain concluded. 'It will fit you out further for the job ahead.' He stood up and offered his hand to her. 'Good luck, Madame Chapelle,' he said, giving her a smile.

'Thank you, Sir.'

As Connie closed the door behind her, he added, 'And may God go with you.'

*   *   *

Connie, Venetia, James and, to Venetia's delight, Henry had apparently made the grade and were sent into the wilds of Scotland to learn advanced guerilla training. Far from habitation, the four of them practised blowing up bridges, managing small boats without sinking them, and learned to load German, British and American arms, then heave them onto trucks in the pitch black. The importance of the Vichy Line was explained in detail and the trainee agents were told how the Germans had created a border that cut France in two, dividing the 'Occupied' zone in the north from the Southern zone.

The basic survival skills they had been taught at Wanborough Manor became a reality as they were left on the Scottish moors to fend for themselves and live off the land for days at a time. A trained assassin arrived to teach them how to kill an assailant outright and silently.

Two weeks into their training in Scotland, Venetia was suddenly removed from the course.

'Thank God for that,' Venetia commented as she hurriedly packed her bags. 'Apparently, I'm being sent off to Thame Park for a quick brush-up on my wireless skills. There's some kind of panic over the Channel and it seems they need wireless operators urgently. Oh, Con—' she flung her arms around her friend's shoulders—'let's just hope we meet again soon over there. And take care of my Henry for me, won't you?'

'Of course I will,' said Connie as she watched Venetia close her suitcase and haul it from the bed. 'But I'm sure it won't take you long to find a replacement.'

'No.' Venetia turned to look at Connie. 'Probably not, but it's been fun.'

There was a knock on their door. 'Miss Burroughs, the car is waiting for you downstairs,' came a voice.

'Time to go. Good luck, Con,' Venetia said as she picked up her suitcase and walked towards the door. 'It's been a pleasure knowing you.'

'And you. Please keep the faith,' Connie begged, 'and believe you will get through this.'

'I'll try,' agreed Venetia, opening the door. 'But I'll die out there, Con, I know I will.' She shrugged. '*À bientôt.*'

9

'So, Constance, you've completed your training, and you're ready to leave for France. How are you feeling?'

Connie was back in London at F Section headquarters, sitting on the other side of the desk from Vera Atkins.

'I believe I'm as prepared as I'll ever be.' Connie gave an automatic answer, which hardly expressed an iota of her thoughts and feelings. After her month in Scotland, she'd been transferred to Beaulieu in Hampshire, another requisitioned estate, where her espionage skills had been further refined. She'd been taught how to distinguish between the different uniforms of both German and the French Milice—the hated police arm of the ruling Vichy government—and learned what to look for in recruiting local French citizens to add to her designated network. She'd also had the importance of never committing anything to paper drilled into her.

'I think I'll feel better when I'm actually in the field,' she concluded.

'Jolly good. That's what we like to hear,' Miss Atkins replied chirpily. 'You're scheduled to fly out at the next full moon. You'll be pleased to know you'll not have to land by parachute, but will be taken by Lysander aircraft and deposited safely on French soil.'

'Thank you.' Connie was relieved for that, at least.

'So, now you have a couple of days to rest and relax. I've booked you in to Fawley Court, a comfortable FANY-run boarding house, whilst you wait to fly over. Now is the time to write a number of letters addressed to your loved ones, which I can send to them over the next few weeks whilst you're away.'

'What should I say in the letters, Miss Atkins?' Connie asked.

'I always advise my girls to keep them brief and positive. Say you are well and all is fine,' Miss Atkins answered. 'I'll come to collect you on the afternoon of your departure, but I'll confirm exact times on the day. When you arrive at the airfield, I'll brief you on your new code name, by which we here at F Section and other agents will recognise you. You'll also be told which network you'll be joining once you arrive in France. Now, Constance, Mr Buckmaster would like to see you before you leave.'

Connie followed Miss Atkins down the corridor and into Maurice Buckmaster's office.

'Constance, my dear!' Buckmaster sprang from his chair behind the desk and walked over with open arms to embrace her. 'All set?' he asked, releasing her.

'As far as I can be, yes, Sir,' Connie replied.

'That's the ticket. From what I've heard, you were the star pupil on your training course. I'm sure you'll do F Section proud,' he enthused, ever positive.

'To be honest, Sir, I'll simply be glad when I'm

116

there.'

'I'm sure. Try not to worry too much, my dear. Last night I spoke to an SOE agent just home from her first tour of duty, and she commented that by far the hardest thing was the miles of cycling every day. She said the travelling had given her thighs the size of an elephant!'

Connie and Buckmaster shared a chuckle.

'Any questions, Constance?' he asked.

'None that I can think of, Sir, except has there been any word from Venetia?' Connie asked eagerly. 'I know she flew out a few days ago.'

'No—' even Buckmaster's face darkened for an instant—'not so far. But I wouldn't worry, it often takes time for a wireless operator to send their first transmission. And there have been a few problems in her region lately. Anyway . . .' He walked back to his desk, opened a drawer and produced a small box, which he duly handed to her. 'A present for you, to wish you luck.'

'Thank you, Sir.'

'Open it,' he urged. 'It's what I give all my girls as a parting gift. Terribly useful and, as I say, if in dire straits you can always sell it.'

Connie pulled a small, silver powder compact from the box.

'Like it?' he asked.

'It's perfect,' she agreed. 'Thank you, Sir.'

'Don't want to let my girls' standards of appearance slip, even when out in the field of operations. Right, Constance, all that remains for me to say is thank you for your diligence so far. I shall no doubt be hearing of your activities in the coming weeks. God speed and *bonne chance*.'

'Yes, Sir. Goodbye.'

Connie turned and left the room.

*   *   *

On the evening of the seventeenth of June, Connie drove down from London with Vera Atkins to Tangmere Airfield in Sussex. Inside the hangar, they sat at a small table at the back and Vera handed Connie a sheet of paper.

'Please spend the next twenty minutes memorising everything written on there. Your code name will be "Lavender", and that will be used at all times when you're in contact with us or other agents in the field of operations, both British and French. You'll be joining the "Scientist" network, which operates mainly in and around Paris. When you land in France at Vieux-Briollay, you'll be met by a reception committee. They will look after you and provide the necessary transportation, plus the contact details of your organiser, wireless operator and other members of your circuit.'

'Yes, Miss Atkins.'

'I should warn you, Constance, that we've had trouble recently communicating with your network,' Miss Atkins continued. 'Your reception committee on the ground in France can probably give you more accurate information than I can at the present time. However, I'm sure that with your intelligence and common sense, you will manage. Now—' Miss Atkins pulled a small leather suitcase up onto the table—'in here is everything you will need. Identity papers, naming you as Constance Chapelle, a school teacher living in Paris. You have many relations in the South of France, which is

118

where you're originally from. You will use this as your reason if at any point it's necessary for you to cross the Vichy Line in or out of the Occupied Zone in the north.'

Connie watched as Miss Atkins then produced a small phial containing a single tablet.

'This is your C pill. You will put it now inside the heel of your shoe,' she instructed.

Having had prior warning, Connie removed the specially adapted shoe from her foot and opened the sole of the heel.

Miss Atkins dropped the pill inside. 'Let's hope you never have to use it.'

'Quite,' agreed Constance, knowing the innocent-looking pill contained a lethal dose of cyanide, in case of arrest and subsequent torture.

'Now then,' Miss Atkins said brightly, 'all set?'

'Yes.'

'Then let's get you on board the Lizzy.'

The two of them walked towards the little plane painted black to avoid detection on a moonlit night. At the bottom of the steps, Miss Atkins paused. 'I nearly forgot,' she said, pulling out an envelope from her jacket pocket. 'This is for you.'

She handed the envelope to Connie, who opened it, then read the words in disbelief.

'Good news, eh?' Miss Atkins commented.

Connie's hand flew to her mouth and her eyes filled with spontaneous tears. 'Miss Atkins, Lawrence is alive! He's alive!'

'He is indeed, dear. And the ship bringing him home docked safely three days ago in Portsmouth. He has a nasty wound to his chest and a broken leg, but the doctors say he's in good spirits and doing well in hospital.'

'You mean he's *here*? Lawrence is in England?' she repeated in disbelief.

'Yes, dear, he's home, safe and sound. Isn't that nice to know?'

Connie looked down at the date of the telegram informing her that her husband had been found alive and was being shipped home immediately. The date was the twentieth of May, nearly a month ago.

'Now then, I thought that would be good news to take with you and it certainly gives you an incentive to return safely. Time to board, dear,' Miss Atkins said briskly as she removed the telegram from Connie's grasp. The propellers on the plane sprang into action. Vera Atkins held out her hand to Connie. 'Goodbye, Constance, and good luck,' she said as she shook it.

In a daze, Connie walked up the steps and into the cramped interior of the plane. As she fastened herself into her seat, she tried to process what she had just been told. Not only was her husband alive, but he was *here*, home safely in England. Maybe no more than a few hours' drive from where she was now.

And they hadn't told her . . .

How could they *not* have informed her that Lawrence had been found and was returning home? Connie bit her lip hard to stem the tears, in danger of flooding the tight, uncomfortable goggles she was wearing.

With a heavy heart, she understood only too well why they hadn't. They'd realised that, if they *had* told her of Lawrence's imminent arrival in England, she would have swiftly turned tail and backed out of the dreadful task she was about to undertake.

But now, as Connie watched another two unidentifiable humans in flight suits and goggles climb inside the plane, and the door shut behind them, there was no turning back. F Section had manipulated her personal circumstances for their own ends. And then, at the last minute, they'd offered her the one incentive she needed to do everything she could to stay alive and return.

'How can I bear this?' she muttered under her breath as the plane began to taxi out of the hangar into the moonlit night.

'Connie? Is that you under all your gear?' shouted a voice from the seat next to her over the roar of the engines. It was a voice she recognised.

'James!' she shouted back, feeling absurdly comforted by the fact he was there.

It was impossible to talk any further as the plane took off into the night sky. Instead, Connie did not resist as a hand reached for hers, squeezed it and held it tightly. She gazed out of the window at the pitch-black English countryside beneath her.

'Goodbye, Lawrence, my darling, darling boy,' she whispered. 'I swear to you, I'll be home in your arms as soon as I can.'

10

The Lysander touched down gracefully into a field, guided by small flashlights held by unseen hands on the ground. The pilot turned round and gave them a thumbs-up signal. 'All seems to be well. Goodbye, ladies and gentlemen. And good luck,' he added as they climbed down the steps and onto the grass.

'*Bienvenue*,' said a man, who scurried past them up the steps of the plane with a satchel. He threw it inside, then sealed the door and ran back down to survey his newest recruits.

The Lysander was already on the move, commencing its return journey. Connie looked at it jealously, wishing she had the courage to run towards it, climb up inside and follow her heart back to England.

'Follow me,' said the man who had dropped the satchel inside the plane. 'And hurry, I saw a Boche truck passing by only a few minutes ago. They may well have heard the landing.'

The three agents, led by their guide, scurried across the field, James bringing up the rear. It was a beautiful French night, clear and warm, and as Connie ran with the rest of them she had a sense of familiar in the unfamiliar. France smelt as it always had: the balmy, dry, pine-scented air, so different from the dampness of the English countryside. She would recognise it anywhere.

Eventually, their guide opened the door to a wooden hut housed in a dense forest. Inside, pallets with blankets atop them lay strewn on the floor. And a gas ring, which their host immediately lit with a match, stood in a corner.

'We must stay here until morning, when curfew has passed. Then we'll send you on your separate journeys from the station in Vieux-Briollay, a twenty-minute cycle ride from here. Please, make yourselves as comfortable as you can. Put your flight suits in the corner over there. You will leave them here with me,' he instructed. 'I'll make some coffee as you do.'

Connie divested herself of her suit and watched as her fellow passengers revealed themselves. The other man, she hadn't met before. They sat down on their pallets as their guide handed them each an enamel mug of coffee.

'No milk, I'm afraid. I know you English like it,' he said.

Connie was glad of the rich, dark liquid; she was used to the strength of it.

'I'm Stefan,' the guide announced, 'and I know you must be "Lavender", Madame, as you're the only woman.'

'I'm "Trespass",' said James.

' "Pragmatist",' offered the unknown man.

'On behalf of France, I welcome you here. We have never been more in need of trained British agents to help us,' said Stefan. 'Many of your fellow agents, especially in Paris, have been arrested in the past few days. We're not sure of their fate, but we believe there must be a traitor amongst them to enable the Gestapo to swoop so successfully. All I can advise is that you trust no one,' he underlined. 'Now, it's time to sleep whilst you can. I'll keep watch and alert you if necessary. Goodnight.'

Stefan stepped outside the hut, lighting a cigarette at the door before he closed it behind him. The three agents made themselves as comfortable as possible on their pallets.

'Goodnight, chaps,' said James, 'sleep well.'

'Doubt I shall get a wink,' said Pragmatist, but soon enough Connie heard faint snores emanating from the other side of the hut.

'Connie?' It was James.

'Yes?'

'This is for real now, isn't it?'

'Yes,' agreed Connie, her empty stomach acidic from coffee and emotion, 'it is.'

*   *   *

Connie must have eventually drifted off to sleep, as she was shaken awake by James and saw light filtering through the small window.

'Wakey, wakey,' said James. 'They're waiting outside for us.'

She had slept fully dressed, so Connie only had to slip on her stockings and shoes to be ready. Outside stood Stefan and a woman.

'Good morning, Lavender,' said Stefan. 'Are you ready to leave?'

'Yes, but—' Connie looked around the forest— 'is there anywhere I can . . . ?' She knew she was blushing.

'We have no facilities here. Please find a place in the woods,' he said with a shrug, turning to speak to James.

Connie scurried off to find a discreet place behind a tree. When she returned, James and the other agent were about to set off on bicycles with the woman.

'Good luck,' Connie whispered to James. 'I hope we'll meet again soon.'

'Hear, hear,' said James, his face taut and tense. 'In the meantime, I'll do my best to blow the Boche to smithereens and get us all back home.'

'That's the spirit,' said Connie, wearing a brave smile for him as he wobbled off through the forest on his bicycle behind the others.

'We'll wait for a while until they're a few kilometres away,' said Stefan. 'Too many cyclists emerging from the forest will attract attention if someone is watching. Coffee?'

'Thank you.' Connie sat on the doorstep of the hut, watching the sun, now risen above the trees, dappling the ground beneath it.

'So, Lavender, I'll tell you what will happen to you next.' Stefan handed her a mug of coffee and came to sit next to her on the step, lighting another cigarette. 'Now, you will have been told you're joining the Scientist network, our largest organisation, which operates both inside and around Paris.'

'Yes,' Connie confirmed.

'Unfortunately, we've had word that various members of Scientist have been arrested by the Gestapo, including Prosper, the leader.'

'I was indeed warned and told you would have further information,' Connie replied, sipping her coffee.

'We've received no word from Prosper's wireless operator either, which may mean he too has been arrested.' Stefan stamped his cigarette out under his foot. 'I had communication three days ago that they were expecting you and would meet you from the train at Montparnasse station, but I can't be sure now who will be there.' Stefan immediately lit another cigarette. 'It's too dangerous for me to accompany you at this time—we've been warned by headquarters to lie low until we know the situation—so you'll have to make the journey alone.'

'I see.' Connie gripped her mug like a talisman to stem her nerves.

125

'As your code name is not yet on any files the Gestapo may have in their possession, it's very unlikely you'll come under any suspicion on your journey. Women are stopped for security checks far less than men,' he reassured her. 'It's a lot to ask of one just arrived, but we need to send someone to Paris who's unknown to the Boche to find out what's happened. Are you willing?'

'Of course.'

'You're due to be met on the station concourse outside the *tabac*. You must buy a packet of Gauloises, and when you have done so, drop them to the ground as if by mistake. Pick them up and then light one with these.' Stefan pulled a box of matches out of his pocket and handed them to her. 'At this point, a man should approach you. He'll then take you on to one of our safe houses.'

'And if he doesn't appear?' asked Connie.

'Then you'll be aware something is wrong. You know Paris well?'

'Yes, I studied at the Sorbonne.'

'Then it will be simple for you to find this address.' Stefan handed her a piece of paper.

'Apartment seventeen, twenty-one, Rue de Rennes,' Connie read the familiar road name. 'I know it well.'

'Good. As you approach the building, you must walk past it to the end of the street and then back along the other side. If you see the Gestapo on the road, or in a truck nearby, you will know the safe house has been discovered. Do you understand?'

'Yes. And if I see no Gestapo outside?' Connie queried.

'Then go up to the third floor, where you'll find the apartment. Knock twice, then three times, and the door should be answered. Tell them your courier hasn't arrived to collect you and that Stefan has sent you,' he instructed.

'Right,' said Connie, committing the address to memory as the piece of paper was taken from her hand and lit with a match by Stefan. 'And if no one is there, where should I go next?'

'There's someone at apartment seventeen twenty-four hours a day. If there's no answer, you'll know the Scientist network is discovered and all have fled to lie low. Therefore, it would be too dangerous to try to make contact with any of its members.' Stefan sighed, taking a deep drag of his cigarette. 'As a last resort, I must send you to a friend of mine. He's not directly part of a circuit, or the SOE, but his loyalty to our cause is beyond reproach. I know he will help you. So, you'll go to this address—' Stefan pulled another small piece of paper from his pocket and handed it to her— 'and ask for "Hero".'

Connie read the new address with surprise. 'It's on the Rue de Varenne. My family used to have friends there.'

'Then your family must have moved in high circles. As you know, it's one of the most prosperous areas of Paris,' said Stefan, raising an eyebrow.

'And—in case Hero isn't there . . . ?' she asked. 'Will I give up and take a train back here?'

'Madame—' Stefan ground the cigarette out aggressively on the forest floor—'at that point, you must use your wits. You will check into a *pension* close by and simply watch and wait for Hero to return. Now, it's time for us to go. And remember, you must not be on the streets of Paris after curfew. That's the most dangerous time of all.'

He went back inside the hut with the coffee mugs and Connie studied the ancient bicycles they would ride to the station.

'Who's your friend Hero?' asked Connie as she climbed aboard, her suitcase wedged precariously between basket and handlebars.

'The rules here are to ask no questions. But he'll be the one who knows everything that has happened and will be able to put you in touch with a safe sub-branch of Scientist. Then you, of course, will be responsible for finding a way to contact London and report back on the situation in Paris as soon as possible. That is if there's a single wireless operator still free in the city,' Stefan added grimly.

The bicycle journey to the station was thankfully uneventful. The town looked much the same as Connie had seen in this area of pre-war France, apart from the swastika flag hanging over the town hall.

Stefan purchased Connie's ticket and handed it to her. She noticed the way his eyes darted constantly around the platform.

'I must leave you here. Goodbye, Madame,' he said, kissing her warmly on both cheeks as if she was a dear relative. 'Keep in touch,' he added and, lighting a further cigarette, ambled off casually towards his bicycle, leaving Connie to wait alone for the train.

It arrived on the dot at eleven o'clock; Buckmaster had once joked that the only advantage of the German Occupation was the sudden promptness of the French transportation system. Connie climbed aboard, stowing her suitcase on the rack above her. As the train left the station, she looked about the carriage and saw the usual melting pot of humanity. Connie's empty stomach growled and she closed her eyes, hoping the soothing familiarity of the train's motion would help calm her frayed nerves. But at every station her eyes flickered open to survey any new arrivals in her carriage.

She changed trains at Le Mans and was able to buy a stale pastry from the kiosk on the platform. Sitting down on a bench to wait for her connection, Connie had her first glimpse of a German officer standing along the platform chatting to the station master.

Finally, at teatime, her train pulled in to Montparnasse station in Paris. Connie joined the rest of the passengers as they alighted and walked along the platform, bracing herself to pass through her first Milice security checkpoint. She saw a number of her fellow passengers being stopped and their cases pulled up on tables to be opened. Connie's heart was in her mouth as she walked through, but none of the French policemen gave her a second glance.

Feeling faint with exhilaration that she had passed through uneventfully, Connie looked around the concourse for the *tabac* kiosk where she was to rendezvous with her courier. The station was crowded with workers returning home, but finally she saw the kiosk in a corner and walked towards it. Doing as requested, she bought a packet of Gauloises. Collecting the change, she dropped the packet onto the floor.

'*Ah, mince alors!*' she muttered as she picked the box up and pulled out a cigarette. She lit it as

129

casually as possible with the matches Stefan had given her, at the same time glancing around to see if anyone was emerging from the crowd and walking towards her.

Connie smoked the whole cigarette, but no one appeared at her side. Stubbing it out underfoot, she looked at her watch and sighed, as if someone she was expecting to meet was late. Ten minutes later, she pulled out another cigarette, using the same box of matches. She smoked that one to the stub too.

After her third cigarette, Connie knew that no one would be coming.

'On to Plan B,' she muttered to herself, and left the station to find herself for the first time on the streets of Occupied Paris. The walk to the Rue de Rennes was only a short one. With few visible signs of anything changed, and being in a city she knew and loved so well, the motion calmed her. On this warm summer evening, the streets crowded with Parisians going about their normal business, it was almost possible to imagine nothing had changed.

Dusk was falling as Connie reached the Rue de Rennes. Locating the building number that she needed, she walked past it on the other side of the street, eyes surreptitiously peeled for danger. Having reached the end of the road, she crossed over and walked back along the other side, feeling horribly conspicuous with her suitcase.

Finally, arriving in front of the entrance to the apartment block, she strode purposefully towards the grand front door and turned the handle confidently. It opened easily and she crossed the marble hall and climbed the stairs, the sound of her feet echoing up the lofty staircase. Pausing on the third floor, she found number seventeen just to her right and, taking a deep breath, knocked on it twice, then three times, as instructed.

Nobody answered. Unsure whether to wait or to knock again, her heart pounding in her ears as her blood pressure rose, Connie decided against it. She had been told to try only once and now she must leave as quickly as possible. It was obvious that Stefan's fears for the network were real. Turning on her heel, she was about to descend the stairs when the door of the apartment next to number seventeen opened very slightly.

'Madame!' a voice hissed, 'your friends are all gone. The Gestapo came here for them yesterday. They are sure to be watching the building now. Do not leave by the front entrance. There's a door at the back which opens into a small courtyard. And a gate, which leads to a path used for the dustmen to remove the rubbish, which brings you out onto a different street. Go now, quickly, Madame!'

The door shut as fast as it had opened and Connie, finally remembering her training, removed her shoes to stop the noise on the stairs and flew down them as fast as she could. Finding the door the woman had suggested at the back of the hall and praying it wasn't a trap, she opened it and saw that it led to a small courtyard. Replacing her shoes, she opened the gate, followed the narrow path and found herself out on a neighbouring street. Turning in the opposite direction from the Rue de Rennes, Connie forced herself to walk slowly and casually away from her first encounter with real danger.

Eventually, faint from hunger and adrenalin, and a good kilometre away by now from apartment

131

seventeen, Connie spotted a café with customers spilling out onto the pavement tables. Concerned her legs would take her no further unless she sat down, she took an empty table and stowed her suitcase beneath it. Studying the limited but welcome menu, Connie ordered a croque-monsieur. As she devoured the food hungrily, she breathed deeply to allow her brain to clear.

In this city of millions, she had never felt more alone. And even though there were many people in Paris whom she knew from her days at the Sorbonne and family members too on her mother's side, any contact was strictly forbidden.

The fact that familiarity and assistance were close at hand, yet so out of reach, made her current situation more poignant. It seemed that Stefan had been right and her network had fled for cover as the Gestapo began their round of arrests. Connie drained her coffee, knowing all she could do was to go to his suggested place of last resort. She paid the bill, picked up her suitcase and walked off along the street.

Jumping out of her skin every time she heard the rumble of a Nazi truck approaching, Connie walked north and finally arrived on the Rue de Varenne—a wide, tree-filled boulevard lined with gracious, elegant houses. Many of them were dark and silent, but as she looked from a distance at the address she'd been given, she saw the house was most definitely occupied. Lights shone from all the windows and she could even see shadowy figures moving about in one of the rooms at the front.

Taking a deep breath, Connie crossed the road, climbed up the steps to the front door and pressed the bell.

A few seconds later, an elderly maid opened the door. Looking Connie up and down, she gave an arrogant, 'Yes?'

'I'm here to see Hero,' Connie whispered. 'Please tell him Stefan sends his regards,' she added.

The maid's attitude towards her changed immediately. Alarm registered on her lined face. 'Please, Madame, step inside quietly and I will go and find him,' she said, ushering Connie in.

'He's here?' Connie's relief was palpable.

'Yes, but . . .' The maid looked uncertain. 'One moment, Madame.'

Whilst the maid disappeared through one of the doors along the corridor, Connie admired the fine antique furniture and elegantly turned staircase which formed the centrepiece to the hall. The occupants of this house were from a world of wealth she knew very well and in which she felt comfortable.

A few seconds later, a tall, dark-haired man whom, with his fine, chiselled bone structure, could be taken for nothing but French, emerged from the room in full dinner dress.

He strode towards her and held out his arms. 'Good evening, my dear!' he cried, enveloping a surprised Connie in his arms, 'I wasn't expecting you.' He whispered into her ear as he hugged her to him, 'We're entertaining and they may have seen you climbing the front steps.' Out loud, he said, 'How was your journey?'

'It was long,' she replied, startled.

'Are you French?' he whispered, still holding her tightly in an embrace and speaking directly into her ear.

'Yes, my family are from St Raphaël,' she whispered quickly.

'What's your name?'

'Constance Chapelle. My aunt is the Baroness du Montaine.'

'I know of the family.' Sudden relief appeared in the man's eyes. 'Then you're my second cousin, come to visit. Go upstairs with Sarah. We'll talk later.' Releasing her, he spoke normally. 'Journeys from the south are so tiresome these days, especially with all the security checks. We will see you downstairs when you're refreshed, my dearest Constance.'

The expression in his eyes gave Connie no alternative. He turned back to the drawing room and then pushed the door open to enter the room.

As he did so, Connie saw a number of German uniforms standing behind it.

11

Having been shown by Sarah, the maid, upstairs to a sumptuous bedroom, then left alone in it whilst Sarah drew her a bath, a shocked Connie sat breathlessly in an armchair, trying to make sense of what she had just seen downstairs. She'd imagined many scenarios, and had even been placed in them during her training course. But never once had she countenanced the thought of spending her first night in Occupied Paris socialising with the enemy.

Sarah led her along the corridor to the bathroom and she briefly luxuriated in the hot water after two days of being unable to wash. She allowed herself a fleeting smile at the irony of the comfortable physical circumstances she had found herself in as she stepped out of the bath reluctantly and hurried back along the corridor to her allocated bedroom.

Sarah was sitting on the chaise longue at the bottom of the bed. She gestured to the seat next to her. 'Please, sit down, Constance.'

Connie did so.

'Édouard, whom you met downstairs, has requested that we speak before you join him for dinner. We don't have long, so please concentrate on what I will tell you. Firstly, my name is Sarah Bonnay, and I have worked for the de la Martinières family for many years. Édouard explained to me that his friend Stefan had sent you, and has asked me to tell you what must happen now.'

'Thank you,' Connie said nervously in reply.

'I can hear the fear in your voice, Constance, and I understand it. But please believe that you're lucky to have fallen into a safe pair of hands at this moment in Paris,' comforted Sarah. 'However, your unexpected arrival puts us all in danger. No one could have known that on this night the household would be . . . entertaining. So Édouard has said we must do all we can to salvage the situation. Constance, on your first night in Paris you must give the performance of your life. Édouard has suggested you are his cousin, up from the south to visit. He said you have family connections there?'

'Yes, my aunt, the Baroness du Montaine, has a château in St Raphaël.'

135

'As he has in Gassin, nearby,' said Sarah. 'So it's perfectly possible that the Montaines and the de la Martinières are related. Your story at dinner is that you have arrived in Paris to see your dear cousins and bring them news of the sad death of your mutual uncle, Albért.'

'I see.'

'Constance, let Édouard do the talking,' continued Sarah. 'Say as little as possible if you are questioned downstairs. If you are yourself, it should be easy for you.'

'I will do my best.'

Sarah appraised her. 'I believe that you're of similar size to the late Emilie de la Martinières, Édouard's mother. You should know she died four years ago, just before the war. Perhaps she was the lucky one . . .' She sighed. 'So, I will bring you one of her gowns. If you would like, I can assist you with your hair. The more beautiful, charming and ignorant you seem, the less danger there will be for all of us. Do you understand, Constance?'

'Yes, I understand.'

'Now, you will hurry to prepare yourself and as soon as possible you must join the party in the drawing room. In the meantime, I shall tell Édouard what we've discussed when he comes to collect his younger sister, whose name is Sophia, and escort her downstairs. Please, do not fail us this evening. It's imperative those gathered here tonight suspect nothing. Otherwise—' Sarah sighed again as she rose from the chaise longue— 'all is lost for the de la Martinières.'

'I promise to do my best,' Connie managed.

'We will all have to pray that you do.'

Twenty minutes later, Connie stood in front of the closed drawing-room door. As Sarah had suggested, she sent up a prayer, opened the door and walked in.

'Constance!' Immediately, Édouard moved away from the crowd in the room and kissed her warmly on both cheeks. 'Are you sufficiently recovered from the rigours of your journey? You certainly look as though you are,' Édouard added admiringly.

'I am,' replied Connie, knowing at least that her physical appearance was the best it had ever been. Sarah had done an excellent job with her hair, then applied make-up, before helping Connie into an exquisite evening dress—made, Connie noticed, by Monsieur Dior. Borrowed diamonds at her ears and her throat completed her disguise.

'Come, let me introduce you to my friends.' Édouard offered Connie his arm and as she walked towards the men a sea of uniforms she'd been trained to identify were directly in her vision.

'Hans, may I introduce you to my dear cousin, Constance Chapelle, who has graced us with her lovely presence for a short stay in Paris. Constance, may I present Kommandant Hans Leidinger.'

Constance felt the eyes of the enormous man, dressed in what she knew was the uniform of a high-ranking Abwehr—a German officer in military intelligence—appraise her.

'Fräulein Chapelle, I am pleased to meet another charming member of Édouard's family.'

'Colonel Falk von Wehndorf.' Édouard had

moved on to the next man, the latter in the uniform of the dreaded Gestapo.

Von Wehndorf was the picture-perfect blond Aryan male. He glanced up and down her body with undisguised interest. Instead of shaking Connie's proffered hand, he took it to his mouth and kissed it. His pale-blue eyes bored into hers for an instant, before he said in perfect French, 'Fräulein Chapelle, where has your cousin Édouard been hiding you away?'

The words, innocently spoken, triggered immediate panic in Connie.

'Colonel von Wehndorf . . .'

'Please, we're all friends here, call me Falk—if I may call you Constance?' he suggested.

'Of course.' Connie gave what she hoped was her most enchanting smile. 'He has not been hiding me, I merely live down in the south and find the journey to Paris arduous.'

'Where in the south does your family live?'

But Édouard was already introducing her to the next man, who was clad in the uniform of the SS—the German State Police.

'Excuse me.' Connie lowered her eyes from Falk and turned her attention to Kommandant Choltitz.

'*À bientôt*, Fräulein Constance,' she heard Falk say softly behind her.

A glass of champagne was thrust into her hand by Édouard as she met another three German officers and a high-ranking official from the French Milice. She was then introduced to two Frenchmen, one a lawyer and the other a professor, whose wife, Lilian, was the only other woman present. Nerves jangling, Connie took a hefty gulp of her champagne and prayed Édouard would have the foresight to place her at the table next to the safety of her fellow countrymen.

'Mesdames et Messieurs, please, pass through to the dining room. I will go to collect my sister,' said Édouard, leading the way to the drawing-room door.

Sandwiching herself as subtly as she could between the French professor and his wife, Connie walked through to the dining room. Sarah indicated her place at the table. She sat down, relieved to see the professor was on one side of her and the lawyer, standing behind a chair, on the other. Then Sarah moved swiftly towards the lawyer, just as he was about to take his seat. She whispered something in his ear and the lawyer moved off immediately to the other side of the table. Connie found Falk von Wehndorf, the German Gestapo officer, suddenly next to her.

'Fräulein Constance, I hope it will not offend you that I asked to be next to you for dinner tonight,' he said with a smile. 'It's not often I have the pleasure of such a beautiful woman as a table companion. Now, we must have more champagne.' Falk signalled to Sarah, who hurried forward with the bottle as Édouard entered the dining room.

On his arm was a beautiful young woman: Sophia, Connie remembered, Édouard's sister. Tiny, almost doll-like in her perfection, Sophia was wearing a midnight-blue evening dress that accentuated the creaminess of her unblemished skin and piercing blue eyes. Her blonde hair was coiled into a chignon, her swan-like neck adorned with a necklace of blue sapphires.

As Édouard guided her to the table, Connie noticed Sophia's arms reach out and search for the chair, her delicate fingers tracing the wooden back of it. Sitting down, she smiled at the assembled company.

'Good evening. It's a pleasure to welcome all of you here again to our home.'

She spoke in a low, musical voice, with the impeccable French of the aristocracy.

Many of the assembled company muttered an affectionate greeting to her in return.

'And cousin Constance . . . Édouard tells me you have finally arrived safely with us.' Sophia's turquoise eyes did not turn towards Connie as she said this.

'Yes, and I'm glad to see you looking so well,' Connie answered blandly.

Sophia's blank gaze turned in the direction of her voice and she offered Connie a dazzling smile. 'And we will have much to catch up on, I'm sure.'

Connie watched as Sophia's neighbour engaged her in conversation. Yet still her eyes did not focus on his face as she talked to him.

With a sudden jolt, she realised that Sophia de la Martinières was blind.

Connie saw Édouard's eyes flick towards her and Falk von Wehndorf, registering the alteration of the table plan. Édouard himself sat on the opposite side of the table to Constance, surrounded by the Germans.

'First, a toast. This dinner is held in honour of the thirty-fifth birthday of our guest and friend, Falk von Wehndorf.' The table held their glasses in readiness. 'To you, Falk.'

'To Falk!' came the chorus of voices.

Falk gave a mock bow. 'And to our host, Comte Édouard de la Martinières, for throwing this party.

140

And it seems,' he said, glancing sideways at Connie, 'that he has also provided me with an unexpected birthday present. To Fräulein Constance, who joins us tonight from the south for this occasion.'

Connie held her nerve as every eye at the table fell upon her. Never had she imagined that her arrival in Paris would be toasted by a group of Nazi officers. She took a sip of champagne, knowing she must keep her wits about her and drink no more. She was grateful as Sarah began to serve the first course and the attention in the room slipped away from her.

*   *   *

In the future, when Connie looked back to her first evening in Occupied Paris, she was convinced that someone had been watching over her. The professor on her left lectured at the Sorbonne, and so she was able, in front of the persistent attention of Falk, to give a true and honest account of her time there. The conversation gave credence to her cover and she noticed Édouard's approving eyes upon her as she managed to circumnavigate questions from Falk and use her charm to divert him with smiles and glances.

At the end of the evening, as the German officers were leaving, Falk again took her hand and kissed it. 'Fräulein, I have enjoyed your company very much this evening. I have learned that not only are you beautiful, but clever.' He nodded approvingly. 'And I like clever women. How long are you in Paris?'

'I've taken no decision,' she answered honestly.

141

'Constance will be staying with us for as long as she pleases.' Édouard came to the rescue as he ushered the men to the door and said goodnight himself.

'Then I hope it will be my pleasure to see you again. And very soon. *Heil Hitler!*' With a last glance at her from his pale-blue eyes, Falk followed the other men out of the front door. It shut behind them and Édouard himself locked and bolted it.

Standing in the hall, her ordeal over, Connie felt all the energy drain from her body. Her legs turned to jelly and she staggered suddenly. Édouard was there to catch her and put a comforting arm around her shoulder.

'Come, Constance,' he said as he steered her towards the back of the house, 'you must be exhausted. We'll take a brandy before bed.' He signalled to Sarah, who was hovering in the corridor. 'Please bring a tray into the sitting room.'

Connie sat down gratefully on the sofa, so tired she felt catatonic. Édouard surveyed her for a while as Sarah brought in the tray of brandy. Once his glass had been filled and Sarah had left the room, he lifted it towards her. 'Congratulations, Constance. You were magnificent tonight.' She saw him smile properly for the first time, his handsome face suddenly alive.

'Thank you,' she said weakly as she garnered the energy to lift the brandy glass to her lips.

'Perhaps all there is to say is—' Édouard smiled again—'welcome to our family.'

They both chuckled at his remark. And, as the dreadful tension of the evening released itself, they laughed until they wept at the coup they had managed to pull off.

'Ah, Constance, you cannot know the shock when you appeared on the doorstep. I thought all was lost. A house full of high-ranking Milice, Gestapo and Abwehr officers, and a lost SOE agent appears here in full view of them all to see me!'

'I couldn't believe it when I saw their uniforms in the drawing room.' Connie shook her head in horror at the memory.

'We'll talk tomorrow about how this happened,' said Édouard. 'But for now I can only extend my grateful thanks to you for rising to the challenge and giving a spectacular performance. Of course, God was on our side tonight in many things. Your background made it easy for everyone to believe you're a member of our family.'

'On the SOE training course,' Connie giggled, 'I was warned time and again that I spoke French in a way that would mark me out as bourgeoise. It would not be suitable for my cover as a schoolteacher from Paris. They said I betrayed too many airs and graces, and I did all I could to remove them.'

'Well, your background came to our rescue tonight. And it seems you have an admirer.' Édouard's face became suddenly taut. 'He's one of the few Nazis I know who comes from an aristocratic family himself. But don't be lulled into a false sense of security by him. Falk von Wehndorf is one of the most lethal and deadly men of all those currently running Paris. He's merciless when it comes to exposing the traitors to the Nazi cause,' Édouard added. 'It was he who was mainly responsible for rounding up many of the members

143

of the network you came here to join.'

A shiver ran down Connie's spine. 'I see,' she said grimly. 'He's certainly well educated and seems to love France.'

'He appreciates the history, culture and elegance of our country, but covets it for himself and his motherland. That makes him even more dangerous. He also, as we both saw tonight—' Édouard raised his eyebrows—'appreciates our women. And if he desires you . . . well, we'll talk of the future tomorrow.' Édouard put his glass down, stood up and walked over to her, patting her shoulder. 'All you need to know for tonight is that you're safe in Paris with us and can sleep peacefully and well in that knowledge.' Édouard offered his elbow. 'Shall we retire?'

'Yes.' Connie stifled a yawn as she stood. They walked along the corridor and upstairs to the landing.

'Goodnight, cousin Constance.' Édouard smiled.

'Goodnight, Édouard.'

Having divested herself of her jewellery and clothes, Connie climbed into the large, comfortable bed. A wave of exhaustion washed over her and she fell deeply and gratefully asleep.

*   *   *

She awoke with a jump the following morning, disorientated for a moment as she looked around the room. Remembering where she was, Connie lay back on the soft pillows with a sigh. Checking the time on her watch, she saw that it was past ten o'clock. She put her hand to her mouth in dismay. Never in her life had she slept in as late. Climbing out of bed, she opened her suitcase and donned the plain blouse and skirt that had been deemed suitable by F Section as part of her schoolteacher wardrobe. Tidying her hair hastily in the mirror, she went downstairs to find Édouard or Sophia.

'The Comte is in his library, Madame,' said Sarah, catching her along the hall. 'He said for you to join him there when you awoke. Can I bring you some breakfast on a tray?'

'Just coffee would be wonderful, thank you,' said Connie, her stomach still full from the sumptuous dinner of the night before. Ration coupons were obviously not a requirement in this house. She followed Sarah to a door, knocked and entered.

Édouard was sitting in a comfortable leather chair in the library, which was lined with floor-to-ceiling bookshelves. He looked up from his newspaper as she came in.

'Good morning, Constance, please take a seat.' He indicated a chair on the other side of the fireplace.

'Thank you,' she said, sitting down. 'What a wonderful collection of books you have in here.' She glanced admiringly at the shelves.

'Inherited from my father, but my passion too. I intend to extend it, if I can. So many thousands of books have been burned across Europe by the Nazis, this collection is even more precious than it was.' Édouard gave a deep sigh and roused himself. Connie could see he looked drained and serious this morning, with none of the ebullience of last night. Studying him in daylight and seeing the fine lines on his face, she guessed he must be in his mid-thirties.

'So, Constance, I would like you to tell me in detail the circumstances which led up to you knocking at my front door last night.'

Connie went on to explain how the courier she was meant to meet at Montparnasse station had not materialised and how she had gone to the address that Stefan had given her on the Rue de Rennes.

'Do you know if you were seen entering the building?' Édouard's eyes filled with alarm.

'I checked very carefully, as Stefan had told me to, and I saw no one in uniform nearby. As I was about to leave, a woman from the next-door apartment told me the Gestapo had been to number seventeen and arrested its occupants. She told me to use the back entrance on the way out,' added Connie.

'Did she see your face?'

'If she did, it was only for a few seconds.'

'Then let us pray she is trustworthy,' breathed Édouard. 'Well, Constance, you seem to have the luck of the blessed on your side so far. Apartment seventeen was one of the main safe houses for the Scientist network. As the neighbour confirmed, it was raided by the Gestapo the night before you arrived here. And they're still continuing to round up sub-circuits and make arrests. It's almost certain that the apartment would still have been under surveillance when you arrived. They would be there waiting to catch agents who hadn't yet heard of the German raid. So—' he sighed—'we can only hope you were not noticed because you were a new face, and hadn't been seen entering the apartment before. Perhaps they assumed you were simply a friend of another resident living at the

146

address.'

'Stefan said I was the only one he could send to Paris because I was unknown and would not be on any Gestapo lists,' Connie explained.

'He's right. At least that's something.' Édouard stroked his chin thoughtfully as Sarah delivered coffee and biscuits for both of them. 'I should point out to you that you were lucky to have Stefan as part of your reception committee. He's a highly trained member of the Maquis, whom your agents support in the field. He knows me through channels other than your organisation. Understanding there were difficulties in Paris, he gave my name as a last resort. The problem is . . .'

'Yes?' Connie was struggling to understand where Édouard fitted in.

'Because of my—' Édouard searched for the right word—'position, any link to the SOE or the Resistance movement must not be discovered. I cannot tell you how vital this is. And, of course, here you are, the link the Germans need: a British SOE agent sitting with me in my library and drinking coffee.'

'I really am most terribly sorry to have caused all this trouble, Édouard.'

'Constance, please, I don't blame you. Stefan needed to send somebody to Paris to find out how serious and far-reaching the situation was. And I can assure you that it's even worse than he thought.'

'Stefan asked me to report back to London on the situation as soon as possible,' she added.

'That will not be necessary. I don't work for the British government, but those at the very top of their Intelligence Services are known to me and we exchange information. I've already contacted London this morning to alert them to what's happened,' explained Édouard. 'Stefan will receive word very soon. Both Prosper, the head of the Scientist network, and his radio operator are under arrest. All other members of Scientist have fled Paris if they could, or are in hiding somewhere in the city until further notice. My dear Constance,' Édouard concluded, 'at present, there's simply no network here to join.'

'Then surely I must be moved out of Paris to another network?' Connie questioned.

'Under normal circumstances, that is what would happen, yes,' Édouard agreed. 'However, through pure coincidence, last night you met some of the most powerful Germans in Paris.' He put down his coffee cup and leant towards her. 'Just imagine this, Constance: you're moved to another network and successfully begin to carry out the mission you've been trained for. Then, *pouf*!' He gesticulated. 'You're arrested and brought in for questioning here at Gestapo headquarters. And then, another coincidence occurs; one of the men you met last night, say Colonel Falk, walks in to interrogate you. And who does he see sitting there, bound to a chair? Why, none other than his good friend the Comte de la Martinières's cousin, Constance, whom Falk met a few weeks ago in his dining room. So what does he think to himself? Does he imagine his friend Édouard does not know of his cousin's activities? Perhaps, at the very least, he would start to take a keener interest in the Comte, look at the other French guests sitting around the table, and perhaps start to question whether they really are the true and loyal supporters of the Vichy and German governments they claim to be.'

'Yes, I see,' agreed Connie, 'but what's the solution? And who do you work with, Édouard?'

'Constance, you don't need to know,' he answered immediately. 'It is indeed better that you don't. But all I do lies with freeing my homeland from the grasp of the Nazi regime; and the puppet Vichy government run by our weak countrymen who agree to everything the Germans say to save their own skins. I've spent the past four years managing to gain their trust. My wealth, combined with their greed, make it sickening, but possible. Never forget what it takes for me to do this, Constance. Every time one of their kind walks over my threshold, I want to take out my gun and shoot him.'

Connie saw Édouard's features were contorted, hands clasped tightly together, his knuckles white.

'But, instead, I invite them into my home, I feed them the finest wine from our cellars, spend money on the black market sourcing the best meat and cheese to fill their mouths and make polite conversation with them. Why, you ask? How can I do this?'

Connie remained silent; she knew he did not require an answer from her.

'I do it because, very occasionally, after too much brandy, I will hear a small titbit of information carelessly dropped from drunken German lips. And, sometimes, that piece of information allows me to alert those in danger and perhaps save the lives of my countrymen. And for that, yes, I will bear their presence at my table.'

Connie sat in silence, understanding now.

'So you see,' Édouard said, 'there must never be a hint of my involvement with any of the organisations the Nazis are desperate to quash. It would not only result in the deaths of the many brave men and women who work with me, but endanger the valuable information which I'm able to relay to those who need it most. It's not so much for my own life I worry, Constance, but that, for example, of Sophia. Living here in this house with me makes it impossible for her not to be a part of my deception. And culpable, if I was discovered. So . . .' Édouard stood up suddenly, walked to the window and looked out at the sunshine bathing the pretty garden beyond in light. 'For all these reasons, I'm afraid it's impossible for you to continue your career as a British agent.'

The words Édouard had spoken slowly sank in. Surely, Connie thought, the weeks of training, the mental and *emotional* preparation, could not be for nothing?

'I see. What will you do with me?' she asked eventually, knowing she sounded plaintive.

'That's a very good question, Constance. I've already informed London you're here with me. And that they must cancel immediately any record of you arriving in France. Word will be sent out to the few who knew of your arrival and there will be no contact with them from now on. You will bring your papers to me immediately and we will burn them together in the fireplace. You will also hand over your suitcase, which I'll dispose of for you. I'm having new papers prepared for you as we speak. From this moment on,' Édouard stated, 'you are simply Constance Chapelle, resident of St Raphaël and known to those who have already met

150

you as my cousin.'

'So what will happen now?' she asked. 'Will I be sent back home to England?'

'Not yet, it's too dangerous. I cannot take the risk of your capture. Constance—' Édouard offered her a grim smile—'I'm afraid that for the next few weeks you must act out the story you gave last night. You will stay here in this house as our guest. Perhaps, sometime in the future, you can travel down to the south, as though you were returning home to St Raphaël, and we can see what we can do to remove you to England from there. But for now, through no fault of your own, you are trapped here with us.'

'And London has agreed to this?' questioned Connie in disbelief.

'They had no choice.' Édouard brushed the question aside as irrelevant. He turned to her, his eyes suddenly softening. 'I can understand your brave wish to help your country and your disappointment that you are not able to carry out your task. But, believe me, sacrificing your career is for a worthy and higher cause. Besides—' he gave a shrug—'there are maybe other ways you can help. You're a beautiful woman, who made a very good impression on a powerful man. Falk is a regular guest here. You never know what he might tell you.'

Connie inwardly shuddered at the thought, but understood what Édouard was saying.

'Meanwhile, Sophia has called her dressmaker and she will be here shortly. You'll need a wardrobe that befits a noblewoman from the line of the Montaines and the de la Martinières. And it will be pleasant for Sophia to have another female

151

in the house. She rarely goes out, due to her . . . condition, and she's lonely. She also misses our mother very much. Perhaps it will be possible for you to spend some time with her?' Édouard suggested.

'Is her condition from birth?' asked Connie.

'Sophia had some sight when she was born, so my parents didn't spot the weakness immediately,' he explained. 'Her vision deteriorated slowly, but by the time they realised the extent of the problem it was too late for the doctors to remedy it. Sophia has adapted to her disability well. She can write, a skill which she learned before she went totally blind, thank God. Her poems are beautiful. Quite beautiful.'

Connie could see the emotion in Édouard's eyes. 'How old was she when she finally lost her sight?'

'Sophia was seven when the light dimmed completely for her. Yet it is amazing how her other senses have made up for that. Her hearing is the sharpest of anyone I know, and normally she can tell who it is entering the room simply by the sound of their movement. She enjoys reading so much; I'm having a number of books from this and my library in Gassin made for her in Braille. She has a special passion for the English romantic poets, such as Byron and Keats. And she can draw too. From feeling her subject, she's somehow able to transfer the shape and colour onto paper.' Édouard gave a gentle smile. 'She's very artistic and she's the dearest thing I have.'

'And very beautiful too,' added Connie.

'Yes. Is it not sad that Sophia can never see that for herself in a mirror? She has no idea of it,' he said. 'Men who meet her for the first time and don't know of her handicap . . . well, I watch the effect she has on them. She's glorious.'

'Yes, she is.'

'Now—' Édouard's expression changed suddenly—'you will go and collect your suitcase and your papers from upstairs. I'm not comfortable whilst they are still in the house.'

This was not a request, it was a demand. Connie did as she was bid and went upstairs to retrieve her suitcase. Ten minutes later, she watched her identity go up in flames. The contents of her suitcase, Édouard transferred to a sack. Then he indicated her shoes.

'Those too, Constance. We both know what one of them hides inside the heel.'

'But I have no other shoes,' stated Connie.

'We'll provide you with new ones immediately,' he answered.

Connie stood in the library in her stockinged feet, now feeling horribly vulnerable. She had not a thing of her own in the world except the clothes she stood up in.

As though he'd done it a hundred times before, Édouard removed the francs hidden in the lining of the suitcase. He handed the money to her, noticing her strained expression. 'You may of course keep this, courtesy of both the British and French governments, for the trials they have put you through. Sophia and I will see to it that you're cared for materially whilst you're here with us. And it will, of course, be of the best. Sophia is waiting for you upstairs to introduce you to the dressmaker. One more thing . . .' Édouard paused at the door. 'It's unlikely that anyone will try to contact you. Few people from your organisation know you're here. But in case by some chance they hear of your location, you must not, and I repeat *not*, attempt to return their messages. Do you understand?'

'Yes.'

'Otherwise—' Édouard's eyes bored into her— 'all this would be for nothing and you would put many lives in grave danger.'

'I understand.'

'Good. Now run along upstairs to see Sophia.'

12

A month had passed since Constance had become a member of the de la Martinières household. She had taken delivery of a beautiful wardrobe of clothes, soft leather shoes—the kind she had not seen since before the war began—and several pairs of silk stockings. As she laid them out in her chest of drawers, Connie sighed at the bitter irony of her situation. She was living like a princess, in a household where money seemed to be no object and where she was waited on hand and foot by the household staff. Yet the outer sumptuousness of the life Connie was now forced to live did nothing to stem the pain of what was no more than captivity. Not only did she lie in bed at night missing Lawrence until her heart physically ached, but tormenting herself with thoughts of the other brave men and women who had trained with her and were now out in the field, constantly in danger, suffering the kind of deprivation she could only imagine. The guilt of her situation ate into her constantly. In this gilded prison, deprived of any contact with the outside world, Connie thought she might go mad.

Her saving grace was Sophia, whom Connie had already grown fond of. With a perception honed from her blindness, she would know when Connie was low in an instant, simply by the tone of her voice.

Sophia, at twenty-five, exactly the same age as herself, was eager to learn and hear of Connie's English life. She had never travelled out of France due to her disability. Connie sat in the heat of a July afternoon describing the bleak but magnificent moors of Yorkshire, and Blackmoor Hall, Lawrence's family home. It comforted and disturbed her in equal measure, but at least it kept her husband alive in her memory.

Recently, as they had sat out on the terrace under a balmy sunset, Connie had confided in Sophia about her husband and how she ached for him. Sophia had been sweetness itself, asking details about Lawrence and comforting Connie with calm words of reassurance.

Afterwards, Connie had panicked. She had said too much; after all, she had no proof that the de la Martinières were not keeping her as a prize to hand over to the Nazis, if and when the whim took them—but she *had* to trust someone.

And then, two nights ago, Colonel Falk von Wehndorf had appeared unannounced on the front doorstep. Sarah had come to find Connie, sitting with Sophia in the library.

'You have a guest, Madame Constance,' Sarah had said, only her eyes giving a warning.

Connie had nodded and, her heart-rate increasing, walked into the drawing room where Falk had been ushered in.

'Fräulein Constance! Why, I think you are looking even more beautiful than when I saw you last.' He'd walked over to her and kissed her hand.

'Thank you, Colonel, I—'

'Please, remember,' Falk had interjected, 'we're to call each other by our first names. I was simply passing on my way back to headquarters, and I thought to myself, I will visit the charming cousin of Édouard to see if Paris is suiting her. And it seems it is.'

'Yes, it's certainly a pleasant change from my rural life in the south,' Connie had replied stiffly.

'I was wondering . . .' he'd paused, 'whether later, after I've concluded an interview, I might pick you up and take you to a club for some dinner and a little dancing?'

Connie's stomach had churned. 'I—'

At that moment, obviously alerted by Sarah to the Colonel's presence, Édouard had entered the room.

'Falk! What a pleasant surprise,' he'd greeted him and the two men shook hands heartily.

'I was just suggesting to your delightful cousin that perhaps I could have the pleasure of her company later tonight,' Falk had repeated.

'Unfortunately, we've already been invited out for dinner near Versailles by a mutual cousin of ours.' Édouard had looked down fondly at Connie. 'My dear, you've been away from Paris too long. It seems you're in demand. But perhaps another time you would like to join Falk and accept his kind invitation?'

156

'Yes, I'm honoured that you ask me, Herr Falk.' Connie had forced a smile.

'Fräulein, it is I who would have the honour. As you say, Édouard, another time.'

Falk had clicked his heels together and, in a parody of what Connie had only ever seen on grainy Pathé newsreels, stuck out his arm in front of him and uttered, '*Heil Hitler!* Now, I must leave.'

'Perhaps we will see you at the Opera on Saturday night?' Édouard had said as he led Falk to the door.

'You're taking a box?' Falk's eyes had settled upon Connie.

'Yes, would you like to join us, Herr Falk?' Édouard had asked.

'That would be most pleasant. Until then, Fräulein Constance.' He'd bowed and kissed her hand.

When he had left, Connie had sunk into a chair as Édouard re-entered the room.

'I'm sorry, Constance, but it seems our Colonel has a penchant for my beautiful cousin.' He had taken her hands in his. 'I suggested he accompany us to the Opera because at least we'll be there to protect you.'

'Oh, Édouard . . .' Connie had sighed helplessly and shook her head.

He'd patted her hands comfortingly. 'I know, my dear. It's a terrible deception. And perhaps it's a pity we did not invent a fiancé down in the south for you on the evening you met Falk. But it's too late now. And you must cope as best you can.'

*   *   *

157

The Place de l'Opéra was humming with a glamorous crowd, consisting of high-ranking Germans, officials from the Vichy government and the bourgeois population of Paris. The French Milice stood guard around the entrance.

The July evening was excruciatingly hot, and Connie, in the tight-fitting bodice of her emerald green evening dress, felt like a trussed-up chicken put on too warm a setting in the oven. She glanced at the Ritz Hotel, a place where she had often met her aunt for tea when she was up from St Raphaël. Now, Nazi flags replaced the Tricolour on the flagpoles. Connie closed her eyes for a second, the lump in her throat immediate and overwhelming. Even though the scenario here tonight was life going on as normal, it was fraudulent—a grim pastiche of what it should be. Of course it wasn't the same . . . nothing was the same.

As Édouard stopped to greet friends on the way to their box, Connie guided Sophia up the grand staircase.

'I'm greatly looking forward to this evening,' said Sophia, her beautiful face creasing into a smile as Connie sat her down in the comfortable velvet chair. 'Although I wish it wasn't a Wagner opera.' She wrinkled her nose. 'But, of course, it's what our friends who rule the country prefer. For myself, I like Puccini.'

Next to arrive in the box was Falk.

'Fräulein Constance,' he said, after the usual kiss of her hand. He surveyed her. 'Your dress is exquisite. It's true that the French ladies are the most elegant in the world. Perhaps some of the French chic can rub off on our own

158

countrywomen.'

He took a glass of champagne from the proffered tray and, as he did so, the door opened again to reveal Édouard and . . . Connie stared in confusion, a facsimile of Falk standing behind him.

Falk smirked at Connie's surprise.

'Fräulein, you think you're seeing double? I assure you, you have not yet drunk too much champagne. May I present my twin brother, Frederik.'

'Madame, I'm honoured to make your acquaintance.' Frederik moved forward to take Connie's hand and shook it politely.

Standing next to his brother, Connie noticed that, although they were identical in build and bone structure, Frederik's eyes were warm as he smiled at her.

'And this,' interrupted Édouard, 'is my sister, Sophia.'

Frederik turned to greet Sophia. He stared at her and opened his mouth to speak, but no words emerged. He stood as if hypnotised, gazing at her in wonder.

In the long pause, Sophia held out her hand towards him and spoke first. 'Colonel von Wehndorf, I'm delighted to make your acquaintance.'

Connie watched as their fingers touched for the first time. Frederik had still not spoken, but he held her tiny hand gently in his for what became an embarrassingly long time. Eventually, Frederik managed an 'Enchanted, Mademoiselle.' Reluctantly, he let go of her hand and Connie saw Sophia offer a radiant smile, as though something wonderful had just happened. Luckily, Édouard's attention was taken with another two guests arriving and Falk's eyes were simply on Connie.

'So, who is the oldest of the two of you twins?' she asked, trying to break the tension.

'Sadly, I'm the youngest,' answered Falk, 'appearing an hour after my big brother. I nearly didn't make it into the world; perhaps he had stolen all my mother's energy for himself!' Falk threw Frederik a look which told Connie there was no love lost between the brothers. 'Would you not agree, Frederik?'

'I'm sorry, I didn't hear what you said, brother.' Frederik managed to drag his eyes away from Sophia to look at Falk questioningly.

'Nothing important. I was merely saying that you arrived in the world first. As you have done many times since.' Falk laughed at his own barbed joke, but his eyes were hard.

'And you will never forgive me for it, will you?' Frederik smiled easily and patted his brother affectionately on the shoulder.

'When did you arrive in Paris, Frederik?' asked Sophia. 'It's a surprise we have not met before.'

'My big brother has had larger fish to fry than looking after one city,' Falk interjected. 'He's been working directly for the Führer as part of his think tank. Frederik is an intellectual, not a soldier, and far above us mere mortals in the Gestapo.'

'I've been sent to visit Paris as an emissary, yes,' answered Frederik. 'The Führer is concerned at the successful amount of sabotage organised by the Resistance recently.'

'In short, Frederik is here because he doesn't think we Gestapo are doing our work well enough.'

160

'Of course it's not that, Falk,' interrupted Frederik, embarrassed. 'It's simply that these people are clever and well organised. And they outwit us once too often.'

'Brother, we have just had our most successful round-up of Resistance members and SOE agents,' said Falk. 'The Scientist network is in chaos. It can do no more damage for the present.'

'And you're to be congratulated on that,' Frederik agreed. 'I'm here simply to take an overview of the intelligence and see how we can continue to net the troublemakers.'

Connie watched the tension between the two brothers, trying to remain impervious to their words. Thankfully, the lights dimmed and the assembled company took their seats, Frederik hastily taking the chair directly beside Sophia. Connie found herself sandwiched between the two brothers.

'You like Wagner, Fräulein Chapelle?' asked Falk as he drained his champagne glass and placed it back on the tray.

'He's not a composer I know particularly well, but I look forward to familiarising myself with him,' answered Connie diplomatically.

'I'm hoping that you, Fräulein Sophia and Édouard will join us for supper afterwards,' Falk added. 'I feel duty bound to show my brother the best of Paris whilst he's here.'

Connie had no need to reply as Falk's words were drowned out by the dramatic opening chorus of *Die Walküre*.

Having always disliked Wagner, finding his music and his stories too heavy, Connie spent much of her time discreetly glancing around the auditorium at the audience. She felt dreadfully uncomfortable being seen in public with the enemy, but what could she do? If, as Édouard had impressed upon her, her actions were for a higher cause, then she must swallow her revulsion as Falk reached a hand towards her silk-covered knee, and somehow bear it.

Connie surreptitiously moved her eyes to the left and saw Frederik's expression of bliss. Then she saw that the direction of his gaze was not on the stage below, but on Sophia.

*　　　*　　　*

After the interminably long performance, Édouard accepted Falk and Frederik's invitation to join them at a club for supper. A black Gestapo limousine waited outside for them.

As Édouard followed the girls into the back of the car, something struck him on the back of his neck.

'*Traître! Traître!*' screamed a voice from somewhere in the crowd.

The chauffeur hurriedly closed the doors as the car was pelted with rotten eggs. As they drew away from the pavement, Connie heard shots ring out behind them. Édouard sighed, took out his handkerchief and did his best to wipe the stinking egg off the shoulder of his black dinner jacket.

Sophia clung to Édouard's other shoulder, her face frozen in fear.

'Pigs!' spat Falk from the seat in front of them. 'Rest assured, the perpetrators will be caught and I will interrogate them personally tomorrow.'

'Really, Falk, it's not a problem,' said Édouard

hastily. 'It was only a few eggs, not guns. Just a bitter patriot who has yet to see the light.'

'The sooner they do, the better for us all,' Falk retorted.

Inside the supper club, as Édouard excused himself to go immediately to the washroom to clean himself up, Frederik guided Sophia carefully down the steps. 'Your poor hand is shaking,' he said gently.

'I don't like violence of any kind,' shuddered Sophia.

'And neither do many of us,' he replied, squeezing her hand tightly and leading her through the crowd to their table. As he sat her down, he put his hands on her shoulders and whispered in her ear: 'Do not worry, Mademoiselle Sophia. You will always be safe with me.'

*　　　*　　　*

Falk's hands ran up and down Connie's back as they danced. Every time his fingers touched the bare skin between her shoulders and her neck, Connie felt a shudder of distaste and terror. Those were fingers, she knew from Édouard, which thought nothing of wrapping themselves around the cold metal of a trigger and shooting a human dead at point-blank range. She smelt Falk's rancid, alcohol-infused breath on her cheek as he tried to manoeuvre her lips towards his.

'Constance, you must know how much I want you, please say I can have you,' he moaned as he nuzzled into her neck.

Filled with disgust, Connie steeled herself not to follow her instincts and break free of his grasp.

163

She realised that, whatever nationality this man might have been, she would still have flinched at his touch. She glanced around at the other French women dancing with Germans in the club, none of them dressed in the expensive way she was herself. By the look of them, some of them were little more than common prostitutes. But how much better was she . . . ?

She saw Sophia across the floor, partnering Frederik. They were not dancing—in fact, they were hardly moving at all. Instead, Frederik was holding her hands in his and talking to her quietly. Sophia smiled, nodded and moved closer into his arms. Connie noticed how he held her tenderly to him, as her head rested naturally against his chest. There was a—Connie searched for the right phrase—an *intimacy* about their body language, a togetherness which belied the fact they had only just met.

'Perhaps next week, we'll escape the clutches of your protective cousin,' Falk said to Connie with a glance at Édouard, who was watching their every move from the table. 'And we can be alone.'

'Perhaps,' said Connie, wondering for how much longer it would be possible to evade this man who was used to choosing what he wanted and getting it. 'Excuse me, but I must go and powder my nose,' she said as the band played the final notes of the song.

Falk gave her a curt nod of his head and followed her off the dance floor.

When Connie arrived back at the table from the powder room, she listened to Falk and Édouard talking.

'My friend would prefer a Renoir, but if that's

not possible he's also fond of Monet.'

'As always, Falk, I'll see what I can do. Ah, Constance, you seem fatigued,' sympathised Édouard as she sat down at the table with them.

'I am a little, yes,' she answered truthfully.

'We'll leave as soon as we have managed to drag Sophia and Frederik from the dance floor,' Édouard said.

'Yes,' grinned Falk, taking a further large slug of his brandy, 'it seems the men of my family are partial to the women of yours.'

*　　*　　*

A Gestapo car took the three of them home and deposited them outside the house on the Rue de Varenne. Connie was silent on the journey, as was Sophia. Édouard's attempts at conversation fell on deaf female ears. As Sarah opened the front door, Connie said an abrupt 'goodnight' to brother and sister and made for the stairs.

'Constance,' said Édouard, stopping her as she began to mount them. 'Come and join me in the library for a brandy.'

It was not an invitation, but an order. As Sarah guided a beatific Sophia up to bed, Connie turned and followed Édouard into the library.

'No brandy for me,' she said as Édouard poured himself one.

'What is it, my dear? It's obvious you're very distressed. Was it the rotten eggs they threw at us? Falk's attentions?'

Connie slumped into a chair and put her fingers to her forehead. Tears came to her eyes and she could not stem them. 'I just . . .' She shook her

165

head in despair. 'I just don't think I can stand this. I'm betraying everything I was taught and believe in. I am living a lie!'

'Come, Constance, please try not to upset yourself. I understand completely what you feel. To the outsider, perhaps many would think you're having an easy war. But what the three of us are living—you, simply through coincidence, myself, through belief, and Sophia through association—is indeed torment to the soul,' Édouard agreed.

'Forgive me, Édouard, but at least you know *why*!' she cried. 'Whereas I have no proof that what you tell me is true! I'm a trained agent of the British government, here to defend the two countries close to my heart, not dine and dance and make small talk with German officers! Édouard, tonight, when I heard the woman screaming "Traitor!", I have never felt more ashamed.' Connie wiped the tears roughly from her cheeks. 'Maybe she will die because of us!'

'Yes, maybe she will,' agreed Édouard, 'and maybe she won't. But perhaps also,' he said, his steady brown eyes fixed on Connie, 'because of tonight, I may be able to warn a dozen men and women who are meeting tomorrow night at a safe house not far from here, that the Nazis know of it. And, therefore, they may not only save themselves, but the other brave souls who number in their hundreds and work for the network.'

Connie stared at him in surprise. 'How?'

'The operatives belong to a sub-circuit of the Scientist network and their names were extracted by torture from the agents who were captured in the last round of arrests. Whilst you were powdering your nose, Falk himself told me. He was

166

full of delight at this development. I know him well—he's always indiscreet after too much brandy. And his arrogance betrays him time and again. He wants me to know how well he performs at his job. And, yes—' Édouard sighed despairingly—'he is indeed far too good.'

Connie was silent for a while, staring at him, wanting to believe him.

'Please, Édouard, I beg you, tell me who you work for, and then at least I can sleep at night knowing I do not betray my country.'

'No.' Édouard shook his head. 'I cannot do that. You'll simply have to trust it's true. And perhaps you'll hear proof from another source sooner than you think. After all, it's not the last we'll be seeing of our friend Falk. If he's gloating over a new round of arrests, then yes, I'm the traitor you accuse me of being. But if, by chance, the safe house is deserted when the Gestapo pounces, then maybe I speak the truth. Constance—' Édouard sighed again—'I accept it's hard for you, as you didn't choose this path. But I can only promise, as I have many times before, that we're both fighting on the same side.'

'If only you could tell me who you work for,' she tried again.

'And risk your life and that of many others?' Édouard shook his head. 'No, Constance, not even Sophia knows the details and that's the way it must stay. And now, it seems the stakes have been raised. Falk's brother, Frederik, is already known to me. He's one of an elite group of SS officers from the SD, the Intelligence branch of the Gestapo. He reports directly to the highest powers. If he, too, is to be a regular visitor to this house, then we must be even more circumspect.'

'He seemed very taken with Sophia,' Connie said, 'and, more worryingly, she with him.'

'As I've mentioned before, both brothers come from an aristocratic Prussian family. They are educated, cultured men, and yet, I saw tonight, very different from each other. Frederik is the intellectual, the thinker.' Édouard paused before he looked up at her. 'I may have liked him, had he been on the right side.'

They sat in silence for a while, lost in their own contemplation. 'And as for Sophia,' said Édouard eventually, 'she's very naive. She's been protected from the world, first by my parents and then by me. She has little knowledge of men or love. Let us hope that Herr Frederik returns soon to Germany. I, too, saw the chemistry between them.'

'And what do I do about Falk?' asked Connie finally. 'Édouard, I'm a married woman!'

Édouard nursed his brandy goblet in both hands, gazing at her steadily. 'We've just agreed that we must sometimes live a lie. And, Constance, you might ask yourself this question: if I was the head of the network you were originally assigned to, and I ordered you to continue and promote your relationship with Falk, hoping he might drop some useful titbit of information that could help compatriots in the fight, would you refuse to obey me?'

Connie avoided Édouard's gaze. She understood clearly what he was saying.

'Given what we have discussed, I would agree, of course,' she answered reluctantly.

'Then perhaps in your relationship with Falk you can separate yourself from your soul and remember each time you wish to move out of his embrace that you're helping a cause larger than your own disgust whilst you are in it. It's what I must do twenty-four hours a day.'

'Do you not care that your countrymen think you are a traitor?'

'Of course I *care*, Constance. But that's hardly the point, is it? I think more about my fellow French citizens locked away in their stinking gaols, being tortured and abused, or losing their lives, than of my reputation. And I believe then that my lot is comparatively easy. Now,' Édouard said, 'I must leave you. I have work to do.'

He stood up, gave her a short smile and left the room.

13

Although Connie could not prove for certain it had been Édouard himself who had managed to alert suspected traitors to the threat of German arrest, both Falk and Frederik were full of the story when they came for dinner a few days later. Falk was furious, perhaps even more so because his brother was present to watch his failure. The emnity Falk showed towards Frederik was palpable; sibling rivalry at its most raw. Frederik had flown far higher and was, on every level, superior. Connie wondered if Falk's legendary aggression towards those he netted in his trap was fuelled by frustration at feeling he could only ever be second best.

'The Resistance are becoming more

troublesome by the day,' grunted Falk into his soup. 'Only yesterday a German convoy in Le Mans was attacked, the officers killed and the arms stolen.'

'They are indeed well organised,' agreed Frederik.

'And it's obvious they're receiving inside information. The Resistance seem to know exactly where and when to attack. We must discover the weak link, brother,' added Falk.

'If anyone can, I'm sure it will be you,' answered Frederik.

Falk left early that night, saying he had business to attend to at Gestapo headquarters. The fact he was preoccupied by his failure to stamp out the Resistance and had been less attentive towards Connie was small compensation for the excruciating two hours of hearing how he would achieve it. Frederik said he would stay on for a while longer, but as he accompanied Édouard and Sophia into the drawing room, Connie excused herself and went upstairs to bed. She closed the door behind her, feeling mentally exhausted with the strain of the constant deception. Even though she was living in the centre of a city that was currently the focus of the world, she had never felt more alone. With radios banned months ago by the Nazis when they discovered that the Allies were using them to communicate with their operatives, and only the propaganda-filled Vichy newspapers to read, Connie felt completely cut off. She had no idea how the Allies were doing, or whether the invasion that had been promised and hoped for just as she flew in to France was still scheduled to take place.

Édouard refused to be drawn into conversation on such subjects; and often, when she joined Sophia downstairs for breakfast in the mornings, Édouard was already out. She had no idea where he went or who he saw. Surely, Connie thought, if F Section had been told by Édouard where she was, they would try to make some kind of contact with her? Not leave her like this, helpless and flaccid, living behind a useless facade of pampered luxury when she had been trained to kill...

'Oh, Lawrence,' she sighed in desperation, 'I wish you could tell me what to do.'

Connie lay down, her thoughts bleak, and wondered for the hundredth time if she would ever see him again.

*   *   *

Connie was at least comforted when August came, and with it the stepping up of Allied bombing raids. The cellar, in keeping with the luxury the de la Martinières were used to, had been furnished with a number of comfortable beds, a gas ring to provide coffee and all manner of parlour games to keep its residents occupied. At least, thought Connie, reading a book as the house shook above them, the dreadful sounds of destruction indicated that perhaps the longed-for invasion was imminent. For her, it could not come soon enough; one way or the other, it would release her from the surreal scenario she was living.

*   *   *

August, as always in Paris, proved unpleasantly muggy, with the barest hint of a searched-for

171

breeze. Connie took to sitting out in the garden every afternoon with Sophia. As Édouard had once mentioned to her, Sophia had a remarkable skill as an artist. Connie would find a flower or a piece of fruit and give it to Sophia to hold for a while. Her tiny hands would explore the shape of the object, and she'd ask Connie to describe it to her. She would then take her charcoal pencil to her sketchbook and half an hour later there would be a perfectly formed lemon or peach on the paper.

'How does it look?' Sophia would ask eagerly. 'Have I captured its shape and texture accurately?'

Connie's answer was always an affirmative 'Yes, Sophia, you have.'

One particularly sticky August afternoon, when Connie felt she would go mad unless the overripe, mackerel-coloured clouds above them dropped their cooling load, Sophia gave a small tush of irritation.

'What is it?' asked Connie, fanning herself with a book.

'It seems I've drawn the same fruits for weeks now. Can you not think of others? At our château in Gassin, we have an orchard full of many different trees, but I can't remember the fruits they bear.'

Having run through the gamut of every fruit she could think of, Connie nodded. 'I'll do my best,' she said, relief flooding through her as she felt the welcome coolness of the first raindrops. 'We must take shelter. The storm is coming, thank goodness,' she added.

Guiding Sophia inside and handing her over to Sarah so Sophia could freshen up, Connie walked into the library. She stood by the window for a while, listening to the unearthly roar of the heavens, comforted that this sound was natural and not produced by the hum of aircraft signalling imminent destruction. The storm was spectacular and, as it continued, Connie began searching the shelves of Édouard's library for inspiration on other fruits Sophia could sketch.

Édouard entered the library, looking unusually tense and drawn.

'Constance,' he gave her a strained smile, 'can I assist you in your search?'

'I'm looking for a book that describes fruit. Your sister is bored with drawing oranges and lemons.'

'I think I may have just the thing . . . I acquired it only a few weeks ago.' His long fingers reached up to a shelf and he pulled out a slim volume. 'Here.'

'Thank you,' Connie said as he handed her the book. '*The History of French Fruit, Volume Two*,' she read out loud.

'That should give you many ideas. Although I doubt you'll be able to find many of its contents available in wartime Paris,' Édouard added morosely.

Connie turned the pages of the coloured plates, which described their subjects in pictures and words. 'These are simply gorgeous,' she said in wonder.

'Yes, and very old. The book was printed in the eighteenth century. My father had already bought the first volume for the library at our château in Gassin,' Édouard explained. 'And, by chance, a dealer acquaintance of mine discovered the second volume here in Paris a few weeks ago. As a pair, they're extremely valuable. Not that I collect books

173

for that reason, merely because I think they're objects of beauty.'

'This is indeed exquisite,' Connie agreed, running her fingers lightly over the delicate green linen binding. 'Over two hundred years old and yet almost untouched.'

'I'll take this copy down to our château the next time I visit,' said Édouard. 'Together, the two volumes will make a perfect reference companion to our orchard there. Please, feel free to use the book. I know you'll take care of it,' he said with a nod. 'Excuse me, Constance, I have some business to attend to.'

*   *   *

As August moved into September, Connie noticed Sophia was distracted. Usually when Connie read to her, she would listen attentively, asking Connie to repeat a sentence if she'd misunderstood it, but now she seemed to be barely listening. There was the same lack of concentration with her sketching; often, when Connie had used all her powers of imagination to describe a bulbous purple damson, Sophia's pencil would hover over the empty paper as her thoughts moved elsewhere.

She had taken instead to scribbling in a small leather-bound notebook. Connie watched, fascinated, as Sophia stared up to the heavens, obviously in search of inspiration, her hands feeling the size of the page and judging the placing of her pen accordingly. But when Connie asked to see what she was writing, Sophia refused to show her.

One afternoon, as they sat together in the

library, the unusually chilly September day engendering the first fire of the season, Sophia said suddenly: 'Constance, you're so good at describing things to me. So, can you explain how love feels?'

Connie's teacup hovered in surprise halfway between the saucer and her mouth as she surveyed Sophia's dreamy expression. 'Well,' she said, taking a sip of the tea and replacing the cup on the saucer, 'that's really very difficult. I think it's a different feeling for everyone.'

'Then tell me how it makes *you* feel,' Sophia urged.

'Goodness,' said Connie, searching her mind for the right words. 'Well, for me with Lawrence, it was as if, when I was with him, the whole world lit up. Even the dullest of dull days felt filled with sunshine, an ordinary walk over the moors was turned into a magical moment, simply because he was by my side.' As Connie conjured up the memories of those heady days when she and Lawrence were first courting, she felt a catch in her throat. 'I longed for his touch, never found it threatening, just exciting and comforting at the same time. He made me feel . . . invincible, special and terribly safe, as though there was nothing to be frightened of if he was there. And the hours in between, when we weren't together, seemed to be endless. Yet, when we were, they would speed past in an instant. He brought me alive, Sophia, I . . . Excuse me.' Connie searched for a handkerchief in her pocket and dabbed her eyes.

'Oh, Constance.' Sophia's hands were clasped together and her enormous, unseeing eyes were misty too. 'May I tell you something?'

'Of course you may,' Connie replied, trying to pull herself together.

'You describe the feelings so eloquently. And now I know for sure that it *is* love. Constance, please, I must confide in someone or I'll go mad! But you must not breathe a word to my brother. You will swear you won't?'

'If you ask me not to, of course.' With a sinking heart, Connie already knew what Sophia wanted to share with her.

'Well . . .' Sophia took a deep breath. 'I have known for some weeks now that I'm in love with Frederik von Wehndorf. And, even better, he's in love with me! There! I've said it, thank God, I've said it.' Sophia gave a laugh of relief, the colour rising to her cheeks.

'Oh, Sophia . . .' This time, Connie truly was lost for words.

'I know, Constance, what you will say; that it's impossible, that our love can never be. But do you not understand? I've fought and fought to deny it, to understand we can never be together, but my heart will not listen. And Frederik—he is the same. Neither of us can help how we feel. We simply cannot live without each other.'

Connie stared at Sophia in horror. Finally, she said, 'But, surely, you must understand that any relationship both now and in the future is impossible? Sophia, Frederik is a high-ranking Nazi officer. If the end of the war comes in the next year and the Allies gain victory, Frederik will almost certainly face arrest, if not death.'

'And if they win?'

'They will *not* win.' It was a thought Connie couldn't even begin to deal with. 'Whatever the outcome to this terrible war, two people from opposing sides could never live a life together afterwards. It simply could not be countenanced.'

'We understand that, of course,' agreed Sophia, 'but Frederik has already suggested ways and means once the war is over.'

'You're seriously talking of a future together?' Connie's jaw was taut with tension. 'But how? Where?'

'Constance,' explained Sophia, 'you must understand that because a country's leader dictates a regime, it doesn't mean that those who are forced to help him create it believe in it too.'

At this point, Connie put her head in her hands and shook it in despair. 'Sophia, are you trying to tell me that Frederik has convinced you he's not a true Nazi believer? That man has been partly responsible for the death and destruction our countries are currently suffering. I've heard from your brother that Frederik reports directly to Himmler. He—'

'No!' Sophia interrupted her. 'Just like us, Constance, Frederik is living a lie. He's an educated, cultured man and a devout Christian who doesn't believe in his leader's ethics. But what can he do?' Sophia sighed. 'If he made his feelings clear, he would no longer be alive.'

Connie's eyes were despairing as she stared at poor, deluded Sophia. A woman who was not only blind physically, but whose feelings had allowed her to believe everything her lover had told her. 'Sophia, I can't believe what you tell me. And my God! Nor should you. Do you not understand what this man is trying to do? He's using you, Sophia; at the worst, perhaps he suspects Édouard and

177

believes you could be the unwitting path to the truth!'

'You're wrong, Constance!' Sophia countered vehemently. 'You don't know Frederik, you haven't heard what we talk of when we're alone. He's a good man and I trust him implicitly! And when the war is over, we plan to simply disappear.'

'No, Sophia, please, there will be no place to run, nowhere Frederik can hide.' Connie wanted to scream at her naivety. 'They will hunt him down then make him answer and pay for his crimes towards humanity.'

'We will find somewhere and we will be together.' Sophia's mouth was set in a pout, reminding Connie of a spoilt child who had been denied a toy she coveted. What Sophia was suggesting was so deluded, she wasn't sure whether to laugh out loud or scream in anger. She tried another tack.

'Sophia,' she said softly, 'I understand that your feelings for Frederik are very strong. But as you said yourself, it's the first time you've been in love. Perhaps, in a few weeks' time, you'll be able to think more clearly. Perhaps this is only a crush . . .'

'Please do not patronise me, Constance. I may be blind, but I'm a grown woman and I know what I feel is real. Frederik must soon return to Germany for a few weeks, but he'll be back for me, you wait and see. Please call for Sarah to take me upstairs,' she ordered imperiously. 'I'm tired and I wish to rest.'

As a shocked Connie left the room, she realised for the first time that underneath Sophia's sweet and vulnerable exterior was a woman who had never been denied anything she desired in her entire life.

14

In the next few days, Connie spent hours tussling over whether she should tell Édouard of Sophia's revelation. If she did, she would be betraying the only friend and companion she currently had. On the other hand, if she said nothing, surely she was putting Édouard, Sophia and herself in further danger?

Sophia had withdrawn from Connie after her confession, and in the afternoons Connie had taken to leaving the house and going for a stroll across the Pont de la Concorde bridge that led eventually to the Tuileries Gardens, simply to remove herself from the claustrophobia of the house and its complex residents. On one of these walks, she was returning home when a familiar face came riding over the bridge on a bicycle. Connie halted in shock as the green eyes registered a second of recognition, but the bicycle continued past her.

Venetia . . .

Connie steeled herself not to turn round and double-check, just in case enemy eyes were watching, and continued walking back towards the de la Martinières's house. Venetia's long black hair had been cut into a neat bob and the clothes she'd been wearing were designed to melt into the background rather than, as the old Venetia had preferred, to steal the show.

The following day, Connie repeated the walk

across the bridge to the gardens at a similar time, sitting on a bench and enjoying the magnificent red-gold carpet of leaves that autumn was providing. Perhaps Venetia lived nearby . . . Connie's heart yearned with longing to see those familiar eyes close-to, to embrace something—*someone*—who was known and familiar from the past.

She repeated the walk at the same time every day for a week, but she did not see Venetia again.

*　　　*　　　*

Frederik was a far more regular visitor to the house these days than Falk. He would drop in unannounced, although Sophia never seemed surprised to see him as she greeted him with undisguised pleasure at the drawing-room door. Connie could only hope that Édouard himself would notice what was happening right under his very nose, but he was often out and, when he was home, seemed drained and distracted. So Connie kept her fears to herself, often trying to join the lovers in the drawing room. When she did, Sophia's unseeing yet expressive eyes told her clearly she was not welcome and, after fifteen minutes of stilted conversation, she would withdraw.

Thankfully, she'd found a welcome ally in Sarah, a woman who had cared for Sophia since birth and was devoted to her. Often, as Connie lurked outside the drawing-room door, Sarah would come towards her. 'Please, Madame, trust me, I will make sure Mademoiselle Sophia is in no danger.'

Connie would gratefully withdraw from her vigil,

knowing Sophia would not come to harm. Sarah was the next best thing to her mother.

*   *   *

Even though nothing had changed outwardly in the day-to-day rhythm of the house, the underlying pulse had quickened. One morning, Connie knew Édouard had not arrived home until dawn. He looked weary as he joined her for breakfast in the dining room.

'I must travel to the south on business,' Édouard announced after they had eaten. He stood up and walked towards the door, then paused. 'If anyone asks my whereabouts, I'm visiting our château in Gassin. I'll be back on Thursday. If there are unexpected guests, Constance, I trust you to protect my sister.' With that, he was gone.

Another empty day loomed in front of Connie. Sophia had not yet arisen, so she took herself into the library and opened an Austen—books were fast becoming her only means of escape and she lived vicariously through the characters she read of. Wandering out of the library to go upstairs and refresh herself before lunch, Connie saw a letter on the doormat. Bending down, she picked it up and, with surprise, saw that it was addressed to her.

Her pace picking up as she mounted the stairs, Connie shut her bedroom door and tore the letter open.

Dear Constance,

I hear you are currently residing in Paris. By coincidence, I find myself here too. As you

*know, your aunt is an old acquaintance of my
family and she has asked me to check on your
well-being whilst I am here. I am staying at the
Ritz, and it would be a pleasure to meet you for
tea this afternoon in the Salon at 3.00 pm. It will
be wonderful to talk over the nights we spent
together at school in our shared dorm.*

V.

Venetia.

Connie hugged the note to her chest in an agony
of indecision, her desperation for contact and guilt
at the betrayal of her promise to Édouard vying for
pole position.

She took lunch in the silent house, Sophia eating
upstairs in her room due to an apparent headache.

Afterwards, still undecided, Connie dressed as
though she was going out then sank onto the bed.
She watched the hands on the clock move round to
half past two. Making a decision, she pinned on
her hat and left the house.

Fifteen minutes later, entering the Ritz Hotel,
Connie moved knowledgeably towards the Salon
d'Été, where she had taken high tea many times
before. The room was full of animated, wealthily
dressed women and thankfully devoid of German
uniforms. Ten minutes passed as Connie
assiduously studied the menu, every second taking
longer than the last. Perhaps this was a trap,
perhaps she was being watched and should leave
now . . . maybe Édouard's tension was a signal that
something was afoot and he'd already been
arrested, and she was next . . .

'Darling! Why, you look even more beautiful

than usual!'

Connie turned round and saw Venetia, glamorous in furs and heavy make-up, unrecognisable from the woman who had cycled past her on the bridge three weeks ago.

Venetia moved closer and embraced her, whispering quickly and clearly, 'Address me as Isobel, I live near you in St Raphaël.' She pulled away and sat down next to Connie. 'How do you like my hair?' she asked, patting it. 'I had it all cut off recently. I thought it was time to grow up!'

'I think it suits you very well . . . Isobel,' Connie replied.

'Shall we order? I'm famished after a morning's shopping,' Venetia drawled. 'And perhaps, as we haven't seen each other for so long, a glass of champagne?'

'Of course,' said Connie, signalling a waiter over. As she ordered, she noticed Venetia's head was down, apparently ferreting in her handbag for her cigarettes, which she produced as the waiter left.

'Smoke?' She offered Connie a Gauloise.

'Thank you.'

'So, how are you enjoying Paris?' said Venetia, lighting Connie's cigarette and taking a long draw on her own.

'Very much, thank you. And you?'

'It certainly makes a change from the slow pace of the south, does it not?'

As the champagne arrived on a tray, Connie watched as Venetia instantly drained half the glass in a most unladylike fashion. Connie also noticed her hands shook as she put her cigarette to her mouth. And, as Venetia removed her fur and hat, Connie saw the razor-sharp shoulder blades outlined under her blouse, her drawn face and the black smudges beneath her eyes that make-up could not hide. Venetia looked a good ten years older than last time she'd seen her.

For the next half an hour, the two of them had an absurd conversation about Connie's aunt in St Raphaël and imaginary friends from school, whom they both 'remembered'. The tea arrived and Venetia pounced on the dainty sandwiches and cakes as if she hadn't eaten for weeks. Connie sat back guiltily, watching Venetia's eyes shadowed by her heavy fringe but, nevertheless, darting back and forth nervously.

'Well, wasn't that delightful?' enthused Venetia. 'Now, I have an appointment with my dressmaker on the Rue de Cambon. Will you accompany me? Then we can continue our talk of the past.'

'Of course,' agreed Connie, knowing the request brooked no refusal.

'I'll see you in the lobby; must pop to powder my nose whilst you get the bill.'

Venetia walked off and Connie signalled for the waiter. Then, having used up most of the francs she had been issued with by F Section on the champagne and cake, Connie stood in the lobby waiting for Venetia to emerge from the powder room. When she did, she tucked her arm into Connie's and they walked out of the Ritz and set off in the direction of the Rue de Cambon.

'Thank heavens for that!' Venetia sighed. 'Now we can talk, couldn't risk it in there. You never know who's watching and listening. Walls really do have ears in this city. Enjoyed the grub though,' she added, 'first proper food I've eaten in days. So, where on earth have you been, Connie? I'd heard from James that you'd travelled over on the Lizzy with him and arrived in France. And then you simply vanished into thin air!'

'You've seen James?' said Connie, thrilled to hear a familiar name.

'I did, but I heard a few days ago he's no longer amongst us, poor chap,' said Venetia. 'Didn't last long, bless him, but then most of us don't.' She gave a harsh laugh.

'He's dead?' whispered Connie, horrified.

'Yes. Anyway, tell me, where have you been hiding yourself? And what on earth are you doing staying in that enormous house on the Rue de Varenne?'

'Venetia, I . . .' Connie sighed, still reeling from the shock of hearing James had died. 'It's a long story and I really can't tell you. Partly because I don't understand some of it myself,' she added.

'That sounds highly unsatisfactory, but I suppose I'll have to accept it. You haven't changed sides, have you?' she asked. 'When I had a friend of mine follow you home from the Tuileries Gardens, he said he saw a Nazi officer entering the house not long after you.'

'Venetia, please,' Connie pleaded, 'I really can't say.'

'So are you still one of us or not? That's a simple enough question to answer, isn't it?' Venetia continued to prod her.

'Of course I am! Look, something happened on the night I arrived in Paris which led to my . . . current circumstances. You of all people will understand, Venetia, that I mustn't say any more,' underlined Connie. 'And if the person who saved me that night knew I was here—well, he would feel I was betraying him.'

'Hardly,' muttered Venetia. 'Making contact with an old friend who has mutual family connections is betraying no one, I would have thought. Look, Con—' Venetia pulled her across the road, taking the opportunity to glance left and right as she did so—'the point is, I need your help. I'm sure you know how the Scientist network has crumbled. At present, I'm the only wireless operator left. And I'm having to move from place to place to send messages back to London so the Boche can't trace my signal. I had a pretty near miss two or three days ago—they came to the apartment where I was staying on a tip-off and I'd left only twenty minutes before. My wireless is currently stashed at another safe house, but it's not secure. I need to find somewhere to transmit urgent messages to London, and also to other operatives here. There's something absolutely huge about to happen, planned for tomorrow night, and it's imperative I get these messages through. Surely, Con, you must know somewhere I could go to do this?'

'Venetia, I'm sorry, but I really don't. I can't explain to you now, but I'm trapped where I am. I've been ordered not to speak to anyone who could trace my association back to the person in question.'

'Good God, Con!' Venetia cried, suddenly stopping in the street. 'What are you saying? You were sent over here as an agent of the British government! I don't care a damn who this "person" you're trying to protect is, or how he's

186

addled your brain. But I and many others involved in tomorrow night know that, if we're successful, it will mean that thousands of Frenchmen are not rounded up and sent to German factories to work as slave labourers there. We need your help! You must know somewhere I can go,' she said desperately. 'I *have* to send these messages tonight and that's an end to it.'

Venetia somewhat reluctantly replaced her arm through Connie's and they continued walking in silence.

Connie felt as though she was caught in a spider's web, the delicately spun silk threads of truths, lies and deception leading everywhere and nowhere. She was in a moral cul-de-sac, not knowing any longer where her loyalty lay, or who she should trust. Seeing Venetia was drawing her back into the realities of the task she had been sent here to complete. Venetia's bedraggled presence, her hunger and desperation, only fed her guilt and confusion further.

'You could come to the house on the Rue de Varenne, but it isn't safe,' Connie stated. 'As you know, it has far too many German visitors.'

'I don't care about that,' said Venetia. 'Often those pigs don't see what's right under their nose.'

'Venetia, surely it's too risky? And I know of nowhere else,' she added.

In one corner of her mind, Connie was privately considering the fact that Édouard was absent tonight, and that there was a separate door from the garden that led down to the cellar. She'd used it in the summer when the air-raid sirens had begun and she'd been sitting outside. But what if there was an air-raid tonight? What if Venetia was seen entering or leaving the house? What if one of the von Wehndorf twins made an impromptu visit, just as Venetia was transmitting from the cellar below?

'To be honest, Con, I'm past caring.' Venetia sighed. 'Nearly all of the safe houses in Paris are gone, although new ones are currently being established. And besides, simply no one would expect a British agent to be transmitting from the cellar of a house which is known to entertain the enemy.' Venetia turned her eyes to Connie. 'Are you absolutely sure you're not turned?' She laughed suddenly. 'Well, if you are, I'm dead anyway, so what does it matter?'

Venetia was asking her to prove herself. Connie sighed as she accepted the inevitable. Her loyalty had to be with her friend and her country, whatever the consequences.

'All right, I'll help you.'

*　　　*　　　*

Connie returned home, then made the excuse to Sarah of leaving a book downstairs in the cellar last time there had been an air raid. She unlocked the cellar door, which led up the steps to the garden beyond, then returned to the drawing room to sit with Sophia. As Sophia's delicate fingers passed lightly over a new Braille version of Byron's poems, a radiant smile on her face, Connie could sit still no longer. She feigned a headache at half past six and said she'd take supper in her room.

Then, at eight o'clock, she returned downstairs to tell Sarah there were no guests that evening and she was free to retire. Sophia was already up in her room. Connie paced the floorboards of her own bedroom, her nerves jangling as the clock ticked forwards. Venetia was almost certainly down below her in the cellar now.

Plagued with guilt at the thought of innocent Sophia, unaware that the woman her family had taken in and given protection to was betraying her safety right under her very nose, Connie watched the next hour pass in an agony of tension.

At ten o'clock Connie crept downstairs. She was at the back of the house in the kitchen on her way down to the cellar to check Venetia had gone, when she heard a soft tap at the front door.

Her heart missing a beat, Connie opened the kitchen door, which led into the entrance hall, and saw the front door had already been opened by Sophia, who had managed to find her way unchaperoned down the stairs. There on the doorstep stood Frederik, his arms wrapped around Sophia. In an agony of tension, Connie slipped back into the shadows to try and decide what to do for the best. She realised that the two of them must have engineered this tryst. Ten o'clock at night was hardly appropriate for anyone to call, let alone a gentleman to visit an unaccompanied lady. Connie wondered whether she should be more concerned for Sophia's virtue or the possibility that there was still a British agent down in the cellar—with a senior Nazi officer only feet above her.

Connie eventually decided the safest thing was to leave them be. Whilst Frederik was looking into Sophia's eyes, at least he was preoccupied. Once she'd seen the two of them enter the drawing room, Connie fled upstairs to her bedroom. She sat ram-rod straight in a winged chair by her window, wishing with every fibre of her body this night would be over and dawn would break.

Then she checked herself. How could she be so selfish? Venetia and her other fellow agents were putting themselves through the most terrible danger every single day. One night of mental agony was hardly a lot to contend with.

Eventually, Connie heard footsteps in the corridor below her and the creak of the stairs. An upstairs door clicked shut and Connie sighed in relief, knowing that Frederik must have left and Sophia had gone to bed. Connie was surprised she hadn't heard him leave, but perhaps he'd taken pains to exit the house as quietly as possible.

She yawned, suddenly feeling the tension drain away and exhaustion replace it. Climbing into bed, Connie fell into a deep, dreamless sleep. And didn't hear the front door being quietly closed as the dawn began to break over Paris.

15

Blackmoor Hall, Yorkshire, 1999

The snow was falling thickly as Sebastian paid the taxi driver and removed Emilie's suitcase from the boot of the car. Emilie turned to survey Blackmoor Hall for the first time and saw a darkly forbidding gothic mansion in red brick. A stone gargoyle was perched menacingly above the arch over the front door, its grin toothless, having been eaten away by the elements, the top of its head clad in a bonnet

190

of snow.

It was impossible to make any judgement of the surroundings in which the house sat; currently the landscape could have been Siberia as much as an English village set on the North Yorkshire moors. The landscape was white, empty and desolate for as far as Emilie's eye could see. She shivered involuntarily, as much from the bleakness as the cold.

'Blimey, only just made it,' said Sebastian, appearing next to her. 'Hope that driver makes it home safely,' he added as the taxi ploughed its way back up the drive through the deepening snow. 'It may be impassable here by tomorrow.'

'You mean we could be snowed in?' Emilie said as they trudged through the snow, now shin deep, to the front door.

'Yup,' he confirmed, 'it happens most years around here. Luckily, we have a Land Rover and a neighbour with a tractor at our disposal.'

'When it snows in the French Alps, they always manage to keep the roads clear,' commented Emilie as Sebastian grasped the large enamel door knob and turned it.

'Say hello to England, my French princess, where any form of unexpected weather can bring the country to a standstill,' he said, smiling. 'And now, Emilie, welcome to my humble abode.'

Sebastian pushed open the front door and they stepped into an entrance hall that was in direct contrast to the white brightness of outside. Everything was clad in dark wood: the panelled walls, the inelegant deep-stained staircase—even the huge fireplace forming the centrepiece of the room sported a heavy mahogany surround.

191

Unfortunately, a fire did not burn brightly in its grate and Emilie felt little change in temperature from that of outside.

'Come on,' said Sebastian, dropping Emilie's suitcase by the bottom of the ugly staircase, 'there'll be a fire burning in the drawing room, I'm sure. I left a message for Mrs Erskine to say we were coming.'

He pulled her along a labyrinth of corridors, the walls covered in deep-green wallpaper and adorned with oil paintings of horses out to hunt. Pushing open a door, Sebastian walked into a large drawing room, its walls sporting a dark maroon William Morris wallpaper and accommodating further paintings crammed haphazardly upon them.

'Bugger!' he swore as he looked at the empty grate, filled only with the greying ashes of a past fire. 'This isn't like her. Don't tell me she's handed in her resignation again.' Sebastian sighed. 'No panic, sweetheart, I'll have this going in a trice.'

Emilie sat on the fender shivering as Sebastian expertly and swiftly built a fire. Her teeth were chattering by the time he'd coaxed the flames into life and she warmed her hands gratefully.

'Right,' he said, 'you sit there and defrost and I'll go and make some tea and find out what the hell has been going on since I left.'

'Sebastian—' Emilie called as he left the drawing room, wanting to know in which direction was the nearest bathroom, but the heavy door swung shut behind him. Hoping he wouldn't be long, Emilie sat and thawed out in front of the fire, watching the snow flurries thicken to a blizzard and settle on the window sills outside.

Her knowledge of England was limited—she'd travelled with her mother on a few occasions to stay with friends in London—but her vision of cosy English cottages adorned with thatched roofs and nestling in chocolate-box villages could not be further removed from this austere, freezing monolith of a house and its surroundings.

Twenty minutes later, Sebastian had still not returned and Emilie was getting desperate. She stood up and ventured outside the drawing room into the corridor, opening doors to further dark rooms in search of the loo. She found one at last, whose vast wooden toilet seat reminded her of a throne. Emerging, Emilie heard raised voices from somewhere in the house. One of them was unknown, but the other was most definitely Sebastian. She couldn't hear what they were saying, but it was obvious he was extremely angry.

She now wished she'd asked for more details of Sebastian's world here in Yorkshire before she'd stepped on a plane with him to come to England. But the two weeks since he'd asked her to marry him had been a whirlwind of activity. Their talk had been more of their fascinating shared past than their future.

Emilie had told him all that Jacques had told her when she'd returned to Paris from the château.

'What a story,' Sebastian had sighed. 'And it sounds like that's only the start. When will Jacques be able to tell you more?'

'He promised he would when I return to put the library into store. I think it drained him emotionally,' Emilie had said.

'I'm sure.' Sebastian had hugged her to him. 'But there's a nice synergy in the way our families have been reunited.'

Emilie's fingers reached to her neck to touch the creamy white pearls—her mother's pearls—remembering when Sebastian had presented her with them on the morning of their wedding.

'I bought them back for you at the auction, sweetheart,' he'd said as he'd fastened them round her throat. Then he'd kissed her. 'Are you sure you don't mind the ceremony being so small? I mean, it's hardly how the last surviving member of the de la Martinières should get married. I'm sure half of Paris attended your parents' wedding.' He smiled down at her.

'Yes, and that's why I'm very happy to get married quietly,' Emilie had answered truthfully, the thought of being the centre of attention horrifying her. The low-key nuptials had suited her perfectly.

After the marriage ceremony, at which Gerard and a Parisian art-dealer friend of Sebastian's had been witnesses, Gerard had insisted on taking the four of them to the Ritz for lunch. 'It's the least your parents would have wanted for you, Emilie,' he'd added. Gerard had raised a glass to their health and happiness, then asked of their plans. Emilie had told him she was off to stay with Sebastian in England whilst the château was renovated. Gerard had caught her as they were leaving the Ritz and urged her to keep in touch with him.

'Anything I can do to help, Emilie, you know that I'm always here for you.'

'Thank you, Gerard, you've been very kind,' she'd acknowledged.

'And, Emilie, please try and remember that even

though you're now married, it's you who owns the château, the proceeds from the sale of the Paris house *and* the de la Martinières name. I would like to speak to you about the details of the estate and the finances in the future, as well as to your husband.'

'Sebastian tells me everything that I need to know,' Emilie had replied. 'He's been wonderful, Gerard, and I couldn't have got through this without him.'

'I agree, he has, but it's still a good thing in a marriage to keep your independence. Especially financially,' he'd added, before kissing Emilie's hand and leaving.

*   *   *

Eventually, when Emilie had been reduced to reading numerous out-of-date copies of *Horse and Hound*, Sebastian re-entered the drawing room looking harassed and apologetic in equal measure.

'So sorry, darling. I had a few things to sort out. Would you like a cup of tea? I could certainly do with one,' he said, sighing and running a hand through his hair.

'What's wrong?' Emilie went to him and he folded his arms around her.

'Oh, nothing out of the ordinary, for this house, at least,' he answered. 'I was right. Mrs Erskine has handed in her notice and gone off home in high dudgeon, swearing never to return. She'll come back, of course. She always does.'

'Why has she left?'

'That, Emilie,' said Sebastian, 'is something I want to try and explain to you over a hot drink.'

*   *   *

Each furnished with a large mug of hot tea, and sitting comfortably on a couple of big cushions by the fire, Sebastian began to explain.

'I want to tell you about my brother, Alex. And I'm warning you, it's a story I don't enjoy relaying. I'm feeling bad I haven't told you before, actually, but then it never seemed relevant. Up until today, anyway.'

'Then tell me now,' Emilie encouraged him.

'Right. So—' Sebastian took a sip of his tea— 'I've already told you our mother dumped us here on our granny when we were toddlers, then disappeared off into the blue yonder. Alex is eighteen months younger than me. And we're polar opposites, rather like Falk and Frederik from the sound of things. As you know, I like to be organised, whereas Alex has always been a . . . free spirit, constantly searching, not prepared or even able to live with routine. Anyway, we were both sent to boarding school, and whereas I loved it and thrived, Alex struggled,' Sebastian explained. 'He got himself expelled and messed up his university place by getting himself a drink-driving conviction. Then, when he was eighteen, he took himself off abroad and we heard nothing from him for a good few years.'

'Where did he go?' Emilie asked.

'We really had no idea, until one day Granny had a call from a hospital in France. Alex had apparently overdosed on heroin. He'd been near death's door when someone had found him, but he'd just pulled through.' Sebastian sighed. 'So

196

Granny flew over to get him and put him into a private rehab clinic here in England. To be fair to him, Alex was as good as his word and came home clean. But then he disappeared abroad again and we didn't see him back until after Granny had died. I think I need a stiff drink. You?'

'I'm fine, thank you,' Emilie replied.

Sebastian left the room and Emilie stood up to close the curtains against the still-falling snow. As she sat back down and stared into the red-hot flames of the fire, Emilie felt sympathy for her new husband. His brother sounded dreadful.

Sebastian came back with a gin and tonic and lay back in Emilie's arms. She stroked his hair.

'What happened next?' she asked.

'Well, just after Granny's death, when Alex had finally returned home and moved back in here, we had a flaming row. He headed for the car and I offered to drive him as I knew he was drunk, but he insisted on driving himself. I foolishly got in the car with him and a few miles down the road on a particularly notorious bend, he took the corner wide and smashed into a car coming in the opposite direction. My brother sustained serious injuries. I had the luck of the blind and escaped with cracked ribs, a broken arm and whiplash.'

'Oh my God!' Emilie breathed to herself. 'You poor, poor thing.'

'As I said, it was Alex who took the worst of it,' Sebastian underlined.

'How sad.' Emilie shook her head. She looked at him. 'You should have told me all of this before, Sebastian.'

'Yes, and given you the chance to get out of marrying me before it was too late.' He smiled harshly.

'No! I didn't mean that,' chastised Emilie. 'But I've learned from you that it always helps to share our problems, not keep them to ourselves.'

'Yes, you're right,' Sebastian agreed. 'You know, the tragedy is that Alex was always so bright. Far brighter than me. He sailed through his exams having done no work, whereas I've had to slog for everything I've ever had. Alex could have had it all if he hadn't been so messed up and irresponsible.'

'I often think people who are too bright suffer as much as those who struggle,' commented Emilie. 'My father always said gifts were best in moderation. Too much or too little of anything brings problems.'

'It sounds like you had a very wise father, and I would very much like to have met him.' Sebastian kissed her on the nose and looked up at her. 'So, there we are. The story of my errant brother. Now then, you must be starving. Why don't you come into the kitchen with me whilst I knock something up from the fridge? At least it's warm in there with the range going full-pelt. And then I suggest we both retire to our icebox of a bedroom. I'm sure we can think of ways to keep warm.' Sebastian pulled her up from the floor with him. 'Come on, let's eat as quickly as possible and then go upstairs.'

As he led her along the icy corridors towards the kitchen, Emilie felt she simply had to ask: 'So where is Alex now?'

'Didn't I say?'

'No, you didn't,' Emilie corrected him.

'He's here, of course. Alex lives here at Blackmoor Hall.'

198

16

Emilie woke early the next morning, having had an unsettled night. This was partly to do with the biting cold, the like of which she'd never experienced before. She felt as if her freezing bones would snap at any moment. Sebastian had apologised profusely, explaining that the reason the ancient heating wasn't working was due to someone forgetting to fill up the oil tank, and that he would sort it out as soon as possible.

Emilie moved her icy toes surreptitiously onto the warmth of Sebastian's shin. The room was completely shrouded in darkness, not a chink of light coming through the fading damask curtains. She wondered if Sebastian would mind if they could sleep with the curtains drawn back. She'd always slept with the windows naked, enjoying waking to the mellow light of a new day.

Emilie mulled over what Sebastian had told her of his brother, Alex, last night. After dropping the bombshell that he lived at Blackmoor Hall, Sebastian had gone on to explain that he'd suffered a broken back in the car crash and was now confined to a wheelchair. He had a carer living in with him on a full-time basis and resided in his own specially converted flat on the ground floor of the east wing.

'Of course, it costs a fortune to have him looked after, not to mention the renovation that was needed to accommodate a disabled person, but what else could I do?' Sebastian had sighed.

'Anyway, please don't worry about Alex. He keeps himself to himself and rarely ventures into the main house.'

'Has he been able to steer clear of drugs and alcohol since the accident?' Emilie had asked tentatively.

'Mainly, yes. But we've been through a succession of carers, two of which I had to get rid of after they'd been coerced by my brother into supplying him with alcohol. Alex can be extremely charming and very persuasive if he wants to be,' he'd added.

Despite her husband's reassurances about the separateness of Alex's existence, Emilie shuddered when she contemplated this drug-dependent paraplegic who lived—whether in a separate apartment or not—very clearly under the same roof.

Sebastian had also mentioned that Alex was a consummate liar. 'Don't believe anything he tells you, Emilie. My brother can convince the brightest mind that black is white.'

*   *   *

'Sweetheart?'

Emilie felt a warm hand snake towards her.

'Yes?'

'Christ!' Sebastian exclaimed as he felt Emilie's shoulder, shrouded in all the layers of clothes she'd put on during the night. 'You're wrapped up like a pass-the-parcel.' He laughed. 'Come here and give me a hug.'

As Emilie settled into his deliciously warm embrace and as he began to kiss her, any early-morning fears that had assailed her melted away.

* * *

'I doubt it's a day for sightseeing,' Sebastian commented as they stood in the kitchen drinking coffee and looking at the hillocks of snow piled up outside the window. 'I reckon it's a good foot deep and that sky is threatening further falls. I'm going to call Jake, my farmer neighbour, and see if he'll bring his tractor here to clear the drive. Supplies are running low and I'll need to get out to the village shop to get us some essentials. How about I install you in the drawing room with a nice fire? There's a library down the corridor and I'm sure you can find yourself a book to keep yourself amused.'

'OK,' agreed Emilie, feeling she didn't have much option.

'And I'll see about having some oil delivered so we can get the central heating going again. It's so bloody expensive these days and most of the heat seems to disappear through the rotting window frames.' He sighed. 'Sorry, darling. As I said, I've rather taken my eye off the work and home ball in the past few months.'

'Is there anything I can help you with?' Emilie asked him.

'No, but I appreciate the offer. I'll also pop in and visit Mrs Erskine, our ex-housekeeper, whilst I'm in the village, and see if I can persuade her to return. I promise I'll have things back on track in the next couple of days,' Sebastian said as they walked together along the corridor to the drawing room. 'You must wonder where the hell I've brought you to,' he added as he bent to clear the grate. 'It gets better, I swear. This is a beautiful part of the world, truly it is.'

'Let me do that.' Emilie knelt next to Sebastian. 'You go off and do what you need to.'

'Are you sure? Sorry about the lack of servants around here,' he teased. 'I know it's not what you're used to.'

'Sebastian . . .' Emilie reddened. 'I can learn.'

'Of course you can, only joking. And feel free to explore the house, although what you'll see will probably horrify you. It makes your old château look positively modern!' Sebastian grimaced and left the room.

*   *   *

Clad in two of Sebastian's thick fisherman's jumpers, Emilie spent an hour wandering around the house. It was obvious that many of the rooms upstairs had not been used for years and, unlike the huge château windows built to let in as much light as possible, this house had small mean ones, designed to keep out the cold. The dreary colours and heavy mahogany furniture were reminiscent of walking onto the set of an Edwardian play.

As she wandered back downstairs, Emilie was aware of how desperately this house needed taking in hand. But, like the château, it would be a huge renovation project. And she realised she had no idea how much money Sebastian had to fund it. However, it hardly mattered; Emilie knew her finances were very healthy and they had enough money to live as they wished for the rest of their lives.

Back in the drawing room, Emilie again pondered why she had never thought to ask about the exact state of Sebastian's finances before she'd married him. Not that she regarded it as relevant to her decision, but now she was his wife, it was important she knew. Perhaps she'd broach the subject later on, she thought, as she saw both the tractor and Sebastian in the Land Rover behind it make their slippery way up the drive and away from the house.

By lunchtime, Emilie was hungry and bored, so she took herself off to the kitchen to see what she could find in the fridge to eat. Making a sandwich with the last remaining crust of a loaf of bread, she sat down at the table to eat it. As she did so, she heard a door slam loudly from somewhere in the house and a raised voice. This time it was female. The door to the kitchen opened and a scrawny, middle-aged woman appeared through it.

'Is Mr Carruthers here? I need to see him immediately,' she stated.

Emilie could see the woman was shaking with anger. 'No, I'm afraid you've missed him. He's gone to the village.'

'Who are you?' the woman asked rudely.

'I'm Emilie, Sebastian's wife.'

'Really? Well, all I can say is good luck to you! And as you're his wife, you can tell him from me that I resign as of now. I'm not taking any more of his brother's rudeness. Or violence! He's just thrown a boiling hot cup of coffee at me. If I hadn't moved out of the way, I could have suffered third-degree burns on my arms. I've called my friend who has a four-wheel drive and she's coming to collect me within the hour. I will not stay another minute in this godforsaken house with that . . . *madman!*'

'I see. I'm so sorry,' Emilie offered, noticing the woman was slurring slightly, probably due to anger. 'Can I offer you a drink? Perhaps we should talk about it before you leave. I'm sure Sebastian won't be long—'

'There's not a thing you or he could say to make me change my mind,' the woman interrupted her. 'He's persuaded me before and I've regretted it. I just hope for your sake your husband doesn't dump his brother on you. Having said that, I can't imagine you'll find anyone else to fill the post. You know Mrs Erskine's walked out too?'

'Yes, but my husband says she'll be coming back.'

'Well, more fool her. She's a nice lady, and it's only out of loyalty to their grandmother that she stays. I knew Constance when I was a young'un and lived in this village. Lovely woman she was, but what those two boys have put her through doesn't bear thinking about. Any road, not my problem any more. I'll be off to pack. He's had his lunch, so he should be all right by himself until your husband gets back. I'd let him be at the moment, anyway. Wait until that temper of his dies down,' she added. 'It normally does.'

'Right.' Emilie didn't know what else to say.

The woman obviously saw the fear in her eyes, for her own softened suddenly. 'Don't worry, love, Alex is all right really, just gets frustrated, like we all would if we was him. He's a good lad at heart, and he's had a rough time of it. But I'm too old to be doing with it all. I want a nice, calm geriatric to take care of, not a volatile little boy who's never

204

grown up.'

All Emilie could think of was the fact this woman was leaving before Sebastian returned. Consequently, she'd be left alone in an unknown and forbidding house, which—due to the snow—she could not escape from. With an as yet unseen, drunken, paraplegic lunatic. Currently her new life resembled something out of a horror film and Emilie had a sudden desperate urge to giggle at the ridiculousness of it.

'Anyway, congratulations on your marriage, love,' said the woman.

'Thank you.' Emile smiled ironically.

The woman walked towards the kitchen door, then stopped and turned back. 'I hope for your sake you knew what you were taking on. Goodbye.'

*   *   *

Back in the drawing room half an hour later, Emilie saw a car steering carefully down the drive and the woman she'd met in the kitchen stomping through the snow and stowing a suitcase in the boot. The car performed a skidding eight-point turn and made its way precariously away from the house.

Emilie watched as the snow began to fall once more, filling the sky with a whirling dervish of thick flakes which built an even more impenetrable wall between her and the out-side world. Her heart began to thud against her chest. The mad brother was now no more than a few feet away from her and they were completely alone. What if the snow became so bad it was impossible for Sebastian to return? At three o'clock, the

January sky was darkening already in preparation for dusk and then dark . . . Emilie stood up, her raised heartbeat signalling its eagerness to move to all-out panic. She'd suffered many attacks in her late teens and, having conquered them, lived in permanent terror that they might strike again.

'Keep calm and breathe,' she told herself as she felt the unremitting waves rushing through her. She began to pant, knowing she was now out of control and it was too late for rational thinking.

Sinking onto a sofa, Emilie put her head between her legs. Her physical strength left her and garish colours assaulted her closed lids as she struggled for breath.

'Please, *mon dieu, mon dieu . . .*'

'Can I help you?'

A deep male voice came from somewhere in the distance as her head spun and her hands and feet tingled wildly. She couldn't look up—couldn't waste the breath she needed to pant.

'I said, can I help you?'

The voice was nearer now, in fact it was almost next to her. Perhaps she could feel hot breath on her cheek, a hand grasping her own . . . she couldn't answer.

'I'm presuming you're Seb's new French wife. Do you understand English?'

Emilie managed a nod.

'OK. I'll go and see if I can find you a bag to breathe into. Just carry on hyperventilating whilst I'm gone. At least it will mean you're still alive.'

Emilie had no idea in her detached existence how long it was before a paper bag was placed over her mouth and nose and she was told by the same, calm voice to breathe in and out slowly. Whether this was part of a dream—or a nightmare—she didn't care. The person seemed to know the right thing to do and, like a helpless child, she followed his instructions.

'Good girl, you're doing really well. Just keep breathing in and out of the bag. There, it's calming. It will stop soon, I promise,' the voice reassured her.

Eventually, the pounding of her heart began to return to a beat resembling normal, her hands and feet began to rejoin her body and Emilie took the bag away from her mouth. Flopping back exhausted onto the sofa, eyes closed, she felt the relief of her body calming down.

It was only after a few minutes of relishing the fact she had survived and it was over that her brain began to question who her knight in shining armour could be. She forced one tired and twitching eyelid open and saw a man who was Sebastian, but not Sebastian. It was a Sebastian in technicolor—eyes a more mesmeric brown, with flecks of amber running through the irises, hair glinting with red-gold lights, a face containing a perfect nose, fuller pinker lips and cheekbones that stood out razor-sharp under the softness of his unblemished skin.

'I'm Alex,' he said. 'Pleased to meet you.'

Emilie immediately closed the eyelid she'd opened and sat very still, not confident that the sight of the mad brother sitting within centimetres of her wouldn't set off a further panic attack.

A warm hand patted hers. 'I understand you don't want to waste your breath speaking to me at present. I know what you've just been through. I've had panic attacks countless times. What you need

207

now is a good stiff drink.'

This man who spoke so gently to her did not match up to the image Sebastian had painted. The hand on hers was reassuring, not terrifying. She dared to open her eyes and study him properly.

'Hello.' The full lips smiled and she saw his eyes were full of amusement.

'Hello,' she managed, her voice still recovering its strength.

'Shall we speak English or *preferez-vous Français?*'

'*Français, merci.*' Her brain was still too fuzzy to start thinking in another language.

'*D'accord.*'

Emilie watched him studying her.

'You're very pretty,' he commented in French. 'My brother said you were. Far prettier with those big blue eyes of yours open though, it has to be said,' he continued in immaculate French. 'Right, your final medicine.' Out of the side of his wheelchair, Alex produced a bottle of whisky. 'The harridan who just left didn't think I knew where she kept her secret tipple. But I managed to rescue it from her suitcase when she was with you complaining about what a complete nightmare I was. Sebastian didn't believe me, but she was a total drunkard—she knocked back a good bottle of this a day. Now—' Alex wheeled himself expertly over to a cabinet and opened it, displaying a dusty array of Edwardian glassware—'we'll both have one, shall we? Never a good idea to drink alone.' He poured two healthy measures of whisky into the glasses and, wedging them expertly between his thighs, steered his wheelchair back towards her.

'I really don't think I should,' Emilie said as

Alex handed her one of the glasses.

'Why not? You can say with complete honesty this is for medicinal purposes only. Come on,' he urged, 'seriously, it's my turn to play nurse for a change and this will help, promise.'

'No, thank you.' Emilie shook her head, not wishing to encourage him.

'Well, I won't if you won't.' Alex placed his glass firmly on the table. 'Right, it's bloody freezing in here and if I can't warm you up with a dram of whisky, at least I can get the fire going again.'

Emilie sat and watched as Alex stoked the fire, too mesmerised to help.

'So where's Seb?' he asked. 'Gone out to beg poor old Mrs Erskine to come back for the umpteenth time?'

'Yes, he said he would visit her while he was in the village buying some food,' Emilie answered.

'Doubt he's going to find much in the shop. All the locals will have seen the snow coming and gone into siege mode, clearing the shelves. It's their most profitable moment of the year, when even the ancient tins of butter beans get snapped up. We'll be lucky if they've even got those this evening. This has really set in,' Alex added, looking at the still-falling snow. 'I rather like it, actually. Do you?'

As the whole weight of his penetrating gaze fell upon her, Emilie tried to remember what Sebastian had said about Alex's ability to charm and convince. 'Not really, I haven't been warm since I arrived.'

'I'd doubt you have. The oil tank's been empty for weeks now. Luckily, I have a secret stash of electric heaters which at least keep my blood circulating. Don't tell Seb, mind you, they'd be confiscated forthwith. Anyway, apart from the fact that we live in an English version of an igloo, I do like the snow. But then—' Alex sighed—'I like anything that breaks the boring monotony of the norm. And this weather is dramatic.'

'Yes,' agreed Emilie feebly.

Alex eyed the two whiskies sitting on the table. 'I think we should both drink this down. It seems a shame to waste it.'

'Really, no.' Emilie shook her head.

'Oh—' Alex raised his eyebrows—'I suppose Seb's mentioned my rampant alcoholism and drug dependency?'

'He mentioned it, yes,' she said honestly.

'It's true that I had a drug problem in days of yore,' Alex agreed companionably, 'but I've never been an alcoholic. However, that doesn't mean to say I don't like a drink. We all do. I mean, you are French; you must have been drinking wine from the cradle, surely?'

'Of course.'

'So, how come you married my brother?'

'I . . .' Emilie was nonplussed by his directness. 'I fell in love. It *is* the reason most people marry.'

'That's as good a reason as any.' Alex nodded. 'Well, I suppose I should say welcome to the family.'

The door to the drawing room opened. Sebastian stood there, his hair dripping with melting snow.

Guiltily, Emilie jumped up to greet him. 'Hello, I'm so glad you're back safely.'

'We didn't hear you come up the drive,' put in Alex.

Sebastian was scowling, his eyes pinned to the two glasses of whisky on the table.

'No, that's because I had to leave the car at the end of it and walk through the snowdrifts with two bloody great bags of shopping. Have you been drinking?' he accused Alex.

'No. Although I admit I did try and persuade your new wife that she should knock one back as she wasn't feeling very well,' Alex said equably.

'That just about sums you up,' said Sebastian, raising his eyebrows. He turned to Emilie, looking angry, not sympathetic. 'Are you feeling all right?'

'I am fine now, thank you,' she replied nervously.

'I told you, Alex, that you were not to enter this house,' Sebastian said, turning on his brother.

'Well, as I was explaining to Emilie here, my carer has walked out on me, so I was just coming to tell you.'

'What! Oh, for God's sake, what have you done this time?' Sebastian expostulated.

'I threw one of her disgusting cups of coffee at a wall. She was so drunk that she'd put salt instead of sugar in it,' Alex explained. 'And she thought I was aiming for her.'

'Well, you've really done it now, Alex.' Sebastian was furious. 'Mrs Erskine has finally refused point blank to come back and I don't blame her. And as for that poor woman who's just left . . . I'm not surprised she's gone too, the way you behave. Where the hell I'm meant to find an immediate replacement to come out in this weather, I really don't know.'

'Look, Seb, I'm not completely incapable, as you know,' Alex shot back. 'I can feed, clothe, wash

211

myself and wipe my own backside. I can even manage to haul myself in and out of bed at night. I've told you countless times I don't need a full-time carer any longer, just someone to help me domestically.'

'You know that's not true,' countered Sebastian angrily.

'Oh yes it is. Honestly.' Alex raised his eyebrows and turned to Emilie. 'He treats me like a two-year-old. I mean—' he indicated the wheelchair— 'I'm hardly going to get into much trouble in this, now am I?'

Emilie felt like an onlooker at a boxing match. She remained silent, unable to add anything to the conversation.

'You seem to do a bloody good job of it, actually,' countered Sebastian. 'Anyway, now you'll be put to the test, certainly in the next few days. Because there's no way I'm going to be able to find someone.'

'That's fine by me, really,' Alex stated categorically. 'I've told you it's a waste of money, but you won't listen. Well, I'll leave you two to it.' He manoeuvred his wheelchair to the door and grasped it. Pausing, he turned back and smiled at Emilie. 'A pleasure to meet you, and welcome to Blackmoor Hall.'

The door closed behind him and silence descended on the drawing room. Sebastian reached for one of the glasses of whisky, picked it up and drained it in one gulp. 'I'm so sorry about that, Emilie. You must be wondering what on earth I've brought you to. He's a nightmare and I'm simply at the end of my tether.'

'Of course you are,' she said. 'And please don't

worry about me. I'll do what I can to help.'

'That's kind of you, but just now I'm all out of ideas. Do you want this?' He indicated the other whisky glass.

'No, thank you.'

Sebastian picked up the second glass and drained that too. 'I think you and I should have a very honest talk, Emilie, because I'm really feeling as if I've married you under false pretences. Everything here is a bloody mess. And if you decide you want to call it quits and ship out, I certainly wouldn't hold it against you.' He sank down onto the sofa next to her and took her hand in his. 'I'm so sorry, I really am.'

'Sebastian, I'm beginning to understand that your life is not as straightforward as I'd believed,' Emilie agreed, 'but I married you because I loved you. I'm your wife now and I share your problems, whatever they are.'

'You haven't heard the half of it,' groaned Sebastian.

'Then tell me.'

'OK, here goes.' He sighed. 'On top of the Alex situation, the bald truth is that I'm stony broke. There wasn't a lot left in the pot when Granny died, but I'd hoped that as my business grew I could at least afford to start to renovate this house. And then, of course, Alex had the accident two years ago and the cost of caring for him has simply eaten its way through my income. I've taken out a mortgage against the house, of course, but I can barely make the repayments on it and certainly the bank won't give me any more. I'm now at the point where the reason the oil tank hasn't been filled so far this winter is that I don't have the money to pay

213

for it. So it looks as though I'm going to have to sell Blackmoor Hall. That is, if Alex will agree. Half of it's his, after all, and he's adamant he doesn't want to leave.'

'Sebastian,' Emilie finally ventured, 'I understand how painful it can be to sell off the family home. But it sounds to me as if you must, that you have no other choice. And neither does Alex.'

'You're right, of course. But—and this is the point—just before I met you, my business was really starting to flourish. I made some good decisions and things were very much going in the right direction. Anyway,' Sebastian continued, 'I suppose all I've said is irrelevant. I'm talking about Point B, but I'm currently at Point A. And how I get from one to the other is the big question. And however much I want to—' he shrugged—'I just don't think I can hold on to this house. What I do with our current next-door neighbour is another story. He'll fight tooth and nail to stay here and we jointly own the house. As you can imagine, the alternative accommodation for someone in Alex's situation is limited.'

'But you wouldn't abandon him, would you?' Emilie asked.

'Of course not, Emilie!' Sebastian's temper flared suddenly. 'What do you take me for? As you've already seen, I take my responsibilities very seriously.'

'Yes,' Emilie replied quickly. 'I didn't mean that. I was simply wondering where he would go if you did sell.'

'Well,' said Sebastian, 'I reckon the proceeds he'd gain from this house would pay for many years of quality care at a suitable establishment. However much he denies it, Alex needs full-time supervision and—'

'Sebastian,' Emilie interrupted, 'throughout our entire conversation, you've talked about "I". Please remember that it's no longer "I". It's "we". I'm your wife now, we're a partnership, and we'll sort out the problems here together, just as you helped me sort out mine in France.'

'You're very sweet, Emilie, but I really don't think, given the circumstances, there's much you can do to help,' he sighed.

'Why do you say that? Firstly, you know I have money. And as your wife, whatever I have is yours. Of course I can help you. I *want* to help you,' she reiterated. 'Especially if, as you say, the finance is only needed to get you through until your business starts to provide a better income. If it makes it easier, think of me as an investor,' she suggested.

Sebastian took his head from his hands and stared at her in wonder. 'Emilie, are you seriously saying you would help me financially?'

'Of course,' she said, shrugging. 'I don't see the problem. You've been there for me in the past few months. Now I can be here for you.'

'Emilie, you're an angel.' Sebastian wrapped his arms around her suddenly and hugged her. 'I feel so guilty I didn't tell you all of this before we were married. To be fair, it was only when we arrived here yesterday that I realised just how desperate the situation is. And I admit to hiding my head in the sand more than I should have done. God, when I opened my bank statement this morning, it resembled the financial equivalent of a car crash.'

'Please, at least don't worry about the money

any longer,' she comforted. 'When you've worked out the amount you need, I'll have it transferred over to your account here in England. Personally, I think there are more urgent problems than money to sort out at present. Like filling the oil tank.' Emilie raised an eyebrow. 'We can pay over the telephone by credit card, I'm sure. Then at least we'll all be warm.'

'Oh, sweetheart.' Sebastian turned to her, his face grey with anxiety. 'You're being so good about all this. I really am so terribly sorry.'

'Hush,' said Emilie. 'Besides the oil, which is an easy problem to solve, the next thing surely is to find someone to take care of your brother's needs. Yes?'

'Absolutely,' Sebastian agreed. 'The most immediate source would be an agency temp, but they really do charge an arm and a leg . . .'

'We've just agreed that money is not the problem,' Emilie repeated. 'Is Alex lying when he says he can look after himself?'

'Well, it's a fair point to say that I've never trusted him to care for himself,' Sebastian admitted. 'He's just so accident-prone, Emilie. Knowing him, he'll end up electrocuting himself by putting a tin of beans into the microwave, or using his computer to order vast quantities of booze from the nearest vintners.'

'So,' Emilie clarified, 'he doesn't actually need a qualified nurse to take care of him medically?'

'Well, he takes some drugs in the morning to help his circulation, but it's more a case of his practical, physical needs.'

'If we fail to find someone, I could help take care of him, at least temporarily,' suggested

Emilie. 'I have some experience with my mother, who was also in a wheelchair in the last few weeks of her life. I'm also a qualified vet, so I know about the workings of the body.'

'But could I trust you not to fall for Alex's charms?' Sebastian eyed the empty whisky glasses and shot her a half-amused glance. 'Or his influence?'

'Of course!' Emilie refrained from pointing out that it had been Sebastian himself who had drained the two glasses, not his wife or his brother. 'Surely it's not surprising he gets frustrated. Does he ever leave the house?'

'Rarely, but I can't really see Alex wanting to go to the community centre every Wednesday and join the rest of the local disabled gang for a game of snap and a cup of squash. Or, at least, that's how he would view it. He's always been a loner. Anyway—' Sebastian let his arms leave Emilie and sank back onto the sofa—'there you have it. Your husband's life out on a plate: unexpurgated and—at present—a bloody disaster.'

'Please don't say that, Sebastian,' Emilie urged him. 'Many of these things are not your fault. You've done your best to help your brother and keep your business and this house going. You mustn't blame yourself.'

'Thanks, sweetheart. I really appreciate your support. You're wonderful, you really are.' Sebastian leant towards her and kissed her softly on the lips. 'Now then, we need to phone the oil company before it closes and put ourselves in the inevitably large queue of snow-bound and oil-less masses. If you don't mind me using your credit card, maybe you could give it to me so I can read out the details when I call them?'

'Of course. It's upstairs in my handbag. I'll go and get it.'

Emilie dropped a kiss on her husband's weary head and left the room. As she walked upstairs, she realised she felt a small glow of satisfaction. She could now help her husband just as he had helped her in the past few months. It was a good feeling.

17

A week later, things at Blackmoor Hall were calmer. The snow, which had fallen solidly for three days and then frozen into great swathes of treacherous ice, was finally beginning to thaw as the temperature went up. The oil company had delivered the day before and Emilie awoke to a subtle lessening of the gnawing cold.

A temporary carer from an agency had been sourced by Sebastian for Alex. Emilie hadn't seen him since the day of her panic attack. In fact, she thought, as she switched on the kettle for a cup of coffee to take back upstairs to bed, she felt much calmer now. Sebastian had admitted how much money he needed to get him through the next few months and she'd had the amount transferred immediately to his bank account. Since then, he'd visibly relaxed.

'As we're snowed in, I think we should treat this imposed hiatus as a kind of impromptu honeymoon,' he'd announced. 'We've got wine in the cellar and food in the fridge, a blazing fire and each other. Let's try and enjoy it, shall we?'

They'd subsequently spent long, leisurely mornings under the covers together, then donned thick coats and wellingtons to brave the short walk into the village to eat hearty British food at the local pub. On the return journey, they'd indulged in heavy snowball fights and arrived back at the house elated from the fresh, icy air of outside. Evenings were spent together curled up in front of the fire, drinking the wine that Sebastian brought up from the cellar, talking and making love.

'You are so very beautiful,' Sebastian would say as he kissed her naked body in the firelight. 'I'm so very glad I've married you.'

The morning before, as the ice had begun to thaw, Sebastian had taken Emilie into the local town of Moulton to stock up on fast-dwindling food supplies. He'd insisted she drive the Land Rover home, which had been a terrifying ordeal for someone who was not used to icy conditions, let alone driving on the left-hand side of the road.

'It's important you can do it, sweetheart,' Sebastian had said as she'd driven them back home at a snail's pace. 'When I'm away in London, you'll need to be able to get out.'

Having made the coffee, Emilie looked with pleasure at the kitchen. The simple action of washing the filthy curtains that had hung drearily at the windows and placing a vase of flowers on the scrubbed pine table had cheered the room enormously. She'd sourced some pretty blue and white china from a selection in one of the cupboards and arranged it on top of the mantelpiece above the range. Climbing the stairs with the mugs of coffee, she could see the sun was shining today and the ice was dripping into invisibility. Perhaps she could even suggest to Sebastian that she decorated the kitchen— primrose paint would lift the room completely.

Getting back into bed beside him, she sipped the hot coffee.

'Sleep well?' Sebastian asked, sitting up and reaching for his mug.

'Yes. I've decided I quite like this house after all,' commented Emilie. 'It's like an ancient, unloved aunt, who simply needs some tenderness and care.'

'*And* lots of cash throwing at it,' Sebastian added. 'Talking of which, now the snow has thawed and you're settled here, I'm afraid I'm going to have to head to London for a few days. Will you be all right without me? Alex seems to be content with his new carer and I'm sure he won't bother you. You could come with me, but I'll be working flat out and won't have any time or the headspace to give you any attention. You'd be bored senseless.'

'Where do you stay when you're in London?' Emilie asked him.

'Oh, I normally put my head down in the box room of a friend's flat. Not exactly the Ritz, but it does for the amount of time I spend there,' Sebastian explained.

'How many days will you be gone?'

'I was thinking that if I left early tomorrow morning, perhaps no more than three. I'll be back late on Friday night,' he promised. 'I'll leave you the Landy, of course, just in case the weather turns again. I have an old banger I use to run myself to the station. And then, perhaps next time, we can think about you coming with me to London.'

'OK,' Emilie replied, trying not to worry at the thought of Sebastian leaving her here alone with the volatile Alex and a car she was terrified of driving. 'I was thinking I might paint the kitchen. Would you mind?'

'Of course not. I've got to pop into town to the bank anyway. We could choose some paint at the DIY place on the way back.' Sebastian turned to her and stroked her cheek. 'You're a miracle, Emilie, you really are.'

*   *   *

Sebastian left for London early the following morning. Full of plans for the day, which included making a start on painting the kitchen, Emilie went downstairs and made coffee, humming to herself. Then she set to work.

By lunchtime, she'd managed to paint the entire wall of the chimney breast and berated herself for not asking Sebastian to help her move the enormous dresser that took up the entirety of one wall. Sitting down to eat the sandwich she'd made, she heard a car arrive and then leave from the front of the house. Presuming it was the postman, she ignored it. After lunch, she tackled the wall that housed the sink.

'Hello again,' a voice said in French from behind her.

Emilie's heart sank as she turned and surveyed Alex sitting in his wheelchair by the kitchen door.

'What are you doing here?' she asked, nerves making her sound harsher than she meant to.

'My house and all that,' he replied affably, 'and I

221

thought I should inform you that my latest carer has buggered off.'

'Oh, Alex! What did you do this time?' Still perched atop the ladder, Emilie began tentatively to climb down.

'Please!' he said in mock horror. 'Don't you start patronising me as well.'

'Well, what do you expect?! I've only been here a week and I've already seen two carers leave,' she countered.

'My brother has got to you, obviously,' Alex said sadly.

'No he hasn't, not at all,' Emilie replied in English to underline how wrong Alex was.

'I love the way you say "not at all" in your beautiful French accent,' he grinned.

'Don't change the subject.' Emilie reverted to French.

'Sorry,' said Alex. 'Anyway, she's gone. And now it's just you and me.'

'Then I must call the agency immediately to find a replacement,' she retorted.

'Look, Emilie, I beg you, please don't. At least, not for a couple of days. I'd like to prove to you and Seb that I really am perfectly capable of caring for myself. If I absolutely promise to behave—no drink, no drugs, no carousing down at the local pub, etcetera . . .' Alex looked at her in desperation. 'Would you grant me a stay of execution? At the first sign of bad behaviour, you can call in the reserves.' He shook his head. 'And you have no idea how much I don't want that.'

Emilie hesitated, in a quandary. Surely, she should call her husband and discuss this with him? On the other hand, Emilie knew that if she did, he

222

would almost certainly race home. And with his business as much in need of attention as he'd described, that was the last thing he needed.

Emilie made a decision. She was Sebastian's wife and would deal with his brother in his stead.

'All right,' she agreed. 'Is there anything you'll need?' She put a foot back on the ladder to return to painting the tricky top corner.

'Not currently, thank you.'

'If you do, let me know.' Turning her back on him, Emilie proceeded up the ladder, stuck her brush in the paint and continued with her task.

There was silence from below. Emilie concentrated on the strokes of her brush.

'Nice colour. Good choice,' Alex commented eventually.

'Thank you. I like it.'

'So do I. And as it's technically half my kitchen, I think that's rather a good thing, don't you?'

'Yes.'

Another silence. And then . . . 'Can I help?'

Emilie refrained from any kind of facetious comment. 'I'm fine, thank you.'

'As a matter of fact, I can wield a roller with the best of them,' Alex confirmed, reading her mind.

'OK. There's one by the sink. Pour yourself some paint into the tray.'

Emilie watched Alex surreptitiously as he moved towards the sink, grasped the paint pot from the top of it and poured it efficiently into the tray. 'Shall I start here?' He indicated a patch to the left of the dresser.

'If you wish,' Emilie agreed. 'It's a shame I can't move that dresser.'

'I'm sure I can help you with that. My upper

223

torso is stronger than most able-legged humans,' Alex stated. 'We can have it moved between us, no problem.'

'OK.' Emilie climbed down the ladder and began to empty the top shelves as Alex cleared the bottom level. Then the two of them together eased the dresser out from the wall.

'Now, tell me about you,' Alex said companionably as Emilie remounted her ladder and he began to roller the wall.

'What do you want to know?'

'Oh, the basics: age, rank and serial number, that sort of thing,' he said, smiling.

'Well, I'm thirty years old and I was born in Paris. My father was much older than my mother and so died when I was quite young.' Emilie was determined to give minimal facts without being rude. 'I became a vet, lived in an apartment in the Marais and then met your brother just after my mother died. That's everything, really.'

'Methinks you underplay yourself,' Alex commented. 'For a start, you come from one of the most aristocratic families in France. The death of your mother even got a mention in *The Times*.'

'You know that from your brother?'

'No, I know it from my research,' he admitted. 'I looked you up on the Internet.'

'Then if you know everything about me, why are you asking me these questions?' Emilie countered.

'Because I'm interested in what you have to say for yourself. We are now related, after all,' Alex said. 'And, to be frank, you're not what I expected. Given your background, I'm surprised you're not the archetypal spoilt French princess, who exudes self-confidence simply because of her surname.

Most young women of your class wouldn't choose to become a vet, would they? Surely they'd prefer to find a suitable wealthy husband and spend their days flitting from the Caribbean, to the Alps, to St Tropez, depending on the season.'

'Yes, you've just described my mother's life very well.' Emilie allowed herself a smile.

'There!' Alex gave a triumphant flourish of his roller. 'So you've chosen to live a life which is the polar opposite of your mother's. And the question is—' he rubbed his chin in a faux pose of thought—'why? Perhaps, Emilie, your mother was so busy being beautiful and social, she didn't have the time to spare on you. And the glitz, glamour and excess of her life you found repugnant, because you always came second to it. She was the ultimate chic Frenchwoman and maybe you felt as though you could never live up to her expectations. You felt unloved and ignored by her. All this meant you grew up with very low self-esteem. So you rejected your birthright, just as you feel *it*— and your mother—had rejected you, and made a decision to live a very different kind of existence.'

Emilie had to grasp the top of the ladder to steady herself.

'And, of course,' Alex continued, unstoppable now in his piercing analysis, 'when it came to choosing a profession, again you decided to be a carer, e.g. a vet, which was something your mother had never been. And as for men . . . I'd doubt you've had many boyfriends. And then my brother tips up, like a knight in shining armour, and you fall hook, line and sinker—'

'*Enough!* Stop! How can you say these things when you don't even know me!' Emilie was

225

shaking involuntarily, the ladder wobbling beneath her. For her own safety, she climbed down the steps and walked over to him. 'How *dare* you presume you can speak to me like this? You know nothing about me! Nothing!'

'Ah now . . .' Alex grinned. 'I see I've stirred a little of the haughty French princess that lurks somewhere in the depths of your soul, however hard you try to hide it.'

'I said *enough*!'

Before she could stop herself, Emilie's hand reached out instinctively and she slapped Alex hard across his face. The sound resonated around the kitchen. She stood there, shocked by what she had just done. It was the first time in her life she had struck anybody.

'Ouch.' Alex reached a hand to his cheek and rubbed it.

'I apologise. I shouldn't have done that,' Emilie said immediately, horrified.

'It's OK, I deserved it.' Alex was cowed. 'I went too far, as always. Please, Emilie, forgive me.'

Without answering, she turned away from him and left the kitchen. When she reached the hall, she began to run, climbing the stairs two at a time. Panting as she slammed the bedroom door behind her, she locked it and threw herself down onto the bed.

She sobbed loudly into the mattress. She felt naked, exposed . . . how *could* he presume to know her? To play with her, as though her inner feelings were simply some kind of game to be used as a tool to humiliate her?

What kind of monster was he?

Emilie put a pillow over her head, wondering if

she should call Sebastian and tell him she couldn't stay here, that she was on her way to London. She'd take the Land Rover to the station, board a train and be in the safety of his arms within a few hours.

No, no, she told herself. She'd been warned about Alex; he was an arch manipulator and she must not allow him to get to her, or go running like an incapable child to her husband, who had so many problems to deal with just now. She must *cope*, somehow . . . Alex was just a bored little boy who enjoyed provoking a reaction. And if he was to be a permanent feature in her future life with Sebastian, she must gain control.

Calmed by these thoughts, but exhausted from the anger which had surged through her, Emilie fell asleep.

But not without thinking first that everything Alex had said about her was true.

*　　　*　　　*

It was dark when she awoke, feeling disorientated and drained. Reaching for her watch, Emilie saw it was just past six o'clock. She crept downstairs, switching lights on as she went, only hoping Alex had gone back to his flat. Opening the kitchen door with trepidation, she saw with relief that the room was empty. As she switched on the kettle, she noticed that the paintbrushes had been thoroughly washed clean and left to dry on the drainer. There was a note propped up against the fruit bowl on the kitchen table.

Dear Emilie, I'm truly sorry for upsetting you. I

227

was too much, as usual. Could we start again?
On this note, by way of an apology, I have
cooked us supper. Please come and join me next
door whenever you are ready.

Sincerely,
Alex

Emilie sighed and sat down heavily at the table, pondering how to react. The note was an obvious peace offering. Despite her antipathy towards him, if they were to live under the same roof together then some state of détente had to be established between them. Besides, she thought, as she made herself a cup of tea, nothing that Alex had said about her had actually been negative. It was simply the fact he'd presumed an intimacy with her that had not yet been established. He hardly knew her, yet knew her so well . . . it was this which had completely destabilised her.

And, on a practical note, Emilie realised she had no idea if Alex *was* physically capable of caring for himself. Tomorrow, she thought, sipping her tea, she'd contact the agency and set about finding him another temporary carer. Sebastian had left the number by the phone just in case. For tonight, she must at least go and check in on Alex. There was no reason why she had to stay for the supper he'd apparently cooked. It was probably beans on toast.

The landline rang and Emilie stood up to answer it.

'Hello, sweetheart, it's me.'

'Hello, "me".' Emilie smiled at the sound of her husband's voice. 'How are you? And how's London?'

'Very busy. I'm still trying to work my way through the pile of paperwork that's been gathering dust on my desk for months. I just wanted to check if everything was all right at home?'

There was a slight pause before Emilie said carefully, 'Yes, everything is fine here.'

'Alex not giving you any trouble?'

'No.'

'You're not too lonely?'

'Well, I miss you, but I'm fine. I've started to paint the kitchen.'

'Great. Well then, I'll say goodnight. You have my mobile if you need to get in touch with me. I'll give you a call tomorrow.'

'Yes. Don't work too hard,' she urged him.

'Oh, I will, but it's all in a good cause. Love you, darling.'

'I love you too.'

Emilie put the receiver back in its cradle and steeled herself to go and see Alex. As she walked along the corridor that led to the east wing, she wondered what she would find. The door leading to the flat was ajar. Taking a deep breath, she knocked on it tentatively.

'Come in! I'm in the kitchen.'

Emilie pushed the door open and walked into a small lobby. Then, following the sound of Alex's voice, she took a right turn and entered a sitting room. The mayhem of disorder she'd expected could not have been a more unsuitable description for the calm room she was standing in. The walls were painted a soft grey, the windows framed by biscuit-coloured linen curtains. A fire burned merrily in a fireplace between two floor-to-ceiling bookshelves, whose occupants were immaculately filed within them. A comfortable modern sofa took up one wall, above which were placed a series of framed black-and-white lithographs. Two elegant, re-covered Victorian chairs stood on either side of the fireplace. A large gilt mirror hung atop it and a vase of fresh flowers stood in the centre of a highly polished coffee table.

The order, neatness and attention to detail of this room was so unexpected—especially set against the miserable, decaying state of the rest of the house—it threatened to again send Emilie into disarray. The soft hum of a classical concerto emanated from hidden speakers, adding to the serenity of the room.

'Welcome to my humble abode.' Alex appeared at a door on the other side of the room.

'This is . . . beautiful,' Emilie could not stop herself commenting. It was exactly how she would wish to decorate a room herself.

'Thank you. My theory is that if one has to spend one's entire life incarcerated, then one should make every effort to make the cell as pleasant as possible. Don't you agree?'

Emilie only had time to nod before Alex said, 'Emilie, I really am sorry about this afternoon. It was unforgivable. I swear it will never happen again. You didn't deserve that. Please, can we forget it and move on?'

'Yes. And I apologise too, for striking you.'

'Oh, it's completely understandable. I seem to be an expert at getting people's backs up. And I fully admit to occasionally doing it on purpose. Must be the boredom.' Alex sighed.

'You mean, you like to test people?' Emilie

countered. 'Push them to their limits? Use the shock tactic of saying out loud the things that most other human beings wouldn't dare to? In order to deflate them, to break down their guard, which immediately puts you in control?'

'*Touché*, Madame.' Alex looked at her with new respect. 'Well now, with that very piercing riposte, plus the slap this afternoon, I'd say we're quits, wouldn't you?' He held out his hand.

Emilie walked over to him and shook his hand formally. 'Quits.'

'You see? I've already brought out your hidden feistiness. You rose to my challenge, not fell.'

'Alex . . . .'

'Yes,' he agreed immediately, 'enough of this mental warfare. Now then, I have a very decent bottle of Raspail-Ay, which I've been saving for a special occasion. Would you like a glass?'

The silky-smooth taste of the Rhône wine that had graced her parents' table on many an occasion was extremely appealing.

'Just a small one, yes,' she agreed.

'Good. And if it makes you feel better, I won't join you. I can assure you I have complete control over my alcoholic intake. The point is, life can be so much more fun with a moderate amount of it. And, in fact, if you look back in history, our ancestors have always used it to soothe their path through life.' Alex turned to wheel himself back into the kitchen. 'Even Jesus was applauded for turning water into wine. And from medieval to Victorian times, everyone would wake to a hop- or grape-based alcoholic beverage in place of our cup of caffeine first thing in the morning. They couldn't drink the water—they'd have died of typhoid, or Black Death, or some revolting parasite eating away at their stomach linings if they had done. They'd then proceed to drink all day and, by bedtime, be completely smashed.' He chuckled.

'Yes, I suppose you're right.' Emilie smiled at the thought.

'And what's wrong with dimming the harsh reality of life a little, anyway?' Alex asked. 'In essence, being alive is a bloody long and hard walk to death. Why not make it as pleasant along the way as you can?'

Emilie had followed Alex into the small, but modern and ergonomic kitchen. Glass, stainless steel and laminated white cabinets shone pristine. On the top of an extra-low centre unit stood the bottle of wine, open, but untouched.

'But everything in moderation, surely?' she suggested, looking at him.

'Yes. And that's where I have sometimes failed,' Alex conceded. 'But no longer. As you can see from my home, I'm a bit of a control freak these days. I like everything, including myself, just so.'

'But what is "so"?'

'Good question.' Alex proceeded to pour the wine out of the bottle and into two glasses. He handed one to Emilie. '"So" is as "so" does. It's a flabby word that covers a multitude of possibilities. But as for me, having spent, or should I say, misspent my youth, never even getting near "doh", let alone "ray", for various reasons which we will discuss another time, the "so" of my life is about controlling what I can. And one of those things is my environment.' Alex took a sip from his glass. 'By the way, if I show any sign of getting at all intoxicated, you can skip away from my clutches, fly back to your Edwardian museum and be done with me. So there's no need to be afraid.'

'I'm not afraid of you, Alex,' Emilie said staunchly.

'Good.' Alex eyed her in the knowing way he had and raised his glass to hers. 'Here's to your marriage.'

'Thank you.'

'And to starting afresh with me. Now, I've banked on the fact that you're French and would rather change your citizenship to British than announce you're vegetarian. So I've prepared us both a steak.'

'Thank you.' Emilie watched as Alex opened the fridge and placed two marinated sirloins on the centre unit. He swung his wheelchair round to the low oven, which was humming with activity and checked something inside it.

'Anything I can do?' she asked.

'No thanks, just enjoy the wine. I've already prepared the salad. Do you mind if we eat in here? The dining room is a bit formal for two.'

'You have a dining room?'

'Of course.' Alex raised an eyebrow.

'No, I don't mind at all. How did you buy this food?' she asked.

'Have you never heard of home delivery?' He smiled. 'I phone in a list and the local farm shop drops it off to me here.'

'That's useful to know,' said Emilie, further disconcerted by Alex's unexpected efficiency. 'So, what can't you do?'

'In terms of practical stuff, I can do mostly everything, which is why I get so frustrated with

233

carers being foisted on me. Granted, at the beginning I was pretty incapable and needed the twenty-four-hour help Seb found for me. However, over the past two years I've adapted and built up a lot of strength in my upper body, which enables me to haul myself around, and in and out of the chair,' he explained. 'Yes, there have been occasional instances when I've misjudged it and ended up on my arse on the floor, but thankfully they're becoming fewer and fewer.' Alex tossed the salad in dressing and placed it on the table. 'One of the main irritations for me is the amount of time it takes to do anything. If I've left my book in the sitting room when I go to bed at night, I have to get back in the chair, wheel myself there and back and launch myself into bed again. Ditto, stuff like taking a shower, or getting dressed. Every normal human function has to be planned like a military operation. But like the adaptable species the human race is, my brain has programmed my unusual bodily requirements in, and the routine works quite well.'

'Do you believe you could do without a carer?' she asked.

'Emilie, look at me.' Alex flung out his arms. 'I'm sitting in my well-ordered flat, cooking you supper. *Alone*. I've told Sebastian this time and again, but he refuses to listen.'

'Well, perhaps he cares about you and doesn't want any harm to come to you.'

Alex sighed. 'I think we should make a pact now not to discuss my brother or his motives. It's best for all concerned if the whole subject remains off-limits.'

'Surely you can hardly criticise him?' said

234

Emilie. 'It's obvious he's spent a lot of money making you very comfortable in here, when he himself lives in a house that urgently needs some money spending on it.'

Alex gave a snort of laughter. 'Yes, well, as I said, it's best we steer clear of the subject of my brother. Now, why don't you sit down and I'll serve up?'

*　　　*　　　*

It was eleven thirty before Emilie said goodnight to Alex and pushed open the door that would take her back into her cold, dreary side of the house, exaggerated by the brightness and modernity of Alex's quarters. As she climbed the stairs to bed, she really did feel as though she had fallen back like Alice through the looking glass.

The heating in the main house had gone off hours before and the bedroom was freezing. Emilie undressed as fast as she could and dived under the blankets. She didn't feel sleepy at all, just exhilarated by having watched the workings of what was obviously a brilliant mind.

As the superb Rhône wine had calmed and relaxed her, the two of them had chatted about Paris, where Alex had spent two years, and their favourite French authors. They had moved on to music and science, and Emilie had listened in awe to Alex's vast and labyrinthine cultural knowledge.

When she'd expressed her admiration, Alex had shrugged nonchalantly. 'One of the advantages to being completely penniless in capital cities as often as I used to be was that the best places to go to keep warm and while away the day were museums, art galleries and libraries. I also have one of those irritating photographic memories.' He'd smiled at her when she'd questioned his amazing recall. 'I'm like an elephant and forget nothing. And that's a warning for you in the future, Emilie,' he'd added.

She also remembered sitting at the kitchen table opposite Alex as they'd eaten, and then later, as he'd deftly manoeuvred himself onto the sofa from the wheelchair, looking as normal as any man would, apart from the odd angle his legs fell at from the knee. She'd realised then how tall he was and commented on it. Alex had confirmed he was indeed six foot three, which, he'd added, had been an enormous bonus since his disablement, as his extra inches gave him more 'reaching' capacity.

Alex was, Emilie admitted to herself, a very attractive man. And, technically, far more handsome than his brother. With his looks, undeniable charisma and intellect, Emilie dreaded to think how many female hearts he'd broken before his accident. Alex's innate masculinity had not been affected by his paralysed legs. He was no victim, that was for sure.

Emilie tried to equate Sebastian's damning description of his brother with the articulate, grown-up man she had just spent the evening with. And then thought of the first time she'd met him, when he'd calmly and efficiently helped her through a panic attack.

So . . . which was the *real* Alex Carruthers?

As she became drowsy, Emilie's last thought was what it must have been like for her husband, growing up with a younger brother who, like Frederik in Jacques's story, must have surpassed him on every possible level.

236

18

Emilie was surprised to see Alex down in the kitchen when she arrived to switch on the kettle the next morning. He had already rollered the bottom half of the wall behind the dresser.

'Morning, sleepyhead,' he commented cheerfully.

Emilie blushed self-consciously, wishing she'd changed out of her nightshirt, Sebastian's fisherman's jumper and a pair of his thick socks. But then, she hadn't been expecting company. 'It's only half past eight,' she said defensively as she switched on the kettle.

'I know, I'm only teasing. One of the unfortunate downsides to having a pair of numb sticks for legs is that they twitch and jerk involuntarily in the night, which means I don't tend to get much sleep. I've also started to get strange tingling sensations in them, which might mean that some feeling is returning. The doctors say it's a very good sign.'

'That's wonderful news, surely?' Emilie leant back against the sink and watched him. 'What was the prognosis originally?'

'Oh, the usual,' said Alex airily. 'That I'd damaged the nerves in my spinal column, that they couldn't tell whether I'd ever regain any feeling in my legs, but that they thought probably not. Blah blah.'

'So they said there was a possibility you might walk again?'

'God no, they wouldn't go that far. False hope from doctors is a suable offence these days, my dear.' Alex smiled. 'But rather than being my normal obtuse self and not listening to anyone in the medical profession, I've been a good boy and worked hard at my physio sessions at the hospital and continued the exercises here at home.'

'So there's a chance you might fully recover?' Emilie confirmed.

'I'd doubt it, but where there's life, there's hope, and all that . . . Now, as I've been slaving away since the dawn broke, I think I deserve a cup of coffee, don't you?'

'Of course.' Emilie filled the cafetière with boiling water and took down two mugs from a cupboard.

'I've obviously left the top half of the wall for you to paint. My ladder climbing could be a spectator sport,' Alex laughed. 'Sleep well?'

'Yes, I did, thank you. Alex?' she asked slowly as she waited for the coffee to brew.

'Yes, Em?' he replied. 'May I call you that? It suits you. It's softer, somehow.'

'Yes, if you wish. I was just thinking how different you were last night from the picture Sebastian paints of you.'

'I simply give my brother what he wants.' Alex shrugged.

'What on earth do you mean? How could Sebastian "want" you to behave badly?' she queried.

'Your husband is a subject you know I'm loath to discuss.' Alex wagged a finger at her. 'Especially covered in primrose paint at this hour of the morning.'

'But, for example, constantly giving your carers so much trouble that they walk out and leave you?' she persisted.

'Em . . .' Alex sighed. 'We said we wouldn't talk about this. All I will say is that, as I don't actually want them, or get a hand in the choosing of them, I have to get rid of them somehow, don't I? I mean, I'm physically unable to prevent Sebastian depositing them in my home. As I mentioned last night, I'm perfectly capable of taking care of myself these days.'

'Are you absolutely sure you can manage alone?'

'Now don't start, please.' He raised his eyebrows. 'Patronising the paraplegic is not an attitude I deserve after my faultless performance in front of you last night.'

'Yes, but I've been left in charge, and I—'

'Em,' Alex broke in, 'nobody, and especially not you, is *in charge* of me. It may suit my brother to believe he is, but as you can see from the short time you've been here, I have a horrible habit of disrupting that illusion.'

'What I'm trying to say, Alex,' Emilie continued, 'is that if I don't follow my husband's instructions to provide you with a new full-time carer and something happened to you, he may never forgive me.'

'I give you my word, Em,' said Alex, serious at last. 'Nothing will happen to me. Now for God's sake, stop fussing and do something useful like pour me that cup of coffee.'

*　　　*　　　*

An hour later, Alex muttered something about

239

having some work to do and took himself off back to his flat. Emilie finished the top half of the wall, then dabbed carefully at the spots she'd missed. Standing by the sink washing the paint off her hands, she looked out of the window and saw the faint greenness of the grass appearing from beneath the fast-melting ice. Having been incarcerated in the house for so many days, she thought she might take herself off for a walk and familiarise herself with the landscape around it.

The sun was shining as she let herself out of the back door. She walked through what she was sure in the summer would be a very pretty formal garden, then made her way through a gate and into an orchard. The ancient trees hung bare, looking for all the world as if they were dead, but the uncollected detritus of mulchy windfall frozen beneath them belied their current state.

Standing at the edge of a grass tennis court, which hadn't seen attention for many years, Emilie realised that the house was set snugly into a gentle valley of rolling hills. In the distance, she could just make out the dark shapes of higher peaks and crags on the horizon. Walking further, she saw the house was surrounded by pasture, obviously inhabited by sheep from the frozen droppings under her feet. Standing atop a grassy hillock, Emilie decided thankfully that this was indeed a beautiful, if rather barren, part of the world.

Later that afternoon, she made some calls to France. It had been agreed with the architect and the builders that she would fly over in the next couple of weeks to meet them. And, most importantly, to oversee the contents of her father's library being put into store before the work began in earnest.

Over a cup of tea in the kitchen, Emilie debated whether she should return the favour and ask Alex in for supper that evening. The puzzle of his relationship with her husband and the animosity that lay between the two of them was something she needed to get to the bottom of. And whilst Sebastian was absent, surely this was the perfect time to do it?

Knocking on the door to his flat, she found Alex tapping away on his computer in his immaculate study.

'Sorry to disturb you, but would you like to come to me for supper tonight? And help put the dresser back in place?'

'Lovely.' He nodded. 'See you later,' he added with a wave, obviously engrossed in whatever he was doing.

*   *   *

'You look pretty tonight,' said Alex admiringly as he wheeled himself into the kitchen later. 'That turquoise jumper suits your skin tone.'

'Thank you,' said Emilie, brushing the compliment aside. 'First of all, can we move the dresser back? Then I can clear the kitchen table so we can eat at it.'

'Leave it to me.'

Emilie watched as Alex hardly broke sweat moving the dresser against the wall. Then he replaced the china back into the lower cupboards as she returned it onto the higher shelves.

'There!' Emilie looked around the kitchen with pleasure. 'Doesn't it look better?'

241

'It's a revelation. It almost makes me want to come in here.' Alex smiled. 'You're a real little homemaker, aren't you, Em?'

'I simply can't bear dreariness. I like warmth and brightness,' she admitted.

'Having lived in the South of France for a lot of your life, I'm sure you do. Now I've brought along another decent bottle of wine, as I happen to know that the cellar here is on its last dregs, so to speak. Oh, and I also brought this in for you to peruse.' Alex produced a small book from the side of his wheelchair and offered it to her. 'I'm presuming they were written by a relative of yours, and I thought you might like to read them. I think they're rather sweet, if naive.'

As Alex opened the wine, Emilie studied the ageing, leather-bound notebook. Turning the first yellowing page, she glanced at the writing, which was in French, trying to decipher it.

'They're poems,' said Alex, stating the obvious. 'The writing is dreadful, isn't it? It took me hours to work out what they said. Here are my typed versions.' Alex handed Emilie some sheets of paper. 'They look as though they've been written by a five-year-old child and, indeed, some of them were written when the poet was young. But the quality of the content as she grows older shows real talent. Have you seen the name at the bottom of the poems?'

'Sophia de la Martinières!' Emilie read, looking at Alex in confusion. 'Where did you get this notebook?'

'Seb pulled out a book from the library a few weeks ago; something to do with French fruit, if I remember correctly. He said he'd found this notebook with it and gave me the poems to read and decipher. Do you know who Sophia de la Martinières was?'

'Yes, Sophia was my aunt, my father's sister. He didn't mention her very often, but I began to learn of her story last time I was in France. She was blind.'

'Ah.' Alex raised an eyebrow. 'That explains the dreadful writing.'

'You say Sebastian found these with a book about French fruit?'

'That's what he said, yes.'

'Jacques, who was telling me the story of your grandmother and Sophia during the war, told me Constance used a book of fruit to describe the shapes and textures to Sophia, so she could sketch them. And that Sophia wrote poetry. Maybe Constance brought both books back to England with her when she returned here after the war.'

'What a sweet story,' Alex commented.

'Yes. Do you know where the book on fruit trees is? I'd love to see it,' she asked him.

'I haven't seen the book since Seb brought it down from the shelf in the library,' said Alex, suddenly guarded. 'Mind you, I'm incapable of checking the top shelves, so it might be there.'

'I'll look for it, and if I can't find it, I'll ask Sebastian when he's home.' Emilie turned her attention back to the poems. 'These are beautiful. Sophia wrote her age at the bottom of this one.' Emilie indicated the signature. 'She was only nine when she wrote it. It's about what she wishes she could see. I . . .' Emilie shook her head, almost moved to tears. 'It's so sad.'

'I especially like this one.' Alex leafed through

the pages until he found it. ' "The Light Behind the Window". It has an elegance in its simplicity and I like the rhyming structure. Em, can you tell me what you know about my grandmother's time in France? I'd be fascinated to hear.'

As she cooked the risotto, Emilie related the story Jacques had told her of Constance. Alex listened intently, asking her questions if he didn't follow something.

'And that's as far in the story as I got,' she said as she served the risotto. 'It's a coincidence that, all these years on, your family and mine are again connected.'

'Yes,' Alex agreed, picking up his fork, 'truly amazing.'

Emilie eyed him, hearing the hint of irony in his voice. 'What do you mean by that? If you're thinking Sebastian had a motive for coming in search of my family, then you're wrong. It was pure coincidence we happened to meet in Gassin when he was down in the Var on business. He recognised me from the newspapers. And he told me at our first meeting of our family connection.'

'Good. Then there isn't a problem, is there?'

'No. There isn't,' stated Emilie firmly.

'Right, let's move on, shall we?' Alex suggested.

After that, the evening had been nowhere near as relaxed as the night before. There was a tension that had hung in the air. Alex had left after he'd eaten and Emilie took a cup of cocoa up the stairs with her.

There was no reason to doubt her husband's motives, Emilie thought as she climbed into bed and sat upright against the pillows, nursing the cocoa. However they had originally met, the facts were that they had fallen in love and subsequently married.

She lay in bed, reading through Sophia's poems, written so sweetly and honestly, wondering again why her father had never talked of his younger sister. She'd only initially discovered Sophia's existence by chance when, as a child, she'd noticed a painting on the wall of her father's study in Paris. It had been of a beautiful young woman, golden hair flowing down her back, turquoise eyes smiling as she stroked the Persian cat resting on her knee.

'Who is that, Papa?' she'd asked.

There'd been a long pause before he'd answered. 'That was my sister, your aunt Sophia, Emilie,' Édouard had finally replied.

'She's very beautiful.'

'Yes, she was.'

'She's dead?'

'Yes.'

'How did she die, Papa?'

'I do not wish to talk of it, Emilie.' And then Édouard's face had closed.

And perhaps at that moment, as Emilie thought back across the years, she had glimpsed tears in his eyes.

*   *   *

The following morning, taking her courage in both hands, Emilie had braved the drive into Moulton and stocked up on provisions for the coming weekend. Sebastian was arriving in York on the nine o'clock train that evening and had said he'd be with her by ten. Emilie went into her husband's arms when he arrived home, feeling very glad to see him.

'How have you been?' he asked.

'I've been fine,' she said as she pulled him towards the kitchen. 'Do you like it?'

Sebastian looked around the newly painted room. 'Yes, what a difference,' he said admiringly. 'How on earth did you move that dresser by yourself?'

'Alex helped me.'

'Alex?' Sebastian's face darkened. 'What was he doing in the house? He's not been bothering you, has he?'

'No. He has behaved perfectly well. I have many things to tell you, but we can talk about them tomorrow. Are you hungry? I made some soup earlier and bought some bread.'

'Lovely,' said Sebastian, sitting down. 'And a glass of wine, if we have any.'

'We do.' Emilie proffered the half-empty bottle that Alex had brought in the night before and poured him a glass.

'This is very good,' he said approvingly. 'Surely you didn't get this in the local Spar?'

'No, Alex brought it in. So—' Emilie moved on quickly, determined not to spend the rest of the evening talking of his brother—'how was London?'

'Well, as I told you on the phone, things are a mess, but I'm getting there. I spent most of today renewing contacts with the clients on my database. It looks like I might have to go to France next week, actually. The client who took me there when I first met you is still interested and I think I may have sourced a Picasso for him in a château near Menton.'

'That isn't far from Gassin,' said Emilie eagerly.

246

'Perhaps I could come with you?'

'A nice idea, but not worth it, as it'll be a flying visit. Besides, I thought you said you were going over yourself to France in a week or so?'

'I am,' Emilie agreed. 'I just miss it,' she sighed.

'I'm sure you do.' Sebastian reached for her hand. 'It's hardly been the most auspicious start to your sojourn in England. I promise you, darling, when the spring comes, this whole place lights up. And I must say, it's rather lovely to have you here to come home to. This soup is delicious. It's going to be a dry weekend, apparently, so I thought we'd go out tomorrow and I can show you a few of the local beauty spots.'

'I'd like that,' Emilie smiled. 'It's strange being here without you.'

'I know, and living here in England is a big change for you. But as I said a few days ago, it's only for a few months—a year at most—before we can make some more firm plans about where we'll settle. And I would have thought that, after the past few weeks, it might be rather nice for you to simply have a break and look after your new husband.'

'If he's here . . .'

'Emilie,' Sebastian sighed, a note of irritation in his voice, 'I've said I'll do my best, but I'm afraid we're both going to have to put up with less than ideal circumstances whilst I get my business back on track.'

Emilie berated herself for being selfish. 'Of course—and maybe after my success here in the kitchen, I could think about painting some of the other rooms to brighten them? Like our bedroom, perhaps?'

247

'Feel free, anything that cheers the old place up is fine by me. I warn you, once you start, you won't be able to stop, but it's lovely that you want to make the effort. Now, I'm exhausted. Shall we go to bed?'

'Why don't you take yourself upstairs for a bath and I'll tidy up down here?' Emilie suggested.

'Thanks,' said Sebastian, standing up. 'It really has been a hard few days.'

Emilie heard Sebastian mount the stairs and then the sound of the ancient pipes groaning as he ran the taps. She immediately left the kitchen and walked along the corridor to Alex's flat, feeling guilty she had not yet told her husband his brother was alone without a carer, but not ready to face the trauma of him knowing. She knocked on the door and a voice called from inside, 'Who is it?'

'Emilie. Can I come in?'

'The door's not locked.'

Alex was sitting in a chair by the fire, reading. He smiled at her as she came in. 'Hello.'

'Hello. I just came to check that you were OK.'

'No, as you can see, I'm blind drunk and about to die by choking on my own vomit,' he quipped. 'I presume you've told Seb I'm without a minder?'

'No, not yet. He's very tired and I didn't want to stress him. I'll suggest to him tomorrow that you're not in need of full-time care. And if he does still insist you must have someone to look after you, I'll say you're capable enough to have someone come in part-time to help domestically. After all, it will save him money.'

'Em, I . . .' Alex raised an eyebrow at this comment then shook his head. 'Nothing. Thank you for batting on my team. It makes a change around here.'

'Yes, but much of it will be down to you to prove to Sebastian that you need little more than domestic support,' she underlined.

'Of course, and admittedly, I'm not too handy at scrubbing floors or making beds. It's normally me who ends up inside the duvet.' Alex smiled. 'But I promise I'll try to be a good boy. Anyway, I appreciate your help. Goodnight.'

'Goodnight.'

*   *   *

Emilie broached the Alex subject as she sat with Sebastian in a cosy pub high up on the moors the following day. Sebastian's face was thunderous as Emilie informed him of the latest carer's departure, but she added quickly that, in her opinion, Alex was capable of doing much more for himself and they should give him a chance.

'Emilie,' Sebastian sighed, 'we've been through this before. It's very sweet of you to try and help, but I just don't think you understand how volatile Alex is. What if he goes on another binge? Or has an accident getting in and out of his chair?'

'We threaten him with another full-time carer if he does. Perhaps—' Emilie persisted—'if he had more independence, he wouldn't get so frustrated. And if we installed a panic button in the main house, at least we would know he was safe.'

'So, actually, you're saying *you* are prepared to take the responsibility for his welfare? Because—' Sebastian sipped his pint—'I'm simply not going to have time in the next few months to pander to my brother's every whim. And let me tell you, from past experience, there'll be many.'

'Alex has asked me for nothing so far. In fact, he's helped me paint the kitchen and cooked me supper.'

'Has he, indeed? Well, he's obviously launched a full-scale charm offensive on you. Sorry, Emilie—' Sebastian shook his head—'I've seen it a thousand times before. I've warned you how manipulative he can be. And he certainly seems to have won you over completely. Perhaps he's aiming for you to take care of him. He's always enjoyed stealing anything that was mine,' he said, pouting like a child.

'Really, Sebastian!' Emilie was shocked at her husband's childish reaction. 'I sometimes think that you two are as bad as each other. Of course it isn't like that. I know it's not for me to interfere, but can I suggest we try it Alex's way for a while? He craves independence and maybe he'll be easier to handle if he gets it. Should we not give him at least a chance to prove himself?'

There was a long pause before Sebastian said, 'All right, I surrender. If that's what you want, then fine. But don't you see, Emilie? He's managed to win you round already and I'll look like a curmudgeon if I refuse.'

'Thank you.' She placed a comforting hand on his and squeezed it. 'I would simply like for things in the house to be calmer than when I arrived. Especially for your sake, because I love you. Now, do we have time to drive across to Haworth? I would so love to see the vicarage where the Brontë sisters lived.'

*　　　*　　　*

250

That evening, whilst Sebastian was sequestered in his study on his computer, Emilie went to see Alex, who was eating his supper in the kitchen.

'Sebastian has agreed to my suggestion.'

Alex's face showed his relief. 'Then you're a miracle worker and I salute you. Thank you, Em, really.'

'I'll try to find you domestic help in the next few days, but if there's anything you need me to do in the meantime, then please, you must ask.'

'Sit down and keep me company for half an hour?' he suggested.

'I can't, I'm in the middle of cooking dinner for Sebastian and me.'

'Of course. Well then—' Alex turned his attention back to his own supper—'have a nice evening.'

'Thank you. And you.'

Sebastian was already in the kitchen when she entered it. 'And where have you been? I was calling you.'

'To check on Alex, and he's fine,' Emilie answered.

'Good.'

He was unusually quiet all through supper. 'Are you all right, Sebastian?' Emilie asked as she cleared away the dishes. 'You seem . . . unsettled. Is there anything wrong?'

'No, nothing. Well, to be honest, yes. Come and sit here.' Sebastian patted his knee.

Emilie did so and kissed him gently on the cheek. 'Tell me.'

'OK . . . this will sound churlish and juvenile, I know: the fact is, I don't want to share you.'

'What do you mean?'

'Well, look what's already happened. Alex has managed to charm you into convincing you he doesn't need anyone to care for him. As he's on his own now, you'll feel duty-bound to check in on him, like you have this evening. He's already luring you in, getting your attention, probably complaining about his cruel big brother and telling you all sorts of lies about me.'

'Sebastian, that's simply not true. Alex never talks of you to me,' Emilie said firmly.

'Well, I'm not comfortable with it at all, Emilie. I'm not always going to be here, and I can imagine the number of cosy tête-à-têtes he will coerce you into having with him. I know you think I'm overreacting, but you have no idea what he's like. As I said earlier, he might try to steal you away from me.'

'That will never happen.' Emilie stroked Sebastian's hair. 'It's you I love. I'm only trying to help.'

'I know you are, sweetheart,' Sebastian agreed. 'And I also know how stupid I sound, but Alex is so manipulative. And I don't want him to destroy our wonderful relationship.'

'He won't, I promise,' she insisted.

'Maybe it wasn't a good idea bringing you back here,' Sebastian sighed, 'but given the circumstances, I can't see that at present we've got any other choice.'

'You know I—*we* can afford an apartment in London, Sebastian. Then we could be together there and—'

'Emilie, *you* said it: "I".' Sebastian's face was taut with tension. 'I'm fully aware that my wealthy

252

wife could buy and sell a small country without denting her fortune, but give your husband his pride. I need to do this for myself, however hard it is on us.' He tipped her face up towards his. 'Do you understand?'

'Yes.'

'Anyway, I'm sorry to be difficult, but I never want anyone to think I married you for money.'

'I know you didn't.'

'Good. Bed?'

*   *   *

Sebastian left on Monday morning to go to London and then on to France. As the morning was bright, Emilie found an old bicycle in the barn and decided to cycle down to the village shop. Parking her bicycle against the wall outside, she went in and waited in the queue of locals to speak to the woman behind the counter.

'May I place this on your advertisement board?' Emilie handed over a postcard, advertising for a cleaner.

The woman took it, read it and then looked up at Emilie, interest suddenly alive in her eyes. 'Yes, it's a pound a week. So are you the new wife Mr Carruthers has brought home from France?'

The Yorkshire accent was very strong and Emilie struggled to decipher the woman's words. News obviously travelled fast around these parts, and Emilie knew her own accent was clearly French.

'Yes, I am. I will pay for two weeks,' she said, digging the coins out of her purse.

'Right-oh.' The woman nodded and took the

postcard from her. 'Doubt you'll be getting much response though. I'd try the local paper if I were you.'

'I will, *merci*—I mean, thank you.'

Emilie left the shop and was walking back towards her bicycle when a woman came hurrying out behind her.

'Mrs Carruthers?'

Unused to being addressed by Sebastian's surname, it took a few seconds for Emilie to realise the woman was talking to her. 'Yes?'

'I'm Norma Erskine. I was the housekeeper for many years up at Blackmoor Hall. I handed in my resignation just before you arrived.'

'Yes, Sebastian told me,' said Emilie.

'He came round the other day to ask me to come back, but I said I'd be having no more of it and he couldn't persuade me otherwise.'

Emilie studied the woman: plump, short, with a pair of lively, warm eyes. 'I'm so sorry Alex upset you,' she apologised.

'Hmmm,' was the reply. 'Well, there's a lot you don't know about what's gone on up at that house and I shan't be telling tales to you, neither,' said Norma. 'All I can say is that their grandmother would be turning in her grave. I stayed for as long as I could, like I promised her, but I couldn't take no more. Anyway, it's nice to meet you. I just hope you know what you've taken on, marrying him. None of my business though now, is it, love?'

'I've already learned it is a difficult situation,' Emilie defended herself.

'And that's not the half of it, I can tell you,' said Norma, rolling her eyes. 'You settling in all right?'

'I'm getting used to it, yes, thank you,' she

answered politely.

'Well, if you ever fancy a cuppa, my cottage is the last one on the left as you go out of the village. Pop down and see me sometime, love, let me know how you're getting on.'

'Thank you. That's kind of you.'

'Right then, goodbye.'

'Goodbye.' As Emilie climbed onto her bike, she missed the glint of sympathy in Norma Erskine's eyes.

*   *   *

In the following couple of days, Emilie painted the bedroom she and Sebastian shared a soft pale pink. She went off into Moulton and bought a thick duvet and sheets, finding the ancient blankets currently on their bed itchy and uncomfortably heavy. She'd taken down the old damask curtains and purchased lengths of voile to hang at the windows, which maximised the light that filtered in wearily from outside. Then she searched the house for less dreary pictures to hang on the wall.

She had checked in on Alex later that evening, issuing him with her mobile number and telling him to call her if there was anything he needed. Sebastian's angst at the weekend had made her determined to stay as uninvolved with his brother as she could. Having put the finishing touches to the bedroom, Emilie went downstairs to find herself something to eat. The house telephone rang and she picked it up.

'Hello?'

'Oh, hello. Is that Mrs Erskine?' asked a female

voice.

'No, I'm afraid she has left.'

'Oh. Is Sebastian there?'

'No, he's in France.'

'Really? In that case, I'll get him on his mobile. Thanks.'

The phone went dead. Emilie shrugged and went back to eating her supper.

*   *   *

'I've found a very nice girl to clean for you,' said Emilie later in the week, finding Alex at his computer.

'Fantastic.' Alex looked up and smiled at her. 'Who is she?'

'She's called Jo and she lives in the village with her family. She's taking a gap year before she goes off to university and wants to earn some extra money.'

'Well, at least it'll make a change that she's under sixty,' commented Alex.

'She's coming in tomorrow afternoon to meet you. Please be nice to her, won't you?' she begged.

'Of course, Em,' Alex agreed.

Emilie could see the different screens that were flashing up continuously on Alex's computer.

'What are you doing?'

'I'm trading.'

'Trading? You mean on the stock market?'

'Yes. But don't you dare tell my brother. He wouldn't approve at all. He'd probably accuse me of gambling and confiscate my computer.' Alex stretched his arms in the air and put them behind his head. 'Fancy a cup of tea?'

Feeling guilty she hadn't gone near him in the past few days, Emilie agreed. 'I'll make it,' she added, heading for the kitchen, which she noted with satisfaction was neat and tidy. 'Do you take sugar?'

'One, please.'

Whilst she waited for the kettle to boil, Emilie had a surreptitious glance in the fridge to make sure it was well stocked. And it was. So far, so good . . . Alex had been true to his word and was behaving. Emilie sighed in relief and put two mugs, the pot, the sugar bowl and some milk on a tray.

'Take them through to the sitting room,' Alex indicated. 'I could do with a break from this screen.'

Emilie did so and Alex wheeled himself through.

'How did you learn to trade?' she asked him as she poured the tea and handed him a cup.

'Trial and error, actually; I'm completely self-taught,' Alex explained. 'It's the perfect way to earn a living if you don't get out much. And for insomniacs, whatever time of the night, there's always a market opening somewhere in the world.'

'Do you have success with it?'

'More and more, yes. I've been doing this for almost eighteen months and I'm over what those in the trade would call beginner's luck. I made some errors to start with, but as a matter of fact I'm doing rather nicely these days.'

'It's something I know nothing about,' admitted Emilie.

'Well, it keeps my brain active and it's beginning to pay quite well too. So, how are you?' Alex asked.

'Very well, thank you.'

'Not getting too bored all alone in your mausoleum?'

'I've been painting the house.'

'That's good.' Alex nodded. 'Thought I might see you occasionally.'

'I've been busy, that's all.'

'Well, how about you stay for supper? I've just had some fantastic foie gras delivered from the farm shop.'

'I have many things to do . . .'

'So he *has* told you to stay clear?' Alex quipped.

'No, it's not that.'

'OK.' He sighed, putting his hands up in surrender.

'I'm sorry.'

'Emilie, for God's sake,' Alex burst out, 'it seems utterly ridiculous that here we are stuck out in the middle of nowhere together and eating alone in separate parts of the house.'

'Yes,' she agreed eventually.

'Good. I'll see you at about seven thirty. And I won't tell if you won't,' he added with a wink as she stood up and walked towards the door.

*   *   *

Before she went back to Alex's flat later, Emilie tried Sebastian's mobile. It was on voicemail, so she left him a message, feeling guilty she wasn't telling him about having supper with his brother tonight. She hadn't heard from him since he'd left the house on Monday morning.

'Come in, come in!' Alex was stoking the fire in the sitting room. 'I've just had some excellent news! One of the fledgling oil companies I

258

invested in ages ago has just struck lucky off Quebec.'

'I'm very happy for you,' Emilie said.

'Thanks!' Alex looked elated. 'White or red?' He indicated the two bottles on the coffee table.

'Red, please,' said Emilie.

'Where's Sebastian, by the way?' he asked as he handed her a glass.

'In France.'

'You really are a bit of a grass widow, aren't you? Perhaps you should suggest you travel with him?'

'I have,' Emilie said, sitting down on the sofa, 'but he says he would be far too busy and I don't wish to bother him while he works. Maybe next time.'

'Well then,' said Alex, 'have you given any thought to what you might do with yourself up here in Yorkshire whilst you're stuck here waiting for hubby to return home?'

'Not really. I've been busy so far and, besides, this situation is only temporary.'

'Yes, I'm sure it is,' Alex replied. 'Cheers,' he added, taking a sip of his wine.

'And what about you? Will you always stay here, do you think?' Emilie asked.

'I hope to, yes. I love this house, I always have.'

'Then why did you spend so much time running away from it when you were younger?'

'Now that, again, is another story.' Alex regarded her. 'And one, given the circumstances, that we best avoid.'

'Please, at least tell me why, even though there seems such . . . animosity between you and your brother, you're still prepared to share the house with him? And what if Sebastian can't continue to keep it? The house needs so much work, and . . .'

'Emilie, don't push me, please. I suggest we move on to neutral territory forthwith,' Alex advised. 'We made a pact, remember?'

'You're right. I'm sorry. There are obviously many things I don't know and I find the situation hard to comprehend.'

'Well, I'm not the one to fill you in.' Alex gave a wistful smile. 'Now, shall we eat?'

After the delicious foie gras, which reminded Emilie so much of home—it had been one of her father's favourites—she made coffee and they retreated back to the warmth of the fire in the sitting room.

'Don't you get lonely here, Alex?' she asked him.

'Sometimes, but I've always been a bit of a loner, so I don't miss company as much as others would. And, as I don't suffer fools gladly either, there aren't many people I would choose as a supper companion. Present company excepted, of course,' he added. 'But wouldn't you agree you're a loner too, Em?'

'Yes,' she acknowledged. 'I've never had many friends, but that's because I haven't felt comfortable in any circle. I found the girls I knew at my private school in Paris spoilt and silly. But at university, because of my surname, most people seemed to be uncomfortable with me there, too.'

'I can't remember who it was that said before you could love anyone else, you had to love yourself. It sounds to me as if we've both struggled with that knotty problem. I certainly have, anyway,' Alex admitted.

'Well, as you pointed out to me once so accurately, I felt like a disappointment to my mother. It was difficult to "love" myself, as you put it,' Emilie said.

'I didn't have parents in the first place, so I can't use them as an excuse,' Alex said with a shrug.

'Yes, Sebastian told me. Surely, the fact that you had none is partly to blame? Do you ever hear from your mother?' Emilie asked.

'Never.'

'Do you remember her at all?'

'I have the occasional flashback, mostly to do with smells. A joint, for example, always makes me think of her. Maybe you're right and that's why I partook so wholeheartedly in drugs.' Alex grinned. 'It was in the genes.'

'I can't understand why anyone would wish to be out of control.' Emilie shook her head adamantly. 'I hate it.'

'Emilie, all us addicts are doing is running away from ourselves. And reality. Anything that eases the pain of being alive helps,' Alex explained. 'The sad thing is, some of the most interesting people I've known have been addicts. The brighter you are, the more you think; the more you think, the more you realise just how futile life is and the more you want to run away from the pointlessness. The good news is, I'm over all that now. I've ceased to blame other people for my problems. It's a road to nowhere. I've stopped being a victim and started taking responsibility for myself. The moment I did that a few years ago, a lot fell into place.'

'Well, it's terribly sad that you and Sebastian grew up without a mother or father. Although—'

261

Emilie sighed—'when I was younger, I used to fantasise that my parents had adopted me. Then I could imagine my real mother might have loved me, or at least liked me a little. I was so lonely, yet there I was, living in beautiful houses with every luxury I could ever want.'

'Most people want what they can't have,' commented Alex soberly. 'The day you wake up and realise that's a totally pointless desire, and look to what you *do* have, is the moment you start on the path to relative contentment. Life's a lottery, the dice are thrown and we all have to make the best of what we've got.'

'You've been in therapy?' Emilie asked.

'Of course.' Alex grinned. 'Who hasn't?'

'Me.' She smiled.

'Well done you,' Alex commented. 'Mind you, I then realised I was becoming addicted to that, too, and so I stopped. A lot of it doesn't work. It tells you why you're messed up, and that normally means there's someone else to blame. Which, of course, gives you an excuse to behave as badly as you want. One therapist actually told me I'd every right to get angry. So, for a year, I did. It felt great—' he sighed—'until I realised I'd upset and alienated everyone I cared about.'

'I never got angry,' Emilie mused.

'You didn't do so badly when you slapped me across the face in the kitchen a little while ago,' Alex pointed out with a smirk.

Emilie blushed. 'You're right.'

'Sorry, that was disingenuous, but I was trying to say that the occasional bout is healthy. However, it should never be a permanent state, like it was with me for a while. We humans, eh, Em?' Alex shook his head. 'What a complex, messy lot we are.'

'You seem to know yourself very well,' Emilie said with genuine admiration.

'Sure do, and I also realise that I'll never cease to surprise myself, either. I've turned from an angry drug addict into an anally organised control freak who gets upset if his routine is disturbed. But then,' Alex analysed, 'maybe that's the only way I can cope. All I can control *is* myself. And I don't want to ever risk going back down the slippery path to addiction.'

'I truly admire your discipline,' said Emilie with feeling. 'Alex, do you mind me asking if there's ever been someone you were close to?'

'A woman, you mean?'

'Yes.'

'There have certainly been countless women I've been "close to" physically, but nobody has ever lasted very long. To be honest, Em, I wasn't fit to hold down a relationship with anyone in the past.'

'But now you're stable, do you think you'd like one?'

Alex looked at her for a moment. 'With the right person, yes. I think I'd like it very much.'

'Well, maybe you'll find her one day.'

'Yes, maybe I will.' Alex glanced at his watch. 'Now, I'm going to be very rude and kick you out, as I need to check on my oil shares. It's after midnight and the markets will be opening in the Far East.'

'I didn't realise it was so late.' Emilie stood up. 'Thank you for the company and the foie gras.'

'It's been a pleasure, Em.'

'I'll bring Jo, the cleaner, through when she arrives tomorrow.' Emilie paused by the door.

'You know, Alex, I only wish Sebastian could see you like this.'

'My brother sees me how he wishes to. And I react accordingly. Goodnight, Em.'

'Goodnight.'

Lying in bed twenty minutes later and enjoying the transformation she had wrought in the room, Emilie mused on the evening.

She had felt very relaxed with Alex. Perhaps that was because there were none of the complexities of a relationship involved. She liked who he was when he was with her. However, the fact they got on so well would not please her husband—even though it should—so she would have to be careful.

Emilie sighed. If only the brothers could forgive and forget the past, whatever it contained, life could be so much more tranquil at Blackmoor Hall.

19

Sebastian arrived home at the end of the week, looking exhausted. When Emilie tried to talk to him over supper, he was distant with her. When they climbed into bed later, she asked him again if he had a problem.

'Sorry, things are just very difficult at present, that's all.'

'You mean, business-wise?' Emilie queried.

'Yes. I've just discovered the bloody bank hasn't been putting through my direct debits. And the chap I'd sourced in France who thought he might be able to lay his hands on a Picasso turned out to be a real chancer. He said he'd already had bids over seven million for it and all I got was a couple of blurred photographs as proof. So no, I'm not in the best of moods,' he grunted.

'You know I'll help financially if you need me to. You just have to ask.' Emilie massaged his shoulders as he lay in bed, his back turned to her.

'Thanks, Emilie, but you understand how I feel about running to you every time I have a crisis.'

'Please, Sebastian, you helped me so much when I needed you. If you love someone, surely it doesn't matter that you turn to them?'

'Maybe it's different for girls.' Sebastian shrugged. 'Anyway, I need to get some sleep.'

*   *   *

For the rest of the weekend, Sebastian was shut away in the study on his computer. Over supper in the evening, he barely talked to her, and there was no reaching for her in bed at night. On Sunday evening, she walked upstairs to the bedroom to find him packing his holdall.

'Are you leaving?' she asked.

'Yes. I'm going to London tomorrow.'

'Then I'll come with you.'

'I'd doubt the hovel I stay in would meet with your approval.'

'I don't care about that,' she stated firmly.

'Well, maybe I do.'

'I could pay for us to stay in a hotel.'

'For the last time, I don't want any more of your bloody money!'

Shocked, Emilie withdrew, feeling as if she had received a slap across the face. She lay in bed next to Sebastian, sleepless, wondering what to say or do and wishing there was someone she could talk to.

Sebastian left for London the next morning, kissing her briefly on the cheek and saying he'd see her on Friday.

The day was miserable, wet and rainy—echoing Emilie's mood perfectly. The house smelt of damp and Emilie thanked God she was leaving midweek for a brighter light in France.

Walking into the library, remembering the book on fruit trees Alex had mentioned, Emilie searched through the shelves, but without success. Instead, finding an F. Scott Fitzgerald on the shelves, she took it into the drawing room and huddled by the fire.

Her mobile rang and she saw it was Alex's number.

'Hello?'

'Hello,' he said. 'You OK?'

'Yes, you?'

'I'm fine,' replied Alex. 'Jo, the girl you got me, is very sweet. She doesn't fuss around and gets on with her job. I like her. I wanted to say thank you.'

'I'm glad.'

There was a pause on the line.

'Are you sure you're OK, Emilie?'

'Yes.'

'All right then. Have a nice day,' said Alex.

'Thank you.'

Emilie pressed the button to end the call, proud she hadn't given away her distress. However much she desired some guidance on her husband's sudden strange and unsettling behaviour, Alex had made it clear he was not the person to discuss it with.

Twenty minutes later, however, there was a tap on the drawing-room door.

'Hello, Alex,' she sighed.

'Hello, Em. If I'm disturbing you, please tell me to bugger off. I just deduced from the tone of your voice that all was not well. I'm simply checking, in a neighbourly fashion, that you're all right.'

'Thank you. And yes,' she admitted, 'I am feeling a little down.'

'Thought so. Do you want to talk about it?'

'I . . . don't know.' She could feel tears pricking at the back of her eyes.

'Sometimes it helps to talk, and I'll gladly act as your very first therapist if you'd like; maintaining, of course, a neutral and unemotional role. That'll make a change for me.' He smiled and Emilie knew he was trying to cheer her up. 'I'm presuming it's my brother who's upset you. I only say that because he marched into my flat the other day without knocking—which really irritates me—and tore me off a strip for bothering you.'

'Oh! But I said nothing to him, Alex. Please believe me,' Emilie urged.

'I'm sure you didn't, but he just wanted to shout at me about something,' Alex replied affably.

'Yes. He was so tense at the weekend. I really don't know what's wrong with him,' she admitted.

'Well, Em—' Alex gave a long sigh—'this is rather a difficult one. I could, of course, give you a run-down of your husband's psyche and help you understand who you've married, but we've agreed it's not right for me to do so. What I will say is that Sebastian has always been prone to sudden, black moods. And I hope for your sake this one will pass

267

soon.'

'So do I.' Emilie was desperate to ask Alex more, but it would be compromising him and, besides, she would feel disloyal to Sebastian. 'The weather here doesn't help. I'm very happy I'm off to France on Wednesday.'

'Lucky old you. That will cheer you up, I'm sure. Perhaps you may be able to find out more about Sophia, and her poems.'

'I'll certainly ask Jacques if he'll tell me more of the story,' agreed Emilie.

'I'd love to see the library at the château you've talked of.' Alex smiled. 'Books are my passion, especially old ones.'

'And I must see them all packed up and put into storage before the renovations begin. I'm dreading it,' she admitted. 'But it's for a good cause.'

'And I'm sure your father would be proud of you, Em. It's sad that the great de la Martinières name will disappear—in fact, *has* disappeared, when you married my brother.'

'Oh, no. I intend to keep it. Sebastian and I discussed it and we agreed I should.'

'But if you two have a child, it will be a "Carruthers", won't it?'

'I'm sure that's a very long way off,' Emilie said abruptly and changed the subject. 'Whilst I'm gone, do you want Jo to sleep in the house? She said she was happy to do so occasionally when I interviewed her.'

'No, it's really not necessary, and she's given me her phone number already in case of disaster. You can trust me, Em, you know you can,' Alex insisted. 'I really am self-sufficient.'

'It's sad you never go out, Alex. Do you miss it?'

'Sometimes I get cabin fever, yes,' he agreed. 'But when the weather gets better, I can at least take a tour around what's left of our beautiful gardens. And don't say anything to Sebastian, but I've been looking into buying a customised car.'

'That's a very good idea,' she said approvingly, 'and when I come back from France, maybe we can get your wheelchair in the boot of the Land Rover and go out somewhere. Would you like that?'

'I'd love it.' Alex gave a big grin of pleasure. 'Oh, for a real pint in a pub.'

'Then that's a promise,' agreed Emilie, vaguely wondering why Sebastian hadn't done this himself before now. But, given the tension that lay between them, the last thing he'd probably want was to face his brother over a table at the pub.

'Now then, I'll be getting back,' said Alex, unlocking the brakes on his wheelchair. 'I have to tend to my ever-growing family of oil shares. Have a good time in France, Em. I'll be interested to hear any titbits of information you pick up about my granny. *Adieu* and *bon voyage*.'

With a small wave, Alex left the room.

*   *   *

Emilie had called the local taxi company Sebastian had recommended and arrived at Leeds Bradford airport with a tinge of excitement running through her. As the plane took off and flew over the grey, industrial heartlands of northern England and headed south down to France, Emilie only wished she'd been able to contact Sebastian before she'd left. But his mobile was permanently on answerphone and, as yet, he hadn't responded to

269

any of her messages.

Alex's mention of his brother's mood swings were all she could find to comfort her. Yet she had still lain awake into the small hours, her stomach churning with fear that something was wrong. The abrupt U-turn from loving, supportive husband to a man who would not even answer her calls was a lot to reconcile.

The weak March sun was shining as the plane landed at Nice. Emilie collected her rental car and set off for what she was fast beginning to feel was the nearest thing she had to a home, the familiar territory calming and comforting her.

At the château, all was a hive of activity. A vast lorry stood sentinel outside.

A flushed-looking Margaux greeted her with a hug on the doorstep. 'Madame, I'm so happy to see you.'

'And you,' said Emilie, returning the hug.

'I've done what I can to answer the questions, but I do not know everything.' Margaux looked harassed. 'They have started on the library.'

'What?! They were told not to start without me,' Emilie exclaimed.

'Well, that's my fault, Madame. They arrived three hours ago and I did not wish to see them idle.'

'Never mind,' said Emilie quickly, stifling her irritation. 'I'm here now.'

'Can I offer you a drink after your long journey?' said Margaux.

'Yes, tea please. Can you bring it into the library for me?'

'Of course, Madame.'

Emilie walked along the passage to find the

library shelves already half empty. The air was thick with the dust of centuries past.

'Hello,' she said to the four or five workers busily stacking the books into water-tight crates. 'I am Emilie de la Martinières.'

'A pleasure, Madame.' A thickly set man stood up and held out his rough palm to greet her. 'As you can see, we're making good progress. It's quite a collection you have here. Some of these books are very old.'

Giles, as he introduced himself, went on to explain how they were numbering each container to the appropriate shelf, which had also been numbered. 'So it will be possible to return the books to their original place,' he concluded.

'Good,' said Emilie, feeling comforted they seemed at least organised and competent and were handling the books carefully. Her eyes moved through the chaos and she started as she saw Margaux's son, Anton, sitting on the floor engrossed in a book, despite the hubbub around him.

'Hello, Anton,' she said as she reached him.

Startled, the boy looked up at her. His eyes betrayed a hint of fear.

'Madame de la Martinières, I am sorry, my mother sent me to help, but I found this and opened it and . . .'

Emilie glanced down at the book. It was an old copy of *Les Misérables* by Victor Hugo, a book she herself had read out of this library when she was younger. Emilie smiled as Anton stood up, reminding her of Gavroche, the young boy from the slums of Paris in the story.

'Please, carry on.' Emilie laid a hand on his

271

shoulder and gently sat him back down. 'You like reading?'

'Oh yes, very much. And I like it in here—' he indicated the library. 'If my mother brings me with her when she's working, I come and look at the books. But I've never touched them before, Madame, I promise,' he added hurriedly.

'Well, I think you should keep that one and finish it at home,' Emilie suggested. 'I'm sure you'll take care of it.'

'Really?' Anton's face lit up. 'I would love to. Thank you, Madame.'

'Please, call me Emilie.'

'Anton! You haven't been causing trouble in here, have you?'

Margaux had brought Emilie's tea into the library and her eyes were full of concern.

'No, of course he hasn't.' Emilie took the tea from Margaux. 'He's like me and my papa; a bookworm. And obviously a very bright boy,' she added with a smile. 'He has chosen *Les Misérables*—a challenge for any adult, let alone a child.'

'Yes!' Margaux's eyes shone with pride. 'He is top of his class and hopes to go on to study literature at a great university. How long are you staying, Madame? All that's left in the rest of the house is the furniture from the bedroom you normally sleep in. Jean and Jacques have offered you a room at their cottage, as you know.'

'Yes, but I'll sleep here tonight. The bed and the armoire in my room are worthless and can be thrown on a skip later. Then I'll move down to the cottage for the night tomorrow. You've been wonderful, Margaux, thank you,' Emilie said gratefully as they walked out of the library and entered the deserted kitchen.

'I have left you some plates, knives and forks and, of course, a kettle,' Margaux explained. 'And they haven't taken the refrigerator—it's very old and perhaps you will wish to replace it anyway?'

The enormity of the project Emilie had undertaken suddenly began to dawn on her. So far, cocooned behind Sebastian's secure and protective shield, it had seemed manageable.

'I'm sure we'll replace it,' agreed Emilie. 'The architect is meeting me here tomorrow morning, along with the project manager who will oversee the building work.'

'How long do you think the process will take, Madame?'

Emilie noticed Margaux looked exhausted today. 'I have no idea. A year maybe? Eighteen months?'

'I see. It's just that . . . sorry, Madame, but I presume I must look for some other employment? After all, there will be nothing to take care of here.'

'Margaux,' said Emilie, realising guiltily she should have spoken to her weeks ago, 'you have worked for our family for over fifteen years and of course I will pay you your normal wages whilst the château undergoes renovation. You can still keep an eye on the builders and the house for me whilst I'm away in England, and let me know if there are any problems.'

'Madame, that's very kind of you, and of course I will,' replied Margaux, obviously relieved. 'If I could take nothing, I would, but you know that I'm not rich. And I save everything for Anton's future education.' Margaux's eyes were suddenly haunted. 'I worry sometimes what would happen if I wasn't here.'

'But you *are* here, Margaux,' Emilie comforted with a smile. 'Don't feel guilty, please. I'm sure you will more than make up for the time you're not working now once the château is finished and the dust must be cleaned away.'

'Well, I think it's a beautiful thing you're doing, and your parents would be very proud of you,' added Margaux, tears suddenly filling her eyes. 'The house will be safe for France and the future generations that you and your husband will produce. Now, I've left you some supper and I must go home with Anton and make ours.'

'Of course. I'll see you before I leave and pay your wages. And thank you again for everything.'

Margaux left the kitchen and Emilie stood alone for a while in its vast, echoing space, then set off back to the library to do what she could to help.

*   *   *

As dusk fell over the château, the books were all on the lorry and ready to leave.

'Madame de la Martinières, I must ask you to sign these forms. They're to say that you have checked over the contents and agreed that there are 24,307 books. Your husband suggested insurance cover of twenty-one million francs when he spoke to me last week,' said Giles.

'Really?' Emilie raised an eyebrow. 'Is that not excessive?'

'It's a very impressive collection, Madame. And if I were you, when it's returned I would have a rare books specialist come and value it properly. These days, old books can be worth a small fortune.'

'Yes,' said Emilie, 'of course.' Sebastian had also advised the same, but she'd never valued the collection financially before, only emotionally. 'Thank you for your help and advice.'

Emilie watched the van drive off into the night then went back to the kitchen to eat the braised oxtail that Margaux had left for her. In front of her were the contents of her father's desk, which she had piled hastily into two black bin bags when the desk had been taken into storage a few weeks before. As she ate, Emilie reached into one of the bags and took out a random clutch of its contents. There were many letters, a mixture of social and business correspondence, dating back to the Sixties. Also, a collection of photographs of her parents in Paris and here in the château garden, enjoying social occasions.

There were many of Emilie as a baby too, a child and then a gawky teenager, with her heavy fringe and plump, hormonal body. Losing track of time, she ploughed through everything, comforted by this very intimate selection of the remnants from her father's life. It brought him closer, and she wept as she read some of the love letters her mother had sent to him.

From these, there was no doubt Valérie had loved her husband, and for that, at least, Emilie was grateful. She wiped her nose on the back of her hand, feeling both moved and ironically happier that some of her pain was slowly being erased as she understood more of the past.

She realised also that, in retrospect, closing

herself off from her family and its history had only served to hinder her present and her future. Of course, there were things that could never be forgiven . . . but, at least, if she understood *why* they had happened, then maybe she could finally free herself.

Glancing at her watch, Emilie saw it was past midnight. She checked her voicemail to see if Sebastian had called her. She had left him a voicemail earlier to say she'd arrived in France.

An electronic voice told her she had no new messages. Emilie sighed as she left the warmth of the range for the chill of the bedroom, glad she'd remembered to pack her trusty hot-water bottle.

Lying in bed, she felt the usual surge of adrenalin at the thought of Sebastian's coldness at the weekend and his subsequent non-communication, but refused to submit to it. If, for some reason, Sebastian had ceased to love her, she would cope. After all, her childhood had taught her how to be alone.

20

The following morning was hectic as Emilie greeted the architect and foreman. After they'd wandered around the house discussing the renovations in detail, Emilie swallowed hard when she saw the revised estimate, but the architect assured her the work was worth every centime in comparison to what the value of the château would be once it was restored.

'I'm sure we'll be in touch on many occasions in the next few months,' said Adrien, the foreman. 'And you must understand that the château will look very forlorn when you next see it—and it will be a very long time before your beautiful house returns to its full glory.'

Eventually, when everyone had left, Emilie closed the front door and took a slow wander around inside. Feeling silly and sentimental as she did so, she assured the rooms that the process of transformation they were about to go through was for their own good.

She had called Jean earlier and he had offered her supper at the cottage, as well as a bed. Wandering back into the scullery where she had stowed her suitcase and the two black bin liners, she pulled the last unread pile of papers and photographs out. Picking up a yellowing envelope, she opened it. Inside was a photograph of a very young Édouard—probably in his twenties—standing on a beach, his arm protectively around the shoulder of a beautiful, fair-haired girl. Emilie recognised her from the portrait in her father's

Paris study. It was his sister, Sophia. There was also another piece of paper in the envelope, torn from a notebook . . . Emilie unfolded it and saw the familiar, uneven, childish writing.

'*Mon Frère . . .*'

'My brother,' Emilie whispered to herself, then did her best to decipher the appalling writing. It was a eulogy to Édouard and was signed, as the other poems she had read, by Sophia de la Martinières, '*âge 14*'.

Realising her fingers were numb with the dense cold of the empty house, Emilie returned to her chair by the range and sat down. This poem illustrated like nothing else could the adoration the young Sophia had felt for her brother. So why had Édouard never talked of her? What had happened between them to render his sadness and silence? Given the obvious affection shown in the photograph between brother and sister, Emilie knew there must be a reason.

Stowing the poem and photograph in her handbag, she picked up the bin bags and her suitcase and closed the door on the château for the last time. As she was steering the car along the gravel drive to Jean's cottage, her mobile rang suddenly. Seeing it was Sebastian, she brought the car to a sharp halt and answered the phone.

'Where have you been? I've been worried out of my mind!' she almost shouted down the phone, a mixture of anxiety and emotion fuelling her anger.

'Darling, I'm so, so sorry. I left my mobile charger in Yorkshire and the battery ran out on Tuesday morning.'

'Sebastian, that's no excuse! Surely there are other phones in the world you could have used to contact me on?' Emilie was unable to control herself.

'I did! I called Blackmoor Hall on Tuesday night, but nobody answered and since then you've been in France.'

'Then why didn't you leave a message on my mobile?' she demanded.

'Emilie, please! Let me explain. It's really very simple. The only place I had your mobile number recorded was *on* my mobile and the battery was flat, remember? So I didn't *have* your number until I arrived back home in Yorkshire this afternoon and charged my phone.'

'Couldn't you have called Gerard? He has it.' Emilie was still shaking with anger.

'His number was also stored on my useless mobile. Please, Emilie—' Sebastian sounded weary—'I'm truly sorry. And before you ask, yes, I did go in search of a replacement charger in London, but my mobile is such an old model that none of the local shops supply it any more. And I really didn't have time to go further afield. Anyway, it's what you might call an unfortunate series of events. And there simply isn't anything more I can say, other than it's taught me how valuable an old-fashioned paper address book is. Besides,' he added, 'what other reason could there be for me not making contact?'

The sense of his words cut through any further frustrated and fearful outpourings Emilie might have uttered. As Sebastian said, what other reason could there be?

'You have no idea how worried I've been. Especially as over the weekend you seemed so . . . odd,' Emilie admitted. 'I even began to wonder

279

whether you'd left me.' Anger abating, she was close to tears now.

This comment elicited a gentle chuckle. 'Left you? Emilie, I only married you a few weeks ago. What on earth do you think I am? Yes, admittedly, I was very low last weekend. But everyone gets down from time to time, don't they?'

'I suppose so, yes.' Emilie bit her lip, feeling wrong-footed and guilty for jumping to conclusions.

'Has that brother of mine been getting to you? Planting seeds in your head that have begun to take root? Yup—' Emilie almost heard him nodding to himself—'I bet that's it.'

'No, Sebastian, Alex never says a word against you, I promise.'

'Don't lie, Emilie, I know what he's like.' Sebastian's voice had a sudden harshness to it.

'He has said nothing,' Emilie underlined, not wanting to get drawn into an argument during the first conversation they'd had in four days. 'You say you're at home in Yorkshire now?'

'Yes, I am. How are things going over there?'

'The books have left the château and it's now awaiting its facelift.'

'Well, I'm sorry I couldn't be there to help you. Things have been incredibly busy here.'

'Well, that's good, isn't it?' Emilie said quietly.

'Yes, not as good as they could be, but . . . when are you coming home?'

'Tomorrow,' she replied.

'Then I shall make you something lovely for supper to welcome you and to try and make up for the débâcle of my mobile,' Sebastian said. 'I'm sorry, Emilie, but really, it wasn't my fault. And I did try and get hold of you on Tuesday night, I promise.'

'Well, let's just forget it, shall we?' she suggested.

'Yes. And if there's anything I can do from here to help you, just let me know.'

'Thank you, but everything is under control so far.'

'OK, sweetheart, please keep in touch,' said Sebastian.

'And *you*!' Emilie managed a weak smile. 'See you tomorrow.'

She sat staring into space for a while, wondering if she believed him. Her father always used to say that the simplest reasons tended to account for the most dramatic circumstances and she hoped she too could take that view. But the four-day silence *had* planted seeds of doubt in her mind.

And even though Alex had said nothing negative or inflammatory about his brother, he had purposely avoided being drawn into a conversation on the subject. Put bluntly, Emilie felt there was far more to say about her husband than Alex was telling her. Turning the car engine back on, she drove the last hundred metres down to the cottage and parked outside.

She left her belongings in the boot and tried the door to the *cave* first, knowing Jean often worked until late. And, sure enough, there he was, sitting at his table, surrounded by his ledgers.

Jean's warm, brown eyes crinkled as he broke into a smile. 'Emilie! Welcome.' He stood up, walked round the table and kissed her on both cheeks. 'It's a pleasure to have you here. Your room is ready and we've made some supper for

281

you. You must be exhausted.'

'It's kind of you to have me, Jean. Where's Jacques?' Emilie peered into the gloom of the *cave* to the large bench at the back where Jacques was usually a permanent fixture, wrapping the bottles.

'I've sent Papa into the cottage to light the fires. It's cold tonight, especially in here, and I don't want him to catch a chill. As you know, he hasn't been well this winter. But then, he's getting very old.' Jean sighed and Emilie noticed the worry in his eyes. 'So, everything is ready at the château?'

'Yes, it will be a new dawn,' Emilie said, nodding.

'Well, I can't tell you how happy Papa and I are that the château will stay in the de la Martinières family. You've not only saved our livelihood, but the home my father and I love so much. I truly think it might have finished Papa if he'd had to leave,' Jean replied. 'Now, let's go through to the cottage, sit by the fire and have a glass of wine. This year's rosé is particularly good. Last season's weather conditions were perfect. In fact, I will know soon whether we have won a medal for the rosé in the forthcoming Vignerons awards. It will be the first time for this vineyard and I have high hopes.'

Emilie helped Jean switch off the lights in the *cave* then they walked along the short passage that led to the cottage. As Jean opened the door into the kitchen, a delicious smell of cooking permeated the air.

'Come through to the sitting room, where I'm sure my father will already have uncorked the wine for us,' said Jean.

Jacques was again dozing in his chair by the fire.

Even Emilie, who had grown up thinking of Jean's father as ancient, noticed his deterioration. She turned to Jean. 'Shall we go into the kitchen and let him sleep?' she whispered.

'No need—' he grinned—'he's as deaf as a post these days. Sit down, Emilie.' Jean gestured to a chair and picked up the open bottle of wine from the table. 'Try some of this.'

Emilie took the glass he handed her, swilled the gorgeous pale-pink liquid inside around its edges and enjoyed its rich, pungent bouquet.

'It smells wonderful, Jean.'

'I added more Syrah grape than usual, and I think the mix is good.'

Emilie took a sip and smiled in pleasure. 'It's lovely.'

'Of course, there's a lot of competition here locally, with huge investment in the latest technology being employed. But I'll do my best to keep up.' Jean shrugged. 'Now, enough of business, we can talk about that later. How's England? And married life?'

Never had the strange, tense, cold atmosphere of Blackmoor Hall seemed so far away than from the familiarity of sitting comfortably with Jean in his cosy cottage.

'It's fine, although it's taking me time to get used to England. And Sebastian hasn't been around very much due to his work,' she replied honestly.

'I know he travels often. Only last week I saw a car I didn't know coming down the drive towards the château one evening. So, in my unofficial capacity as security guard when Margaux leaves for the day, I went to investigate when I didn't see it return,' Jean explained. 'It was your husband.'

'Really? Sebastian was here last week?' Emilie did her best to disguise her shock and not let it show on her face.

'Yes. You didn't know?' Jean gazed at her thoughtfully for a moment.

'I knew he was in France, so perhaps he found himself nearby and decided to check on the château,' she equivocated quickly.

'Yes, I'm sure. I'm afraid I startled him when I arrived at the house. He was in the library, surrounded by piles of books.'

'Oh! Well, he was obviously trying to help me by beginning to pack them,' said Emilie, relief flooding through her.

'He was here for two days, although I didn't see him after the first time as I didn't want to disturb him. He is your husband after all, and therefore has a right to be at the château whenever he chooses.'

'Yes.' But, privately, Emilie wondered why on earth Sebastian hadn't mentioned spending two days at the château to her. Yet again, anxiety began to churn in her stomach. 'It was kind of him to spare the time to help with the library,' she managed weakly.

'I know he's helped you through a very difficult time and offered you support.'

'Yes, he has. Now—' Emilie was desperate to change the subject—'I wanted to show you something that I found at the house in Yorkshire.' She produced the envelope containing the poems Alex had given her. 'These were written by my aunt, Sophia de la Martinières. Jacques mentioned she wrote poems when he spoke of the past last time.' She handed them over to Jean and, as she did so, saw one of Jacques's eyes open.

'They're beautiful . . .' murmured Jean quietly, reading through them. 'Papa, would you like to see them?'

'Yes.' Jacques's eyes were fully open now and Emilie wondered if his apparent deafness was conveniently exaggerated. Jean placed the poems in Jacques's shaking hands. They sat in silence as he read them. When he looked up, there were tears in his eyes.

'She was so very beautiful . . . so tragic, the end . . . I—' Jacques shook his head, emotion getting the better of him.

'Jacques, can you tell me how she died?' Emilie asked gently. 'And why my father never spoke of her? And why Constance had these poems in her house in Yorkshire?'

'Emilie—' Jean put a gentle hand on her arm— 'slow down a little. I can see Papa is shocked by seeing these poems. Shall we eat and perhaps give Papa some time to get his thoughts in order?'

'Of course.' Emilie was chastened. 'My apologies, Jacques. Having lost my family, I'm excited that you know of their past.'

'We will eat first,' said Jacques gravely as Jean handed him his walking stick and helped him to stand.

Over supper, Jacques said very little. Jean pointedly changed the topic of conversation back to the vineyard and his plans for modernisation and expansion.

'With the right level of investment, I know that within five years we could be turning in a good profit. It would be a beautiful thing to add a

285

positive contribution to the domaine, rather than a negative one,' he enthused.

As Emilie listened to Jean, seeing him full of enthusiasm for his passion, she thought what an attractive man he still was; with his smooth skin— nut-brown even after a long winter—and his chestnut hair hanging in wavy tendrils and framing his face, he looked younger than his thirty-nine years. When she'd been a teenager, and they'd spent time together, she'd developed a girlish crush on him for a while.

As she helped Jean clear away the plates, Jacques yawned.

'Papa, shall I help you up to bed?'

'No!' Jacques spoke loud and strong. 'I don't wish to sleep. It's emotion making me yawn. Jean, find the Armagnac and I will try to tell Emilie more of what I know. And, unfortunately for me—' Jacques made a sound somewhere between a groan and a chuckle—'it is everything. I've been thinking since you left, Emilie, whether the rest of it should go with me to the grave. But then—' he shrugged—'how can you make sense of the present if you do not know of the past?'

'Jacques, that's a lesson I'm learning too,' said Emilie softly. 'And, if you remember, you'd told me of Constance's arrival in Paris. She'd just met Venetia and had agreed to help her . . .'

My Brother

Strong above me, arm protective,
Round my shoulder, leading me.
Always caring, ever loving,
Do you see me, do you see?

Enigmatic, strong and stoic,
Leaning forward over me.
Book in one hand, reading quietly,
Do you see me, do you see?

Light glows brightly, shining from
you,
In your shadow, always be.
I am here now, I am growing,
Do you see me, do you see?

So you'll leave me, one day finding,
Life beyond our sanctuary.
Never knowing how I loved you,
Did you see me, did you see?

Sophia de la Martinières
1932, age 14

21

Paris, 1943

Édouard arrived back home from the south two days later. He seemed exhausted and went straight up to his room, pausing on the stairs to tell Connie they were entertaining that evening. She would be required in the drawing room at six thirty.

She wondered who the guests would be that night—and sent up a silent prayer it wouldn't be Falk and Frederik. She was slowly calming down after the trials of two nights ago, when Venetia had been transmitting from the cellar and Frederik had arrived at the house unexpectedly.

When Sarah had gone out shopping the morning after, Connie had run downstairs and checked the cellar, intending to relock it. But there was no key with which to do so. She searched for it both inside and out, but had found no trace. Comfortingly, neither was there evidence of Venetia's presence—not a hint of stale Gauloises in the air and nothing touched or removed that she could see. And so far, no reprisals, which she knew from experience were fast. If the Boche had picked up a radio signal from the locality, they would have conducted a house-to-house search immediately, aware that the wireless operator would usually pack up and leave within hours.

At six thirty that evening, as requested, Connie was on parade in the drawing room. A dreamy Sophia, looking heartbreakingly beautiful in a new lilac cocktail dress, was led in by Sarah.

As Sophia sat down in the chair, Connie studied her and realised she'd recently gained an aura that distinguished between longing and knowing. She was simply radiant: a young woman at the full height of her physical powers.

Édouard arrived downstairs in the drawing room looking rested and refreshed, seemingly back to his untroubled self. He kissed his sister, commented on her beauty that evening and relayed the guest list. It was the usual mixture of bourgeois French, Vichy officials and Germans.

By seven thirty, all the guests had arrived, apart from Falk. Frederik had delivered his brother's apologies that he was delayed, but would arrive later.

'There was a break-in last night at the STO office on the Rue des Francs-Bourgeois,' Frederik explained. 'The Resistance stole sixty-five thousand files and got clean away. Under-standably, this has not pleased my brother.'

The STO programme was one that Connie had been made aware of during her SOE training course. It was a system by which a register of young Frenchmen—totalling almost 150,000 names—was kept on file. Large numbers of them were continuously rounded up and sent to Germany to work in munitions factories and on production lines. The deportation of these thousands of young men had caused growing dissent amongst the French public and had rendered the Vichy government extremely unpopular. The STO programme had made many previously law-abiding French citizens look to and support the Resistance. Connie's concerned face as she listened to Frederik gave away none of the inner delight she felt at the success of the Resistance's mission. And Venetia's obviously successful part in it.

'Of course there will be reprisals,' added a high-ranking Vichy official. 'We will become even more vigilant to stamp out these rebels who tear our country apart.'

*   *   *

As coffee and brandy were being served in the drawing room, the front doorbell rang. A few seconds later, Falk entered the room.

'My apologies, Édouard, I have been kept from your table by the militants of this country who continue to undermine our regime.'

As Édouard poured him a brandy, Connie noticed Falk's face was set hard and there was a glint in his eye. Connie gritted her teeth as he walked over. 'Fräulein Constance, how does this evening find you?'

'I'm well, thank you, Falk. And you?'

'As you have heard, there has been some trouble from the Resistance, but rest assured, we are dealing with it and they will not get away with what they have done. Anyway, enough of work. I'm in need of some entertainment.' His fingers reached out to stroke Connie's cheek.

His touch was like iced water dripping down her face.

'Fräulein, perhaps you can—'

'So, you have had to deal with a big problem.' Édouard appeared by their side to defuse the situation.

'Yes, but the perpetrators will be caught and

291

punished. We already have intelligence coming in from the French public who do not approve of the Resistance and wish to alert us to traitors. And we believe they are operating very close to here. One of our listeners picked up a strong signal two nights ago, which was being transmitted from one of the houses in this street. A full search was conducted immediately of your neighbours' properties but nothing was found. Of course, I told my officers not to trouble you with such an intrusion,' Falk said.

Connie's blood froze in her veins as Édouard looked genuinely surprised. 'Where could the signal have come from?' he questioned. 'I know for a fact that all my neighbours are loyal and law-abiding people.'

'Brother,' Frederik interrupted the conversation suddenly, 'if this was two nights ago, I was here for a short time visiting Mademoiselle Sophia and she said she longed to hear some music. The gramophone would not work, so she mentioned there was a radio in the house. Of course she does not use it, she understands it's illegal,' Frederik added hastily, 'but for that moment, wanting to please her, I switched it on and tuned it to find some classical music for Sophia to listen to. So, Falk—' Frederik sighed penitently—'I think that perhaps this is my fault. I apologise for causing you extra work. But I can assure you, the full might of the SS was present in this house that evening and I only saw the cat enter and leave.'

Even Édouard's calm demeanour seemed ruffled by Frederik's strange confession. Falk also looked suspicious. 'Well, I can hardly arrest my own superior for carrying out an illegal operation

292

in his mission to please a lady,' he replied, irritation clear in his voice. 'We shall, of course, forget it, but I suggest, Édouard, that you hand in your radio immediately, so there can be no more confusion.'

'Of course, Falk,' said Édouard. 'I was not here at the house on the night in question. Sophia, you should not have encouraged such behaviour.'

'But the music we listened to was beautiful.' Sophia smiled from the chair behind them. 'Mozart's "Requiem" must be worth all the trouble, surely?' she said, and her innocent charm broke the tension.

Connie noticed that Frederik's gaze rested on Sophia constantly, tenderness in his eyes. The juxtaposition of an identical pair of eyes on the other side of her—steely and devoid of warmth—was evident. If the eyes truly were windows to the soul, she knew that Frederik and Falk, for all their identical outer packaging, did not share a similar one.

* * *

Édouard came to Connie in the library the next morning.

'So, Frederik was here whilst I was away?' he questioned.

'Yes. But I didn't invite him, your sister did. And I knew nothing of the arrangement.'

'I see.' Édouard folded his arms and sighed. 'I saw last night that the relationship has grown. They're deeply in love. Has Sophia spoken to you of it?'

'Yes,' Connie replied truthfully, 'and I tried to

293

warn her of the hopelessness of pursuing any relationship with Frederik. But she won't be reasoned with.'

'We can only hope that Frederik returns to Germany soon, for Sophia's sake.' Édouard turned to her. 'You were with them the night he was here?'

'No, Frederik arrived after I retired. I was in bed.'

'My God!' Édouard put a hand to his forehead in horror. 'Sophia has truly gone mad! To entertain a man alone is unacceptable, but to do it in secret, late at night, is unthinkable!'

'Édouard, please forgive me, but I really didn't know what to do,' Connie explained. 'Even if I had told Sophia it was inappropriate to entertain Frederik alone here at that hour, I'm only a guest in her house. I don't have the right to tell her what she may or may not do. And especially not whilst she's with a German officer, so high in rank,' she added. 'I'm so very sorry.'

Édouard slumped into a chair, suddenly despairing. 'Is it not enough they rape and destroy our beautiful country and steal its treasures? Do they have to steal my sister too? Sometimes I . . .'

'Édouard, what is it?'

He stared into space for a while, then said, 'Forgive me, Constance, I'm tired, and shocked at my sister's behaviour. I feel I have been fighting this war for a very long time. So, we will see if Frederik leaves for Germany soon. If not, more drastic action must be taken.'

'At least it was wonderful news about the STO files being successfully removed by the Resistance, wasn't it?' said Connie.

'Yes.' He turned to her, an odd expression on his face. 'And there will be more, rest assured, there will be more.'

Édouard left the library and Connie sat with her book on her lap, at that moment certain Édouard de la Martinières had been a part of the STO raid the previous night. And she was comforted by the thought. But it didn't change the fact that she was trapped in a web which was not of her own making; passive when she had been trained to be active . . . going slowly mad . . .

And why had Frederik covered for the household by mentioning the radio? Could it be that Sophia was speaking the truth when she said Frederik did not believe in the Nazi cause? Or had he known already that there was a signal being transmitted from the house and had come to investigate for himself?

Connie put her head in her hands and wept. The cause she had been enlisted to fight for had been lost in a blur of confusion. Everyone else seemed to know the game they were playing and their role in it. But she felt no better than a piece of flotsam, tossed to and fro on the whims and secret objectives of others.

'Lawrence,' she whispered, 'help me.'

She looked around the library and the books stared back at her, hard, cold and inanimate, their outer skins so similar, betraying little of their contents. A perfect metaphor for the life she was currently being forced to live.

*   *   *

At lunchtime, Sophia, whom Connie had seen little

of in the past few days, looked tired and pale. Connie watched as she picked at her food, then stood up from the table and excused herself.

Two hours later, when Sophia had not emerged from her bedroom, Connie knocked on her door. Sophia was lying on her bed, her face grey, a cold flannel pressed to her forehead.

'My dear, are you unwell?' Connie sat down on the bed and took Sophia's hand in her own. 'Is there anything I can do to help?'

'No, I'm not ill. Physically at least . . .' Sophia sighed and gave a weak smile. 'Thank you for coming, Constance. It feels as if we haven't spent time together recently. I've missed you.'

'Well, I'm here now,' she comforted.

'Oh, Constance.' Sophia bit her lip. 'Frederik has told me he must leave within the next few weeks to return to Germany. How will I bear it?' Her sightless eyes brimmed with tears.

'Because you must.' Connie squeezed Sophia's hand. 'Just like I must bear being without Lawrence.'

'Yes,' she agreed. 'I know you think I'm naive and that I don't understand the meaning of love. That I will get over Frederik, because there's no future for us. But I'm a grown woman and I know my own heart.'

'I'm only trying to protect you, Sophia,' Connie said. 'I understand how difficult it is for you.'

'Constance, I know Frederik and I will be together. I know it here—' Sophia put her hand on her heart—'inside me. Frederik says he will find a way and I believe him.'

Connie sighed. Set against the hardships of the past four years, when millions of people had lost either their own lives or their loved ones to the war, Sophia's romance could be seen as trivial. But to Sophia it was all-consuming, simply because it was *hers*.

'Well, if Frederik says he will find a way, he will,' Connie consoled, realising there was little else she could say. If Frederik was leaving soon, she could only pray the situation would be resolved naturally.

*   *   *

The next few weeks were full of broken nights as air-raid sirens shattered the still Paris air and its residents yet again retreated underground for safety. Connie heard of RAF attacks on both the Peugeot and Michelin factories in the industrial heartlands outside Paris. At home in England, she would have greeted this news with joy as she read it in *The Times*, but here, the papers were full of the numbers of innocent French civilians working there who had been killed.

As she took her daily stroll down to the Tuileries Gardens, Connie could almost feel the weakening heartbeat of a city and the people who were slowly losing their faith that the war would ever end. The promised Allied invasion had still not materialised and Connie was beginning to wonder whether it ever would.

Sitting down on her usual bench, the air already heavy with mist, as though also in a hurry to rid itself of this miserable day, Connie saw Venetia walking towards her.

They went through the usual polite rigmarole of a greeting and Venetia sat down next to her.

Although she was in her 'wealthy woman' uniform, today she had not bothered with her make-up mask. Her skin was translucently pale, her face desperately thin.

'Thank you for your help with the cellar that time. Much appreciated.' Venetia pulled out a Gauloise. 'Smoke?'

'No. Thank you.'

'I live on these bloody things, they stem the hunger,' Venetia added, lighting up.

'Do you need money to buy some food?' Connie asked, feeling that at least this was something she could provide.

'No thanks. The real problem is I always seem to be haring around, never able to stay at the same place twice in case the Boche pick up my signal. I'm always in transit on my wretched bicycle, so it's hard to find the time to sit down and eat.'

'How are things going?' asked Connie.

'Oh, you know, Con,' said Venetia, drawing heavily on her cigarette, 'one step forwards, two steps back. At least our lot are a little more organised than they were when I arrived in the summer. But we can always do with an extra pair of hands. And I was thinking, perhaps it doesn't matter if you're no longer officially an agent. There's no reason why you couldn't lend a hand as an ordinary French citizen. And then, perhaps, if you met the people I work with, they might be able to help you leave France.'

'Really?' Connie's deadened spirits lifted immediately. 'Oh, Venetia, I know my life is a picnic compared to yours, but I'd do anything, *anything* to try to get home and out of that house.'

'Well, I've already told my network that you

helped me and I'm sure they might be able to help you get out of France. What I suggest is that you join us at the next meeting. I can't promise anything and you must remember there's always a risk there's a traitor who will inform the Germans of our whereabouts, but a favour deserves a favour. Besides,' she added, 'you're my friend. And I feel sorry for you, stuck in that house entertaining those pigs.'

Venetia gave Connie a warm smile, and she saw a sudden flash of her friend's beauty appear through the veil of exhaustion. 'By the way, I think the chap you're staying with may be extremely high up in the Resistance. I've heard there's a very wealthy man in Paris who's number two only to Moulin, our late and revered Resistance boss. If it is your chap, sweetie, it's understandable why London had to sacrifice your glittering career as an agent when you appeared on his doorstep in full view of the Gestapo. Anyway, must fly.' Venetia stood up. 'I'll bring you exact details of where and when the meeting is taking place on Thursday. So, tally ho, and see you here then.'

22

As arranged, Connie was in the gardens on Thursday, but Venetia did not appear. Finally, after sitting on the bench at the appointed time for the following four days, Venetia arrived, wheeling her bicycle. She did not acknowledge Connie, merely paused, stared straight ahead and said under her breath: 'Café de la Paix, ninth arrondissement, nine o'clock tonight.' Then she was gone.

Connie spent the next few hours pondering how she could leave the house unnoticed. As sure as eggs were eggs, Édouard would not allow her out in the evening unaccompanied. She decided the best thing for it was to announce she had a headache and retire to her room after dinner. Édouard usually shut himself away in his study at this point. And when she knew he was safely inside, she would go to the kitchen and let herself out through the cellar, which still remained unlocked due to the lost key.

That night, after dinner, just as Édouard had left the table and she was following suit, the doorbell rang and Sarah answered it. She came into the dining room. 'It is Colonel Falk von Wehndorf to see you, Madame Constance. He is waiting in the drawing room.'

Almost weeping at the bad timing, Connie walked into the hall and painted on a bright smile as she entered the drawing room. 'Hello, Herr Falk. How are you?'

'I'm well, but I haven't seen you for the past few days, Fräulein, and I have missed your beauty. I wish to ask you if you would give me the pleasure of accompanying me out for some dancing later on this evening?'

Connie began to utter an excuse, but Falk shook his head and put a finger to her lips. 'No, Fräulein, you have refused me once too often. Tonight, I will not be dissuaded. I will collect you at ten o'clock.' Falk began to leave the room then stopped as in afterthought. 'I hope to be in a very good mood. My officers have an important appointment at the

Café de la Paix tonight.' He smiled at her. 'Until later, Fräulein.'

A horrified Connie watched him leave, her heart thudding against her chest. This was the café where she too was headed. She had to warn Venetia that the Gestapo knew of their meeting. Running upstairs and pinning on her hat, Connie raced back down and walked towards the door. Opening it, she had one foot on the doorstep outside when a hand grabbed her arm.

'Constance, where are you in such a hurry to go at this hour?'

She turned towards Édouard, knowing her face betrayed the panic she felt. 'I have to leave now! It's a matter of life and death! Please, you don't understand!'

'Come, we'll talk in the library and you'll tell me what it is that has upset you.' Pulling her firmly back down the hall in a way that brokered no dissent, Édouard closed the door behind them.

'Please,' begged Connie, 'I'm not your prisoner! You can't keep me here against my will. I must go out now, otherwise it may be too late!'

'Constance, you're not my prisoner, but neither can I risk letting you out without knowing where it is you're going. Either you tell me or I will indeed be forced to lock you in your room. Do not think your activities, such as your meeting with a "friend" at the Ritz, went unnoticed,' Édouard said grimly. 'I've told you time and again we cannot risk any connection with the Resistance being made to this house.'

'Yes,' confessed Connie, horrified he knew. 'The woman I met at the Ritz trained with me in England. She asked for my help. She's my friend

301

and I couldn't deny her.'

'So, now tell me, where must you go tonight?' Édouard repeated.

'My friend told me this afternoon that her network is holding a meeting at nine o'clock tonight at the Café de la Paix. Falk has just informed me he knows of it, too. The Gestapo will be waiting there for them. I must go and warn them, Édouard. Please,' Connie begged, 'let me go!'

'No, Constance! You know I can't let you do that. If you were caught and arrested, we know the consequences for the rest of us here in this household.'

'But I can't just sit here whilst she's walking into a death trap! I'm sorry, Édouard, whatever you say, I'm going.' Connie walked determinedly towards the door.

'NO!'

Édouard gripped her shoulders and she struggled against him, bursting into tears of frustration as she realised it was a physical fight she could not win.

'Constance, calm down, please, or I'll be forced to slap your face. *You* will not be going out tonight to warn them.' Édouard looked at her and gave a deep sigh. 'I will.'

'You?'

'Yes, I have far more experience in these kinds of situations than you will ever have.' He checked his watch. 'What time did your friend say the meeting was planned for?'

'Nine o'clock. One hour from now.'

'Then I may be in time to contact someone who can pass on a message before it begins.' Édouard

302

gave a brief, forced smile. 'If not, I'll go there myself. You must leave it to me. I'll do all I can, I promise.'

'Oh God, Édouard.' Connie's last shreds of veneer crumbled and she put her head in her hands. 'Forgive me for betraying your trust.'

'We'll talk later. I must leave if I'm to be in time. If anyone should call here—' he raised his eyebrows—'then I'm in bed with a migraine.'

'Édouard!' Connie suddenly remembered. 'Falk is collecting me from here at ten o'clock to take me dancing.'

'Then I must make sure I'm back home by then.'

As Édouard left the library, Connie collapsed into a chair and, a few minutes later, heard the sound of the front door closing.

'Please—' she wrung her hands as she spoke to the heavens—'let Édouard get there in time.'

*   *   *

Connie sat sentinel in the drawing room by the window so she could watch for Édouard returning. The night was not cold, but she shivered unnaturally with fear. The clock on the mantelpiece ticked the seconds away, and when the doorbell rang, Connie jumped, suddenly remembering her appointment with Falk. Yet it was only just past nine.

Moving out into the hall, Connie watched Sarah open the door and saw Falk.

'You're early, Herr Falk, I'm not quite ready,' she said to him.

'You're mistaken, Fräulein Constance.' The man gave her an unusually warm smile. 'It is Frederik standing here. I wondered if Mademoiselle Sophia was in? Perhaps she has told you that I leave tomorrow, and I wish to say goodbye.'

'Yes, of course,' replied Connie, 'she's in the library.' She indicated the door. 'And I apologise for thinking you were Falk. I'm expecting him later.'

'Please do not apologise,' Frederik comforted her, 'it has happened many times before and I'm sure it will happen again.' He nodded at her as he walked past and entered the library, shutting the door behind him.

As she climbed the stairs to prepare herself for her forthcoming ordeal, Connie wondered if things could get any worse. When she was ready, she walked back downstairs and resumed her vigil in the drawing room so she could alert Édouard immediately to Frederik's presence in the house.

The hands of the clock read a quarter to ten before Connie heard footsteps climbing up to the front door. Running to it immediately, she opened it and Édouard fell through it into her arms. Panting, he staggered upright, and she gave a gasp of horror at the blood seeping through his jacket on his right shoulder.

'Oh my God, Édouard, you're hurt! What happened?' she hissed.

'I wasn't there in time. As I walked down the steps, the place was surrounded by Gestapo. The café was in chaos, both sides opening fire . . . I'm not sure who shot me. Don't worry, Constance, it's only a flesh wound and I'll be fine. Unfortunately, I cannot vouch for your friend,' he said weakly.

'Édouard,' Connie said urgently, 'we have a guest, and you must not be seen . . .'

It was too late. Édouard's eyes were no longer looking at Connie, but instead at Frederik and Sophia, who were standing at the other end of the hall. Frederik was gazing at Édouard in surprise.

'Édouard, are you hurt?' asked Frederik.

'No, it's nothing,' he answered quickly. 'I was simply coming out of a restaurant and got caught in a skirmish in the street.'

'What's happened, Frederik?' Sophia asked, unable to see Édouard's wound. 'Are you badly hurt, brother? Should we take you to hospital?' she asked, panic in her voice.

'Not at all,' Édouard managed, drunk with pain, 'I'll go upstairs and clean myself up.'

'I'll help you,' said Connie.

'No, send Sarah up to run me a bath,' grimaced Édouard as he began to mount the stairs. 'I'm sure I'll be well in the morning. Goodnight.'

The three of them watched Édouard make his way gingerly to the top of the stairs. As he disappeared along the corridor, the doorbell rang.

'It will be your brother,' said Connie, hurriedly collecting her coat from the peg. 'Please carry on, Herr Frederik, and I'll see you, Sophia, later.'

Connie opened the door to Falk. With a bright smile, she said, 'I'm ready! Shall we go?'

Surprised and gratified by her eagerness, Falk agreed, took Connie's arm in his and they walked down the steps to his waiting car. The chauffeur opened the door for Connie and Falk climbed into the back with her. She could smell his acrid breath, as usual, tinged with stale alcohol. The swastika on the arm of his jacket brushed up against her flesh and a hand laid itself firmly on her knee.

'Attcchh! It's good to be away for a while. It has

305

been a busy day,' Falk commented.

'But successful?' Connie asked as calmly as she could.

'Extremely. We caught twenty of them, although sadly they took out their guns and we lost a good officer, who was a friend of mine. Some of them got away, of course . . . but it's interesting how, when we poke them, they squeal and give us their friends' names. Rest assured, we'll find the others who escaped. Now—' he patted her knee—'that is for tomorrow. Tonight, many are safely behind bars and I wish to relax.'

Connie could feel Falk tingling with triumph. As they entered the club, Connie excused herself, walked into the powder room and locked herself inside a cubicle. She sat down on the lid and put her head between her legs. She felt horribly faint and her breath was coming in short, sharp bursts. Surely, the game was up? When Frederik told his brother of Édouard arriving home with an obvious gunshot wound, Falk's suspicions would be raised. Frederik may well have left and alerted the Gestapo already.

And this was all due to her—she had broken Édouard's trust and, in trying to warn Venetia, had compromised his hard-won and fiercely protected cover and placed him in irrevocable danger.

'Oh God, oh God, what have I done . . . ?' Connie keened. And Venetia—had she been one of the lucky few who, like Édouard, had managed to escape? Or was she locked up in a cell at Gestapo headquarters, awaiting the dreadful round of torture SOE and Resistance agents were subjected to? Before they were shipped off to the death camps or, if they were lucky, shot then

306

and there.

Connie left the cubicle and splashed her face in the basin. She reapplied her lipstick and gave herself a good talking to in the mirror. Tonight, Connie knew she must give Édouard, if he hadn't already been arrested, as much time as possible to recover.

Whatever it took . . .

*   *   *

Édouard lay on his bed, gritting his teeth against the pain in his shoulder. After his bath, Sarah had cleaned the wound for him and placed on an antiseptic, then a dressing.

'Monsieur Édouard,' said Sarah desperately, 'you know you should go to hospital to have this properly tended to. It's a flesh wound, yes, but it's deep and perhaps there's still shrapnel from the bullet inside you.'

'Sarah, you know I cannot.' He grimaced as the antiseptic stung like a thousand bees. 'We must do the best we can here. Has Frederik left the house?'

'No, he's still in the library with Mademoiselle Sophia.'

Édouard reached for Sarah's hand. 'You know now, don't you, that it's almost certainly all over for me? I was seen by at least two of the Gestapo officers in the café. And the rest of the household will be under equal suspicion. I . . .' Édouard tried to sit up but fell back onto his pillows in pain. 'Sarah, as we have always planned in these circumstances, you must leave as soon as possible and take Mademoiselle Sophia and Constance down south to the château. The Gestapo could be

307

here for us all at any minute.'

'Monsieur—' Sarah shook her head—'you know I will not do that. I've worked with this family for thirty-five years and I salute your courage and bravery. My husband was shot two years ago by those pigs. I will not desert you now.'

'You must, Sarah, for Sophia's sake,' Édouard urged. 'Please make ready for you all to leave as soon as you can. There's money in the bureau in the library and identity papers I have prepared for you all. They will, with luck, take you out of Paris, but you must obtain new papers before you cross the Vichy Line. I'll send word to those I know that you're coming. They will help you, I—'

There was a knock on the bedroom door.

'Open it. Then do as I've just said.'

Sarah walked to the door and opened it. Standing on the threshold was Frederik, with Sophia's arm tucked into his.

'Your sister wished to see you, Édouard,' explained Frederik. 'She's very concerned for your health, as am I. May we enter?'

'Of course.'

Édouard watched as Frederik, tender as a father, steered Sophia towards the bed and sat her down.

'Oh, brother, what happened?' Sophia felt for his hand and clasped it, her face a mask of fear. 'Are you badly hurt?'

'No, my dearest. As I said, it's only a flesh wound. There was a skirmish and I was caught in the middle of it.' Édouard was aware that every word he uttered could be his death sentence, and his sister's. Yet Frederik's eyes were not fo-cused on him, or the tiny pieces of shrapnel which Sarah had painstakingly picked out of the wound and were lying on a dish on his bedside table. They were on Sophia, full of concern.

'Yes, I hear there were a number of raids in the city tonight.' At this point, Frederik moved his eyeline to Édouard and the two men glanced at each other. 'Now, I must leave you. Please, Édouard, if there's anything you need, you can call me directly on my private line at Gestapo headquarters. Here, I'll write it down.' Frederik retrieved a pencil and paper from the inside of his jacket and wrote out his number. 'Goodnight, Sophia,' he said. 'Take care of your brother.' He kissed her hand gently, nodded at Édouard and left the room.

*   *   *

Connie had managed to return to Falk with a smile painted as falsely on her lips as the red vermillion adorning them. Falk ate heartily as Connie picked at her supper. He asked her more of her life before the war, about her home in St Raphaël and her plans for the future.

'I think it's difficult for us all to plan further ahead until this war reaches a conclusion,' she said as Falk refilled her wine glass.

'But the conclusion is inevitable, is it not?' Falk's eyes bored into her.

'Of course,' Connie replied quickly, 'but until the French people understand what is best for them, these are dangerous times.'

'Yes, quite so.' Falk was pacified. 'So, what of your cousin, Édouard? He's an interesting man, is he not?'

'He is indeed interesting,' Connie replied blandly.

'A member of the French bourgeoisie, with a family history stretching back hundreds of years. A family tree full of men of valour, who have risked their lives defending the country they love.'

'His family has indeed been full of brave men,' she agreed.

'And yet, Édouard has been able to switch allegiance to Germany and its growing Empire. I've often wondered how, and why, such a man as he should do this?' Falk pondered, still holding Connie's eye.

'Perhaps because he sees the future as you do,' she enthused. 'He knows that the old France cannot survive as it was, and he embraces the Führer's ethos.'

'Admittedly, our right-wing sentiments are beneficial to wealthy men such as he. But—' Falk sighed—'there have been occasions when others have doubted that his support for our cause is all it seems. His name has been linked to a certain undercover organisation of intellectuals and, lately, the Resistance. I, of course, have ignored these comments as gossip.'

'And you're right to do so, Falk. It seems no one in Paris is not under suspicion from time to time. Perhaps even myself!' Connie gave a small chuckle.

'No, Fräulein, I assure you that your record has no question marks against it. Is Édouard home this evening?' Falk enquired. 'Perhaps when we've finished here, I can speak with him, warn him that his name has been mentioned to me in a recent Resistance activity. After all, it's only what one friend must do for another. Édouard has offered great hospitality to myself and my brother.'

'Of course he'll be there, but it's so late, he will surely be in bed. Besides—' Connie steeled herself and put a light hand on Falk's forearm—'I thought tonight was for relaxation?' She tipped her head coyly and smiled at him flirtatiously.

Falk's eyes cleared and he banged the table. 'Yes! You're right. Tonight is for pleasure. Let us go and dance.'

Connie pressed her body hard against his as they swayed to the music. She accepted his caresses as though she'd been longing for them. She could feel his excitement against her thigh as he kissed her hard on the lips, his lizard-like tongue sweeping around her mouth.

'Let's go somewhere we can be alone,' Connie whispered into his ear, wishing to take Falk's mind off his suggestion of visiting Édouard.

'At once.'

Falk called for his car and they stepped into it. Having barked his address to the chauffeur, he lost no time in roughly exploring the parts of Connie's body that were within his grasp. Stopping in front of a bland apartment block a few minutes from Gestapo headquarters on the Avenue Foch, Falk dismissed the driver, pulled Connie inside and up in the lift to the second floor. As they entered the apartment, Connie was led hurriedly into a darkened bedroom.

'*Mein Gott!* I have waited for this ever since I set eyes on you.'

Tearing the clothes from her body and stopping only to remove his jacket, he threw her onto the bed and opened the zip of his trousers. Connie closed her eyes tightly to stop the tears as he forced his way inside her, kneading her breasts aggressively as he did so. She moved her hips up to meet his to indicate pleasure, so that perhaps this might be over faster.

She listened to him moaning expletives in German, his breath foul on her face. Her dry insides were screaming in pain as he continued to pummel her delicate inner flesh. Just as she was beginning to believe she would faint, Falk gave a roar, and collapsed on top of her.

As his breathing steadied, he propped himself up on one arm and looked down at her. 'For a French aristocrat, you fuck like a prostitute.' He rolled off her and closed his eyes.

Connie, lulled into a false sense of security, thanked God it had been over relatively quickly.

But ten minutes later, Falk was awake. He looked at her and started stroking himself. Grabbing her by the shoulders, he dragged her across the bed, tipping her off it roughly onto the floor. Swinging his own legs round, he positioned her between them.

'Herr Falk! Please, I—' She could speak no more as he forced himself into her mouth.

'You French bourgeoisie, you think you're superior to us.' Falk placed Connie's head in a vice-like grip as he thrust into her. 'But no, you women are all the same: whores and prostitutes!'

As the night wore on into a weary dawn, Connie was subjected to a series of degrading and unnatural sexual acts. And throughout, Falk's tirade on women continued. She cried, she begged, but her words fell on deaf ears as he continued to abuse her. At one point, when he'd turned her over and was invading virgin, intimate orifices not designed for the purpose, the agony was so great that Connie lost consciousness.

She woke to a dim light emanating from the window and found Falk was no longer in the room. Tears cascading down her cheeks, she collected her clothes, staggering dizzily as she did so, and dressed her bruised and bleeding body in them. She checked her watch and saw that it was just after six o'clock. Managing to stand, every step she took making her violated muscles scream indignantly, Connie opened the bedroom door. Looking desperately for the way out, she found herself in the sitting room.

She saw a photograph, one of the only adornments in the utilitarian space. It was of a woman, comely, plump and motherly, pictured with two cherubic young children—miniature facsimiles of Falk.

Connie staggered back to the bathroom to vomit, wiped her face and swallowed some water from the tap. Then she left the apartment.

23

As Connie stumbled through the front door of the de la Martinières house, Sarah greeted her.

'Madame, we've been waiting for you. Where have you been? What has happened to you?' she asked in horror, seeing Connie's dishevelled state.

Connie gave no reply, brushed past her and ran up the stairs. In the bathroom, she turned on the taps and stepped into the tub, scrubbing every part

313

of her body until it was red raw.

Downstairs, the doorbell rang again. This time, it was Frederik.

'I must see the Comte, Madame,' he said to Sarah.

'But he's still asleep.'

Again, Sarah was ignored as Frederik took the stairs two at a time and entered Édouard's bedroom.

Édouard, eyes bright with fever from a wound that was fast becoming infected, stared at him from his pillows in fear. He did not know immediately which brother it was.

'Monsieur le Comte, Édouard, I apologise for bursting in like this,' Frederik said hurriedly. 'But I come to warn you that you and your family are in grave danger. My brother has long suspected you of being part of the Resistance. He came to my office this morning and told me that one of his officers recognised you when members of the Psychology network were arrested at the Café de la Paix last night. He will come any minute to arrest you, your cousin and Sophia. Please, Monsieur, you must leave now,' Frederik implored. 'There's no time to lose.'

Édouard stared at Frederik in shocked fascination. 'But . . . why would you tell me this? How can I trust you?'

'Because you have no choice, and because I love your sister. Listen,' said Frederik, coming closer to the bed and staring down at Édouard, 'your hatred of our race is justified, but there are many of us who have had no choice but to take part in a cause in which we no longer believe. And many more are joining us. Édouard, just like you, I've used my

314

position in any way I can to minimise the amount of deaths. I, too, have links with those of your acquaintance, who fight to stop our beautiful countries from turning to rubble, and their history from being ground under the weight of Nazi boots. But now is not the time to talk of this. You must get up and leave the house immediately.'

Édouard shook his head. 'I cannot, Frederik. Look at me, I'm sick. It is the ladies who must leave. I would be too noticeable and hinder their escape.'

'Frederik!' Sophia stood at the door, searching for her lover's whereabouts. 'What's happening?'

He walked swiftly towards her and held her against him. 'Don't worry, my Sophia, I'll make sure you're safe. I'm telling your brother that this household is under suspicion and that the Gestapo will be here at any moment. You must leave immediately, *mein Liebling*.'

'Sarah has already packed for me. My brother told her to do so last night. We are ready. Édouard, now you must rouse yourself and dress,' Sophia called to him.

'I have the car downstairs. I can take you anywhere you wish to go in Paris,' added Frederik. 'But we must leave now.'

'Surely, Frederik, you put yourself in great danger by doing this?' said Édouard as he tried to sit up but, failing, fell back onto the pillows.

'We do what we must for those we love,' said Frederik, still clasping Sophia to him.

Sophia pulled herself from his grasp and made her way towards the bed, feeling for Édouard's hand and then his forehead. 'You have a fever, but you must get up! Dear God, Frederik says they will

315

be here at any second!'

'Sophia, you know very well it's impossible for me to travel,' Édouard stated as calmly as he could. 'But please believe I will find a way to reach you. You'll have Sarah and Constance with you on your journey and I'll follow as soon as I can. Now, go!'

'But I can't leave you . . .'

'For once you will do as you are told, Sophia! God speed, my beloved sister, and I pray we will meet again soon.' Édouard reached up and kissed her on both cheeks, then signalled to Frederik to take Sophia from the bedroom. The door closed behind them and Édouard tried to turn his feverish mind to a plan.

Downstairs, Sarah and Connie were waiting for them. Frederik led them out to the car and they climbed inside.

Édouard, painfully upright now, watched them from the window as Frederik drove off.

*   *   *

'Where should I take you?' asked Frederik, looking strange in his chauffeur's cap.

'Gare de Montparnasse. We'll first go to my sister's house where we can obtain new papers,' said Sarah, the only one of the three women who was in a fit state to answer.

'And then where will you go?' he asked.

Connie shot Sarah such a look that she closed her mouth and remained silent. Sophia, who couldn't see this, said, 'We will travel down to our family château in Gassin.'

Frederik caught Connie's look of horror in his

316

mirror. 'Constance, I know it's impossible for you to trust a German. But please believe that I risk a lot too, simply by doing what I have done so far. It would be easy for me to arrest all three of you now and take you straight to Gestapo headquarters. I can assure you my actions this morning will not remain unnoticed. This may well be my death sentence.'

'Yes,' agreed Connie, her nerves still in shreds from the past few hours. 'I apologise, Frederik, and I appreciate your help.'

'Even though we share the same blood, I'm very different from my twin,' Frederik continued. 'Doubtless he will suspect me of aiding your escape and will do all he can to convince others of my actions, too.'

At Montparnasse station, the three women climbed out of the car. Frederik handed them their suitcases from the boot.

'Good luck to you all,' he breathed quietly.

Sophia made a move to touch him, but he stopped her. 'No, I'm the chauffeur, remember? But, *mein Liebling*, I swear to you I will come and find you soon. Now, get out of Paris as fast as you can.'

'I love you, Frederik,' Sophia told him urgently, before they joined the crowds in the station.

'I love you too, my Sophia. With all my heart,' Frederik murmured as he climbed back into the car.

*   *   *

Falk arrived at the de la Martinières house on the Rue de Varenne one hour after the women had

317

left. There was no answer to his banging on the front door, so he had his storm troopers break it down. Scouring the house from top to bottom, he and his men found it deserted.

Swearing under his breath, Falk left the house to return to headquarters.

As he walked into Frederik's office, he saw that his brother was packing his briefcase to leave for Germany.

'I've just called on the de la Martinières household to arrest them. It seems they have vanished. It's as if someone warned them. How can this be?' Falk asked, fury on his face. 'The only one I told of my suspicions was you, brother.'

Frederik clicked the clasp on his briefcase shut. 'Really? That is indeed troubling. But as you always say, in Paris, walls have ears.'

Falk leant closer. 'I know it was you—do you think I'm stupid?! You make me look like a fool when it's *you* who's the traitor to the cause. And I know this is not the first time. You should watch out, big brother,' he sneered. 'For all your clever words and ideas, which you use to confuse others into believing your loyalty, I know who you really are.'

Frederik stared back across the desk, his eyes benign. 'Then, brother, you must speak of what you know. I will say goodbye now. I'm sure we will meet again soon.'

'Attchh!' As always, Frederik's calm superiority irritated Falk to breaking point. 'You think you're so much higher than me, with your degrees and your doctorates and the paper plans you've drawn up to impress our Führer. But it is I who works tirelessly every day for the cause.'

Frederik lifted his briefcase from the desk and walked towards the door. He stopped and turned back in afterthought. 'It's not me who thinks I'm high, brother, but you who believes you are low.'

'I'll find them!' Falk called down the corridor after him as he left the room. 'And that whore you're so entranced by!'

'Goodbye, Falk,' Frederik sighed as the lift removed him from sight.

Falk slammed his fist full-force into the office door.

*　　*　　*

Édouard awoke from a feverish sleep. It was pitch black and he felt for the matches he had brought with him. He lit one to look at his watch and saw it was past three o'clock; five hours since he had heard the storm troopers enter the house above him. He moved his stiff limbs to stretch them and his feet touched the wall on the other side of the confined space.

This tiny brick hole, deep under the ground, accessed from an invisible trapdoor in the cellar, had been dug originally to protect his ancestors during the Revolution. There was only enough space for one or two people. Although legend had it that one particular night, as Paris burned above them and aristocrats were taken by the dozen on open carts to face the guillotine, Arnaud de la Martinières, his wife and two children had taken shelter here.

Édouard crouched on his knees as he lit another match to locate the edge of the trapdoor above him. And, finding it, used what little energy he had left to release it.

Hauling himself out into the cellar, he lay on the damp stone floor, panting in agony. Dragging himself across to the cupboard where flagons of water were kept for the nights the air-raid sirens forced them down here to shelter, Édouard took some large gulps. Shivering and sweating in equal measure, he looked down and saw that liquid from the wound on his shoulder was seeping through his shirt, the fluid tinged with yellow. He needed medical help urgently or the infection would slowly poison his blood. But that was an impossibility. He knew they would be watching the house to see if anyone returned. He was trapped.

Édouard thought of his sister and only prayed that she, Sarah and Connie were now on their way to safety.

He looked up to the rough, cracked ceiling of the cellar, but it swam in front of his eyes. So he closed them, and found comfort in sleep.

*   *   *

Connie was only too glad that Sarah had taken charge. As they sat in their First Class carriage, she closed her eyes to block out the faces of the two German officers sitting opposite. Sarah made polite conversation with them and Connie was grateful for the older woman's calming presence. Sophia was silent, staring sightlessly out of the window as they passed through the industrialised outer reaches of Paris as the train headed south. If she lived or died, Connie thought, what did it matter? Last night, her very soul had been violated; she had been treated as an animal—a useless bag of flesh and bones, degraded beyond endurance.

How could she ever face Lawrence again? And what had it been for? She had fought to protect Édouard, to give him the night to make plans of escape. But Édouard was still in Paris, alone and wounded. Even now, perhaps he was in Falk's clutches at Gestapo headquarters.

'I tried, Édouard,' she cried silently.

Exhausted, Connie dozed as the train pulled its passengers into the flatness of the French countryside. At every station, she felt Sarah tense up next to her, her eyes alert for Gestapo who may have been warned about their flight south. The officers opposite them left the train at Le Mans and, whilst the enclosed compartment was empty of other travellers, Sarah spoke in hushed tones to her two charges.

'We'll leave the train at Amiens and stay with my sister nearby, where we can buy new identity papers. Édouard arranged last night for us to be met there by a friend of his who will take us over the Vichy Line. It's too risky for us to cross at an official checkpoint. Undoubtedly, by now, Colonel Falk will have alerted the authorities to be on the lookout for us.'

Sophia's sightless eyes gazed in fear at Sarah. 'But I thought we were going down to the château?'

'We are.' Sarah took her hand and patted it. 'Do not worry, my dear, all is well.'

Hours later, as night was falling, the three women left the train. Sarah strode confidently through the narrow streets of the town, approached the front door of a village house and knocked on it.

A woman of similar appearance to Sarah opened the door and looked at her in surprise and delight.

'Florence,' said Sarah, 'thank God you're at home!'

'What are you doing here? Quickly, come inside.' Florence glanced at the two women accompanying her. 'And your friends.'

Once the door was closed, Florence led them to a table in the small kitchen and sat them down, fussing over them, and disappearing to bring a jug of wine and some bread and cheese.

'Who is Florence?' asked Sophia imperiously.

'She's my sister, Sophia,' said Sarah, her eyes dancing with happiness at the reunion. 'And this town is where I grew up.'

Connie sat at the table sipping her wine and listening to the two sisters talking. Her body was still protesting from the brutality of the night before. She forced the bread and cheese down her throat and did her best to blank out the dreadful pictures that kept appearing in her head.

Florence was talking of how the Gestapo had recently rounded up a number of young men from the village and shipped them to labour camps in Germany, in retaliation for the Resistance blowing up a railway bridge very close to the town. In return, Sarah spoke of Paris and her employer, Édouard, whose fate was currently unknown.

'At least you're all safe with me here tonight,' Florence said, patting her sister's hand. 'But we'll put your two friends up in the attic, just to be sure.' She glanced over to Sophia, who sat at the table, her bread and cheese untouched. 'You must forgive me, Mademoiselle de la Martinières, if the accommodation does not compare with what you're used to.'

'Madame, I'm simply grateful that you provide a roof over our heads tonight. And at risk to yourself. My brother, I'm sure, will reward you if—' Sophia's eyes filled with tears and Sarah put an arm around her shoulder.

'My Sophia, I've known Édouard since he was a seed in your mother's stomach. He will have found a way, I know it here.' Sarah thumped her breast.

Later, Sophia and Connie were shown upstairs to the attic, Sarah helping Sophia climb the steep stairs, then undressing her and tucking her into bed as if she were still a small child.

'Sleep well, my dear.' Sarah kissed Sophia. 'Goodnight, Madame Constance.'

When Sarah had left, Connie undressed, not daring to look down at what she knew would be a mass of ugly black bruises, and pulled her nightshirt over her head. She climbed into her narrow bed, grateful to rest her aching body, and pulled the patchwork quilt around her, feeling the bitterness of the December night.

'Sleep well, Sophia,' she called.

'I'll try,' came the reply, 'but I'm so cold, and my thoughts are with my brother. Oh, Constance, how can I bear it? I've lost Édouard and Frederik in the same day.'

The sound of pitiful tears encouraged Connie to leave her own bed and walk over to Sophia's. 'Here, move over, I'll climb in with you to warm you up.'

Sophia did so, snuggling into Connie's open arms.

'We must both believe that Édouard is safe and will find a way to come to us,' said Connie with a conviction she did not feel. Eventually, both women fell into a troubled sleep, their bodies huddled together for warmth and comfort.

*   *   *

Édouard saw his mother standing over him. He was seven years old and she was urging him to drink some water because he had a fever.

'Maman, you're here,' he murmured, smiling at her wonderful, comforting presence. Then her face changed and she was Falk, wearing a Nazi uniform, pointing a gun at his chest . . .

Édouard woke with a jump and groaned as he saw the cellar ceiling above him. He needed water desperately—the thirst he felt was unbearable. But when he ordered his body to move towards the cupboard containing the flagons, it would not obey him.

As he fell in and out of consciousness, he accepted that death would soon be upon him. And he would be glad of it. He only wished he could know before he died that his treasured sister was safe.

'Dear God,' he rasped, 'take me, but let her live . . . let her live.'

And now, again, he knew he was hallucinating as his soul prepared to depart his body, for an angel with raven hair was hovering above him, placing a blissfully cool cloth on his fevered brow and dripping water between his parched lips. Something on a spoon, which tasted unpleasant, was being forced down his throat. He gagged, but

324

swallowed and fell asleep again. The same dream persisted endlessly as the angel stayed with him. At some point, he felt the angel heaving him onto a bed and he began to feel calmer, cooler and more comfortable.

And then he awoke to find the cracked ceiling of the cellar still above him, but no longer spinning and blurred. For the first time, it looked solid. So, Édouard thought miserably, he was still not dead, but trapped in the hopelessness of life.

'Don't tell me you've actually woken up!' said a female voice from beside him.

He turned his head and stared up into a pair of beautiful green eyes. The pale face that surrounded them was fringed by a jet-black halo of hair. This was the angel he had dreamed of. Yet, in fact, she was a living, breathing woman, who somehow seemed to have found her way into his cellar.

'Who—' Édouard cleared his throat to find his distant voice—'are you?'

'Which name would you prefer?' The eyes glinted in amusement. 'I have a number I can offer you. My official name here is Claudette Dessally, but you may call me Venetia.'

'Venetia . . .' The name rang a far-away bell in Édouard's exhausted mind.

'And you, Sir, I presume, are Édouard, le Comte de la Martinières? The owner and, at present, lone resident of this house?'

'Yes, but how can you be here? I . . .'

'It's a long story.' Venetia waved the question away airily. 'We can talk about that later when you're stronger. All you need to know for now is that when I found you, you were on the brink of death. Somehow, and not being renowned for my nursing skills, I've managed to save your life. I'm rather proud of that.' She grinned as she stood up and seized a flagon of water from the cupboard and put it down next to him. 'Drink as much as you can. I'm going to endeavour to warm some soup on this gas hob. Although, I warn you in advance, my cooking skills are even worse than my nursing!'

Édouard tried to focus on the slim body of the young woman kneeling over the gas flame, but his eyes closed once more.

Later, when he woke again, she was still there, sitting by him in a chair reading a book.

'Hello . . .' She smiled. 'I hope you don't mind, but I nipped upstairs and found the library. It's been pretty tedious down here in the past few days.'

Édouard was immediately on the alert. He tried to sit up but she stopped him, shaking her head. 'Please, relax. I swear that nobody saw me, even though they're still watching the house. Take comfort in the fact I was trained especially for this kind of thing. I'm one of the best,' she announced proudly.

'Please, tell me who you are? And how you found me?' he begged.

'I did tell you my name is Venetia, and I'll explain everything, if you promise to drink every bit of this soup. Your infection seems to have gone, but you're still very weak and need to build up your strength.' Venetia stood up and retrieved the tin saucepan, then she sat down on the bed and spooned it into his mouth.

'I know,' she commented as Édouard's face twisted in disgust. 'It's gone a little cold. I did warm it up earlier for you, but you fell asleep before you could drink it.'

Édouard refused more than a few spoonfuls, his stomach complaining at the sudden influx and threatening to protest.

'Right.' Venetia put the saucepan down on the stone floor. 'I'm not good with vomit, so we'll have to leave it until later.'

'Now, will you tell me how you found me?' Édouard begged, desperate to know how this woman had saved his life.

'I'm sure you'll be jolly annoyed if I tell you but, on the other hand, if I hadn't tipped up here, you wouldn't be having this conversation now. With me, or anyone else for that matter,' she added. 'I'm an SOE wireless operator. When most of my network were arrested, I tracked Connie down— we trained together in Blighty—and begged her to let me use this cellar to transmit urgent messages home to London. And you should be very glad I did, Édouard, as it was the night before the raid on the STO office, which I happen to know you were heavily involved in organising.' Venetia raised an eyebrow. 'Whilst I was here, I removed the key to the cellar door—' she pointed to it—'just in case I needed to find sanctuary again. And after the night of the Café de la Paix when, as you know, many operatives were rounded up, this is where I ran to hide. Of course, when I got here, I realised that the house had been raided. So I bided my time, and when I saw the patrol outside nip off for supper, I hopped in through the garden, opened the cellar door and found you half-dead on the floor.'

Édouard listened without surprise. 'I see.'

327

'Don't be miffed with Connie, please,' Venetia added. 'She was only trying to do the job she'd been sent here to do. And, all in all, given where you and I are now, the fact she did help me has proved a blessing in disguise.'

Édouard felt too exhausted to ask for further details. His shoulder ached and he altered his position to try to make himself more comfortable. 'Thank you for saving my life,' he said.

'God bless iodine,' smiled Venetia, 'and the fact there's a houseful of supplies up above us. Your wound seems to be healing well, but you must have a pretty strong constitution. Perhaps it's all that wonderful food you and your Boche friends eat. I hope you don't mind, but I raided the fridge last night and enjoyed a wonderful foie gras sarnie.'

'Venetia, you understand, of course, that the enemy I entertained here are not my friends,' Édouard said pointedly.

'Course I do. Only teasing.' She grinned at him.

'You know,' Édouard sighed, 'the reason I came to the café that night was because your friend, Constance, had been told by a Gestapo officer there was to be a raid there. She was insisting on going herself to try and warn you, but I came instead. I was too late, as it happens. And I got shot for my trouble.'

'Well, there we are then. You tried to save my life, and I've saved yours. We're quits,' Venetia said, nodding. 'Mind if I smoke?'

'No.' Édouard shook his head and Venetia lit up a Gauloise. 'Are they still watching the house?'

'No. They left a couple of hours ago and haven't returned. The Boche have got enough problems without wasting time on birds they presume have already flown the nest. By the way, where is Constance?' Venetia enquired.

'She left with my sister and her maid the morning after the raid,' Édouard explained. 'I sent them off down south but, of course, I have no idea where they are at present.'

'Where are they headed?' asked Venetia.

Édouard eyed her. 'I would prefer to say nothing.'

'Oh, please!' Venetia looked insulted at his words. 'I think it's pretty obvious we're on the same side. And I know now exactly who you are. The Resistance speak your name in reverential tones. The fact that your cover has been blown is a huge loss to the cause. And I apologise for my part in that. But it's a tribute to you that you've managed to keep it for so long. I think, Hero—' Venetia emphasised Édouard's code name—'you'll have to leave the country as soon as possible. You're almost certainly top priority on the Gestapo's "wanted" list at present.'

'I can't do that. My sister is blind and therefore extremely vulnerable. If the Gestapo get hold of her to try and discover my whereabouts . . .' Édouard shuddered. 'I can hardly bear to think of it.'

'I presume you've sent them into hiding?'

'We had little time to discuss anything,' Édouard sighed, 'but they know where they're headed.'

'Well, your sister's in very capable hands. Constance was the star pupil on the SOE training course,' comforted Venetia.

'Yes, Constance is an exceptional woman,' Édouard agreed. 'And what of you, Venetia? Where do you go from here?'

'Well, unfortunately, when I made my escape from the safe house, I had to leave my wireless behind. London are aware and are presently organising another for me. I've been told to lie low for a while. So, here I am, making myself useful playing nurse to you.' She smiled.

Édouard looked at Venetia in admiration. Her spirit was unbroken, despite the danger she faced. 'You're a very brave young woman, and we're lucky to have you,' he said weakly.

'Well, thank you, kind sir.' Venetia batted her eyelids at him. 'Only doing my job. And what can you do but laugh? The world's in such a mess, so I try to live every day as though it's my last. Because it might well be,' she added. 'I try to see it all as one awfully big adventure.'

She smiled brightly, but Édouard could see the suffering in her eyes.

'Now, I reckon that in a few days' time you might be strong enough to think about your plan of escape,' Venetia suggested. 'If you're happy for me to do so, I can involve my lot in the operation of removing you from France. But for the moment, as we're stuck here, I'm going to nip upstairs, get another book and use the lavvy. At some point, you could do with a decent wash.' Venetia wrinkled her nose. 'I'm afraid I draw the line at a bed bath. Anything you want, Édouard?'

'No, thank you, Venetia. Take care up there,' he called as she climbed the stairs which led up to the house.

'Don't worry, I will,' she replied airily.

Édouard lay back, exhausted, and thanked God that, through a series of lucky coincidences, this extraordinary woman had walked into his life and

330

saved him.

24

Sarah had advised the following morning that the three of them must stay where they were for the time being.

'We must wait for the next crossing over the river,' she explained to Connie over breakfast the next morning. 'Now, Madame Constance, I suggest that your new papers show you are a housekeeper from Provençe. Is there any name you would prefer to use?'

'Hélène Latour?' Connie suggested, thinking of the daughter of her aunt's neighbour, whom she had played with on the beach long ago in St Raphaël.

'Then Sophia can be your sister, Claudine. Of course—' Sarah lowered her voice—'when we arrive at our destination, Sophia must go into hiding. There are too many local people who will recognise her.'

'Surely the Boche are bound to come looking for us there?' said Connie. 'Falk knew all about the château.'

'Édouard has told me there's a place where we can hide Sophia and keep her safe. Of course, it would be better if we could all leave the country immediately, but with Sophia's disability the escape route would be far too arduous for her. And at least at the château we'll only be relying on ourselves. Even safe houses are no longer safe. The Gestapo pay a great deal of money for information regarding any neighbours they suspect of housing people like us. So just in case they do visit us, you and I will change our appearance for the photograph on our papers.' Sarah brandished a bottle of peroxide at Connie. 'You think you have a problem,' she chuckled, seeing Connie's face. 'My hair is to turn red! And then we must do something about Mademoiselle Sophia's clothes. They're too fine and will draw attention to her.'

Connie looked at her in amazement. 'Sarah,' she said, 'you are a true professional. How do you know what to do?'

'My husband worked with the Maquis for two years, until he was caught and shot by the Gestapo. And I, of course, have assisted the Comte with his many dangerous missions. It's a question of survival. When you have to, you learn quickly. Now—' Sarah indicated the latrine at the back of the house which also held a small sink—'you must wet your hair before you apply the peroxide.'

As Connie left for the outside facilities with the bottle in her hand, she felt humbled. For all her grand training, Sarah, a simple serving woman, was far more equipped to deal with the situation than she.

*   *   *

Two days later, when Connie had glimpsed the third German patrol car cruising down the narrow street in as many hours, Sarah came to her and said they were leaving that night.

'I cannot put my sister in danger any longer,' she added. 'So, we have our new papers and will move on. Everything is organised for this evening.'

'Right.' Connie nodded and glanced at a listless Sophia, who was sitting at the kitchen table. She seemed lost in a world of her own, not equipped by birth or physicality to deal with what was happening to her. Connie reached towards her and squeezed her hand. 'We're leaving this evening, my dear, and you'll soon be at the home you've talked so much about,' she comforted.

Sophia responded with a nod, wretchedness emanating from her. She was dressed in peasant attire, a thick beige woollen cardigan accentuating her paleness. Connie had hardly seen her eat since they'd arrived and on more than one occasion had accompanied her to the outside toilet and stood by as she vomited. Even when they had crossed over the Vichy Line safely, Connie knew they had hundreds of kilometres to journey before they reached sanctuary. Connie prayed Sophia would survive it. She was obviously extremely unwell.

* * *

At ten o'clock that night, Connie, Sarah and Sophia joined six others huddled together on the bank of the River Saône. They were loaded onto a flat-bottomed boat, Connie climbing in first and Sarah carefully handing Sophia down to her. As the boat set off in complete blackness on its short journey to the other side of the river, no one spoke. When they reached the opposite bank, the passengers disembarked silently and scampered off immediately across the frozen field, disappearing into the night.

'Take Sophia's hand and I'll take the other,' instructed Sarah. 'Sophia, you have to run with us now, for we must not be spotted out here.'

'But where are we going?' whispered Sophia as

the two women guided her across the field as fast as they could. 'It's so cold, I can hardly feel my feet.'

Sarah, breathless, her plump body not used to physical exercise, did not waste breath replying.

Finally, Connie saw a flickering light shining in the distance.

Sarah's pace slowed as the outline of a building came into view. The light Connie had seen was an oil lamp, hanging from a nail on the side of a barn.

'We're to shelter in here for the night until dawn breaks.' Sarah pushed open the door of the barn and unhooked the lamp from its nail to take it inside with her. In the dim light, Connie could see the bales of hay stacked around her.

'There now—' Sarah led Sophia to a bale at the back of the barn and sat her down on it, still panting from the exertion—'at least it's dry and safe in here.'

'We're to sleep in a barn?' said Sophia, horrified. 'All night?'

Connie almost laughed out loud at her outrage. This was a woman who had laid on the best of horsehair mattresses and feather-filled pillows for almost every night of her life.

'Yes, and we must all make the best of it,' said Sarah. 'Now, you lie down and I'll make you a warm bed of hay.'

When Sophia was finally settled in the hay bale, Sarah lay down next to her. 'You too must sleep, Madame Constance,' she called to her. 'We have a long, hard journey ahead of us. But before I forget, just in case anything should happen to me, take this.' Sarah passed Connie a slip of paper. 'It's the address of the de la Martinières's château. When you arrive, go directly to the *cave* in the grounds of the domaine. Jacques Benoit, so Édouard says, will be expecting you. Goodnight.'

Connie read the address, committed it to memory, then lit a match and burned it, grateful for the fleeting warmth on her fingertips. Burying herself in the hay, Connie clasped her hands about her shoulders and prayed for morning to come soon.

*   *   *

When Connie awoke, she saw that Sarah's hay bed was already empty. Sophia was still fast asleep. She went out of the barn and round to the side to relieve herself, then saw Sarah coming back with a horse and cart clopping behind her.

'This is Pierre, the farmer from next door, and he's been persuaded to take us down to the station in Limoges. It's too dangerous to board the train any closer to here,' Sarah said.

Sophia was roused and eventually helped on top of one of the bales of hay in the back of the cart. The driver, a weather-beaten, silent Frenchman, set off.

'These people, they get greedier the longer the war continues,' grumbled Sarah. 'Even though I explained to him the young lady in my care is blind, he still charges me a fortune for the ride. But at least I'm assured he can be trusted.'

Connie thought what a pleasant journey this would make in high summer, as the horse and cart clopped through the fields of Burgundy. In a few months' time, the now-frozen ground would be full of burgeoning vines. They travelled for four cold and uncomfortable hours until the farmer stopped just outside the town of Limoges and turned to them: 'I must leave you here, I dare not go any further.'

'Thank you, Monsieur,' replied Sarah wearily. The three of them climbed off and began the walk towards the centre of the town.

'I am so tired . . . and faint,' moaned Sophia as the two women on either side of her took most of her weight.

'Not much further, my dear, and we'll be on the train that will take us all the way to Marseilles,' comforted Sarah.

At the station, Sarah purchased the rail tickets and they went to a café just by the entrance. Connie sipped her warm coffee gratefully and chewed on a baguette, even though it was stale. Sophia picked up her coffee, then gagged and pushed it away. On the platform, having sat Sophia down on a bench, Sarah moved away out of earshot to speak with Connie.

'She's not at all well, is she, Sarah?' Connie said anxiously. 'And she's been like this for weeks now, so it can't simply be the shock and the hardship of the journey.'

'You're right. That's not the problem,' replied Sarah grimly. 'Unfortunately, it's much more serious than that. Look at her: so pale, so often sick . . . did you not see her push her coffee away just now because she cannot stand the smell? Madame, what do these symptoms indicate to you?'

It took a while for Connie to register what Sarah was implying. She put her hand to her mouth. 'You're suggesting that . . . ?'

337

'I'm not suggesting,' said Sarah, 'I *know*. Remember, I must help Mademoiselle Sophia with many things. And there has been no bleeding for weeks.'

'She's pregnant?' Connie whispered the words in horror.

'Yes, but I don't know when it could have happened,' Sarah sighed. 'I can't think of an occasion on which the two of them were unchaperoned for long enough to . . .' Sarah's words trailed off in disgust. 'But I do not doubt it's the truth. She has every symptom of being with child.'

With a sinking heart, Connie knew *exactly* when the opportunity had presented itself, and it had been on her watch. But not for a moment had she even dreamed that Sophia, being from the background she was, could have done such a thing. She was so innocent . . . a child . . .

No, Connie corrected herself. Sophia was a woman, full of the same dreams and physical desires as any other—the same age as Connie herself. It was the de la Martinières household, including herself, who had treated her as a child. And—Connie's stomach turned at the ramifications of the news Sarah had just imparted—she knew the baby's father was a high-ranking German officer in the SS.

'Sarah,' Connie turned to her, 'I cannot think the circumstances could be much worse.'

'No,' Sarah agreed. 'It's bad enough she finds herself pregnant out of wedlock, but if anyone discovers the father's identity . . .' Sarah's voice tailed off, too distressed to continue.

'At least nobody else knows,' comforted Connie

as the train pulled into the station and they walked back towards Sophia.

'Madame, you will learn that there is always somebody who does,' sighed Sarah. 'And will tell what they know. We must simply concentrate on getting Sophia to a place of safety and then we can decide what's best to do.'

Rather than the luxury of First Class, the three women boarded into Third Class as befitted their lowly status. The crowded carriage was dirty and smelt of stale bodies. Eventually, the train pulled out and Connie sighed with relief. Every step they took was one nearer to sanctuary.

At each station, Connie's body tensed. Germans were swarming down to Marseilles, fearing invasions from the south of the country, and the platforms were full of troops. The carriage was unheated and uncomfortable, though she could see that both Sarah and Sophia had managed to sleep. Apart from the fear of being apprehended, every time Connie closed her eyes the horror of three nights ago continued to assail her senses.

At the station before Marseilles, the ticket collector passed by, warning that the Germans were on board, checking papers on the train. Connie's heart thudded in her chest as she roused the others to warn them. Everyone in the carriage was braced for danger, the scent of fear palpable. Connie wondered, as she looked at the motley collection of humanity, just how many other passengers were travelling illegally.

A German officer entered the carriage and barked for everyone to produce their papers. All eyes were on him as he checked each row of passengers. Sarah, Sophia and herself were in the last row and the agony of waiting for him to reach them seemed endless.

'Fräulein, papers!' he snapped at Sarah, who sat on the end of the row.

'Of course, Monsieur.' Sarah handed them to him with a friendly smile. He perused them then looked up at her.

'Where were these papers issued, Fräulein?'

'At the *mairie*, in my local town of Chalon.'

He read them again then shook his head. 'These papers are forged, Fräulein. They do not have the correct stamp on them. Stand up!'

Sarah stood, shaking with fear, and the German pulled his gun out of his holster and stuck it in her stomach.

'Monsieur, I'm an innocent citizen, I do no harm, please . . . I—'

'*Aus!* Out now!'

As Sarah was marched off the train at gunpoint, she did not turn back towards Sophia and Connie. Any signal that they had been travelling together and they too could have been arrested. A few seconds later, the whistle blew and the train moved on.

Everyone in the carriage was staring at where Sarah had been sitting. Connie squeezed Sophia's hand hard to warn her to say nothing, and gave a nonchalant shrug to the others in the carriage. The woman had simply been another passenger sitting next to them.

At Marseilles, the two of them left the train to wait for their connection to Toulon. Connie sat Sophia down on a bench on the platform.

'My God! Constance,' Sophia breathed in desperation, 'where will they take Sarah? What

340

will happen to her?'

'I don't know, Sophia,' Connie replied, trying to remain calm, 'but there was nothing either of us could have done. At least I trust Sarah not to say a word about us, or who she works for in Paris. She loves you and your family so very much.'

'Oh, Constance, she's been with me since I was born,' cried Sophia. 'How will I cope without her?'

'You have me with you,' Connie said, patting her hand. 'And I'll take care of you, I promise.'

When the train for Toulon arrived, Connie stepped on with trepidation. If Sarah's papers had been noticeably forged, then theirs were too. And it was only by chance that Sarah's were looked at first and theirs hadn't been checked afterwards. As the train chugged east across Provençe and towards the Côte d'Azur, Connie had to face the fact that the protective arm of Sarah was no longer around her. Sophia's safety, and her own, now depended entirely on her.

*   *   *

'How are we today?' Venetia asked as she brought Édouard some coffee and placed it by his bed. 'We've run out of milk. I'm afraid I've used up all the tinned stuff I found in the cupboard upstairs.'

'I'm better, thank you, Venetia,' Édouard said, nodding.

In the past two days, Édouard had done little more than sleep and eat whatever sustenance Venetia had offered him to try to regain his strength. But, today, his brain was alert and he definitely felt he was on the mend.

'Good,' said Venetia. 'Time for a bath, methinks.

341

A good wash always makes you feel more human and will please those who are currently sharing the same quarters with you.' She wrinkled her nose to emphasise the point.

'You think it's safe to go upstairs?' Édouard asked.

'Yes, perfectly. Besides, the bathroom is at the back of the house and has shutters. I've enjoyed a candlelit soak every night so far. Heaven!' Venetia stretched and smiled. 'Now, drink your coffee and I'll go and run it for you.'

An hour later, after a long soak, Édouard was indeed feeling refreshed. Venetia had procured some clothes from his bedroom and had applied a fresh bandage to his healing wound.

'Goodness, Édouard!' Venetia commented as he walked down the cellar steps. 'You're awfully tall when you're upright. Now, I think I'll have to venture out as we're down to the cat food in the kitchen. And even I have my limits.' She smiled.

'No, let me go,' he urged.

'Don't be silly, Édouard. I'm practised at melting into a crowd, whereas you, Monsieur le Comte, unfortunately stick out like a sore thumb. Leave it to me. I'll be back in a jiffy.'

Before Édouard could stop her, Venetia left by the cellar door, but was back twenty minutes later with two fresh baguettes. For the first time, he ate hungrily and thought the return of his appetite a very good sign.

'I've been in touch with my network and they're coming up with a plan to get you out of France as soon as possible,' Venetia explained. 'How do you fancy a sojourn in London? My people have been in touch with De Gaulle's Free French headquarters over there. They would all very much like the pleasure of your company and a debrief. If we can get you over there in one piece, of course. Just a shame you're so tall,' Venetia added, 'your height makes you far more difficult to conceal.'

'But what about my sister, Sophia? And your friend, Constance?' Édouard shook his head. 'No, I can't simply abandon them and escape myself!'

'To be blunt, Édouard, for your sister's sake, it's probably the best thing you can do,' Venetia stated. 'As I've mentioned, you're high on the Boche's "most wanted" list at present. And we're all hoping your sojourn won't be for long; plans are still moving forward for the Allied invasion.'

'I wish, in retrospect, that I'd kept Sophia here in Paris with me,' Édouard sighed.

'Well, there's no turning back now,' Venetia said stoically. 'I've managed to send a message down south to alert our friends there to your sister's imminent arrival. They'll be looking out for her and will assist in any way they can.'

'Thank you, Venetia,' Édouard said gratefully. 'I sent them in good faith, presuming I would be able to follow on.'

'Well, you can't, and that's that,' Venetia replied briskly. 'I saw your face on a fly poster when I was out. You're famous in Paris, Édouard. You must leave the country as soon as you can.'

'Then you'll take a risk in helping me.'

'No more than usual.' Venetia raised her eyebrows and grinned. 'But it's time we moved on before our luck runs out. We'll be leaving tomorrow.'

Édouard nodded reluctantly. 'It goes without saying that I appreciate everything you've done

343

and are doing for me.'

'Well, "Hero",' Venetia replied brusquely to hide her emotion, 'from what I hear, given the countless lives you've saved in the past four years, it's my honour.'

*　　　*　　　*

Connie pulled a weary Sophia from the train at Toulon station. It was pouring with rain and pitch black as they emerged from the platform. Connie went to the ticket office and spoke through the grille to the clerk behind it.

'Excuse me, Monsieur, but when is the next train along the coast to Gassin?'

'Tomorrow morning at ten o'clock,' the clerk rasped.

'I see. Then would you know of a hotel where we could stay for the night?'

'Turn left and there's a place on the corner of this street,' said the clerk, looking at Connie's dishevelled appearance and snapping down his blind.

Connie took hold of Sophia's arm and they trudged along the street until they reached the hotel the clerk had suggested, both of them now drenched by the torrential rain.

Inside, at least the hotel was warm, if shabby. Connie was offered a room at a price that would normally secure accommodation at the Ritz, and helped an exhausted and dripping Sophia upstairs. An hour later, after both women had washed and dried themselves as best they could in the limited facilities, Connie led Sophia into the small restaurant and sat her down.

'Nearly home,' said Connie comfortingly. 'Please, Sophia, try to eat something.'

Both of them picked at their food, Connie thinking of Sarah, Édouard and Venetia. She told herself how lucky she and Sophia were to be at least free, warm and dry tonight. Besides, this was the kind of operation she'd been trained for and she must finally prove her worth.

A voice broke into her thoughts: 'You are travelling far, Madame?'

She turned and saw a young man sitting at the table next to her, watching them both with interest.

'We're returning home,' Connie replied cautiously. 'We live further along the coast.'

'Ah, the Côte d'Azur. I think there's no place more beautiful on earth,' he said.

'No, Monsieur, I agree.'

'Have you been visiting relatives?' the man asked.

'Yes,' said Connie, stifling a yawn, 'and it's been a long journey back.'

'Any journey undertaken these days is fraught with difficulty. I myself am an agricultural engineer, so I travel widely and see many things.' The man raised his eyebrows. 'You're travelling unchaperoned?'

'Yes, but we're almost there,' Connie answered, nervous now at so many questions.

'That's very brave in these difficult times. Especially as I notice your companion . . .' The young man mimed a pair of closed eyes.

Connie immediately panicked. What was she doing sitting openly in a restaurant with an obviously blind sister of a man wanted by the Gestapo? 'No, my sister is not blind, she's simply tired. Come, Claudine, it's time we were in bed. Goodnight, Monsieur,' she said as she allowed Sophia to stand from the table alone, and only at the last minute took her elbow and led her out of the room.

'Who was that man?' Sophia whispered fearfully.

'I don't know, but I'm not sure we should stay here, I—' As her foot touched the bottom step to walk upstairs, a hand grasped her shoulder and Connie jumped in fright. It was the man from the restaurant.

'Madame, I know who you both are.' He spoke in a low voice. 'Do not fear, your secret is safe. A friend alerted me to the fact that such a young lady—' he indicated Sophia—'would be travelling down this way and I was asked to look out for her and help her and her companions. I spotted you at Marseilles station and would have introduced myself sooner, but I saw what happened to your friend on the train. I'm to see you safely to the end of your journey. Mademoiselle Sophia's brother is well known to me,' the man added.

Connie stood silently in an agony of indecision.

'He is a hero, Madame,' the man added, gazing at her intently.

At the use of Édouard's code name, Connie nodded.

'Thank you, Monsieur. We're grateful to you.'

'Tomorrow I'll escort you down the coast to Mademoiselle's home. My name is Armand and I'm at your service. Goodnight.'

'Can we trust him?' asked Sophia as she climbed into bed a few seconds later.

If the Gestapo hadn't burst in by morning, then

Connie knew they could. But she didn't say this to Sophia. 'Yes. I think we can. Your brother, with his many contacts in the Resistance, must have sent word down the line.'

'I wonder when Édouard will join us?' sighed Sophia. 'Oh, Constance, I can't stop thinking of poor Sarah. What can we do?'

'We have to hope she is questioned, then released and returned to us. Sleep now, Sophia, and know that tomorrow evening we'll be in a place of safety.'

*   *   *

The following morning, after a breakfast of the freshest bread and even a croissant still hot from the oven, Connie felt somewhat restored. Armand had nodded at her across the restaurant as he drank his coffee, then stood up and looked at his watch.

'It has been a pleasure to make your acquaintance, Madame. I'll be leaving now to walk to the station to catch the train along the coast.' He smiled at them and left the room.

A few minutes after Armand had left, Connie guided Sophia down the street towards the station and Armand tipped his hat as he saw them arrive. Having purchased two tickets and taken Sophia to sit on a bench on the platform, Connie watched Armand as he read a newspaper nonchalantly. The little train drew in and everyone clustered around the doors in a very un-British fashion. Leading Sophia onto the train, Connie settled her in a seat by the window. She looked for Armand, but he had obviously disappeared into the second carriage.

347

The journey to Gassin took just over two hours. Connie looked at the raft of pretty coastal villages which, in high summer, faced on to an azure-coloured sea. Now, in early December, the waves below were an angry grey. Connie shivered, hoping only for warmth when they arrived; she was chilled to the bone.

The train journey was thankfully uneventful, and the two of them disembarked at Gassin station in further torrential rain. When the train had trundled off and the small number of passengers had dispersed, only they and a donkey and cart waited patiently for further guidance. A few minutes later, Armand appeared out of nowhere wheeling two bicycles with him.

Connie looked at him in horror. 'Monsieur, you must understand that Sophia cannot cycle. How about the donkey and cart?' she suggested.

'Charlotte, the donkey, takes the post up the hill to Gassin village.' Armand looked at the animal fondly. 'But her disappearance might alert the villagers to Sophia's presence.'

'But, surely, Monsieur, she would say nothing?'

'Charlotte, certainly, is trustworthy,' he agreed, a glint of a smile appearing in his eyes as he and Connie shared the absurdity of the statement. 'But her master, the postman, I cannot vouch for. The château is a short bicycle ride of five minutes. Sophia will hold tight to me.'

'No!' Sophia was aghast. 'I cannot.'

'Mademoiselle, you must. Now—' he glanced at Connie—'take this.' Armand handed her Sophia's small holdall, which she placed in the bicycle basket in front of her. 'And help me get Mademoiselle aboard.'

'Please don't make me!' Sophia moaned in fear.

By now dripping wet, Connie lost her patience. 'Sophia, for goodness' sake, get on, before we all die of pneumonia!'

The sharpness in Connie's voice quietened Sophia's protests and the two of them helped her climb onto the saddle.

'Put your arms about my waist and hang on tight,' Armand instructed, standing astride the bicycle in front of Sophia. 'Right. Here we go!'

Connie watched as Armand wobbled off along the bumpy road, Sophia clinging on for dear life behind him. She followed on after them, and several minutes later, as raindrops cascaded from Connie's white-blonde hair, Armand turned off the main road. A few yards down the narrow track, he stopped to let Connie catch up with them.

'There, Mademoiselle! Your first bicycle ride.' He handed a shaking Sophia from the bicycle and laid it down, indicating Connie to do the same. 'We must walk from here, the track is too rough for wheels. We're entering by the back of the château, which takes us through the vineyards and directly to the *cave*. The good news is that we haven't passed a soul since we left the station,' he said as he led Sophia carefully along the potholed, puddled track. 'The rain has been on our side.'

'We're here?' asked Sophia.

'Yes, we'll be at the *cave* in a few minutes,' he said reassuringly.

'Thank God,' cried Sophia, panting with fear and exhaustion.

'Jacques is expecting you,' said Armand.

The sound of the name seemed to spur Sophia's feet forward. A large, rendered building came into view, and Armand pulled open the high wooden doors in the centre of it. Connie felt like crying with relief herself as they stepped inside out of the rain.

The interior of the building was a vast, dim space, filled with the scent of fermenting grapes. Huge oak barrels lined its sides and a figure appeared through a side door between two of them.

'Sophia? Is that you?' a voice whispered from the shadows.

'Jacques!' Sophia reached out her thin, childlike arms and a tall, heavy-set man in his thirties, his face lined and tanned brown as a nut by the relentless sun, walked up to her.

'My Sophia, thank God you're safe!' The man clasped her against his wide, strong chest and Sophia sobbed onto his shoulder. He stroked her soaking hair and whispered to her tenderly. 'Don't worry, Jacques is here now. I'll look after you.'

Connie and Armand watched this display of affection silently. Then Jacques looked towards them.

'Thank you for bringing her home,' he said to both of them, his voice cracked with emotion. 'I didn't believe she would make it. Did anyone see you arrive here?'

'Jacques, we couldn't see two centimetres in front of us in this rain,' Armand laughed, 'it couldn't have been better.'

'Good. So now, ladies, there's a fire lit in my cottage and you must both change out of your wet clothes.' Jacques took his arms from around Sophia and strode over to Armand. 'Thank you, my friend. I'm sure the Comte will never forget what you've done for him.'

'I did very little—it's this lady you should thank.' Armand indicated Connie.

'Where is Sarah, Sophia's maid?' enquired Jacques of Connie.

'Monsieur, I—'

'Sarah was arrested just before Marseilles,' interjected Armand.

'Then who is she?' Jacques's eyes narrowed at Connie.

'A trusted friend of le Comte and one of us. But no doubt Constance herself will explain in good time,' said Armand.

'Right.' Jacques seemed pacified. 'Come, Sophia, we must get you warm. I'll no doubt be hearing from you soon,' he said, nodding in the direction of Armand.

'Of course. Goodbye, Madame Constance. I'm sure it will not be the last time we meet.' Armand smiled at her pleasantly.

'Thank you from both of us for your help,' Connie said with feeling. 'Do you have far to go?'

'That's not a question we ask in these times. I have many homes.' He winked at her and, pulling his dripping jacket up pointlessly around his ears, Armand left the *cave*.

'Follow me,' said Jacques, nodding to Connie as he led Sophia through the door between the huge barrels and along a passage to another door. Opening it, he led them through a neat kitchen and a blissful warmth assailed Connie as she stepped into a tiny sitting room with a log fire burning in the grate.

'I'll go upstairs and find you both some warm clothes to wear. Those you've brought with you will be just as sodden as the ones you're wearing,' said Jacques, indicating the leather holdall, which had made a puddle on the flagstone floor.

'Oh, Constance!' exclaimed Sophia as she removed her coat and handed it to her. 'I've never been so grateful to arrive anywhere!'

'Yes, it's been a terrible journey,' she agreed, 'but we're here now, Sophia, and you can rest.'

Jacques came down the stairs with two thick fleece shirts and woollen jumpers for both of them. 'They'll do for now,' he said gruffly as he handed them each a cloth to dry their soaking hair. 'I'll make coffee and prepare some food while you change,' he added as he left the room, closing the door behind him.

'I wonder why Jacques doesn't take us straight to the château?' said Sophia as Connie helped her out of the rest of her soaking garments. 'I have a wardrobe of fresh clothes hanging there.'

Connie, having no idea where the château was in relation to the cottage or, in fact, what the plan was, shrugged. 'I'm sure he felt the most important thing was to get you warm and dry.'

'Yes, and I'm so happy to be here. The château is my favourite place on the earth,' said Sophia as her fingers felt for the buttons on Jacques's shirt, which fell to below her knees.

'Now, sit down here beside the fire and dry your hair,' said Connie, undressing herself and collecting the pile of dripping clothes, which would need to be wrung out in a sink before being placed in front of the fire. Jacques re-emerged from the kitchen with a tray of coffee and placed it on the table in front of them.

Connie sipped it silently, listening to Sophia as

she chattered to Jacques, asking after the workers at the vineyard.

'Sadly, Sophia, there's only me here now. All the rest of the men have either gone off to fight or have been sent to Germany to work in the Boche factories. They keep me here in the *cave* as the schnapps I make powers their torpedoes. There's a factory making hundreds of them only a few kilometres away from here. Last time they came, I said I couldn't give them what they needed. I told them they'd drunk too much schnapps themselves and I'd run out.' Jacques's eyes twinkled. 'I was lying, of course.'

'But I thought there were few Germans down here?' said Sophia. 'That it was safe?'

'Sadly, much has changed since you were here last.' Jacques sighed. 'Everyone lives in fear, just as they do in Paris. There was a public execution at the La Foux racecourse near St Tropez only a few weeks ago. The Boche shot four members of the Maquis, of which our brave friend, Armand, is a member. These are troubled times and we must all be very careful,' he warned.

'But what about the château? The housekeeper? The maids?' asked Sophia.

'All gone away,' Jacques told her. 'The château is shut up and has been so for the past two years.'

'But who will take care of us when we're living in it?'

'Mademoiselle Sophia—' Jacques reached for her hand—'you won't be living in the château. It's far too dangerous for you to do so. If Édouard has managed to escape, it's the first place they will come looking for him. And if they find you there, they will undoubtedly arrest you and take you in for questioning. You were, after all, living under the same roof when your brother was conducting his brave double life.'

'But I know nothing.' Sophia wrung her hands in despair. 'What would they want with me?! Besides, I don't even know if my poor brother is alive or dead.'

Connie realised just how protected Sophia had been by Édouard. In terms of physical deprivation, nothing had changed for Sophia in the past four years. She'd still lived the same comfortable life as before the war began. The cotton wool in which her brother's indulgence and the family wealth had wrapped her had shielded her from any danger she might have faced.

'Sophia, my dear, you must understand that you can't be seen here by anyone. Did your brother not explain this to you? He wasn't sending you to the château to live in it openly. You would be removed by the Boche the moment they knew of your presence here,' Jacques explained again. 'No, he sent you down to me because he knows, like I do, that there's a safe hiding place here for you to use until the war is over. And it shouldn't be for long, I promise.'

'Where is this hiding place?' Sophia asked fearfully.

'I'll show you later, after we've eaten. As for you, Madame Constance—' Jacques turned to her—'you'll live in the cottage with me. We will say you are my niece, if anyone cares to enquire.'

'Are you sure it isn't best if I go my own way from here?' suggested Connie. 'Perhaps Armand could help me contact a local network and eventually find my way back home to England. I—'

'But who would care for the needs of Mademoiselle Sophia?' Jacques looked horrified at Connie's notion. 'As a man, I can only do so much.' He shifted with embarrassment. 'As her presence here must never come to light, I simply cannot find someone else from the village. I trust nobody.'

'Constance! Don't leave me here!' cried Sophia. 'I can't manage alone. You know that. Please, you must stay with me,' she begged, searching for Connie's hand.

Yet again, any thought she'd had of extracting herself from the grip of the de la Martinières family disappeared into thin air. Connie took Sophia's hand and, resigned, nodded. 'Of course I won't leave you, Sophia.'

'Thank you,' she said with relief, and Connie noticed she instinctively covered her stomach protectively with her hand as she said it. Sophia turned her attention back to Jacques. 'Is the hiding place here with you, in your cottage?'

'No, that would not be possible. The Boche visit here when they wish to fill their bellies with the wine and their torpedoes with the schnapps the *cave* produces.' Jacques gave a long sigh. 'As I said, I'll show you after we've eaten.'

*   *   *

Connie was at least glad to see that Sophia ate every mouthful of the rich bean and vegetable stew Jacques had prepared.

'I'm suddenly so hungry,' Sophia said, smiling. 'It must be the Provençal air.'

Connie took Sophia back to the chair by the

fireplace and sat her down. Sophia yawned. 'I feel so sleepy, Constance, almost as if my eyes can't stay open.'

'Then close them,' Connie suggested.

When she was certain Sophia was asleep, Connie went through to the small kitchen and helped Jacques wash up the pots from supper. Jacques's face was grave as he stowed the plates in a small cupboard.

'The place that Sophia must hide won't be to her liking, although I've tried to make it as comfortable as possible. But it's underground and cold, with little natural light. Perhaps the one saving grace is that Sophia doesn't have light in her life anyway,' sighed Jacques. 'For any sighted human, I think it would indeed be a fate worse than death. Let's hope it won't be long before this war is won and Sophia can be free.'

'That we can all be free,' murmured Connie to herself in English.

'She must go down there as soon as possible; I didn't mention it in front of her, but the Gestapo were here only yesterday conducting a search of the château and the *cave*. Word must have reached them from Paris of Édouard's disappearance. But,' he comforted, 'they'll never find where she's hidden. And what of you, Madame? How have you ended up playing maid to Sophia?'

'Well, I . . .'

Jacques read the trepidation in her eyes. 'Madame, my family has run the de la Martinières *cave* for the past two hundred years. Édouard and I grew up together as boys. He was the brother I'd always wished for. We both share the same dreams for our country. As you will be living under my

356

roof for the foreseeable future, I think you must trust me.'

'Yes.' Connie took a deep breath and told her story. Jacques listened calmly, his eyes never wavering from her face.

'So,' he concluded, 'you're an elite, trained agent, whose talent has so far been wasted. It is indeed a pity,' he agreed. 'But at least if the Gestapo visit again and find you here with me, I won't be dealing with an amateur. Is it likely they have a photograph of you on file?'

'No,' confirmed Connie. 'Besides, I look very different now. I've dyed my hair.'

'Good. Tomorrow, I'll have a new set of papers made for you, stating that you're my niece come from Grimaud to lend a hand with bottling the wine and keeping house for your uncle. Does that suit you?' Jacques asked.

Connie wondered just how many aliases she would acquire before she left France. 'Of course, Jacques, whatever you believe is best.'

'And, happily for you, you can take the small bedroom upstairs next to mine,' Jacques continued. 'It's terrible Sophia cannot enjoy the same luxury, but you must understand, Madame Constance, that if the Gestapo decided to arrive here in the middle of the night, her blindness would pre-vent us from hiding her fast enough. And I've sworn to her brother I will keep her safe. She, and we, must do whatever it takes.'

'Of course. And I'm afraid there's something else you should know . . .' Connie had decided she must tell him the whole truth about Sophia. 'She's pregnant.'

Jacques's face went through a gamut of emotion,

357

ending in horror. 'How? *Who?* Does Édouard know of this?' he asked eventually.

'No, and in fact, Sophia herself has yet to tell me. It was Sarah, her maid, who confirmed it. She knows her intimately. And that, Monsieur, is not the worst of it.' Connie took a deep breath. 'The father is a high-ranking German officer in the SS.'

This last piece of information rendered Jacques completely silent.

'I'm so sorry to tell you this,' said Connie, reading his shock.

'My little Sophia . . . I simply cannot believe it.' Jacques shook his head. 'And I was thinking she was only in danger from the Boche. But if it was known that the father of her child was an SS officer, she would have the entire wrath of France down on her too. Only a few weeks ago, a woman known to be sleeping with the enemy disappeared in the night from her house in the village here. Her body was found washed up on the shore further down the coast. She'd been beaten to death and her corpse thrown into the sea.' Jacques shook his head. 'Madame, it could not be worse.'

'I know,' Connie replied sombrely. 'But what can we do?'

'You're sure that nobody else knows of her liaison with this officer? Or what has come about because of it?'

'Yes, I'm sure.'

'Thank God,' Jacques breathed. 'Then it must stay that way.'

'Perhaps all I can say is that Édouard once told me he liked the man in question. That if life had been different, they might have been friends. Frederik helped us escape from Paris,' Connie added. 'I believe he's a good man.'

'No!' Jacques shook his head vehemently. 'He's a German, and he has raped our country and our women!'

'I agree, but sometimes the badge you're forced to wear in life does not necessarily indicate the kind of person you are. Or your true loyalties.' Connie sighed. 'So, there it is.'

'Then it's even more imperative that Sophia stays hidden. Although what the consequences will be for her when this war is finally ended, I cannot say,' said Jacques gravely. He shook his head and put his hand to his brow. 'You must understand, I've loved her like she's my own flesh and blood since she was a baby. I cannot bear to think of . . .' He shuddered and shook his head. 'The war makes fools of us all in many different ways. And it has now ruined the life of a vulnerable and beautiful young woman. It's not for me to make any decision on her future, but simply as an unmarried mother, she will face a difficult time. Let us hope that Édouard survives the manhunt for him and is able, once again, to take up the reins of Sophia's life. For now, you and I must do our best to protect her.'

*   *   *

Later that night, Jacques led Sophia back into the *cave* where the vast Russian oak barrels of wine stood, six metres high, towering above Connie, protecting and encouraging the juice to ferment inside.

Jacques stopped in front of a barrel towards the back of the *cave*, then stood atop a small ladder in

359

front of the huge tap, removed the front of the barrel and climbed inside. As Sophia and Connie stood waiting, they heard the sound of boards moving in the barrel. Finally, Jacques's head peered out. 'It will be hard for you to climb in, Mademoiselle Sophia, but don't worry, I'll be here to help you. Madame Constance, can you hand her up to me and then follow her?'

'We're going inside the wine barrel?' said Sophia in confusion. 'I don't have to hide there for the next few weeks, do I?'

'Take Jacques's hand and he'll help you over the edge,' urged Connie as she assisted Sophia up the ladder and inside, where Jacques had gone. Sophia disappeared into the black interior and Connie could hear Jacques talking gently to her.

'You now, Madame Constance,' said his echoing voice from inside the barrel.

Connie climbed up and repeated the same process. When she looked down inside the barrel, she saw that three of the planks in the base had been removed. Sophia and Jacques, who was holding a lantern, were now standing in the darkness underneath the barrel itself. She levered herself into the hole below and stood beside them.

'Follow me,' said Jacques, grasping Sophia with one hand and the lantern with the other.

Connie crouched low as she made her way along the narrow passage, thanking God that Sophia was blind and used to the intense darkness. The tunnel—for it was no more than that as they went further—seemed to go on forever. Not normally claustrophobic, even Connie was shaken by the time Jacques reached a low door and unlocked it. They stepped into a square room, which, Connie

360

noted, had a small, grilled window set high on one bare brick wall. As Connie's eyes adjusted, she saw a bed, a chair and a chest of drawers. There was even a mat placed on the rough stone floor.

'Where are we, Jacques?' said Sophia, gripping his arm as he sat her down in the chair. 'It's so cold and smells terribly of damp!'

'We're in the cellar of the château,' said Jacques. 'Next door is the wine cellar. You'll be safe in here, Sophia.'

'You mean, I must stay down here? In this cold, damp place? And come through that long tunnel every time I wish to leave my room?' Panic registered on Sophia's face. 'You can't leave me down here, Jacques, *please*!'

'Mademoiselle Sophia, as long as you're never seen entering the château from the outside, I can't see why, with all the shutters closed, you shouldn't sometimes venture upstairs. And perhaps take a walk in the walled garden, where nobody will spot you. But for your own safety, and certainly for now, this is where you must stay.'

'But what about washing?' Sophia's voice was nearing hysteria. 'And all the other things a lady must do?'

Jacques pushed open a door and shone the lamp inside it. 'In here, there are facilities for you.'

Connie looked inside and saw a basin placed under a tap and a commode. The paraffin lamp Jacques was holding suddenly went out, and the three of them stood in total blackness.

This is Sophia's world; that of darkness, Connie thought, as Jacques struggled to relight the lantern. And for now, standing in the unlit room that would form her prison, she was for once glad it was.

'I can't stay down here alone,' said Sophia, wringing her hands, 'I can't!'

'You have no choice,' said Jacques, suddenly brusque. 'During the day, as I said, you'll be able to come out, but for the nights, we cannot risk it.'

'Connie!' Sophia reached out a hand to find her. 'Please, don't leave me here. I beg you!' she cried in desperation.

Jacques ignored Sophia's pleas and continued. 'I'll also show you, Madame Constance, how to access the château itself from here. The designer of this hiding place was clever; it has two exits.'

He went to the wall on the other side of the room and turned a key in the lock of a tiny door. He pushed it open and, as it swung back, Connie saw an enormous wine cellar beyond. Jacques led her to the end of it and indicated a set of steps. 'These take you directly up into the back of the château itself. As long as you never open the shutters in the house, it will be possible for you to use the kitchen for water and to prepare food for Sophia. Never, ever light a fire. We're in a valley and the smoke would be seen in the village above,' he warned.

'Of course,' Connie agreed, feeling a little comforted that there was another and far more palatable way out of the underground cell below.

'I'll leave you here with Mademoiselle Sophia to settle her for the night. Tomorrow, you can take her up inside the château, where she can have a bath and collect some clothes. I say again, there must be no light shining behind the château windows at night. It would be seen for miles around and alert others to her presence,' he

362

reiterated.

'I understand,' said Connie.

'Are you confident of finding your way back? I'll leave you a lamp,' said Jacques as they went back into the cell where Sophia was weeping softly, head in her hands.

'Yes.'

When Jacques had left them, Connie sat on the bed next to Sophia, taking her hand.

'Dearest Sophia, please try to be brave. It's only for the nights that you must be down here. I think it's a small price to pay for your safety.'

'But it's so dreadful! The smell . . . .' Sophia sighed, laying her head on Connie's shoulder. 'Constance, will you stay here with me until I fall asleep?'

'Yes, of course I will.'

As Connie sat with Sophia in her arms, rocking her like a baby, she wondered how life had transpired to send her to France as an SOE agent, then subsequently have her act as protector and nursemaid to a spoilt, aristocratic child.

*   *   *

Édouard sat with Venetia at the edge of the thick woods which led on to a large, flat field. They were somewhere just west of Tours, although, due to the various and extremely uncomfortable methods of transport he'd endured to get there, his sense of direction was fuzzy. However, got there he had, and now the man crouched next to Venetia was shooting across the field with his torch as the low hum of an approaching aircraft was heard. The man signalled three times with his torch to let the pilot know all was well and the plane began to descend towards them.

'Right, Édouard, looks like you're going to make it out of here. Send my love to Blighty, won't you?' said Venetia cheerfully.

'Of course. Do you wish you were coming with me?' Édouard turned to look at her. And for a moment saw the softness beneath the bravado in her lovely green eyes.

'In a perfect world, of course.' She nodded. 'I haven't seen Mup and Pup—that's my parents—for over a year. But the world isn't perfect, is it? And I still have a job to do here.'

'How can I ever thank you enough for what you've done for me?' Édouard said, sudden tears blurring his eyes at the thought of leaving her behind to face further danger. Despite his illness, incarceration in the cellar and the hazardous journey, Venetia's humour, bravery and, above all, her spirit, had amazed and enchanted him. 'I'll miss you,' he added.

'And I'll miss you too.' She smiled at him suddenly.

'If, by any chance, we both come out of the other side of this war, I would so very much like to see you again, Venetia.'

'Me too.' She lowered her eyes, suddenly embarrassed.

'Venetia, I . . .' On instinct, Édouard took her in his arms and kissed her hard and passionately on the lips.

As the plane landed, she pulled away from his grasp. And Édouard saw there were tears in her eyes too. He tipped her chin up to him. 'Be brave, my angel. Keep safe, for me.'

'After that kiss, I will most certainly try,' she said. 'Come on, time to go.'

They ran together across the field towards the Lysander, which would take Édouard safely away from his homeland to hers.

As Édouard was about to board, he handed Venetia a package. 'Please, if there's any way that you or another member of your organisation can contact my sister at the château, this will tell her that I'm safe.'

'I'll get it to her, one way or another,' promised Venetia, stowing it in her satchel.

Édouard climbed the steps of the aircraft, then turned back. 'Good luck, my angel, and I pray we'll meet again soon.'

He stepped inside and the small door closed behind him. Venetia watched as the plane taxied, then picked up speed and flew out across the Channel towards home.

'Come, Claudette, we must leave,' said Tony, her companion, grasping her arm and dragging her away across the field.

Venetia looked up wistfully at the night sky, the full moon turning the frost on the field into a fairyland of glistening whiteness. And decided that Édouard de la Martinières was a man she knew she could finally love.

*   *   *

A day later, having entrusted Édouard's package to a courier who was travelling down to the south, Venetia set off by train to make her way back to Paris. Arriving at the new safe house, she threw her satchel down with a sigh of relief and went into

365

the kitchen to boil some water for a hot drink.

'Good evening, Fräulein. I'm so very glad to make your acquaintance at last.'

Venetia turned and froze, recognising the icy pale-blue eyes of Colonel Falk von Wehndorf.

* * *

A week later, having been held at Gestapo headquarters, interrogated and then brutally tortured for refusing to reveal the information they required, Venetia was led out into the yard.

The officer who tied her to the post looked at her in disgust.

'Give a girl a last ciggy,' she asked him, staggering a little and forcing a smile.

He lit one and stuck it in her mouth. She took a couple of drags, and sent her love across the Channel to her family.

As the officer went to take his marks and pointed the gun at her heart, Venetia's last living thought, as she closed her eyes, was that of the kiss from Édouard de la Martinières.

25

Gassin, South of France, 1999

Jacques was grey with exhaustion.

'Enough, Papa. You must rest,' ordered Jean, seeing his weariness. 'I'll help you upstairs now.'

'But I must get to the end of the story . . . I haven't finished, I . . .'

'No more, Papa,' said Jean as he helped Jacques out of his chair and led him towards the door. 'There's plenty of time. Maybe you can continue tomorrow.'

As they left the room, Emilie sat staring into the fire. Thoughts of Venetia, who had perhaps found love with her father only days before her death, assailed her. Emilie felt humbled and awed by Venetia's strength and courage.

Jean came back down the stairs and perched on the fender opposite Emilie. 'It's quite a story, is it not?' he murmured.

'Yes. And now I'm thinking that my aunt's early death is connected to her love affair with Frederik,' sighed Emilie.

'Well, we both know what happened to French women who consorted with the enemy after the war. Tarred and feathered, or shot by their angry neighbours,' agreed Jean.

Emilie shuddered. 'Of all the men Sophia could have chosen . . .'

'But no one can choose who they love, Emilie, can they?' Jean said quietly.

'And Sophia's baby? Did it die too?' she

pondered.

'Who knows? We can only wait until Papa shares the rest of the story with us,' said Jean. 'But it's obvious to me already that Frederik was a good man. And Papa's story only underlines how one's place of birth and the timing of it is a matter of chance. Does any human really choose to fight and kill?' he said. 'At that time, at least, they simply had no choice, whichever side they were on.'

'The suffering and deprivation our forefathers knew . . .' Emile shook her head. 'It puts our own existences into perspective.'

'It does indeed. Thank God, after the two world wars, certainly the West learned its lesson. For a while anyway,' Jean mused sombrely. 'But war will always begin again; it's the human condition to wish for change and be unable to sustain peace. Sad, but true. On the positive side, the extreme circumstances it creates can bring out the best in us. Your father almost certainly saved Constance's life by going himself to the café to warn Venetia. And, in return, to protect Édouard, Constance subjugated herself to the most terrible fate a woman can suffer. Alternatively, of course—' he exhaled—'it can bring out the very worst, as it did with Falk. Great power often corrupts.'

'Then I'm glad I have none.' Emilie smiled.

'But of course you do, Emilie.' Jean raised an eyebrow. 'Stop underestimating yourself. You're an intelligent and beautiful woman. This alone can often be enough, but you were also lucky and were born into a well-respected and powerful family. As these things go, you were given many gifts. Now, it's late, and I must be up, as always, with the birds.'

'Yes, of course. And you're right, Jean. I was given many gifts. Maybe it's only now that I'm starting to appreciate them,' said Emilie quietly.

'Good.' Jean stood up. 'I'll see you in the morning.'

'Sleep well, Jean.'

Twenty minutes later, she was lying in the old bed in the small bedroom which Constance must have used during the time she was here. She heard Jean use the communal bathroom then close the door to his room.

Emilie realised that Jean and his father were the nearest thing she had left to a family. Comforted by that thought, she fell asleep.

*   *   *

The following morning, she came into the kitchen to find Jean looking grave.

'Papa's breathing is terrible and I have the doctor coming. Coffee?' he offered.

'Yes, thank you. Is there anything I can do?' Seeing the disappointment on Emilie's face, Jean put an arm around her.

'No, he's simply very old and weak. I'm sorry, Emilie, but Papa can't tell you any more of the past today.'

'Of course. I'm being selfish,' she apologised. 'It's your father's health that matters most.'

'It simply means that you must return very soon if you wish to hear any more.' Jean smiled at her. 'You know there will always be a bed for you here whilst the château renovations are undertaken.'

'Perhaps I can bring my husband with me next time,' Emilie suggested. 'After all, it's his

369

grandmother's story too.'

'Yes. Can I leave you to make your own breakfast? I have some work to complete before the doctor arrives. I can only hope Papa doesn't have to return to hospital. He hated it there so much last time. Anyhow, I'll see you before you leave.' Jean nodded and left the kitchen.

After breakfast, Emilie went upstairs to pack her few belongings. She could hear Jacques coughing in the next room. She knocked on his door tentatively, then opened it and peeped inside.

'May I come in?'

Jacques raised a hand to acquiesce.

She could see his eyes were open, and as she walked towards him, the sight of his pale, shrunken body in the big bed reminded her of her mother just before she had died. She sat down on a corner of the bed and smiled down at him. 'I just wanted to say thank you for sharing the story of my family's war. I hope, when you're better, you can tell me the rest of it.'

Jacques opened his mouth and a rasping grunt came out.

'Please don't try and speak now,' Emilie said comfortingly.

Jacques grabbed her hand with his claw-like one, showing strength for someone so frail. He gave a ghoulish parody of a smile and nodded at her.

'Goodbye, and please get better.' Emilie leant towards the papery skin and kissed him lightly on his forehead.

*   *   *

Jean was upstairs with his father and the doctor

370

when it was time for Emilie to leave for the airport. So as not to disturb him, she left a note on the kitchen table thanking them both, climbed into her car and set off for Nice. She felt guilty that Jacques's relapse may have been caused by the exertion of telling his story. The energy and emotion it had taken for him to relate it had obviously had an impact.

*   *   *

As the aircraft took off from Nice, Emilie prayed that Jacques would recover, but resigned herself to never knowing the rest of the story. And somewhere over northern France, Emilie turned her thoughts to home—or the home that was now.

The idea of returning to Blackmoor Hall after spending two days where she felt she belonged was not an enticing one. The cold, grey English skies and the depressing, tense atmosphere of the house were something she needed to steel herself for. She also had to ask her husband why he had spent two days at the château, but hadn't told her . . .

As the plane landed, descending through thick rain clouds and into the gloom on the ground, Emilie rallied her strength. This was the man and the life she had chosen, however difficult it currently felt. As she walked out of the airport and climbed aboard the Land Rover, she checked herself. A miserable, cold house and a couple of brothers at war was nothing compared to the dreadful suffering which Jacques had related last night.

When she arrived at Blackmoor Hall, there was no sign of the old banger Sebastian used to run to the station sitting in the drive and Emilie entered a silent house. It was freezing again, so she dropped her holdall and went into the boiler room to turn the heating back on. This told her that Sebastian hadn't been here for at least a few days. Which was odd, as when they'd spoken yesterday, he'd said he was calling from home . . .

Perhaps, Emilie shrugged, ready to forgive, he was used to living without the heating and hadn't thought to switch it back on. She climbed the stairs to their bedroom and found the room exactly as she'd left it two days ago. Back in the kitchen to make a cup of tea, Emilie saw the half bottle of milk she'd left in the fridge was still there and untouched.

'Stop it!' Emilie scolded herself. It may well have been that Sebastian had simply returned in the evening, slept overnight and disappeared back to London. Whatever, she would need to go and buy some urgent supplies to feed them tonight.

Just as she was about to open the front door to get back into the Land Rover, Sebastian's old banger pulled into the drive. Emilie paused uncertainly in the doorway as she saw him climb out.

'Darling!' Sebastian threw his arms open as he walked towards her and enclosed her in them. 'It's so good to have you back.' His lips immediately bent to hers and he kissed her. 'I missed you.'

'And I you, Sebastian, I was so worried. I—'

'Hush, Emilie.' Sebastian put a finger to her lips. 'We're together now.'

*　　　*　　　*

Thankfully, Sebastian seemed to be much more back to his usual self and the two of them spent a pleasant weekend rebonding. They made love, rose late, cooked when they were hungry and, on Sunday afternoon, wandered around the land which belonged to the house. The gardens, even though unkempt, were beginning to show the very first signs of spring.

'There's so much out here to put right, I hardly know where to begin,' Sebastian sighed as they walked across the main lawn and into the house.

'I like gardening,' said Emilie. 'Perhaps I could see what I can achieve. It would give me something to do when you're away.'

'It would,' Sebastian agreed as they entered the kitchen. 'Tea?'

'Yes, please.'

'It's not very satisfactory all round, is it?' Sebastian said. 'And I'm afraid I'm going to be away a lot in the next few months.'

'Then perhaps I really should think about moving with you to London,' Emilie said firmly as he handed her a mug of tea. 'It's not good to be apart so much, and so early in our married life. And ridiculous that you won't let your wife use her money to help our relationship,' she added, amazed at her sudden courage.

'Yes, you're right. Why don't we think about it in a few weeks' time?' Sebastian said, kissing Emilie on the nose. 'We could look around for a small apartment. I certainly wouldn't want you anywhere near my ghastly little box room, my five-star girl,' he said, smiling.

Emilie wanted to say that, really, she didn't care where they lived, but as he was finally amenable to the idea of her moving down to London with him, she decided to let it rest.

That night, however, she did broach the subject of his appearance at the château in France.

They were lying in bed and Sebastian looked down at her oddly. 'You don't remember me telling you I was going?' Then he chuckled. 'You're not getting early dementia, are you? Why on earth wouldn't I have told you?'

'Sebastian, I'm sure you didn't.' Emilie determinedly stuck to her guns.

'Well, either way, would it have mattered? I mean, I wouldn't expect you to ask my permission to come here, Emilie. My visit to the château wasn't planned. I had a little spare time and thought I'd go and help make a start on the library. That was OK with you, wasn't it?'

'Of course.'

'Good. Night, sweetheart, got to be up for the early train in the morning. I'm going to try and get some sleep.'

As Sebastian switched off the light, Emilie lay there, wondering at her husband's power to make every one of his actions completely plausible, which rendered her sounding stupid and in the wrong.

Or maybe she *was* wrong . . .

She gave a small sigh and closed her eyes, remembering that everyone had to work at marriage and be prepared to give and take.

*   *   *

Sebastian left for London at six the following morning and Emilie did her best to go back to sleep. In the end, she surrendered, got up and went downstairs to make some coffee. She switched on her mobile for the first time since she'd arrived back in Yorkshire and listened to her messages. There was one from Jean, telling her Jacques had been admitted to hospital in Nice, but was responding to the antibiotics and doing well. He'd let her know as soon as Jacques was home and fit enough to continue his story.

The day was bright and Emilie decided to take another trip around the garden to see how she could make a start. It was important she kept busy and did something useful with her time whilst she was here. Walking out into the garden, she realised that most of what was needed was work well beyond her physical capacity. The lengths of flowerbeds needed weeding, pruning and fertilising. It would be spring before she knew what could be salvaged out of years of neglect, she thought, as she moved into the orchard and looked at the chaos there.

Feeling disheartened at the enormity of the job, Emilie walked back inside to make some more coffee, and decided the most she could do was to try to make something of the pretty terrace that sat outside the kitchen and caught the morning sun. The old paving stones had moss covering each crack, their green snail-trails painting the stone. She made a list of supplies she would need to buy from the local garden centre, which she had spotted a few miles down the road. She was sure that, with a little bit of elbow grease and some new planting, she could make the small area a pleasant outside space to sit in.

Back from the garden centre and the supermarket, Emilie knew she must check on Alex. Her feelings towards him were a mass of confusion. She liked him very much, but every time she saw him, although he said nothing negative about Sebastian, the unspoken undercurrent unsettled her. Having just managed to get her relationship back on track with her husband, she didn't want to risk destabilising it.

At seven that evening, she knocked on Alex's door.

'Come in.'

Alex was in the kitchen, eating supper. He looked up at her and smiled. 'Hello, stranger.'

'Hello.' Emilie felt uncomfortable and embarrassed. 'I came to make sure you were well.'

'Very well, thank you. You?'

'Yes.'

'Good. Would you like to join me?' Alex indicated the shepherd's pie sitting on the hob. 'I always make far too much.'

'No thank you. I've prepared my own supper next door. Is there anything you need?'

'No thanks.'

'Right. I'll leave you in peace to eat. Any problems, please call me on my mobile.'

'Yes.'

'Goodnight, Alex.' She threw him a forced smile as she turned to leave.

'Goodnight, Emilie,' Alex replied sadly.

For the next few days, Emilie busied herself clearing the small terrace and cleaning up the moss-covered pots filled with dead remnants of past flowers. For now, she filled them with winter pansies, but in a few weeks' time she could add petunias and busy Lizzies and plant sweet-smelling lavender in the beds.

Jean had called to say Jacques was back at home and eager to continue telling his story, so Emilie booked a flight to France for the following week. She also cornered Jo, the young girl she had employed as Alex's cleaner, and asked her how she was settling in to her job.

'Oh, I love it, Mrs Carruthers,' she said as they walked together towards Jo's bicycle. 'Alex is such a nice man. And so clever. I'm studying Russian next year at Uni and he's been helping me.'

'He speaks Russian?' Emilie replied in surprise.

'Yes. And Japanese and a little Chinese and Spanish. And French, of course.' Jo sighed. 'It's such a shame he's stuck in that chair and not able to get out much. He never complains though, Mrs Carruthers. I would, if I was Alex.'

'Yes,' agreed Emilie. Waving to Jo as she cycled off down the drive, she felt even more churlish for steering clear of her brother-in-law.

*   *   *

Emilie was glad when Friday arrived. Sebastian had phoned in once, but she was beginning to accept that when he was away he was too wrapped up in work to contact her. He arrived home in a good mood, saying he'd managed to sell a painting by one of his new artists and received a healthy

377

commission. Emilie suggested he came with her to France next week to hear the rest of Jacques's story, but he said he'd be too busy. As for Alex, Emilie assured Sebastian he was fine and she'd hardly seen him.

'He really is self-sufficient, Sebastian.'

'Well, seems you were right and I was wrong,' he commented brusquely.

'I didn't mean it like that,' she replied.

They were sitting outside on her newly renovated terrace at the back of the house. She shivered as the tiny slice of Yorkshire sun disappeared behind a cloud, then stood up. 'I'll go and make supper.'

'By the way, it may be that I need to go to Geneva in Switzerland for a few days and I might not be home next weekend,' Sebastian said.

Emilie nodded thoughtfully. 'Then maybe I could join you there from France? I could drive across to Geneva. It isn't far.'

'I'd love you to, but really, this isn't a trip for pleasure—I'll be in meetings all the time.'

'OK.' She sighed, not wanting to argue, and went inside to begin supper.

*   *   *

Sebastian left again on Monday morning and Emilie lay in bed feeling genuinely disgruntled. Even though she was doing her best not to complain and to be supportive about Sebastian's dedication to resolving his business and not be demanding of his time, the fact was that she was seeing less and less of him. What was she meant to do with her life here in Yorkshire all by herself?

Filling her days painting over the cracks of a house that might be sold and wasn't hers anyway suddenly seemed completely pointless.

Her decision to avoid Alex meant that she was spending all her time here alone. Emilie sighed as she got up and dressed. She could stay in her nightshirt all day if she wished, as no one would be coming to see her. It was a depressing thought.

On that note, having taken the bicycle down to the village to buy milk and bread—or what masqueraded as bread in England—Emilie cycled off past the shop until she reached the last cottage on the left-hand side. Parking her bicycle against the rough Yorkshire stone of the exterior, she walked to the front door and knocked. If Mrs Erskine wasn't there, she would simply go away. But the woman had invited her to pop in, and it was about time she gleaned some more information on the brothers and their relationship.

The door was opened after a second knock and Norma Erskine's warm smile of welcome made Emilie feel comfortable that she wasn't intruding.

'Hello, love, I was wondering when you'd be along to see me,' she said as she led Emilie down the narrow hallway. 'Come in, I were just putting the kettle on, any road. Sit yourself down at the table.'

'Thank you.' Emilie did so and saw she was in an old-fashioned but immaculately kept kitchen. The melamine yellow cabinets, Baby Belling cooker and Electrolux fridge with its hallmark rounded corners were all remnants of the Sixties.

'So, love, how are those terrible twins of mine treating you?' She smiled at Emilie.

'Fine, thank you,' she said politely.

'That's good to hear. Not fighting amongst themselves as usual, then? Mebbe you're having a good influence on them.' Norma placed a coffee in front of Emilie and sat down herself on the other side of the small table. 'Though I'd be surprised if anyone could sort those two out.'

'I'm not quite sure what you mean,' said Emilie neutrally.

'Well, you must have noticed the tension that hangs between them. You would have thought with them being grown men, they'd have got past it. But I say there's nowt that will ever change them now.'

'I agree they're not close.'

'And that's an understatement,' sighed Norma. She reached over and patted Emilie's hand. 'And I understand you're married to one of them, love, and you don't want to be disloyal.'

'No,' Emilie agreed, 'but you're right, the atmosphere in the house is difficult. As I don't know the history behind it, it's hard for me to understand. So I've come to ask you if you would explain things to me. If I know what causes the problem between them, then it might be easier for me to cope.'

Norma paused and studied her for a while. 'The problem is, love, it would mean saying some pretty unpleasant things about the man you've just gone and married. And I'm not sure you'd want to hear them. Because once I start, I'd have to tell the truth as it is. I wouldn't be able to lie to you, Mrs Carruthers. Are you sure that's what you want?'

'No, of course not,' Emilie replied honestly, 'but it would be better than guessing.'

'I suppose Master Alex has said nowt about it?'

'Nothing. He refuses to talk of his brother or the

380

past to me.'

'He's a loyal one, I'll give him that. Right-o, then.' She slapped her sturdy knees. 'I can only hope I'm doing the right thing by telling you. But, likewise, remember that it was you that asked in the first place.'

'I will,' Emilie promised.

'Now, I suppose you know that both boys were brought back from America by their mum from the hippy commune she lived in?'

'Yes.' Emilie was concentrating hard to decipher the strong Yorkshire accent.

'Like two peas in a pod they were, only eighteen months between them and the sweetest little things you've ever seen. Of course, even though it was Master Sebastian who was the older lad, right from the start it were obvious the exceptional one of the two was the young'un. Master Alex were reading and writing before his fourth birthday. As a child he were a charmer, he could always manage to wangle a slice of Victoria sponge cake out of me in the kitchen, even before dinner!' Norma chuckled. 'He looked like a little angel, he did, with those big brown eyes of his. Don't get me wrong, Mrs Carruthers, your husband, he were a sweet lad too, but without sounding disrespectful or rude, he hadn't been given the gifts that his younger brother had in spades. He were bright enough, and not bad-looking, but it was obvious then he could never match up to Alex. Of course, Sebastian competed constantly to be the best, but Alex always won hands down without even breaking sweat.' She sighed and shook her head. 'And it didn't help, neither, that little Alex was the apple of his grandmother's eye.'

'I see. It must have been hard on Sebastian.'

'Oh, it was, love, and as they got older, nothing improved. In fact, it got a great deal worse. Any time Sebastian could manage to get Alex into trouble, he did it. He had to "win" sometimes, didn't he? Of course, Sebastian would always say 'twas Alex who'd started the ruck, but there were never a bruise on him.'

'I see,' said Emilie again, shocked but understanding. 'Did Alex fight back?'

'No,' grimaced Norma, 'not once. He idolised his older brother, you see, just wanted to please him, and if Sebastian told Alex it was all his fault, he'd accept it without a murmur. Your husband always did have a gift for convincing others that black is white.' She shook her head. 'It all calmed down for a while when Sebastian left to go away to boarding school and could come home bragging about his success. But then Alex went and won the academic scholarship at the same school, didn't he? He left here in a blaze of glory with all of us expecting great things of him. Then Constance— Mrs Carruthers as was—started getting letters from the school saying Alex were constantly in trouble. None of us understood it here, the boy were one of the most gentle souls I've ever met; more interested in a book than a fist fight. Any road, a year later he was expelled and sent home in disgrace. Apparently he'd set fire to the newly built gym.'

'And had he?'

'The school said he had and Alex would never utter a word about it, even though me and his granny tried to get out of him what had happened. I, for one, have my suspicions.' Mrs Erskine raised her eyebrows and Emilie knew what she was implying.

'The upshot of the expulsion was that Alex was sent to the local secondary school here. Which even I'd admit I'd not have wanted my kids to go to. Rough as old boots, it was, and Alex stuck out like a sore thumb. He hated it, but his examination marks were always exceptional, even with the poor level of teaching, and he were offered a place at Cambridge. His granny was thrilled that her golden boy had still pulled it off. Sebastian, who'd had the best education money could buy, but was a lazy one, had been lucky to get a place studying History of Art at Sheffield.'

Norma broke off from her tale to have a sip of her coffee. Emilie sat quietly, waiting for her to continue.

'Now then,' she said, 'that summer before Alex was meant to go up to Cambridge started well, with both boys enjoying a taste of adulthood. Alex had saved up for a car and they used to take themselves off in it to the pub. Alex was as proud as punch of that old Mini.' She smiled. 'Then one night, it weren't Alex who arrived home that evening, it was the police. Alex had been involved in a crash. He were blind drunk apparently, and the police had him in the cells sobering up. Thank the Lord no one was seriously hurt, but both his car and the other one were write-offs. Alex was charged with dangerous driving and Cambridge refused to accept him because he had a police record.'

'That's terrible! But then,' Emilie speculated, 'Sebastian told me Alex has had a drinking problem. Maybe that was the start of it.'

383

'Well, love—' Norma shook her head—'before then, if he were driving, I'd never known Alex touch a drop of alcohol. That proud of his car he was, he wouldn't have done nowt to risk it. He still swears blind to this day he only drank orange juice that night, but all that alcohol got into his system somehow, didn't it?' she said. 'Anyway, with his university place scuppered, in the autumn he used all the money he'd saved from working in the local shop here in the village and took himself off and away abroad. And that was the last we saw of him for five years.'

'Yes, Sebastian told me he disappeared.'

'We had no idea where he was. His granny was out of her mind with worry, wondering if he were even alive, because he never contacted her. Then we got a call from a hospital in France to say he was there and more or less at death's door. I'm not up on drugs myself, love, but suffice to say, apparently there wasn't much that Alex hadn't tried. Constance got on a plane immediately and went over to sort him out.'

'Constance put him in a private rehab centre, didn't she?' asked Emilie.

'She did, and he came home clean, as they say, but it weren't long after that he disappeared off again and it was another four years until I next saw him. He missed his granny's funeral.' Tears came to Norma's eyes. She took a hanky from her sleeve and blew her nose. 'Sorry, love, it's just that Constance kept asking before she passed away if he was coming back. But we didn't know where he was. So she never did get to say goodbye to her boy. And I don't think Alex has ever forgiven himself for not being there, either. Whatever he'd got up to on his travels, he still adored his granny.'

'I'm sure.'

'He kept saying over and over that he'd written letters home with a forwarding address, but we never got them, love, we really didn't.' She sighed. 'Any road, perhaps it was the shock of losing Constance, but after that Alex stayed put here and began to get himself back on track. He talked of perhaps training to become a teacher. He was a changed soul. Or should I say—' Norma smiled through her tears—'back to the soul he'd been as a boy. Sebastian was off in London, and I were glad Alex was back to sort things out, because I'd have had no idea what to do. Then, one weekend, not long after Constance died, your husband turns up from London. They had a flaming row over something or other, and I saw Alex get in his car and start the engine. Before he could leave, Sebastian had climbed in next to him. The car shot off down the drive, and the next thing I know, there's another call from another hospital and both the boys are in it this time. As I'm sure you know, your husband escaped with minor injuries, but it was Alex who was so badly hurt.'

'Alex was drunk again, wasn't he?'

'No, love—' Norma shook her head—'you're getting confused. That was the *first* time he had a crash. This time, it were the other driver who was drunk. When it went to court, hospital records showed Alex's blood was clean and he was in the clear. Except, of course, he wasn't, being paralysed for the rest of his life,' she explained. 'I sometimes wonder if tragedy follows that young man around. Anyway, when Alex finally came back here from hospital, your husband told me very clearly that he

385

was to be in charge of his brother's care. I'd like to point out that I said I were quite happy to look after Alex, but he insisted I had enough else to do.'

'So why did you finally decide to leave the house?' asked Emilie.

'If you want the truth, I know your husband tried to do his best by his brother, but he'd employ carers I wouldn't have given the time of day to.' Norma wrinkled her nose in disgust. 'And certainly Master Alex didn't, either. It were almost as though your husband chose the worst he could find. And then, if there were a good one who Alex liked and began to trust, Sebastian would find fault and sack her. I can understand in the beginning that Alex needed full-time care, but he's much stronger and more capable now. I happen to know your husband himself is getting a full carer's allowance for Alex. Maybe he felt he had to use it or something.' She shrugged.

Emilie sat silently, digesting the facts. So Sebastian was taking money for Alex's care.

'As I said, I must believe—' Norma looked at Emilie guiltily—'*must* believe that your husband has his brother's best interests at heart. After all, he was often away in London. But besides the fact I was always there, all that chopping and changing of carers did no one any good, especially not me. And the last one . . .' She rolled her eyes. 'If Master Alex hadn't chucked a cup of coffee at her, I think I would have done. Blind drunk, she was, on many an occasion. I tried to tell your husband, but he didn't listen. And that was when I decided I'd finally had enough.'

'I see.'

'And now,' sighed Norma, 'you have to cope with

it all. You have my sympathy, love. You really do.'

Emilie didn't know how to reply. 'Thank you for telling me. I appreciate your honesty,' she said.

'Well now, I hope I haven't said anything out of turn about your husband. I've just told it how it is. They're both good men at heart,' she added feebly.

The two women sat in silence, Emilie knowing there had been a lot of subtle diplomacy used in the telling of Norma's tale.

As if Norma was reading her mind, she said, 'I watched them grow up, you see. And I love them both, however they've behaved.'

'Yes. Thank you for the coffee.' Emilie rose from the table, feeling suddenly exhausted. 'I must go home now.'

'Of course.' Norma led her to the door and put her large, roughened hand on Emilie's shoulder. 'I hope I haven't set the cat amongst the pigeons,' she said, and when Emilie looked at her questioningly added, 'I mean, told you things it would be better for you not to know.'

They both knew what she meant.

'I can only be grateful for what you've explained to me. I needed to understand and now I do.'

'Good. And just you remember, love, there's always a brew waiting for you here.'

'I will,' said Emilie as she stepped over the threshold and pulled her bicycle away from the wall.

'Look out for Alex, won't you? He's very vulnerable.' Norma's eyes said everything as they entreated Emilie to realise what she meant.

Emilie nodded in response, climbed on her bicycle and cycled off back to Blackmoor Hall.

26

Emilie did not visit Alex that night. Instead, she sat by the fire in the drawing room and wrote down everything Mrs Erskine had told her so she would not forget it.

It was hard to doubt the housekeeper's perception of the brothers, as it completely mirrored her own. Sebastian's ability to turn black to white was a phrase she had herself used to describe him. Twisting the facts to put a different slant on any subject was, she knew from experience, something he was a past master at.

Was her husband, as Mrs Erskine had hinted, a liar, a cheat and a bully, who would stop at nothing to destroy his own brother? And if it *was* true that Sebastian held a grudge against Alex, did that mean he was a bad person overall?

Emilie thought back to the mobile phone disaster, when Sebastian had managed to convince her that she was being ridiculous for becoming upset when he hadn't contacted her. And although he'd assured her that he'd mentioned going to the château to make a start on the library, she knew he hadn't.

And why was it he didn't want her to accompany him to London or on his travels, but left her—his new wife of less than a month—alone here in Yorkshire?

No! She had to stop this, her imagination was running riot now. It was what her father had always called 'small hour-itis'—when the human body was at its lowest ebb and the mind lost all logic and ran away with itself.

Upstairs, Emilie rooted in her washbag for one of the sleeping tablets the doctor had prescribed for her after her mother's death and swallowed it down. She needed to sleep more than anything. And, tomorrow, she would take further steps to find out the truth.

*   *   *

Emilie tapped on Alex's door at six the following evening. She had spent all day trying to process the facts into some kind of logical order. Armed with a bottle of red wine, she heard his voice welcoming her into the flat.

'I'm at my computer,' he called. 'Some of my children have suffered considerable losses today, due to the disastrous sugar crop in Fiji. Come through.'

'Hello, Alex.' Emilie stood in the doorway of his study, fascinated by the screens that blinked red and green and moved constantly in front of him.

'Hello,' he replied, his attention still on the screens. 'Long time, no see.'

'I brought this.' Emilie proffered the bottle. Alex turned his head towards her, saw the bottle and looked suitably surprised.

'Are you sure?'

'Yes, I am.'

'Well, this is a pleasant treat,' he said, wheeling himself backwards and turning towards her. 'You, I mean, not the wine.' He smiled at her.

'I'm sorry I haven't been in to see you before,' Emilie offered.

'That's all right, I'm used to being a pariah. But

still, I'm very happy to see you, Em. Shall I get the glasses or will you?'

'I will.'

'Thanks.'

Finding a corkscrew and two glasses in a kitchen cupboard, Emilie followed Alex into the sitting room and watched as he leant forward to stoke the fire. She uncorked the bottle, poured the wine into the glasses and handed him one. She watched his intelligent eyes appraising her with interest.

'*Santé*,' said Emilie, taking a sip.

'So—' Alex was still staring at her—'spit it out, then.'

'What do you mean?'

'You have something to say to me, or possibly ask me. I'm all ears.'

'Yes.' Emilie set her wine glass down on the table and sat on one of the fireside chairs close to him. 'Alex, are you a liar?'

'What?!' He chuckled. 'Well, of course I'm going to say no. To be fair, I probably was when I was on the hard stuff during my addict years, but then that's normal.'

'Sorry, but it felt like the right thing to say, given that I must ask you, indeed beg you, to tell me the truth.'

'Yes, your honour, the whole truth and nothing but. Em, what's going on?' he asked.

'I went to see Norma Erskine yesterday.'

'Oh, I see.' Alex sighed then took a sip of his wine. 'And what did she have to say for herself?'

'She told me only because I asked,' Emilie added quickly, 'about your childhood here.'

'Right. And?' Alex said guardedly.

'She was very diplomatic, but I have some

questions I want to ask you because of our conversation, to help me make sense of the confusion I feel.'

'OK . . . I think I can see where we're headed. And it's towards a conversation I've purposely steered clear of,' Alex said sombrely. 'Are you sure you wish to continue? I'll only be able to tell you the truth. But, like all of us, the truth will be from my perspective, which may well be warped. And biased,' he added.

'Then I think it would be simpler if I asked you short questions first. I believe they have a yes or no answer.'

'Emilie, have you ever thought of a career as a lawyer? I think you'd be remarkably successful,' he said, smiling and trying to break the tension.

'Alex, this is serious.'

'Well, your honour, nothing in life is *that* serious, as long as you're alive and kicking.'

'*Please*, Alex.'

'Sorry. I will answer "yes" or "no" and not elucidate unless you ask me to. Fire away.'

Emilie looked down at her list. 'The first question: when you were a child were you bullied by your brother? And did he constantly lie about who caused an argument or a fight to get you into trouble?'

'Yes.'

'When you won your scholarship and went to the same school as your brother, did he again try to make it look as if you were to blame for bad things that happened there? For example, did he start the fire that got you expelled from the school?'

There was a slight hesitation from Alex. Eventually, he said, 'I have to believe so, yes. It

391

certainly wasn't me, although four boys and a master swore they saw someone who *was* me making a hasty exit from the gym once I'd started the fire. And, from a distance, Seb and I could definitely be physically confused.'

'Why didn't you defend yourself?' she asked.

'I thought you wanted "yes" or "no" answers?' Alex raised an eyebrow. 'Well, I was hardly going to point the finger at my brother, was I? Besides, no one would have believed me. Seb had somehow managed to garner a reputation for being whiter than white. He's always been like Macavity from the poems of T. S. Eliot. When there was trouble, he simply wasn't there. But there's no proof it *was* him, so the jury is out on that question.'

'I understand. OK, next question: did you drink alcohol the night the two of you went out in your car together when you were eighteen, and you ended up being charged with dangerous driving?'

'Not that I knew of, no. I asked for orange juice at the pub, as I always did,' stated Alex.

'Do you believe that your brother spiked your drink?'

'Yes.' There was no hesitation on this one.

'Did you ever confront him?'

'No. How could it be proved?'

'Do you think he did this to stop you going to Cambridge?'

'Yes.'

'Did you leave Yorkshire and go abroad to escape from a brother who you realised was so consumed with jealousy, he'd stop at nothing to sabotage anything you achieved?'

'Yes.'

'When you went out on the night of your

accident, you and Sebastian had already had a dreadful argument. Was it because he wanted to sell Blackmoor Hall and you did not?'

'Yes.'

'Do you blame Sebastian for the accident?'

'No,' Alex said firmly. 'The accident was an accident and nothing to do with him.'

'Are you sure?'

Alex paused then sighed heavily. 'Well, put it this way. I was furious with him and we continued to argue because he wouldn't get out of my car. I'd parked up on a grass verge along a country road, and was about to turn the car round to head home when a maniac came round the corner and smashed straight into us. So—' he shrugged—'you could look at it either way; normally I wouldn't have been sitting on a grass verge if I hadn't been having a rabid argument with my brother. But then one can say that about anything. The upshot is, it was simply bad luck, and I can't lay the blame at your husband's door. Pray continue,' encouraged Alex.

'In your opinion, since the accident, has your brother gone out of his way to make life as difficult as possible for you? For example, employing carers whom he knows you don't even need any longer and you'll dislike. And getting rid of the ones you did like?'

'Yes.'

'Is he doing this, in your opinion, simply because he can, or because there's another reason? Does he wish to make life as difficult as possible for you here so you'll agree to sell this house?'

Another pause. Alex took a sip of his wine and looked at her thoughtfully. 'Probably. The house is in our joint names and he has to have my agreement to sell. For all sorts of reasons, I don't want to. Is that everything?'

Emilie glanced down at the list in front of her. There was another section she had written out—a brutal list that related very personally to her relationship with Sebastian. She was too disturbed by what she'd heard to even begin to tackle those questions. She nodded. 'It is.'

'You do realise, don't you,' commented Alex, 'that if you were to put the same questions to my brother, you would get the polar opposite response in terms of answers?'

'Yes,' she agreed. 'But please remember, Alex, I have eyes and ears . . . and a brain too.'

'Poor Em,' Alex said suddenly, 'dragged into a game of cat and mouse, not knowing who or what to believe.'

'Please don't patronise me, Alex,' Emilie said irritably. 'I'm simply trying to work out the facts. I already know that neither of you are quite what you seem.'

'That's certainly the truth,' he agreed. 'I apologise if I sounded patronising. I actually feel genuinely sorry for you. More wine?'

Emilie let him fill her glass and sat watching him silently. Eventually she said, 'Why do you stay here? You tell me you have money. Surely it would be healthier and safer for the both of you if you agreed to sell the house and go your separate ways?'

'Yes, that's the sensible answer, but it's also leaving out emotion. My grandmother's dearest wish was for us brothers to mend the rift between us. She thought—misguidedly—that bequeathing

Blackmoor Hall to us jointly might do that,' Alex said. 'I've tried, really I have, but it's impossible. And, to be honest, I'm slowly running out of steam. Sebastian will win eventually. I accept that.'

'Why does my husband want to sell it so badly?' Emilie asked. 'He tells me he loves this house and wants to earn the money to restore it.'

'Em, I can only go so far,' Alex stated. 'And I really think that's a question you'll have to ask him. But, yes, I wanted to give my best shot at reconciliation, because it was what my grandmother wanted. I let her down so terribly in my earlier life.' He sighed. 'I adored Constance and I caused her so much worry and pain when I ran away and went down the slippery slope to oblivion.'

'She must have known why you left?'

'Possibly, but to be fair, Emilie, despite the fact that I have a brother who managed to sabotage me during my formative years, I can't blame him for my subsequent decline into drugs. It was my choice completely,' Alex admitted. 'I wanted to blank out the pain of losing what could have been. I'd reached the point where I felt that nothing in my life would ever turn out right. That no matter what I achieved, however hard I worked, somehow it would all come to nothing and go wrong. Do you understand?'

'Yes, I do,' nodded Emilie.

'But through that process, I hurt my beloved grandmother, and I can never forgive myself for that. Staying here and reconciling with Seb made me feel I was at least doing something to make amends.'

'I understand,' she said.

395

'Listen, Em,' said Alex after a pause, 'I'm worried about you, now. You must remember that just because my brother has a problem with me, it doesn't mean that he can't go on to forge successful relationships with other people. I'd hate to think that what has happened between us brothers in the past will prejudice your view of him. I'd like to think of Seb and you being happy together.'

'But how can you still care for him after all he's done to you?' asked Emilie.

'I've learned that growing up as second best, whether real or imagined, is a tough one. I understand now that's how Seb felt. And maybe still feels. You, of all people, should understand that emotion.' He stared at her and she blushed.

'Yes,' she agreed, 'we all carry secrets and we all have flaws.'

'*And* strengths. Seb may not have my academic mind, but he's amazingly streetwise. He's lived on his wits for most of his life. Please, give him a chance, Em. Don't give up just yet,' Alex begged.

'I won't,' she promised.

'Now, how about some supper?' Alex suggested. 'I had a delivery from the farm shop earlier today. And perhaps you could also tell me what you learned about my grandmother's past whilst you were in France?'

Over supper, Emilie related what she'd discovered from Jacques as accurately as she could.

'None of it surprises me,' Alex said when she'd finished. 'Constance was such a wonderful woman, Em. I wish you could have met her.'

Emilie saw the love in his eyes. 'There's little I

can say, except I'm so sorry.'

'Thanks, Em.' Alex gave her a weak smile. 'It'll never stop hurting, but maybe that's the way it should be. The shock of losing her certainly brought me up short. It's made me a better person.'

Emilie saw it was after midnight. 'I must go, Alex. I'm off to France tomorrow to hear the rest of the story, but I'll see you when I get back. And thank you so much for being so honest and *fair* about Sebastian. Goodnight.' Bending down, she kissed him lightly on the cheek.

'Night, Em.'

Alex watched her leave with a sigh. There was so much more he felt he should tell her, but he understood his hands were tied. It would be down to her to discover the truth of the man she had married. He could do no more.

*   *   *

Next door, Emilie climbed into bed feeling unsettled but relieved she knew the truth of the relationship between the brothers. Armed with the facts, she at least felt more capable of dealing with the situation. Her husband wasn't a madman, merely an insecure little boy who had always harboured a deep jealousy of the younger brother who had bested him at everything.

Did this make him a bad person?

No, *no* . . .

Now she understood Sebastian, surely it was possible to help him get over his problems? He needed to feel loved, valued and secure.

Unlike Frederik and Falk, surely one character

did not have to be pure evil and the other good? Neither life nor people were usually so black and white.

Or—Emilie sighed as she switched off the light to prepare for sleep—was she making excuses for her husband's behaviour simply because she couldn't bear the truth?

Which was that she had made a dreadful mistake . . . ?

*   *   *

When Emilie arrived at the château the following afternoon, the sight of its windows and doors boarded up and covered in scaffolding was almost too painful to bear. She spent two hours with the architect going through what they had achieved so far then drove down to the cottage, where Jean sat as usual at his desk in the *cave*, completing paperwork.

'Emilie, it's good to see you again.' He smiled as he stood up and kissed her.

'How's your father?' she asked.

'He's coming back to life as the spring begins to arrive. He's resting at the moment, ready to continue his story tonight. He's told me he wishes for you to know—' Jean sighed—'that it's not a happy ending.'

After the past week of mental and emotional confusion, contrasted with the current joy of being back in the light and balmy air of the Provençal spring, Emilie was ready to deal with it. 'Jean, this is my *past*, not my present or my future. I promise I can cope.'

He looked at her intently, pausing before he

spoke. 'My Emilie, you're different somehow. I feel you've grown up. Forgive me for saying so.'

'No, Jean, I think you're right,' she agreed.

'People say that the death of the older generation means you truly become an adult. Maybe that's the prize from the sadness of losing them.'

'Maybe,' agreed Emilie.

'And now, whilst my father rests, can we talk about the vineyard, Emilie? I want to explain my plan for expansion.'

Emilie did her best to concentrate on the facts and figures Jean put in front of her, but she didn't feel qualified to have an input. She knew nothing about the wine business and her inadequacy made her feel embarrassed that Jean had to come to her to ask for permission to expand it when she was not sure how to advise or help him.

'I trust you, Jean, I know you'll do everything you can to make the *cave* more financially successful,' she said as Jean tidied his papers away.

'Thank you, Emilie, but of course I must talk through my ideas with you. You own the land and the business.'

'Then maybe I shouldn't.' The idea sprang out of nowhere. 'Perhaps you should own it yourself.'

Jean looked at her in surprise. 'Listen, shall we go and take a glass of rosé and talk further?'

They sat out on the terrace at the back of the cottage and discussed how Emilie's idea could be made possible.

'Perhaps I could buy the business, but continue to rent the actual land, which would mean that anyone who came after me to the *cave* would never be able to separate it from the château,' suggested

399

Jean. 'I can't offer much, because I'll borrow from the bank and it will take some time to pay back the interest. But, in return, I could offer a percentage of any profit I make to you.'

'I think that in principle it all sounds sensible,' Emilie agreed. 'I would have to ask Gerard what he thinks of the idea and also to check if there were any covenants put in place by past generations to prohibit it. But I'm sure that, even if there were, I could remove them, as I'm suddenly all-powerful.' She smiled.

'And it suits you,' said Jean, laughing.

'Maybe it does.' Emilie sipped her wine thoughtfully. 'You know, when my mother first died, I was terrified of handling the estate and its complexities. My initial instinct was to sell. I've learned so much in the past year. Perhaps I'm more capable than I believed.' She checked herself. 'Forgive me, I don't want to sound arrogant.'

'Emilie, part of your problem has always been your *lack* of belief in yourself,' commented Jean. 'Anyway, if you're happy to investigate the idea, I'd be keen to reach an agreement. Now, you must be hungry. Let's go inside and eat, and then it won't be too late for my father to tell you more of his story.'

Jacques, thought Emilie, looked much improved from the last time she'd seen him.

'It's the spring air warming my bones,' he chuckled over a supper of fresh sea bream from the local market. 'Now, are you ready Emilie?' he asked her as they settled themselves in the sitting room. 'I warn you, the story is . . . complex.'

'I'm ready.'

'If I remember correctly, Constance and Sophia had arrived at the château and Édouard had managed to escape to England . . .'

Paradise

A glowing dawn, a sweet, ripe
   peach,
A blue sea lapping on the beach.
A hint of spring, a dewy rose
Whose scent assails an eager nose.
Beauty now at every sight.
A feast for senses to delight.

A darkened cell, the fear of night,
A mistral blows with all its might.
A winter's chill in barren land,
The bitter cold through frozen hand.
Beauty now has closed its door.
And swept away for distant shore.

A touch of cheek, a lingered kiss
So soft remembered, soon to miss.
A tender arm around me thrown,
The beauty of a heart's true home.
In black despair, a shooting star,
For Paradise is where you are.

           Sophia de la Martinières,
                April 1944

27

Gassin, South of France, 1944

'There's someone coming!' cried Jacques. 'Where's Sophia?'

'In the cellar, sleeping,' replied Connie, immediately alert.

'Go and warn her she's not to cry out . . .' Jacques's eye was pinned to the peephole in the *cave* door. 'Wait—it's Armand!' He turned to Connie with a sigh of relief and opened the door for him. Connie watched as Armand put his bike against the wall and walked inside. After a month of seeing no one except Jacques and Sophia, Connie was extraordinarily glad to see his bright face.

The two men embraced in their peculiarly intimate French way and Jacques led Armand along the passage to the cottage.

'Sit down, my friend, and tell us all the news. We are starved of it here. Constance, can you make coffee?'

Connie nodded reluctantly, wanting to hear every snippet Armand had to offer. Her current role playing comforter and maid to Sophia—a Sophia who, for the past month, had refused to rouse herself from her bed in the cellar to take some fresh air in the walled garden, and who was not eating or responding to Connie's pleas that she must not give up—was becoming more difficult by the day.

Hurriedly placing three cups on a tray and

pouring the coffee into them, she took them into the sitting room.

'Thank you, Constance, and a happy new year to you!' Armand said as he took the cup from the tray and drank the coffee with relish.

'And let us all pray that 1944 will finally see the deliverance of our country,' added Jacques fervently.

'Yes,' nodded Armand as he pulled a package from his satchel. 'This is for Mademoiselle Sophia, but I'm sure she won't mind if you open it, Madame. It contains good news.'

Connie took the package from him and unwrapped it. She looked at the faded green linen of the cover and the title of the book and smiled.

'It's Volume Two of *The History of French Fruit.*' She looked at Jacques with shining eyes. 'A book I loved from Édouard's library in his Paris house. I presume this means he's safe?'

'Yes, Madame, Édouard is safe,' Armand confirmed. 'And even from his place of hiding, aiding us in our fight. I'm sure it will raise Mademoiselle Sophia's spirits to know that her brother is alive and well. And who knows? He may return sooner than we think. But he stays away purely to protect his sister.'

'Do you know how he managed to escape? He was so sick when we left.' Connie continued to clasp the book to her like a talisman.

'I do not have the details, Madame. But, sadly, I've heard that the British agent who saved his life was recently shot by the Gestapo. These are dangerous times, Madame, but at least "Hero" is safe.'

'Any news of Sarah?'

'None, I'm afraid.' Armand shook his head sadly. 'Like so many others, she has simply disappeared. So, how goes it with Sophia?'

Jacques and Connie looked at each other.

'She's well enough,' said Jacques gruffly. 'She pines for her brother and misses her freedom. But what can be done until this war is over?'

'Tell her she must not give up hope. It will be over soon and then all of us will step into the light. The Allied invasion is coming and we here on the ground are doing all we can to aid it.' Armand smiled at Connie, the faith and hope in his eyes restoring hers. 'Now, I must be going.'

They watched him cycle away, both grateful for the diversion from the solitary life they currently led. Sophia might feel imprisoned downstairs but, above ground, her gaolers felt equally constrained by the need to protect her.

'How is she today?' asked Jacques as Connie cleared away the coffee cups.

'The same; it's as if she has given up.'

'Perhaps the news that her brother is safe and well will help.' Jacques shrugged.

'I'll go down and tell her,' said Connie.

Jacques nodded silently as Connie walked back into the kitchen. She took a sealed flagon of milk from the pantry, placed it in the canvas bag she used to transport supplies down to the cellar and strapped it across her chest.

'Try to encourage her to come upstairs for a while,' added Jacques.

'I will try.'

Connie clambered inside the oak barrel, removed the false floor, lit the oil lamp and made her way along the tunnel. The journey that had sent fear into her the first time she had attempted it was now an everyday routine. Reaching the door, she opened it and saw, in the dim, shallow light of the small window, that Sophia was still asleep. It was almost lunchtime.

'Sophia—' Connie shook her gently—'wake up, I have good news.'

Sophia rolled over and stretched. In her white lawn nightdress, the thickening of her waist was now evident. 'What is it?' she asked.

'A courier has just brought wonderful news. Your brother is safe!'

At this, Sophia sat up. 'And is he coming here? Is he coming to take me away?'

'Maybe soon,' Connie lied, 'but isn't it wonderful that we know he's well? He sent us his book on fruit trees. Remember, you made sketches from it in Paris?'

'Yes!' Sophia tucked her knees into her chest and wrapped her arms around them. 'They were wonderful days.'

'And they will come again, Sophia, I promise.'

'And soon he will come—' she stared off into the distance—'and take me out of this hell. Or maybe Frederik . . .' Sophia grasped Connie's hand suddenly. 'You don't know how much I miss him.'

'I do, because there's someone I miss just as much.'

'Yes, your husband.' Suddenly, all Sophia's energy left her and she lay back down on the bed. 'But I cannot believe this war will ever end. And I think I will die down here in this miserable place.'

These were words Connie had heard over and over in the past few weeks. From experience, she knew there was little she could say or do to pull

407

Sophia out of her torpor.

'Spring is on its way, Sophia, and the dawn of a new era. You must believe that,' she entreated.

'I want to, really I want to—but down here, alone at night, I find it so hard to believe.'

'I understand how difficult it is for you, but you must not give up hope.'

The two women sat silently in the gloom, Connie pondering why Sophia had not yet mentioned the fact that she was pregnant. Surely she must know, given the changes in her body? It had been on the tip of her tongue so many times to talk of it with her. Perhaps being so protected by Édouard and Sarah meant that the girl didn't know what was happening to her. By her reckoning, there would be a baby born from this woman's body in under six months. And, today, Connie felt with a certainty that perhaps it was the only thing that could bring Sophia out of her slough of despondence. And it had to be addressed.

'Sophia,' Connie began gently, 'you do know that, very soon, you'll be having a baby?'

The words hung in the damp, fetid air for so long that Connie wondered if Sophia had gone back to sleep.

Finally, Sophia spoke.

'Yes.'

'And it's Frederik's baby?'

'Of course!' Sophia was indignant at the question.

'And you know that women who are carrying babies need to make sure that their child is nourished? Not just with food, but with fresh air and good spirits?'

A further silence ensued.

'How long have you known?' Sophia asked finally.

'Sarah knew immediately. And she told me,' Connie replied.

'Yes, she would know.' Sophia sighed and moved position to make herself more comfortable. 'I miss her so much.'

'I know you do. I try to do my best, but I understand I'm not Sarah.' Constance could hear the tinge of frustration in her own voice.

'Forgive me, Constance.' Sophia must have sensed the sudden drop in an already chilly temperature. 'I understand how you've cared for me, and I'm truly grateful. As for the baby . . . I was too ashamed to tell you. I understand what it means, what I've done.' Sophia wrung her hands in despair. 'Perhaps it's better if I die. What will my brother say when he knows? My God, what will he say?'

'He will understand that you're human and did what you did out of love,' Connie lied. 'And now, from that love, there's to be a new life born into the world. Sophia, you mustn't give up. You must fight, like you've never fought before, for the sake of your child.'

'But . . . Édouard will never forgive me, never. And you, Constance, how could I tell you that the night my brother was away from Paris, I deceived you and I took Frederik to my bed and laid with him willingly? You must hate me!' Sophia shook her head in despair. 'And yet here you are caring for me, simply because you're a kind woman and have no choice. But you cannot understand, Constance, what it's like to be a burden to everyone around you. From early childhood, I

409

could never be left alone in case I fell. Every day of my life, I cannot do the simple things that others can, I must rely on everyone to help me, ask if I wish to climb the stairs or use the bathroom, or simply get dressed in a new garment that is unfamiliar to me. I can never, as you can, step out of the front door and walk along the street.' Sophia put her tiny fingers to her head. 'Forgive me, Constance, for my self-indulgence.'

'Of course.' Connie laid a comforting hand on Sophia's shoulder. 'It is indeed terrible for you.'

'And then,' Sophia continued, 'I meet a man who does not see me as firstly blind, who does not treat me as my family treat me, like a helpless child. No, Frederik treats me like a woman, he ignores my impairment, listens without patronising me, loves me for who I am inside and long to be on the outside. But it's bad luck for me he's on the wrong side, that he's the enemy. And because of that, I must not, *should* not, love him or I'm betraying my family—my country even—causing them another problem. And now he's gone and I carry his child; yet another burden for those around me to bear. Constance, you question why I lie down here and wait and want to die? I know how much easier everyone's life would be without me!'

Connie sat in shock at the force of Sophia's outburst. Her words made her realise for the first time the depth of Sophia's understanding and her feelings of guilt for her dependence on others.

'If it hadn't been for me,' Sophia continued, 'Sarah would not have been on that train and then arrested. She's probably dead by now, or sent off to one of those terrible camps where she will die anyway.'

Connie searched for the right words. 'Sophia, your presence in your family's life is so valuable that no one even thinks about the care they give you. They love you.'

'And how do I repay that love? By disgracing my family.' Sophia shook her head, tears streaming down her face. 'Whatever you say, Édouard will never forgive me for this. How will I ever tell him?'

'We'll worry about that later, Sophia,' Connie concluded. 'For now, the most important thing is you and your child's health. You must do all you can to help your baby come into the world. Sophia, do you want this child?'

There was a long pause before Sophia spoke. 'Sometimes I think it's best if we both lie down here and die. But then I think that everyone I love has gone and the life inside me is all I have. And it's part of him, part of Frederik . . . Oh, Constance, I'm so confused. Do you not hate me for what I've done?'

'No, Sophia.' Connie sighed. 'I don't hate you, of course I don't. You must realise that you're not the only woman who has found herself in this predicament, nor will you be the last. I agree that the circumstances couldn't be more complicated, but just remember that tiny, innocent life growing inside you knows nothing of this. And whatever his or her heritage, or what the future holds, surely you owe it to your baby to at least give it a fighting chance to have a life? There's been so much death, so much destruction. And new life is new hope, whatever the circumstances of conception. A baby is a gift from God, Sophia.'

As she paused, Connie wondered if it was her latent Catholic upbringing putting these

411

passionate words into her mouth. She realised she meant every one of them. 'I think that, for now, all you can do is to cherish what's growing inside you,' she added quietly.

'Yes, you're right,' said Sophia. 'You're so kind and wise, Constance, and I cannot thank you enough for what you've done for me. And, one day, I hope to find a way to repay you.'

'Well, maybe you can do that by not lying down here wishing to die,' Connie suggested. 'Please, Sophia, help me to help you and your baby.'

'Yes.' Sophia sighed. 'I've been self-indulgent, when so many others are suffering far worse. I'll try to have hope from now on. And perhaps when Frederik comes we can make a plan.'

Connie stared at Sophia, incredulous that she still thought this possible. 'You believe he will?'

'I know he will,' Sophia replied with the certainty of love. 'He said he would come to find me and my heart tells me that he won't let me down.'

'Then, Sophia,' Connie encouraged, 'you mustn't let Frederik down, either.'

*   *   *

In the next few days, Sophia roused herself. She began to eat properly and climbed the stairs up to the château and out into the walled garden, where she would walk with Connie to take exercise.

One morning, she sniffed the air. 'Spring's on its way. I can smell it. Then life will become so much more pleasant.'

March came and the mimosa grew wild in the walled garden. There were no visitors to the château, and Jacques refused to let Connie leave the grounds to cycle to the village for supplies, insisting he did it himself. They lived on constant alert of a visit from the local Gestapo, but all the attention they'd received recently was from a German minion who had arrived to demand a hundred bottles of wine and two barrels of schnapps for the torpedo factory.

'Our solitary life is a safe life,' said Jacques one evening. 'No one can be trusted and whilst Sophia is under my protection we cannot become complacent. So we must suffer the loneliness and monotony of each other's company until this is over.' Jacques raised his eyebrows and smiled at her.

Connie could do little more than agree. Yet, forced together with this stranger, she had grown very fond of Jacques. His peasant skin and bearing belied a clever and thoughtful mind. Once Sophia was sleeping downstairs in the cellar, many evenings were spent tussling over a chessboard. Connie also learned much from Jacques about the complex process of producing wine and never failed to be moved by his total devotion to his dear friend and master, Édouard. In return, she talked to him of her life in England, and her darling Lawrence, who had no idea where she was.

Connie felt she existed in perpetual darkness, either downstairs in Sophia's cellar bedroom or in the shuttered rooms of the château. Occasionally, she would lead Sophia up the stairs and sit with her in the wonderful library Édouard and his father had created. She would take a book off the shelf and read it to Sophia by the flickering light of the oil lamp. On one of the shelves, Connie had

413

found the first volume to *The History of French Fruit*, and had taken it back to the cottage to show Jacques.

'They're beautiful books,' he acknowledged as he turned the fragile pages of the exquisite coloured plates. 'Édouard showed me this first volume which his father had bought some time ago. At least *they* have been reunited after hundreds of years.'

As the spring arrived, Sophia's body burgeoned too. Now in the full bloom of pregnancy, her cheeks were pink from afternoons of sitting underneath the protective branches of the chestnut tree in the walled garden. Whenever Sophia was taking the air, Jacques was on patrol for unwanted visitors. He was as protective as any father could be.

One night, when Connie had helped Sophia to bed in the cellar, Jacques took out a jug of wine and poured both himself and Connie a glass.

'Do you have any idea when the baby is due to be born?' he asked her.

'By my calculations, sometime in June,' Connie answered.

'And what will we do then?' sighed Jacques. 'Can a baby really spend the first few weeks of its life in a cold, dark cellar? Besides, what if it cries and somebody hears it? And how can Sophia take care of a baby when she cannot see it?'

'Under normal circumstances, she'd have a nursemaid to help her. But these are not normal circumstances,' said Connie.

'No.'

'Well—' she sighed—'it seems I will be the nursemaid, although I don't have any idea of how

414

to look after a baby.'

'I've wondered, Constance, whether it would be best if the baby was taken straight to an orphanage. Then no one except you and me and Mademoiselle Sophia would know of its existence. What future can there ever be for it?' Jacques shook his head in despair. 'When Édouard discovers the truth, I dare not think what he will do.'

'That's certainly an idea, yes,' Connie agreed tentatively, 'but not one that should be put to Sophia at this moment. She's doing very well.'

'Of course—' Jacques nodded—'but I do know of a convent orphanage in Draguignan which takes cases such as this one.'

'Perhaps.' Connie did not think it appropriate to mention the attachment Sophia had recently formed to the unborn child inside her; the way she saw it as part of Frederik and a symbol of their love—an attitude which she herself had encouraged, to try and spring Sophia out of her torpor. Jacques was a man. He wouldn't understand. 'We will see,' was all she said.

*   *   *

In early May, Armand appeared at the cottage on his bicycle. He sat with Jacques and Connie in the small garden, drinking the new batch of rosé from the barrel. Exhausted and gaunt, he told them how his branch of the Maquis, based up in the thickly wooded hillside of La Garde-Freinet, was preparing for the southern invasion.

'The Boche are being fooled into thinking the attack will come in from the shores of Marseilles

415

and Toulon, but the Allies are planning to land down here on the beaches around Cavalaire and Ramatuelle. And we, the Resistance, are doing all we can to confuse the Boche and make their life difficult,' he said, smiling. 'We're cutting telephone lines, blowing up railway bridges and hijacking their convoys of arms. There're many thousands of us now, all fighting for the same cause. The British are secretly dropping as many weapons as they can to us down here and we're well organised. I've heard the Americans will head up the southern attack by sea. Constance, I know you're trained in this kind of work. Can you help us? We need a courier to—'

'No, Armand, so far she hasn't been out of this house,' Jacques replied firmly, 'and we've been left alone. If Constance was seen cycling in and out of here, it would be too dangerous for Mademoiselle Sophia.'

Connie was crestfallen. 'But couldn't I use the back way, Jacques? I want to help.'

'I know, Constance, and maybe in time you can. But, for now, it's important for you to be close to Mademoiselle Sophia.' Jacques gave her a warning glance.

'But perhaps there are other ways you could assist us, Jacques,' continued Armand. 'We often have British airmen we're smuggling out of France through Corsica, and occasionally we need a safe house where they can wait until the boat comes for them. Would you be prepared to take them in?'

Jacques sighed doubtfully. 'I don't want to attract any attention to us here.'

'Surely, Jacques, we could do this safely?' Connie insisted. 'Sophia is hidden in the cellar

416

away from the *cave* and we must do all we can to help the greater cause. It's what Édouard himself lived by, even if it meant putting his family in danger,' Connie emphasised, determined to do something of use.

'Yes, Constance, you're right,' Jacques answered eventually. 'How can I refuse? We can put the airmen up in the attic.'

'Thank you,' nodded Armand gratefully.

'And I'm sure, Constance, that you'll look after them,' Jacques said as he stood up.

'Of course.' Connie was selfishly thinking of how much she would like to join the airmen on the boat to Corsica.

'I—or one of my men—will be in touch when the need arises,' said Armand. 'Now, I must be on my way.'

*　　　*　　　*

The first two British airmen arrived at three o'clock in the morning a week later. The sound of their British accents brought tears to Connie's eyes as she fussed around them, giving them food and wine. They were to stay for twenty-four hours before leaving by boat to Corsica. Both men, though frail and exhausted from being on the run for the past few weeks, were in good spirits at the thought of returning home.

'Don't you worry, old girl,' one of them said to her as she showed them up to the attic, 'the Nazis' hold on France is weakening. Hitler is losing his grip—there was even a foiled plot to kill him by some of his senior men recently. One way or another, it'll be weeks rather than months before this is all over.'

When they left in the small hours of the following morning, Connie handed one of the English pilots an envelope. 'Please, when you're home, could you post this for me?'

'Of course I can. A small price to pay for the first decent nosh I've had in weeks,' he said with a smile.

Connie retired to bed, a renewed sense of hope in her heart. If the airman did make it back, then at least Lawrence might hear she was safe and well.

*　　*　　*

As Sophia's time grew closer, she struggled to mount the steep cellar steps with her swollen stomach. Yet she had an air of tranquillity about her and was glowing with health.

Connie had managed to find some wool and a pair of knitting needles in the old housekeeper's store in the château and sat in the walled garden with Sophia in the afternoons making tiny jackets, hats and booties for the baby. She sometimes looked at Sophia in envy; after all, her own dream with Lawrence was to have a family. Now she was living vicariously through another woman's journey into motherhood.

In the warm evenings, she and Jacques often sat outside at the table in the cottage garden, surrounded by the tender young vines that protected the tiny green berries which would soon grow into fat, bulbous grapes.

'It's not long now until the *vendange*, when the grapes must be picked, but whether I can get the help I need to do it, I don't know.' Jacques sighed. 'Everyone's thoughts are on more important things than making wine.'

'I'll help you as much as I can,' Connie offered, knowing it was a futile gesture. Jacques would normally have a dozen men and women picking the grapes from dawn until dusk.

'It's kind of you to offer, Constance, but I think your help may be needed elsewhere. Do you have any knowledge of bringing babies into the world?' Jacques asked.

'No. Surprisingly, that wasn't part of my training course before I came out here,' she replied with irony in her voice. 'In books I've read, everyone fusses around with hot water and towels. Why, I'm not exactly sure, but I expect I'll cope when the time comes.'

'I worry that something may go wrong and Sophia will need proper medical help. What would we do then? We cannot risk taking her to hospital,' worried Jacques.

'As I said, I'll do my best.'

'And that, my dearest Constance—' Jacques sighed—'is all we can both do.'

*   *   *

A steady trail of airmen passed across Jacques's threshold, using the holding bay of the attic in the cottage to wait for the boat to Corsica. Connie gleaned from them that the Allied invasion plan for Normandy was close to fruition. The southern invasion would follow a few weeks later. Every time the airmen left, she handed them an envelope to send to Lawrence.

419

The letters always said the same thing:

*My darling, do not worry about me. I am safe
and well and I hope to return home soon.*

Surely, Connie thought, as she wrote the fifth
letter one June evening, ready to hand to an
airman when he left in the small hours of the
morning, one of them must find its way safely to
Lawrence?

Jacques suddenly entered the sitting room, his
face concerned. 'Constance, someone is prowling
around outside. Go up and tell the airmen to stay
silent and I'll see who it is.'

Jacques took his hunting gun from its position
by the front door and left the cottage.

Having warned the airmen, Connie came back
downstairs to find Jacques standing in the sitting
room, his gun pointed at a tall, painfully emaciated
blond-haired man whose arms were held upright in
surrender.

'Stay clear! He's German!' Jacques poked the
gun in the man's chest. 'Sit down! Over there.' He
indicated the chair by the fire, where the man
would be safely pinned into a corner.

As the man sat down, Connie looked at his eyes,
huge in his gaunt face, his matted, filthy blond hair
and what was left of his shirt and trousers hanging
off his skeletal frame. She stared at him and her
heart began to beat. She thought she might faint
from shock.

'Constance, it's me, Frederik,' the man croaked
hoarsely. 'Perhaps you do not recognise me out of
my uniform?'

Connie forced herself to drag her gaze back up

to his face. The expression in his eyes was the only clue as to which twin he was. She read the gentleness and the fear in them and, with a sigh of relief, realised he was telling the truth.

'You know this man?' Jacques turned to Connie, disbelief on his face.

'Yes.' She nodded. 'His name is Frederik von Wehndorf and he's a colonel in the SS. He's known to Sophia also.' Connie eyed Jacques, hoping he would understand without her speaking the words.

'I see.' Jacques gave a nod of comprehension, but did not relax the gun. He turned to Frederik. 'And what are you doing here?'

'I've come to see Sophia, as I promised her I would. Is she here?'

Neither Connie nor Jacques answered him.

'As you can see—' Frederik indicated his clothes—'I'm no longer an officer in the German army. In fact, I'm a wanted man. If they find me, they will take me back to Germany, where I will be shot immediately as a traitor.'

Jacques gave a harsh laugh. 'You seriously expect us to believe your story? How can we know this is not a trick? You Boche will lie endlessly to save your own sorry skins.'

'You're right, sir,' Frederik agreed calmly. 'I cannot prove it to you. I can only tell you *my* truth.' He turned to Connie. 'After I took you, Sophia and her maid to Gare de Montparnasse, I did not return to Germany. I was aware that my brother, Falk, would not rest until I was brought to justice for helping you escape. It's not the first time he's doubted my allegiance to the cause. It seems I have many enemies and no friends.'

The pain and exhaustion in Frederik's eyes were

palpable. Out of his uniform, he looked far more vulnerable.

'Where are you headed, Frederik?' Connie interjected.

'Constance, my only thought was to get here to see Sophia, as I promised her I would,' said Frederik. 'When I left Paris, I went into hiding. I fled to the High Pyrenees and used a mixture of bribery and the kindness of strangers to stay alive. I lay low, even milking goats and feeding chickens, waiting until I felt it was safe to travel through France to find Sophia. I left—' Frederik gave a desperate shrug—'many weeks ago to make my way here.'

'You've done well to come this far without being caught by either side,' said Jacques, still disbelieving.

'It was the thought of seeing Sophia that drove me on. But my luck is sure to run out soon. There's one in particular who could have guessed where I would eventually head and care enough to hunt me down.' Frederik sighed then shook his head. 'No matter—I know my death is inevitable, whether by French or German hands. I simply wanted to see Sophia one last time. Please, Constance, at least tell me if she's safe and well? That she's alive?'

Connie could see Frederik's eyes were filled with tears. As he sat there at gunpoint, hardly recognisable as the man he used to be, her heart went out to him. He had chosen to risk his life to see the woman he loved, rather than escaping and saving his own skin. Whatever his nationality, political persuasion or even what he may have done over the past few years, this was a human

422

being who currently deserved sympathy.

'Yes, she's safe and well,' Connie stated.

Jacques shot her a look of warning, but Connie ignored it. 'Are you hungry? I doubt you've eaten much over the past few weeks.'

'Constance, anything you have to spare would be welcome, but tell me, is Sophia here? Can I see her?' Frederik pleaded.

'I'll bring you food and then we'll talk. Jacques, you can lower your gun. Frederik will do us no harm. You have my word. Why don't you go upstairs and tell our friends in the attic there's no need for panic. It's simply a visiting relative, but they're to stay out of sight anyway.'

'If you believe we can trust him,' Jacques said slowly, lowering his gun reluctantly, 'I will do so.'

'I do,' nodded Connie, enjoying the feeling of taking charge for a change. 'Now, Frederik, come into the kitchen and we'll talk whilst I prepare some food.'

With effort, Frederik stood up and Connie noticed how every step he took was a struggle. He had reached his journey's end and exhaustion, hunger and desperation were replacing adrenalin. Connie closed the kitchen door firmly behind her and indicated Frederik should sit down on a wooden chair at the small table.

'Constance, please,' he implored her again, 'is she here?'

'Yes, Frederik. Sophia is here,' Connie confirmed.

'Oh God, oh God.' Frederik put his head in his hands and began to weep. 'Sometimes, as I made my way here, sleeping in ditches and looking through rubbish to find some morsel of food, I thought to myself that maybe she was dead. I have imagined it so often, I . . .' Frederik wiped his nose on his sleeve and shook his head. 'My apologies, Constance, I understand you can have no sympathy for me, but you cannot know what hell I've been through to find her.'

'Here, drink this.' Putting a glass of wine in front of him, Connie patted him gently on the shoulder. 'I'm amazed you've made it here alive.'

'I was helped by the fact that both the French and my own kind know something is coming. France is in chaos, the Resistance have grown stronger. We—*they*—' Frederik immediately corrected himself—'are struggling to keep them at bay. And perhaps the last place anyone thought to look for me was in France. Except for one . . .'

'There, eat.' Connie put a roughly cut piece of bread and some cheese in front of him.

'Have they been to search the château yet?' asked Frederik as he stuffed the bread and cheese into his mouth, swallowing without chewing.

'Yes, they've searched and found nothing. Jacques and I have taken great care to make sure the château stays closed and Sophia hidden. At present, they don't suspect she's here.'

'And Édouard? Is he here too?' Frederik asked.

'No. He knew his presence would put his sister in even greater danger.'

'Well, I cannot stay for long; I'm aware every second I'm here is putting your lives at risk. So—' Frederik washed down his bread and cheese with large gulps of wine—'I will see Sophia, then I will leave. Will you take me to her now? I beg you, please, Constance.'

'Yes, I will. Follow me.'

Connie took Frederik into the *cave*, up and inside the oak barrel, then led him along the tunnel.

'My poor, poor Sophia,' he grunted as his height hampered his progress. 'How can she bear it? Does she ever feel the warmth of the sun on her face?'

'She has had no choice but to suffer this for her own safety.' Connie had reached the door. 'She's in there and she may be asleep. I'll go in first so as not to startle her. And, Frederik—' she turned to look at him—'I think that you too are in for a shock.'

Connie tapped on the door three times then opened it softly. Sophia was sitting in the chair by the mean window, a Braille book resting on her stomach.

'Constance?' She looked up.

'Yes, it is I.' She walked across to where Sophia sat and put a gentle hand on her shoulder. 'Don't be afraid, but you have a visitor. I think you'll be very happy when you realise who it is.'

'Sophia, Sophia my love, it's Frederik,' a voice whispered from behind Connie. 'I'm here, *mein Liebling.*'

For a moment, Sophia could not speak. 'Am I dreaming? Frederik?' she whispered. 'Is it really you?'

'Oh yes, my Sophia, it is.'

Sophia reached out her arms wide, the book dropping to the floor.

Connie backed away, watching from the door as Frederik walked to Sophia and took her in his arms. Tears filled her eyes as she quietly left the room, closing the door behind her.

28

All that night, Connie sat up in Jacques's sitting room, keeping watch. When the airmen left at two, Jacques joined her, yawning.

'At least that is part of our trouble removed from the house. What about the other?' He indicated below the floorboards. 'Is he still with her?'

'Yes.'

'Have you been down to check on them?'

'Once. I could hear them talking.'

'Forgive me, Constance, but can you really trust him? It may be a trick to fool us, using a love-struck young girl.'

'I can assure you it isn't. You only need to look at him to see he's telling the truth. It's obvious he's been on the run for weeks. We wouldn't be here if it wasn't for him aiding our escape from Paris. And he loves Sophia with every fibre in his body.'

'But what if he's been followed?'

'Of course, it's a strong possibility—'

'Constance! From what I've heard from you about his brother, it's a certainty,' Jacques interjected.

'But whilst they're both down in the hidden room, surely they're safe? And Frederik knows he must leave as soon as possible. But to deny them what may well be their last few hours together would be terribly cruel. Please, Jacques, give them this time,' Connie pleaded. 'I think they'll have a lot to talk about, given the circumstances.'

'He must leave quickly,' Jacques said with a shudder. 'If it's ever known we have harboured a

Nazi here, it will be the end of me.'

'Please, Jacques, he'll move on tomorrow,' Connie replied staunchly.

*   *   *

Sophia lay on the narrow bed that barely sufficed for her, let alone the man in whose arms she was currently held. She continually stroked his face, his neck, his hair, to convince herself Frederik was really there. He was so exhausted he sporadically fell asleep, then woke with a jump and tightened his loosened grip around Sophia's shoulders.

'Tell me, my love, what can we do?' she asked him. 'There must be somewhere in the world we can run to?'

Frederik gently stroked the outline of his child underneath the thin, white skin of Sophia's stomach. 'You must stay here until our baby is born. You have no choice. I'll leave tomorrow and, God willing, find a safe harbour until the war is over. I promise you, it won't be long now.'

'I've heard that for years and it never seems to end.' Sophia sighed.

'It will end, Sophia, I swear, and you must believe it,' said Frederik. 'And then, when it's over, and I've found a place we can be, I'll come to find you and our child.'

'Please don't leave me! I cannot bear it without you, *please* . . .' The words that even she knew were fruitless were muffled as she buried her face in his warm chest.

'It's only for a few more months and you must hold on. Be strong for the baby. And, one day, we'll sit with him and tell him of the bravery his

427

mother showed to bring him into the world. Sophia—' Frederik kissed her forehead, nose and lips tenderly—'I said I'd come to find you this time and I have. I will not let you down in the future. Believe me.'

'I believe you. So let us talk of happier subjects. Tell me about your childhood,' Sophia suggested, suddenly desperate to glean all the information she could of the man she loved—the father of her child.

'I grew up in East Prussia, in a small village named Charlottenruhe.' Frederik closed his eyes and smiled as he pictured it. 'We were lucky, for our family lived in a beautiful *Schloss*, surrounded by the many acres of fertile land that we owned and farmed. East Prussia was known as the Corn Chamber, for it had hundreds of miles of land on which crops grew. And from that, we who lived there became prosperous. I had a beautiful childhood, wanting for nothing, loved by both my parents and blessed with an excellent education. Perhaps the only trouble I had was from my brother, who resented me from the start.'

'Two brothers, born an hour apart, brought up in the same family, and yet you're so very different,' Sophia mused. She patted her tummy. 'I can only hope our little one takes after his father, not his uncle. Where did you go when you left school?'

'Falk went straight into the army and I went to university in Dresden to study politics and philosophy. It was an interesting moment in time—the Führer had just come to power,' Frederik explained. 'After years of poverty for so many Germans since the end of the First World

War, Hitler began making reforms to provide wealth and a better standard of living for his citizens. Like the rest of the young radical thinkers, and with a particular interest in politics because of my degree, I became swept up in the excitement.' Frederik sighed. 'You won't want to hear this, Sophia, but in the first years that Hitler became Chancellor, he made a lot of changes for the better and his ideas to build our nation into a strong economic and industrial international force were enticing. I went to one of his rallies in Nuremberg and the atmosphere was incredible. The Führer had a magnificence, a charisma that made him irresistible to a downtrodden nation. And when he spoke, we believed every word of it. He offered us hope for the future and we worshipped him. I, like the rest of my friends, hurried to sign up to his party.'

'I see.' Sophia shuddered. 'So how did it change?'

'Well—' Frederik searched for the words in his exhausted mind to try and explain—'it's hard for you and me to imagine the thought of millions of people hanging on every word we uttered, to be the subject of such frenzied adoration, with hardly a dissenting voice amongst them. Surely we would feel omnipotent, a God?'

'I understand, yes,' murmured Sophia into his shoulder.

'Even before the war began, I was horrified at what he was doing to the Jews in Germany, and the way he was outlawing religion. I'm a Christian, as you know, a fact I had to keep hidden for my own safety. But by that time, I'd already been chosen to join the Intelligence Service. I had no

429

choice, Sophia. I would have been shot if I'd refused.'

'My Frederik, what you have suffered,' comforted Sophia, her eyes full of tears.

'My suffering is nothing compared to thirteen-year-old boys who have a gun forced into their hands to kill for a cause they don't even understand!' Frederik began to weep too. 'And I, too, through my actions, knowingly sent people to their deaths. You don't know the terrible things I've done . . . God forgive me for them. And you, Sophia—' Frederik looked at her with agonised eyes—'how can *you* forgive me? How can I forgive myself?'

'Frederik, please . . .'

'Yes, you're right, enough of that now,' he murmured, caressing her hair with his lips. 'Down here with you, I finally feel safe and peaceful. And if I died right now, I'd die happy.'

Frederik settled back down next to Sophia and looked up at the reflection of the oil lamp on the darkened ceiling. 'I think I'll remember this night for always. I understand that Paradise is not being in a beautiful place like the Garden of Eden as the Bible suggests, or amassing great wealth to provide power and status. Those things are only outer beauty and mean nothing. For here I am, in a damp, dark cellar, already sentenced to death. Yet, with you in my arms, I'm at peace.' Frederik gave a sob of emotion. 'My soul is in Paradise because I'm with you.'

'Frederik,' Sophia begged, 'please, hold me like you can never let me go.'

*　　*　　*

430

The residents of the de la Martinières château awoke to a soft Provençal dawn. The occupants above the ground prowled nervously, and those below lay wakeful too, dreading the sun rising in the sky.

*   *   *

In London, at first light, Édouard de la Martinières was disturbed by a low and insistent hum, which turned as it passed overhead to a deafening roar. He went to the window and saw the aircraft flying in massed formation in a never-ending stream across the capital. It was the sixth of June, 1944. D-Day had just begun.

*   *   *

At seven o'clock, Connie heard a tentative tap on the kitchen door. She opened it and saw Frederik standing there, his eyes still alight with the fire of love.

'I must leave soon, Constance. Could I trouble you for some coffee and perhaps some bread for breakfast? It may be the last food I get for a long time,' he said.

'Of course,' said Connie. 'And I'm sure we can provide you with some fresh clothes to wear. You're a similar height to Jacques.' Even from this distance, Connie could smell Frederik's staleness.

'That's most kind of you, Constance. Sophia has asked you to go to her. She says there's a garden in which it's safe for her to sit. She would prefer to say goodbye to me there.'

431

'Of course.' Connie indicated a kettle close to boiling on top of the range and the bread left over from the night before. 'There are washing facilities just outside the kitchen door. I'll bring you some clothes down.'

Jacques had cycled off to the village to buy fresh bread, so Connie went to his wardrobe, brought down a pile of clothes she thought suitable and offered them to Frederik. 'Take what fits. I'll help Sophia into the garden and then re-turn. I'll also see if we can give you some francs to aid your journey.'

'Constance, you're an angel of mercy and I'll never forget what you've done for Sophia and myself. Thank you.'

*   *   *

Connie knocked on the door of Sophia's cellar room fifteen minutes later. She was sitting on her bed, her face serene and beautiful.

'Frederik said you would like to say goodbye to him in the garden.'

'Yes. It may be a long time before we're together again. And I'd like to remember the last moments we have together as if both of us were simply free to go wherever we chose.'

'I understand, but you must be ready to move quickly if anyone should come.'

'Of course. Now, Constance, can you make sure I have no smudges on my face and my hair is neat?' she asked.

When Connie had done her best in the dim light the small window provided, thinking that, with love lighting her face, Sophia would look beautiful without any attention, she led her upstairs into the walled garden and sat her at the table under the chestnut tree.

'I'll bring Frederik here to you,' said Connie.

'Thank you. It's a beautiful morning,' said Sophia.

'Yes, it is.'

Connie left the garden and Sophia sat alone, enjoying the warmth of the sun on her face. She breathed in the scented air, recognising the strong smell of lavender planted profusely in the borders of the garden.

'Sophia.'

'You're back so fast.' She smiled, opening her arms to greet him. 'Has Constance left us alone?'

There was a slight pause, before he said, 'Yes.'

'Come and hold me, Frederik. Our time runs out.'

He did so, and Sophia breathed in his scent, different from an hour ago. She traced the familiar structure of his face and then the roughness of a strange jacket. 'I think you've washed and Constance has provided you with new clothes,' she said.

'Yes, she's very kind.'

'Must you leave immediately? Perhaps we could sit here for a little longer.' She patted the chair next to her and felt for his hands as he sat down. Their grip seemed tighter than usual, his hands less calloused, probably from the soap.

'How will I know how to reach you when you leave?' she asked.

'I'll contact you. Perhaps if you tell me where your brother is hiding, I can send a message to him too.'

'Frederik, I told you last night, I don't know where he is. He stays away to protect me.'

'You really have no idea where he is?'

'No!' She shook her head in frustration. 'Why do we talk of this when at any minute you're leaving? Frederik, please, we have so little time left, let us talk of our plans for the future. Perhaps we should decide on a name for our child, depending on whether it's a girl or a boy.'

'How about Falk, after his uncle?' It was the same voice, but it came from a distance. Sophia did not understand. Her arms flailed out as she searched for him.

'Where are you? Frederik? What's happening?'

Frederik surveyed his brother, who had stood up from the chair next to Sophia and now pointed a pistol at him.

'So, you have come, Falk,' Frederik stated.

'Of course.'

'And have you brought the might of your Gestapo friends with you? Are they waiting at the entrance of the château to march me back to Germany?' Frederik asked wearily.

'No.' Falk shook his head. 'I thought I would enjoy this pleasure alone. Give you one last chance to explain. After all, you are my brother. I felt it was the least I could do.'

'That's most kind of you.' Frederik nodded. 'How did you find me?'

'It would take a fool not to know where you would head. You've been followed for the past few weeks,' Falk informed him. 'I knew you would eventually lead me to the others I'm interested in questioning. For example, the young lady who sits before us. Unfortunately, she refuses to divulge

434

the whereabouts of her brother. Although she knows where he is, of course.'

'Monsieur, I do not! He does not tell us for our own protection!' Sophia cried.

'Come now, Fräulein, even a whore like you—' Falk indicated her stomach—'who has her brains elsewhere, would not expect me to believe that.' He turned his attention back to Frederik. 'You know I have a warrant for your arrest in my pocket. It would be a shame if I had to kill you now to force your girlfriend to talk.'

'Perhaps you have anticipated this moment since we were children, brother.' Frederik looked at his twin with sadness in his eyes. 'And I would die happily at your hands if it wasn't for the woman I love. If I surrender to you peacefully and accompany you back to Germany, where you can be lauded for your cleverness in hunting me down, would you spare her? I swear to you on our mother's life, Sophia knows nothing of Édouard de la Martinières's whereabouts. So do we have a deal?' begged Frederik. 'I will come freely and give you the glory you've always sought, if you will spare both the woman I love and our child.'

Falk looked at his brother then gave a harsh snort of laughter. He laughed so hard his gun wavered and he pulled himself up short. 'Ah, brother, you're such an idealist! Those poems you used to read as a child—romantic rubbish! Your belief in God, your much vaunted intellect and skill at philosophy, when you do not see what life is really about. Life is cold and hard and cruel. We do not possess the soul you have always talked about. We're nothing better than ants who crawl around blindly across the planet. You have never understood reality. It's dog eat dog in this world, brother. Everyone for themselves. You think your little life matters—or hers? You really believe that *love*—' Falk spat the word out—'can conquer all? You're deluded, Frederik, as you always have been. And now it's time I taught you what reality is about.'

Falk's gun swerved away from Frederik as he pointed it at Sophia.

'*This* is "reality"!'

Frederik dived in front of Sophia as a shot rang out in the quiet dawn.

And then another.

Frederik turned round, unhurt, to see if Sophia had been hit. But it was Falk who dropped to the ground. He shuddered a little, mortally wounded, as the gun fell from his fingertips. Frederik ran to him and knelt over him, looking down into his brother's eyes, which were rolling in their sockets.

Falk opened his mouth and managed to focus on his twin. With difficulty, he formed some words.

'You won.' And with a small smile of surrender, life left him.

There was silence in the garden apart from the birds in the trees above, who still welcomed in the new day. Eventually, having closed his twin's eyes and kissed him on the forehead, Frederik looked up.

Connie stood behind Falk, Jacques's hunting gun still pointing at where he had been standing.

'Thank you,' Frederik mouthed to her, tears in his eyes.

'He'd earned it,' she said. 'And I thought it was about time I used some of my expensive training,' she added quietly, a ghost of a smile playing on her lips. 'I did the right thing?' Her eyes begged him to answer in the affirmative.

Frederik looked down at his dead brother and then turned his head to Sophia, who was ashen with shock.

'Yes,' he said, 'you did. Thank you.'

Jacques appeared beside her. 'Give me the gun, Constance.' He took it gently from her hands. As he did so, Connie began to shake violently. Jacques put an arm around her shoulders and led her to the chair next to Sophia.

'He's dead?' Jacques asked Frederik, looking down at the body on the grass.

'Yes.'

'I didn't know you were such an accurate shot, Constance,' said Jacques as he bent over Falk and saw the blood seeping through his uniform.

'I was trained to kill,' Connie replied.

'He was your brother?' said Jacques to Frederik.

'Yes. My twin.'

'I suppose many others knew of his presence here?'

'I doubt it. He wanted the glory of my capture all for himself.'

'Well, we cannot risk that he didn't tell someone where he was going,' said Jacques. 'Frederik, you must leave immediately. At the very least, anyone passing by the château may have heard the shots. Mademoiselle Sophia, you must hurry downstairs and stay there for now, whilst we decide what is best to do. Constance will take you,' he added.

'Thank you,' said Sophia as Connie helped her up and the two women held on to each other for support.

Frederik left his twin's body and walked slowly

437

towards Connie. 'I won't let you take the blame for this. Falk came for me and it's I who should have ended it. When his death is discovered, I wish you to say that it was I who shot him.'

'No, Frederik, I didn't kill him just to save Sophia and yourself.' Connie stared into the distance. 'I had reasons of my own. At least now I'll know that no other woman will ever be subjected to what he did to me.' She lifted her eyes up to Frederik. 'I've wished him dead for many months.'

'We must dispose of the body immediately, Frederik,' said Jacques. 'I'll need your help to dig a grave.'

'Of course,' Frederik agreed.

'Here in the walled garden is safest, so we don't take the risk of moving him and being seen. I'll collect the shovels. Perhaps you could remove your brother's clothing and I'll burn it on a bonfire,' Jacques suggested to him. 'Constance, when you've taken Sophia down to the cellar, there's brandy in the kitchen. Take a drink—it will help. You're not needed here.'

After she had taken a shaken Sophia back to the cellar, and assured her Frederik would be down to see her to say goodbye, Connie did as she was told. The brandy helped although, even in the heat of the June day, she continued to shiver.

Half an hour later, Jacques arrived back at the cottage. 'Falk has been buried and his uniform burned. Frederik is down in the cellar saying goodbye to Sophia and then he will leave.'

'Thank you, Jacques.'

'No, Constance, it's us who should thank you.' Jacques looked at her with new respect. 'Now, I'll collect supplies to help Frederik on his way and, when he's gone, we'll talk.'

*   *   *

'Goodbye, my love.' Frederik held Sophia to him. 'I'll send word to you, I swear, but for now you must concentrate on your own safety and that of our child. Take advice from Jacques and Constance—they're good people and I know they will protect you.'

'Yes.' Tears ran down Sophia's face from her sightless eyes. She reached for the signet ring on the fifth finger of her right hand and pulled it over her swollen knuckle. 'Here, take this. It has the de la Martinières insignia engraved upon it. I wish for you to have it.'

'Then you must have mine. It carries my family crest. Here, I'll put it on your finger for you.'

Sophia held out her hand and Frederik placed the ring on her ring finger.

He smiled. 'We're exchanging rings, down here in this terrible place, on this terrible day. It's not where I would choose, but it's better than nothing. Wear that ring, Sophia, and never forget how much I love you. You will be in my heart, always.'

'And you in mine.'

'I must go.'

'Yes.'

Reluctantly, Frederik took his arms from about her, kissed her on the lips one last time and walked towards the door. 'And whatever happens, please tell our child that his father loved his mother so very much. Goodbye, Sophia.'

'Goodbye,' she whispered, 'and may God go

439

with you.'

*   *   *

Later, when Frederik had finally left, Connie went down to the cellar to comfort what she knew would be a distraught Sophia. And found her instead crouched over her bed, panting.

'My God!' Sophia exclaimed. 'I thought you would never come. The baby . . .' Sophia screamed as a contraction ripped through her body. 'Help me, Constance, help me!'

As the liberation of France began and the Allies stormed onto the beaches of Normandy, the battle raging for days, the cries of a newborn infant echoed around the darkened cellar.

29

Three Months Later

On a mellow evening in late September, Édouard de la Martinières stepped into the walled garden of the château just as the sun was setting. He saw a woman sitting under the oak tree, cradling a baby. Her eyes were lowered to the child, her full attention on soothing it.

He walked towards the woman, momentarily confused.

'Hello,' he said with a question in his voice, a question which was answered the minute the clear brown eyes looked up in surprise at his unexpected intrusion.

440

'Édouard!'

He walked over to her and she stood up, the baby in her arms.

'Forgive me, Constance, your hair colour . . . you look very different. For a moment, I thought you were Sophia.' He smiled.

'No . . .' Connie's eyes clouded then she said, 'I can't believe you're here! You should have sent word, Édouard.'

'I didn't want to risk announcing my presence,' he explained. 'Even though Paris is liberated and De Gaulle is back in control, there's still danger until the whole of France is free.'

'After the Allied invasion down here on the beaches nearby, the Germans fled away like a plague of locusts, with the Resistance snapping at their heels,' said Connie. 'Does Jacques know you're here?'

'No, he wasn't at the *cave*, or in his cottage, but I saw the shutters of the château were open. I came here to see Sophia and Sarah.'

'It has been wonderful to finally live here freely,' acknowledged Connie.

'Is Sophia inside?' Édouard asked her.

'No, Édouard, she is not. Please . . .' Connie sighed. 'Sit down. I have so much to tell you.'

'So it seems.' Édouard indicated the baby.

Connie, unprepared for his visit, was at a loss to know where to begin. 'Édouard, it's . . . not what you think.'

'In that case,' he replied, 'I should fetch a jug of rosé from the *cave*. I won't be long.'

Connie watched Édouard disappear through the door of the walled garden. She'd wished for, yet dreaded, this moment so many times in the past few weeks. Now it was here, she wondered how she would find the words to tell him what she must. Even though his long-awaited presence would at last set her free, it was with a heavy heart that Connie watched him return with the jug of wine and two glasses.

'First of all, before we talk, I want us to drink to the end of hell. France is almost free again and the rest of the world will be following shortly.' Édouard clinked his glass against hers.

'To new beginnings,' murmured Connie. 'I can hardly believe it's nearly over.'

'Yes, to new beginnings.' Édouard took a sip of his rosé. 'Tell me, where's Sarah?'

Connie explained how she'd been arrested on the journey south across France. 'We've made investigations in the past few weeks and believe she was sent to a German work camp. We will simply have to wait for further news.' Connie sighed.

'Let us pray we get it,' Édouard said with feeling. 'Since the northern and southern invasions, the new spirit of the people is palpable here in France. We must hope the Germans officially surrender soon. But the devastation of the country and the mourning for the hundreds of thousands lost to the war will take many years to recover from. Now, Constance, please tell me about . . . *that*.' Édouard indicated the baby. 'I can't pretend I'm not shocked. How . . . ? *Who?*'

Connie took a deep breath. 'The child is not mine. I've only been taking care of it.'

'Then whose child is it?'

'Édouard, this baby is your niece. The child is Sophia's.'

442

He stared at Connie as if she had gone mad. 'No, no! This cannot be! Surely, Sophia could never have . . .' Édouard shook his head. 'No,' he repeated. 'It's unthinkable!'

'I understand you find it impossible to believe, just as I did when Sarah told me. But, Édouard, I helped bring this baby into the world. Sophia went into labour on D-Day, so we thought it appropriate to call her daughter Victoria.'

Édouard still had his fingers to his brow, trying to take in what Constance was telling him.

'I understand your shock, Édouard,' she continued. 'And I'm sorry it's me who has to tell you. You must remember that we all treated Sophia like a child. But, in fact, she was the same age as me, and a woman. A woman who fell in love,' she added.

Édouard looked up at Connie suddenly. 'Why do you keep talking of Sophia in the past tense, as though she's no longer here? Where is she? Tell me, Constance, where is she?' he demanded.

'Sophia is dead, Édouard,' Connie said slowly. 'She died a few days after Victoria was born. The labour was long and hard, and afterwards, although we did everything, we couldn't stop the bleeding. And, of course, it was impossible to take her to a hospital. Jacques called a doctor who did what he could for her here, but nothing would have saved her.' Connie's voice cracked with emotion. 'Oh, Édouard, forgive me. I've been dreading this conversation with you ever since it happened.'

Édouard was silent. Then a guttural howl from deep inside him shattered the still evening air.

'*No! No!* It cannot be!' He stood up and turned

443

on Constance, taking her by the shoulders and shaking her. 'Tell me you're lying. Tell me I'm dreaming this, that my dear sister is not dead when I still live! It cannot be, it cannot be!'

'I'm so sorry. But it's true, it's true!' Connie was terrified now by the look in his eyes. As he shook her, she gripped the baby tighter in her arms.

'Édouard! Stop that at once! You have nothing to reproach Constance for, and every reason to thank her!'

Jacques strode across the garden and pulled Édouard away from a frightened Connie. 'Édouard, listen to me, the woman you attack was your sister's saviour! She protected her at great risk to her own life—even *killed* for her! I will not have you behaving like this towards her, however deep your shock and grief.'

'Jacques . . .' Édouard staggered backwards, turned round and looked at his old friend as if he barely recognised him. 'Tell me, please tell me what she says isn't true,' he entreated him desperately.

'It *is* true, Édouard. Sophia died three months ago,' Jacques confirmed. 'We tried to get a message to you, but everything has been in chaos since the Allied invasion. I'm not surprised you didn't get it.'

'Oh God, oh God! Sophia . . . my Sophia!'

Édouard began to sob. Jacques put his arm around his friend's shoulders and held him as he wept.

'I cannot bear it, I cannot bear it. The thought that *I* did this! If I hadn't tried to save France before her, there's no doubt that Sophia would still be alive. It shouldn't have been her life that was

444

sacrificed, it should have been mine, *mine!*'

'Yes, it is indeed terrible she did not live,' agreed Jacques quietly, 'but you must not blame yourself. Sophia idolised you, Édouard, and she was so very proud of the part you've played in helping France achieve its freedom.'

'But, Jacques—' Édouard wept—'there was I, sitting safely in London for months as she suffered here alone. I believed I must stay away from her, that my presence would only endanger her. And now she's dead!'

'Please remember, my friend,' Jacques said gently, 'that Sophia did not die at the hands of the Gestapo, she died in childbirth. Whether you had been present or not, it's doubtful you could have saved her.'

Édouard's sobbing ceased suddenly and he looked up at Jacques.

'Tell me, who was the father?'

Jacques looked to Connie for help. She stood up and tentatively took a step towards him. 'It was Frederik von Wehndorf. I'm sorry, Édouard.'

Silence hung long in the garden as Édouard processed the further revelation. This time he sighed, staggered over to the chair and sat down abruptly as if his legs would carry him no longer.

As he sat in catatonic silence, Connie said softly, 'Even you said Frederik was a good man, Édouard. He aided our escape from Paris and helped others at great cost to himself, like you. And whatever his uniform, he loved your sister very much.'

'I saw the love too,' added Jacques.

'You met him?' Édouard's eyes were glazed over with shock.

'Yes. He came here to find Sophia,' explained

Jacques. 'At least she had a few hours of joy and comfort in the time before she died. There is more. Falk—'

'No more!' Édouard opened his mouth to continue speaking then shut it as if no words he could say would express his feelings. 'Sorry.' He stood up and walked drunkenly to the door of the walled garden. 'I need to be alone.'

*   *   *

That evening, when Connie had fed Victoria her bedtime bottle and was settling her down for the night in the airy nursery she had created in one of the château bedrooms, she heard footsteps coming up the stairs. Édouard stood at the door, looking grey and haggard, his eyes red from weeping.

'Constance, I have come to offer my sincerest apologies for my treatment of you earlier. It was unforgivable.'

'I understand,' said Connie, only glad that Édouard seemed calmer. 'Would you like to see your niece?' she offered. 'She's a beautiful little girl, the image of Sophia.'

'No . . . no! I cannot.'

With that, Édouard turned and walked away.

*   *   *

In the next few days, Connie rarely saw Édouard. He'd installed himself in the main bedroom of the château, just along the corridor. She'd hear him pacing the floors during the night, but he was out by the time she emerged in the morning. She glimpsed him from the windows of the château as she fed Victoria at dawn; a distant figure disappearing through the vines, his body language underlining his misery. He'd often be gone all day, returning home when it was dark and going straight up to his bedroom.

'He's grieving, Constance. Let him be. He just needs time,' Jacques advised.

Connie understood, but as the days passed and Édouard showed no signs of rousing himself from his despair, her patience began to run out. She was desperate to finally return home. It was safe for her to travel now that the city of Paris was free and she wanted to see her husband. And, for the first time in four years, take up the reins of her *own* life once more.

But until Édouard was over his grief and could take responsibility for his niece, she could not walk out on Victoria. Her arms had been the first to hold her, and with Sophia initially too ill to acknowledge her child, followed by her death a few days later, Connie had seen to Victoria's every need since.

Connie looked down at Victoria's cherubic face, a tiny facsimile of her mother. She had been nervous that Sophia's blindness might be hereditary, but she saw that Victoria's beautiful blue eyes followed any bright colours Connie placed in front of her with grave interest. Recently, Victoria had learned to smile, and a huge beam would arrive on her face when Connie came to collect her from her cot. The wrench when she eventually had to say goodbye was something Connie currently couldn't contemplate. She had become the child's mother, and the overwhelming surge of love she felt for Victoria frightened her.

447

Connie prayed that one day, very soon, she'd have her own babies with Lawrence.

* * *

After a week of Édouard's constant solitary mourning, Connie decided she had to address the problem. Up early one morning with Victoria, she heard Édouard's footsteps along the landing. She caught him as he was descending the stairs.

'Édouard, I'm afraid we must talk.'

He turned back slowly and regarded her. 'What about?'

'The war is practically over. I have a husband and a life and I must go home to England.'

'Then go.' He shrugged and turned to continue down the stairs.

'Édouard, wait! What about Victoria? You will need to make arrangements for her to be cared for when I've gone. Perhaps you would consider hiring a nursemaid? I could help you find someone suitable.'

At this, Édouard turned again. 'Constance, I wish to make it clear to you that I have no interest in *that* child.' He spat the words out. 'It is the reason, along with its bastard father, why Sophia is no longer here.'

Connie was horrified by his coldness. 'Édouard, surely you must see it's not the child's fault? She's an innocent baby, who didn't ask to be born. I . . . it's your responsibility as her uncle to take charge of her care!'

'No. I said no! Why don't you make the arrangements, Constance? Perhaps there's a local orphanage who will take her.' He sighed. 'From what you say, you'll wish this to happen as soon as possible. The faster that child is out of the house, the better. Please, do as you see fit with it. I will, of course, reimburse any costs.'

Édouard turned and continued down the stairs, leaving Connie reeling in shock.

*   *   *

'How can he say such terrible things?' Connie wrung her hands in despair as Jacques listened grimly an hour later.

'He's grieving, as I said. Not just for Sophia, but for all he has lost in the war. His refusal to acknowledge the baby is because her presence gives him a focus for his blame. Of course he knows that the child is not responsible. He's a man of integrity, who has never shirked his duty in his life,' Jacques underlined. 'He'll come round, Constance, I know he will.'

'But, Jacques, I *have* no more time,' Connie said despairingly. 'Forgive me, but you must understand I have loved ones too whom I'm desperate to see. And knowing that if it wasn't for Victoria I could travel home to England this very minute if I wished is proving almost impossible. Yet I love Victoria, and I can't abandon her. How could Édouard mention an orphanage?' Tears spilled freely down Connie's face as she looked at Victoria, gurgling happily on her blanket on the grass.

'Perhaps it doesn't help that the baby resembles her mother so strongly,' sighed Jacques. 'Constance, I swear to you, Édouard will eventually discover that this child could be the one

449

thing he needs to bring him hope and joy for the future. But he's lost in his own sorrow and can't see anything.'

'So what do I do, Jacques? Please, tell me,' she begged. 'I must go home! And I can't wait much longer.'

'Let me talk to Édouard myself, see if I can knock some sense into him, bring him out of his self-pity,' Jacques suggested.

'I'm glad you used those words,' Connie admitted. 'I'm afraid that's how I'm starting to feel about him too. There's been so much suffering. For all of us,' she added.

'As I said, Édouard is not normally a self-indulgent man.' Jacques nodded. 'I'll talk to him.'

*   *   *

That evening, waiting on tenterhooks in the cottage, Connie watched as Jacques marched through the vineyard when he spotted Édouard returning home. She sent up a prayer. If Édouard would listen to anyone, it was Jacques. He was her only hope.

Putting Victoria to sleep in the bassinet she kept in the cottage for when she visited Jacques, Connie waited in an agony of suspense for him to return. When he did so, she knew at once from his expression that it was bad news.

'No, Constance—' he sighed—'he won't be moved. He's so full of bitterness and hatred . . . he's a changed man. I don't know what to suggest. I still believe that in time, as I've said, Édouard will come round. But you don't have that time. I understand that. And you, of all people, who have given so much to this family, should not feel guilty that you wish to return to those you love. So, perhaps the orphanage I mentioned—'

'No!' Connie shook her head firmly. 'Never would I abandon Victoria! I couldn't live with myself if I did.'

'Constance, I don't know what you imagine, but the convent orphanage I'm talking of is clean and the nuns are kindly. There's every chance a beautiful baby such as Victoria would find a suitable family immediately,' said Jacques, with far more conviction than he felt. 'And please try to remember, Victoria is not your responsibility and you must now think of yourself.'

Connie gazed down silently at Victoria. 'Then whose responsibility is she?'

'Listen to me—' Jacques put a hand gently on hers—'war is a time of cruelty, when there are many casualties. Not just the brave soldiers who have fought for their countries, but Sophia and her daughter too. Édouard is another. Maybe he'll never be the same, for even though he lashes out at others so angrily, blaming them for Sophia's death, it is in fact himself he holds responsible. You've done enough, my dear. You can do no more. And as someone who has come to admire and respect you, I think you must now walk away.'

'What about Victoria's father?' Connie asked Jacques. 'Surely, if Frederik knew Sophia was dead and Édouard was refusing to acknowledge the child, he would take her?'

'Yes, I'm sure he would, but how do you intend to go about finding him? He could be anywhere, or even dead, like Sophia.' Jacques shook his head. 'Constance, the entire world is in chaos, displaced

451

people everywhere. It would be a fruitless task and not one to even contemplate.'

'No, you're right. It's all . . . hopeless,' said Connie sadly. 'There are no solutions.'

'Tomorrow, I'll visit the convent in Draguignan and speak to the nuns to see if they're able to take Victoria,' Jacques said gently. 'You must believe that I care for her too. And I wouldn't suggest she was left in a place which did not provide for her needs. But it's time someone took the burden away from you. And as Édouard cannot seem to do that at present, then I will.'

*   *   *

Connie lay sleepless that night, tossing and turning, not knowing what was right or wrong any more. The war seemed to have turned any sense of morality on its head and she was struggling to hang on to hers.

Then she suddenly sat upright, an idea springing to her mind. What if *she* took Victoria back home to England with her . . . ?

Climbing out of bed, she paced the floor restlessly, thinking it through.

No, it was ridiculous . . . apart from anything else, if she arrived home with a baby, years after she'd last seen her husband, would Lawrence believe the story she'd tell him? Or would he assume, like anyone would, that she was lying and the baby was hers?

Whatever Lawrence believed, presenting him with a child on her return after four years of separation would hardly be conducive to their relationship. It simply wasn't fair on him.

Miserably, Connie crawled back into bed, hearing Jacques's words again and knowing that, not just for her own sake, but for Lawrence's too, she had no choice but to accept the inevitable. Jacques was right. There was always sacrifice during war. And she and her husband had made enough of their own for a lifetime.

*   *   *

Jacques returned the following evening from his trip to the orphanage.

'They will take her, Constance,' he said as he found her in the walled garden. 'They're full, but I offered them a considerable donation and they accepted. Édouard will pay, of course.'

Swallowing back tears, Connie nodded. 'When will you take her?'

'I think it's best for everyone if Victoria goes as soon as possible. I'll ask Édouard for the money tonight and give him a last chance to change his mind.' Jacques grimaced. 'And if he doesn't, I'll take Victoria in the morning.'

'Then I will accompany you,' insisted Connie.

'Is that a good idea?' said Jacques, frowning.

'None of it's a good idea, but at least if I see where Victoria will be looked after for myself, I might feel better.' She sighed despairingly.

'As you wish.' Jacques nodded. 'If Édouard has no change of heart, we'll leave mid-morning.'

That evening, Connie laid Victoria in her cot and sat watching the familiar movements for the last time as she fell asleep.

'Precious, precious child,' Connie whispered, 'I am so very sorry.'

453

'Édouard will not change his mind.' Jacques shook his head sadly the following morning. 'I asked for the money and he handed it to me without a word. Please ready yourself and the baby to leave as soon as possible.'

Connie had already packed Victoria's things—anything to make the long sleepless hours pass until the morning—and went to collect Victoria herself. As she walked downstairs from the nursery, Connie prayed for a last-minute reprieve; that Édouard might emerge from somewhere in the house or garden when he saw them taking Victoria away. But he was nowhere to be seen.

There was an old Citroën parked in front of the cottage.

'I've saved the petrol for an occasion when it was really needed,' said Jacques. 'We have just enough to get us there and back.'

As the little car shuddered into life and they drove away from the château, Connie sat next to Jacques with Victoria in her arms. Usually such a good baby, Victoria screamed relentlessly all the way to Draguignan.

They arrived at the convent and Jacques took the small case Connie had packed for Victoria and led them towards the entrance. A nun ushered them inside into a calm waiting room, but the baby continued to scream in Connie's arms.

'Hush, Victoria!' Connie looked up at Jacques with anguished eyes. 'Do you think she knows?'

'No, Constance, I think she doesn't like cars.' Jacques gave a ghost of a smile, trying to lighten the tension. Eventually, a nun dressed in a starched white uniform came into the room.

'Welcome, Monsieur.' She nodded in recognition at Jacques, then surveyed Connie and Victoria. 'And this is the baby and her mother?'

'No.' Connie shook her head. 'I'm not Victoria's mother.'

The nun gave a short, disbelieving nod and opened her arms. 'Come, give me the child.'

Taking a deep breath, Connie handed Victoria to her. The baby screamed louder.

'Does she always cry like this?' The nun frowned.

'She never normally cries at all,' Connie assured her.

'Well, we'll take care of Victoria now. Monsieur?' The nun's eyes looked questioningly at Jacques, who hurriedly produced an envelope and gave it to her.

'Thank you.' The nun acknowledged the receipt of the money and tucked it away in a voluminous pocket. 'Let us hope we can find her a suitable family soon. It's difficult, with all in turmoil and no one with the money to spare for an extra mouth,' she said. 'But she's a pretty baby, even if she howls. Excuse me, we're very busy and I must return to the nursery. Please see yourselves out.'

The nun turned and walked away with Victoria towards the door. Connie made to get up and follow her, but with a firm hand Jacques held her back. With an arm around her shoulder, as the tears dripped down her face, he led a distraught Connie out of the convent and placed her tenderly in the front seat of his car.

Like Victoria, Connie sobbed the whole way

home.

When Jacques had halted the car in front of the *cave*, he placed a hand on Connie's knee and patted it.

'I loved her too, Constance. But it's best she goes now. If it's any comfort, babies have little memory of who cared for them at a few months old. Please, don't punish yourself any longer. Victoria has gone and you're finally free to go home. You must look to your future and think of your return to the country and the man you love.'

*   *   *

Two days later, having packed her few possessions, and with Jacques ready to use the rest of his petrol and drive her the short distance to Gassin station, Connie descended the stairs of the château. She pushed open the door to the library, intending to put the second volume of *The History of French Fruit* back on a shelf. She had Sophia's notebook of poems also, and had decided to leave it on Édouard's desk, hoping that he might read them and understand the deep love his sister had felt for Frederik. And that her heartfelt words might comfort and soften him.

The room was shrouded in darkness, the shutters firmly closed. She made her way to a window to pull back a shutter, so she could see to replace the book.

'Hello, Constance.'

She almost jumped out of her skin as she turned and saw Édouard sitting in a leather armchair.

'I'm sorry if I startled you,' he said.

'And I apologise for disturbing you. I wanted to

456

return this book before I left,' she explained. 'And Sophia's book of poems. I thought you might like to read them. They're beautiful, Édouard.' Connie offered the notebook to him, feeling such resentment towards him that she wanted to be out of his presence as soon as possible.

'No. You take both of them with you to England as a keepsake to remind you of all that happened here in France,' Édouard suggested.

Connie could not find the strength to argue with him. 'I'm leaving now, Édouard. Thank you for helping me when I arrived in France,' she managed, and walked away from him towards the door.

'Constance?'

She paused and turned round. 'Yes?'

'Jacques told me how you saved Sophia's life when Falk von Wehndorf came here to find his brother. I am grateful.'

'I did what was right, Édouard,' she said pointedly.

'And your brave friend Venetia saved my life. And through that bravery, lost her own,' he added sadly. 'I heard she'd been shot by the Gestapo whilst I was in London.'

'Venetia is dead? Oh God, no!' Tears springing to her eyes, Connie wondered when the pain of the aftermath of war would cease.

'She was a wonderful woman.' Édouard's voice softened. 'I'll never forget her. You know, I've thought recently the better option would be to have died with those I've loved and lost.'

'It was not your destiny, Édouard, nor mine,' Connie said firmly. 'And it's up to all of us left behind to rebuild a future in their memory.'

'Yes. But there are some things—' Édouard shook his head—'that I cannot forgive or forget. I'm sorry, Constance. For everything.'

She paused, trying to think how to respond. But there were no words, so she opened the door, walked through it and closed it firmly behind her. Leaving Édouard de la Martinières locked in the past as she took her first tentative steps into the future.

*   *   *

Three days later, the overcrowded train full of weary, returning soldiers chugged into York station. Connie had sent a telegram to Blackmoor Hall, alerting the house to her imminent arrival, but had no idea if they'd received it or, in fact, whether Lawrence was back at home. Alighting from the train and shivering most happily in the autumnal English air, Connie walked along the platform full of apprehension.

Would he be there to meet her?

She looked anxiously at the throng of people who stood waiting to greet their loved ones. Coming to a halt, she searched the concourse for his familiar face. After fifteen minutes looking for him to no avail, she was about to leave the station and join the queue for the bus that would take her across the moors. Then, suddenly, she saw a lone figure still waiting at the end of the now-empty platform. His hair had turned prematurely grey and he held a walking stick in his right hand.

'Lawrence!' she called.

He turned at the familiar sound of her voice, then looked at her in astonishment, recognition

458

dawning. She ran towards him and flung herself into his arms. The smell of him, which conjured up all that was safe and wonderful and good, brought tears to her eyes.

'My darling! I'm so sorry, I didn't recognise you! Your hair . . .' Lawrence murmured, gazing at her in wonder.

'Of course.' Connie understood. They were both changed. 'I've had this colour so long now, I'm used to it.'

'As a matter of fact—' he studied her with a grin—'I think it rather suits you. You look like a film star.'

'Hardly,' sighed Connie, looking down at the crumpled clothes she had worn all the way from the South of France.

'How are you?' they both said at the same time, and then giggled.

'Very tired,' said Connie, 'but, oh, so glad to be home. I have so much to tell you, I simply don't know where to start.'

'I'm sure,' said Lawrence. 'So why don't you begin once we're in the car? I've used all my ration coupons on the petrol to drive you home.'

'Home . . .' whispered Connie, the simple word conjuring up all she had longed for in the past eighteen months.

Lawrence gave her another tight hug as he read her emotion. Then picked up her bag and tucked her arm through his.

'Yes, my darling.' He hugged her. 'I'm taking you home.'

*   *   *

Three months later, Connie received a letter from F Section, asking her to travel to London for an appointment with Maurice Buckmaster.

He greeted her cheerfully as she was led into his Baker Street office and shook her hand heartily.

'Constance Chapelle, the agent that never was. Sit down, my dear, sit down.'

Connie did so as Buckmaster perched, as usual, on his desk. 'So, Constance, good to be back in Blighty?'

'Yes, Sir, it's wonderful,' she answered with feeling.

'Well, now you're here, I can officially let you know that you're demobbed.'

'Yes, Sir.'

'I do apologise that we had to drop you like a hot potato when you arrived in France. Unfortunately, you happened to knock on the door of one of the most powerful and valuable members of De Gaulle's Free French movement. Orders came from on high, I'm afraid. They couldn't risk "Hero's" cover being blown, unfortunately. Nothing to be done, under the circumstances. Glad you eventually arrived home safely, anyway.'

'Thank you, Sir.'

'Out of the forty of you girls that went, fourteen have unfortunately not returned. Your friend Venetia was one of them.' Buckmaster sighed.

'I know,' Connie said sombrely.

'As a matter of fact, it's testament to you all that the number of survivors is so high. I was expecting fewer,' he added. 'Terrible shame about Venetia. When she left for France, we were all concerned about her devil-may-care attitude. But she proved

460

to be one of our finest and bravest agents. She's currently under review for a posthumous award for bravery.'

'I'm very glad, Sir. No one could deserve it more.'

'Well, the good news is that France is finally free. And the SOE played a major part in its victory. A shame you didn't get a chance to be more involved, Connie. Under the umbrella of the de la Martinières, you probably ate better than I did.' He smiled. 'Hear you ended up living at their rather grand château in the South of France?'

'Yes, Sir, but—'

Connie stopped herself. On the train on the way down from York, she'd wondered whether she would tell him the true story of her life in France. And what she had sacrificed. But Venetia, Sophia and so many others were dead, whilst she lived on to continue her life, whatever the scars she carried.

'Yes, Constance?'

'Nothing, Sir.'

'Well then, all that remains to be said is congratulations on your safe return home. And thank you on behalf of the British government for being prepared to put your life at risk for the sake of your country.' Buckmaster stood up from the desk and shook her hand. 'Seems you were lucky enough to have a quiet war.'

'Yes, Sir,' Connie replied as she stood up and walked towards the door. 'I had a quiet war.'

30

Gassin, South of France, 1999

Jean stood up and went to the kitchen to collect the Armagnac bottle and three glasses. Emilie watched as Jacques blew his nose and wiped his tears away. He had shed many during the telling of the tale. She tried to gather her thoughts . . . there were so many questions. But only one she wanted an immediate answer to.

'Are you all right, Emilie?' Jean returned, handed her an Armagnac and placed a gentle hand on her shoulder.

'Yes, I'm all right.'

'Papa, some Armagnac?' he asked.

Jacques nodded his assent.

Emilie took a large gulp to give her the courage to ask the question that burned on her tongue. 'So, Jacques, what became of Sophia and Frederik's child?'

Jacques remained silent, looking past Emilie into the distance.

'You understand that, if I could find her, I would no longer be the only surviving member of the de la Martinières family?' she continued.

Still Jacques said nothing, and eventually Jean said, 'Emilie, it's unlikely anyone would know who adopted the baby. There were so many orphans after the war. The world was in chaos. Victoria would have had no birth certificate to prove who she was when she went to the orphanage anyway. Is that not right, Papa?'

'Yes.'

'So even though the baby's mother was a de la Martinières,' Jean thought out loud, 'Victoria herself was illegitimate and therefore would have no claims on the estate.'

'That's immaterial to me,' said Emilie, 'all that matters is I know there may be another human being out there who's related to me, someone who carries the de la Martinières blood in her veins. And she may since have had children . . . So many questions.' Emilie sighed. 'Jacques, please, answer me one thing: did Frederik do as he promised and come back to find Sophia?'

'Yes.' Jacques finally found his voice. 'A year after the war finally ended, he appeared here at the cottage. I was the one who had to tell him Sophia had died.'

'Did you tell Frederik he'd had a daughter?' Emilie asked.

Jacques shook his head and put a shaking hand to his brow. 'I did not know what to tell him. So I lied and said—' his voice cracked—'that the child had died also. I felt—' Jacques's chest heaved with emotion—'it was best for everyone.'

'Papa, I'm sure you did the right thing,' Jean comforted him. 'If Frederik loved Sophia as you say, he would have stopped at nothing to try and trace their child. And if the baby was already settled in a new family who had no knowledge of her Nazi parentage, it must have been for the best.'

'I had to protect the child, you see . . .' Jacques crossed himself. 'God forgive me for the terrible lie I told him. Frederik was completely broken. Distraught beyond all rational thought.'

463

'I can only imagine,' shuddered Jean.

'Jacques, where did you bury Sophia?' asked Emilie.

'In the graveyard at Gassin,' he answered. 'She had no headstone until after the war ended. We could not arouse suspicion. Even in death, Sophia had to be hidden.'

'And do you know where Frederik is, Papa?' questioned Jean. 'Maybe he's dead. He must be over eighty at least?'

'He lives in Switzerland under an assumed identity. When he eventually returned to his home, his family's lands had been seized by the Poles when the borders changed and East Prussia was returned to Poland. Both his parents had been shot by the Russians. Like many after the war, he had to begin again. But what I subsequently learned was that Frederik had aided those he could over the German border to escape the death camps before the war began and there were many eager to repay his kindness. They helped him start a new life.' Jacques chuckled. 'Would you believe he became a clockmaker in Basel! And a lay preacher in his spare time. He has taught me much about forgiveness during our correspondence and I'm proud to have him as my friend. I told Édouard often he should make contact with Frederik. They were not dissimilar—both doing what they could in a time of dreadful destruction. I thought that, perhaps, they could take comfort from each other over the loss of the woman they loved. But—' he sighed—'it was not to be.'

'Do you still hear from Frederik?' asked Jean.

'He still writes to me sometimes, but I haven't heard from him now for over a year, so maybe he's ill. Like me . . .' Jacques shrugged. 'He never married again. The love of his life was Sophia. There could be no one else for him.'

'And my father . . .' For Emilie, this had been the most painful part of the story. 'I find it so difficult to believe he could have abandoned his sister's baby. He was such a kind, loving man—how could he have washed his hands of her?'

'Emilie, your father was all those things you say of him,' said Jacques slowly, 'but he had idolised and protected his sister for her entire life. The thought of her purity and innocence being sullied by any man, let alone a German officer, was too much for him. How could he look at the product of his sister's affair, be faced every day with a living, breathing reminder of what she had done? And feel that he had failed to protect her? You must not blame him, Emilie. You cannot understand how it was . . .'

'Papa,' Jean said as he saw his father's exhausted expression, 'I think that's enough now. Emilie can ask you more questions in the morning. Come.' He offered his father his arm.

Jacques stood then turned to Emilie in afterthought. 'Édouard sacrificed everything for his country. He was a true Frenchman and you have every reason to be proud of him. But the war changed us all, Emilie, it changed us all.'

Emilie sat pensively staring into the fire as Jean took his father upstairs.

'How are you?' asked Jean, when he came back down.

'I'm shocked at the horror of the story. It's a lot to take in.'

'Yes. And all of this happened only fifty-five

years ago,' he sighed. 'It's hard to believe.'

'Your father knows where Sophia and Frederik's baby is, Jean, I'm sure of it,' Emilie added.

'Perhaps,' Jean agreed, 'but if he does, then he'll have his own reasons for not telling you. And if he wishes to continue keeping her whereabouts a secret, you must respect that.'

'I know. But the past is the past, and let us hope we've all learned lessons from it. The world has moved on now.'

'I agree, but for my father, and many others of his age who lived through that terrible time, it isn't so easy. We're the younger generation and can look back on it logically as it becomes history, but those who suffered because of it cannot be quite so unemotional and detached. Now—' Jean patted Emilie's hand—'I think it's time for us to follow my father upstairs.'

*   *   *

Surprisingly, Emilie slept the moment her head touched the pillow, but she was awake early the following morning. Pulling on her clothes, she walked down the drive to the château, wanting to have some peace there before the building work began for the day. Pushing open the door to the walled garden, Emilie walked across the lawn and stood in front of the small wooden cross, which Jacques had told her Frederik had erected for Falk on his return after the war. She had always presumed it had been the grave of a family pet. The thought that underneath the soil right in front of her lay Falk's remains made her shudder. It was hard to conceive that in this beautiful spot, so much hatred and violence had taken place.

Emilie wished Sebastian *and* Alex had been with her to hear the story of their courageous grandmother, who had won no plaudits for her actions and had not even chosen to share them with her family. She had been a remarkable woman, unsung like so many during that time. And her two grandsons, one of them eaten up with jealousy for the other . . . The irony of her newly discovered family past was not lost on her present circumstances. And neither could it have been lost on Constance.

Being an only child, sibling rivalry was not something Emilie had ever encountered. But hearing the story last night, she'd truly understood its strength.

Shaking her head suddenly as if to clear it, only able to cope with one complex scenario at a time, Emilie walked back across the lawn. She thought of the dreadful cellar she and Sebastian had found that first afternoon, where Sophia had been a virtual prisoner, given birth and then died. The physical and emotional pain her aunt must have suffered brought tears to her eyes, but yet again reinforced her sense of how lucky *she* was. As she left the château and walked back down the drive, Anton, Margaux's son, came cycling towards her on his bicycle. He halted and gave her a shy smile.

'How are you, Anton?' she asked him.

'I'm well, thank you, Madame. Maman said I was to bring this back to you.' Anton reached into his basket and handed her the book she had lent him. 'Thank you for letting me borrow it. I enjoyed it very much.'

'I'm impressed that you read it so quickly. It

467

took me months,' she confided.

'I read very fast, sometimes right into the night. I love books—' he shrugged—'although now I've read almost everything suitable in the local library.'

'Then when the château library is back in place, you must come down and choose some more. I doubt you will ever run out in there,' she said with a smile.

'Thank you, Madame,' he replied gratefully.

'How is your mother?' Emilie enquired.

'She sends you her regards. If there's anything you need, she asks you to call her. I think she'll be happier when all is back to normal.'

'Yes, we all will be. Goodbye, Anton.'

'Goodbye, Madame Emilie.'

Emilie arrived back at the cottage and made herself some coffee. Wandering through to the *cave*, she saw Jacques was in his usual position at his table, wrapping the bottles, as Jean worked away at his desk. So as not to disturb them, she took her coffee out into the garden. She didn't want to push Jacques to tell her if he did know where the adopted child had ended up, but she was desperate to know. And Frederik, the father of the baby and muse of Sophia's beautiful love poems— Jacques said he thought he was still alive . . .

An idea formed in her mind, which she expounded to Jean and Jacques over lunch.

'Why not?' agreed Jean. 'Papa, what do you think about Emilie going to Switzerland to meet Frederik?'

'I don't know.' Jacques looked uncomfortable.

'But surely it can do no harm, Papa?' asked Jean. 'If Emilie gave Frederik the poems, at least he would have a physical memory of Sophia's undying love for him? It might comfort him.'

'Would you give me the address, Jacques?' she asked.

'I'll see if I can find it, Emilie.' Jacques was still reticent. 'He may not be alive now, of course.'

'I know, but at least I could write to him and find out.'

'Will you tell him that I lied about the death of his baby girl all those years ago?' Jacques asked tentatively.

Emilie looked to Jean uncertainly for advice.

'Papa, if Frederik is the man you say he is, he will understand why you kept his daughter's birth a secret from him. You were protecting the child.'

'And accept I denied his right to know his daughter for the whole of his life?' muttered Jacques.

'Yes,' said Jean, 'if that's what it took. Papa, if you do know who and where she is, I think the time has come to tell. Emilie has a right to know. It's her family, after all.'

'No!' Jacques shook his head. 'Jean, you don't understand . . . You don't understand. I—'

'Jacques,' Emilie put a hand on his arm, 'please don't upset yourself. If you feel so strongly that you can't, I'm sure you have your reasons. Just answer me one question: tell me you know where she is.'

Jacques paused, the agony of indecision on his face.

'Yes! I know!' he admitted finally. 'There! I've told you. I've broken the promise I made to myself all those years ago.' He shook his head despairingly.

'Papa, it *was* years ago,' said Jean. 'No one will judge Sophia's daughter now. You won't be putting her in any danger.'

'Stop! Enough!' Jacques slammed his fist down on the table, then heaved himself to his feet and grabbed his walking stick. 'You don't understand— I must think, I must think.'

Jean and Emilie watched him stagger as fast as he could out of the cottage.

'We shouldn't have pressurised him, Jean,' said Emilie guiltily. 'He's very upset.'

'Well, perhaps it may be good for him to unburden the secret. He's carried it alone for long enough,' said Jean. 'Now, I must continue working. Can you keep yourself amused for the afternoon?'

'Of course,' she said. 'You go back to the *cave* and I'll take care of things in here.'

When Jean had left, Emilie cleared away the lunch and washed up, then took out her mobile phone. She saw there were a number of missed calls from Sebastian, but it was her turn to be disinclined to call back. The story last night had affected her on many levels and the distaste for Sebastian's abuse of his brother was growing, not dwindling.

Needing some fresh air, Emilie took a walk through the vines, her head spinning in confusion. Then a thought hit her and she came to an abrupt halt, trying to process it . . .

Jacques had said how devastated Constance had been about having to relinquish the baby she'd cared for since her birth. Emilie completely understood the rationale of why Constance hadn't taken Victoria home to England with her. In the days before genetic tests, there would always have

470

been a doubt in her husband's mind, no matter how many times Constance had reassured him that Victoria wasn't her child.

Victoria . . .

Emilie sat down abruptly in the middle of the vines. But what if Constance *had* told her husband about the baby in the orphanage when she'd arrived back in Yorkshire? And what if Lawrence, seeing his wife's distress, had agreed that they must go back to France and adopt her themselves?

She was sure that Sebastian had once mentioned his mother's name . . . Emilie searched her mind to recall it but, unable to do so, she took her mobile from her jean pocket and hesitated over which brother to call for confirmation.

Trying her husband first, she received his voicemail. So she then rang Alex on his mobile. He answered immediately.

'Alex? It's Emilie.'

'Emilie! Great to hear from you, how are you?' he asked.

'Well, thank you.' Emilie came straight to the point. 'Alex, what was your mother's Christian name?'

'Victoria. Why?'

A shocked Emilie put a hand to her mouth.

'I . . . it's a long story, Alex. I promise I'll explain when I see you. Thank you so much, goodbye.'

Emilie pressed a button to end the call and sat in the vines trying to take in the new information.

Victoria was Sebastian and Alex's mother.

Which meant that—Emilie worked it out as fast as she could—she was currently married to her first cousin, once removed . . .

'Nooo!' she howled into the still air. She lay

471

down flat, resting her head against the hard, stony soil and tried to think rationally.

What if Constance, near her death, had told Sebastian that his mother, Victoria, had been adopted? And was, in fact, a blood member of the de la Martinières family? Constance had also mentioned the book on French fruit and the poems, written by Sophia—perhaps *his* grandmother—to him. Had Constance done this as proof to help the two brothers make their claim?

Sebastian could have subsequently investigated and discovered who the de la Martinières were. And when he'd read of her own mother's death, he'd thought he might be in line to inherit something.

But, as Jacques had mentioned, establishing his right as an illegitimate heir would be a long and drawn-out legal battle. How much easier and more convenient to marry the natural heiress? And, at some point, persuade her to move the château and bank account into both of their names?

Emilie shuddered, more at her cold, analytical pragmatism than Sebastian's possible duplicity. It all fitted so well, but there was no proof she was right. Besides, could Sebastian have knowingly married his own cousin?

Emilie lay there, wondering at her own naivety. Even if there was another explanation and she was conjuring up some Machiavellian scenario of which Sebastian was perfectly innocent, what on earth had possessed her to go ahead and marry him, knowing as little about him as she had?

Maybe, she sighed, it had been as simple as the fact that he had shown her affection and support when she'd been so vulnerable. And the Sebastian she'd known in France could not have been more loving, tender or supportive. But had that simply been an act to seduce her?

Emilie sat up. 'Oh God, oh God . . .' She shook her head despairingly. Even if she was wrong about Sebastian's motives, she was dreadfully unhappy. And she no longer trusted her husband at all.

Feeling drained, exhausted and shaken, Emilie picked herself up and began to walk back to the cottage. There was only one way to find out. She must beg Jacques to tell her if she was right.

'Where have you been, Emilie? It's almost dark.' A concerned Jean was in the kitchen cooking supper.

'I needed to go out and think,' she answered.

'You look very pale, Emilie.' Jean studied her with concern.

'I must speak to your father as soon as possible,' she said.

'Here, drink this.' Jean passed her a glass of wine. 'I'm afraid my father has taken himself up to his room and has asked that he's not disturbed. He doesn't want to see you tonight, Emilie. Please, you must understand how hard this is for him. You're asking him to release a secret kept for over fifty years. He needs time to think about it. You'll simply have to be patient.'

'But you don't understand . . . I *must* know before I return home. I must!'

Jean could see and feel her tension and distress. 'Why, Emilie? How can what Papa has to tell you have any relevance to your current life?'

'Because . . . because it *does* . . . Oh, Jean, please would you ask him if I could see him?' she begged.

473

'Emilie, try and calm yourself. You and I have known each other for many years. Perhaps you could trust me enough to tell me what it is that's upset you? Come, let us sit down.' Jean led her into the sitting room and pushed her gently into the chair.

'Oh, Jean.' Emilie buried her head in her hands. 'Perhaps I really am going mad.'

'I doubt it.' He smiled. 'You've always been the sanest woman I've ever known. So, I'm listening,' he encouraged.

Emilie took a deep breath and began from the first moment she'd encountered Sebastian in Gassin. She told the full story of their courtship and of her husband's recent bizarre behaviour with her. Then of his relationship with his brother and the strange atmosphere in Yorkshire. Finally, when a bowl of very good rabbit stew had been pushed in front of her and she had gulped it down, still talking, she told Jean of her suspicion that Victoria was Alex and Sebastian's mother.

'What if Sebastian married me because he thought it was an easy route to what he believes is rightfully his anyway?' Emilie asked.

'Emilie, slow down,' Jean advised. 'We have no hard facts, apart from a Christian name, to think that any of this is true.'

'So am I mad to believe this of my husband?' Emilie asked sadly.

'Well, I think we know that Sebastian didn't arrive here out of coincidence, despite telling you he was in the area on other business,' agreed Jean. 'You say he mentioned the connection his grandmother had to your family immediately. And, yes, I agree his mother being named "Victoria"

474

makes your story a plausible possibility. However,' Jean continued, 'whether or not there is a blood tie . . . do you mind if I speak the truth?'

'Of course not. I would welcome it,' Emilie said gratefully.

'Well, to put it simply, I think you're missing the point. Whether Sebastian has an ulterior motive for marrying you or not, you're extremely unhappy. And your husband's character does not sound—' Jean shrugged—'solid.'

'But as Alex said, it may be that my husband's bad behaviour is confined to him,' Emilie replied.

'I would say he's being too kind. He doesn't wish to compromise your relationship with your husband. This Alex sounds very sensible. Perhaps you have married the wrong brother?' Jean's eyes twinkled.

'Alex is extremely clever, yes,' she agreed uncomfortably.

'Emilie, I understand.' Jean nodded, serious now. 'You've married this man, you've made your choice and you want it to work. Of course, the thing to do now is confront him with all your fears when you arrive home.'

'But he'll lie, of course! He'll protect himself.'

'Then surely,' Jean replied sadly, 'you have just answered your own question? Emilie, if you feel you can never get the truth from your husband, then what hope do you have of a successful relationship?'

Emilie sat silently, knowing Jean was right. 'We've been married such a short time, Jean. Surely I must continue to give us a chance? I can't just give up!'

'No, I agree. Normally your heart does not rule

your head, Emilie. You were impulsive, for the first time in your life, but you mustn't punish yourself for that. And it may still work out. *If* you can discover the truth from him.'

'I'll feel better when I've spoken to your father.' She sighed. 'The fact he's so reluctant to tell us must indicate the revelation will impact on someone.'

'I promise to talk to Papa for you tomorrow,' Jean said. 'If you try to calm down.'

'You're so close to your father,' she sighed wistfully. 'It's unusual and wonderful to see.'

'What's unusual about wishing to put the person who brought you up and cared for you first, when they need you? Like you, Emilie,' Jean explained, 'I was born late in my father's life, and then my mother died when I was young. Perhaps it's because I grew up with older parents that I learned the moral values of previous generations. Rather than our own, which it seems to me has lost a reliable compass.'

'It's strange that both our fathers decided to marry late,' mused Emilie. 'I wonder if that had anything to do with their experiences in the war?'

'Perhaps,' agreed Jean. 'They both witnessed the darker side of human nature. I'm sure it took many years to restore their faith and trust in love again. Now—' he yawned—'it's late and time for bed.'

'Yes.'

They stood up and kissed goodnight.

'Thank you, Jean. I can't tell you how much I appreciate your advice. And I'm sorry for boring you with my problems,' she added.

'Emilie, you did not bore me. We're almost

family,' Jean said gently.

'Yes, Jean, we are,' she agreed.

*   *   *

Emilie was up early again the following morning, knowing there were only a few hours to go before she had to leave for Yorkshire.

Finally, Jacques arrived in the kitchen for breakfast. He nodded at Emilie as she passed him some coffee.

'How did you sleep?' she asked.

'I did not,' he said as he raised the cup to his lips.

'Have you seen Jean this morning?'

'I have. He came to see me earlier and has told me that you've managed to work out a reason why I'm reluctant to tell you who your cousin is.'

'Jacques, please, I beg you. I must know if I'm right,' Emilie urged. 'You understand why, don't you?'

'Yes.' He looked at her and then suddenly chuckled. 'You're a clever girl, Emilie. It's a good story. And, indeed,' he nodded, 'Constance named her one child after the baby girl she had left behind.'

'But . . .' Emilie stared at him for confirmation, 'her daughter wasn't Sophia's child?'

'No, Emilie, it was not Constance who adopted Victoria,' said Jacques. 'And even though, from the little I've seen of your new husband, I would not trust him, I can assure you he didn't marry you because he believed he might be an illegitimate heir to the de la Martinières fortune.'

'Oh. Thank God!' Emilie felt near to tears.

'Thank you, Jacques.'

'I'm happy at least to put your mind at rest on that score,' he said as he sipped his coffee.

Emilie was immediately torn between relief that the story she'd conjured up was not true and guilt that she had managed to think Sebastian capable of such a plot.

'Then, Jacques, please, will you tell me who Victoria is?'

Jacques paused, took another sip of his coffee and looked at her. 'I understand your eagerness to know. But, Emilie, it isn't your life that will be turned upside down. It's hers, and her family's. If I decide to speak, it will be her I tell first, not you. Do you understand?'

Emilie understood that Jacques was telling her she was being selfish. Cowed, she bent her head and nodded. 'I do. And I'm sorry.'

'There's no need to apologise, Emilie. I can see why you wish to know.'

Jean walked into the kitchen and felt the tension. 'My father has told you your story was wrong?' he asked.

'Yes.'

'You must be relieved, Emilie,' said Jean.

'I am, of course.' She stood up, feeling uncomfortable and embarrassed that these two men were blatantly aware of how fast she'd jumped to dishonourable conclusions about her husband. 'I must leave,' she said, suddenly needing some time alone. She could sit at Nice airport for a couple of hours and think. 'Excuse me.'

The two men gazed at her with sympathy in their eyes as she left the kitchen to collect her holdall from her bed-room.

'She's made a mistake by marrying that man, and she knows it,' whispered Jacques. 'He may not be a de la Martinières by blood, but he's after something.'

'I agree. But then she had just lost her mother, the last of her family. It's hardly surprising she fell into the first pair of arms that came along,' said Jean. 'She was so vulnerable.'

'On the positive side, she's had to grow up fast in the past year and is stronger. She's learned many lessons.'

'Yes,' agreed Jean. 'She's indeed even more special now.'

Jacques gazed at the pain in his son's eyes. 'I know how you feel about her. But she's a clever girl, like her father, with good instincts. She'll make the right decision and come home, where she belongs.'

'I wish I could be so sure.' Jean sighed.

'I am,' said Jacques.

Emilie appeared in the kitchen with her holdall, looking strained and pale. 'Thank you again for your hospitality and I'm sure I'll see you both soon.'

'As you know, there's always a bed for you here with us,' said Jean, feeling her distress and trying to comfort her.

'Thank you.' Emilie put her holdall down. 'Jacques, I'm so sorry that I pressured you to tell me the identity of Sophia and Frederik's baby. Of course it's your decision. I promise I will never ask again.' She bent down to kiss him on both cheeks and Jacques snatched at her hands before she could move away.

'Your father would have been proud of you.

479

Trust in yourself, Emilie. And God bless, until we see you again.'

'I'll be back very soon to check on the progress of the château. Goodbye, Jacques.'

She left the kitchen with Jean as he carried her holdall out to the car.

'Keep in contact, Emilie,' he said as he slammed the boot closed. 'You know we're always here for you.'

'I know—' she nodded—'and thank you for everything.'

31

On the drive to Nice airport, Emilie came to a decision. She couldn't face going back to Yorkshire and waiting there alone until Sebastian came home. Instead, she would fly straight to London and go to his gallery to see him. And ask him to tell her the truth.

Standing at the sales desk paying for her ticket to Heathrow, Emilie pondered whether she should let Sebastian know she was coming. But maybe it would be better to surprise him. The flight arrived in London at half past two, plenty of time to get to his gallery before it closed. She'd tell him she'd missed him and wanted to see him straight away.

As Emilie boarded the plane, although still confused about her husband's behaviour, she felt better. At least she was being proactive, *doing* something to try to close the chasm that had opened up between them. She needed to confront him about his relationship with Alex and find out

480

the real reason he was disinclined to have his wife by his side in London.

*   *   *

After landing at Heathrow, Emilie climbed into a taxi and gave the driver the address of Sebastian's gallery on the Fulham Road. Having a sudden attack of cold feet that she was arriving unannounced, Emilie took out her mobile and tried Sebastian. A mechanical voice told her his mobile was switched off.

Twenty minutes later, she arrived in front of Arté. Paying the driver, Emilie lugged her holdall out of the taxi and perused the windows. The art was modern, as Sebastian had described, and the gallery was extremely smart. Pushing the door open, a bell tinkled and an attractive, willowy blonde came forward to greet her.

'Hello, Madam, just browsing?'

'Is the owner here?' Emilie asked her, abrupt from nerves.

'Yes, he's in the office at the back. Can I help you with anything?'

'No, thank you. Please could you tell him that Emilie de la Martinières is here to see him?'

'Of course, Madam.'

The girl walked through a door at the back of the shop and Emilie browsed the canvases on display. A few seconds later, an elegant, middle-aged man appeared from the door at the back of the gallery.

'Madam de la Martinières, it's a pleasure to meet you. I heard of the sale of your Matisse last year. Can I help you with anything?'

481

'I . . .' Emilie was confused. 'Are you the owner?'

'Yes, I'm Jonathan Maxwell.' He held out his hand and she shook it weakly. He eyed her with interest. 'You seem surprised. Is there a problem?'

'Maybe I have the wrong address,' she stuttered. 'I thought Sebastian Carruthers was the owner of this gallery?'

'Sebastian? No.' Jonathan chuckled. 'What stories has he been telling you? Sebastian is an agent who has a couple of artists whose work I display here occasionally. I've not seen him for a while, though. I think he's been concentrating more on his sourcing of French artists for his clients. Didn't he discover your unsigned Matisse?'

'Yes, he did.' Emilie felt at least comforted that *something* Sebastian had told her was actually true.

'Nice work if you can get it,' commented Jonathan. 'I'm presuming it's Sebastian you want to speak to?'

'Yes.'

'I'll go and get his telephone number for you,' Jonathan offered. 'I've got it on file.'

'Thank you. You wouldn't by any chance have the address of his office as well, would you?'

'I'd say "office" was rather an exaggeration. He works out of the apartment he shares with his girlfriend, Bella. She's one of his artists.' Jonathan pointed to a large vivid canvas, filled with extravagant red poppies. 'I have the address; it's where I send Bella's cheques when I sell a painting of hers. It's probably better to call him first and make an appointment.'

Emilie's legs were buckling under her, but she couldn't give in now.

'If you have the address, I'll take it anyway,' she

said brightly. 'I like . . . Bella's work very much. Perhaps she has others I could see.'

'Her studio is in her flat. She's in one of those wharf developments by Tower Bridge. Hardly a garret in Paris, lucky girl . . .' Jonathan shared a glance with Emilie. 'Let me get you the address.'

Aware that she was a few seconds away from having a panic attack, Emilie took a number of deep, slow breaths as she waited for him to return.

'There you are,' said Jonathan, handing her the address and telephone number he'd scribbled on an envelope. 'As I say, probably best to call first to make sure they're in.'

'Of course. Thank you for your help.'

'No problem. Here's my card too,' said Jonathan, producing one from his shirt pocket. 'If there's anything in the future I can help you with, I'd be delighted to. Goodbye, Madame de la Martinières.'

'Goodbye.' Emilie turned to leave.

'Oh, and if you do see young Sebastian, you can say from me I'll be having words with him about telling you he owned this gallery.' Jonathan raised his eyebrows, smiling. 'He's a nice chap, but he can be a little frugal with the truth.'

'Yes, thank you.'

Emilie left the gallery and looked down with shaking hands at the address Jonathan had given her. Before she could rationalise what she was doing, she hailed a passing taxi, gave the address to the driver and climbed inside. As the taxi set off, she began to pant at the thought of where she was headed. She took out a paper bag from the front of her holdall, containing a half-eaten croissant from Nice airport, and began surreptitiously blowing into it.

'You all right, love?' asked the driver.

'*Oui*—yes, thank you.'

'My son used to have panic attacks,' he said, glancing at her in the mirror. 'Just breathe deeply, love, and you'll be all right.'

'Thank you.' The kindness of a stranger brought tears to her eyes.

'Something upset you, has it?'

'Yes,' said Emilie, the tears of shock and despair stinging her face.

'There we go.' The driver passed a box of tissues through the window to her. 'Never mind, I'm sure it will all come out in the wash, whatever it is. Lovely-looking girl like you . . . life can't be too bad, eh?'

*   *   *

Forty agonising minutes later, the driver pulled into a narrow cobbled lane between two tall buildings.

'These used to be where they stored the tea when it was shipped in from India. Never thought they'd end up as desirable homes—these cost millions now, they do. I'm afraid that's thirty-six quid, love,' the driver added.

Emilie paid him and staggered out with her holdall, her heart still thumping in her chest. She walked to the entrance and saw there was an intercom button for each apartment. Double-checking her piece of paper and gathering every ounce of strength she had left, she pressed the buzzer for number nine.

'Hello?'

'Hello, is that Bella Roseman-Boyd?'

'Yes?'

'I've come from the Arté gallery in Fulham. Jonathan sent me as I was interested in seeing more of your work,' Emilie lied as smoothly as she could.

'Really?' said the voice. 'I wonder why he didn't call to warn me. I wasn't expecting anyone.'

'No, I said I'd come immediately . . . because I am leaving to go back to France tomorrow and I wanted to see your work before I did. Please, you can contact him if you wish. He would tell you it is the truth.'

In the pause that followed, Emilie only hoped what she'd said was enough to gain her entry.

'You'd better come up, then.'

The buzzer sounded and the door opened. Emilie took the large gated lift up to the third floor, walked out into a corridor and saw that the door to number nine was already ajar. Garnering her courage, Emilie knocked on it.

'Come in, I'm just trying to clean the paint off me,' called a voice.

Emilie stepped inside the vast lofted space, the huge windows giving a panoramic vista of the Thames. One end of the room was obviously where Bella painted, the rest of it divided into an area with sofas and a kitchen.

'Hello.' A strikingly beautiful girl with jet-black hair emerged from a door. The paint splatters on her skin-tight faded jeans and T-shirt did nothing to detract from her sylph-like figure. 'Sorry, your name is?'

'My name is Emilie. Are you alone or am I interrupting you?' she asked, needing to know immediately if Sebastian was actually there.

'No, I'm alone,' Bella confirmed. 'Well, Emilie, it's very good of you to come out all this way to see my work. I'd offer you some tea, but I'm pretty sure I've run out of milk. And to be frank, I haven't got much to show you either. I've been getting quite a lot of private commissions recently.' She smiled, showing a perfect set of white teeth.

'Who is your agent?' Emilie enquired politely.

'Sebastian Carruthers, but I'm sure you won't have heard of him. Anyway, come and have a look at what I've got,' she offered.

'Before I do, may I use your bathroom?' Emilie asked.

'Of course, it's just along the corridor on the right,' Bella indicated.

'Thank you.'

Emilie walked out of the room and along the corridor as instructed. There were three doors, all of which were ajar. The first one housed a large, unmade double bed. Emilie gasped in horror as she saw Sebastian's holdall sitting on a chair, his favourite pink shirt in a heap on the floor, entangled with discarded feminine underwear.

Moving along the corridor, she saw the next room was used for storage, with books, paintings, a vacuum cleaner and a rail of clothes taking up its limited space. There was certainly no room for a bed in this 'box room', Emilie thought grimly. Staggering slightly, she entered the bathroom, closed the door behind her and locked it. On the shelf over the sink sat Sebastian's washbag, containing his shaving kit and aftershave. His blue toothbrush was abandoned on the basin.

Emilie sat down on the toilet seat, brutally trying

to push away emotion and think logically what she should do from here. Even though her instinct was to leave the apartment instantly and run, she knew she must use this moment to glean as much information from the horse's mouth as she possibly could. Confronting Sebastian later would only result in the usual veil of lies and deceit. Standing up and flushing the unused toilet, she turned and walked back out of the bathroom and into the sitting room.

'Look,' Bella called, 'the sun's past the yardarm, I'm out of milk for tea and gagging for a glass of wine. Will you join me?'

'OK, thank you,' Emilie agreed.

'Feel free to wander down to the studio and take a look at the paintings,' Bella said as she walked towards the kitchen.

Emilie did so and, despite herself, saw that Bella was an extremely accomplished artist. The paintings had a life and vibrancy which couldn't be taught. She was obviously a talented young woman.

'Come and sit down for a bit.' Bella patted the comfortable leather sofa. 'I've been painting all day, so it's nice to take the weight off my feet for a while. What do you think?' She indicated the current painting on her easel, a lively splash of huge purple irises. 'Obviously, as the artist, I'm massively critical and full of self-doubt, but I think it's going rather well.'

'I love it,' said Emilie genuinely, sitting down.

'I'm afraid you can't have it as it's a commission for some City guy Sebastian met. But I could certainly paint you one similar if you wished. Not for the next three months, mind you, I'm chocker.'

'I would definitely be interested,' agreed Emilie. 'What do you charge?'

'Oh, Sebastian deals with all that, you'd have to speak to him.' Bella waved the question away airily. 'I think it's normally between five and twenty thousand, depending on the size of the canvas.'

'It's a shame you must pay someone to do that for you when I'm sitting here right now and we could agree a price,' said Emilie.

'I know.' Bella nodded. 'Agents are all vultures, feeding off the talent of us artists, but at least it's sort of "in the family" in my case. Which helps.'

'Sorry, it is my bad English.' Emilie forced a smile. 'You mean Sebastian is a relative of yours?'

'Not a relative, exactly. More—how would you say in French—*mon amour*,' said Bella.

'Ah yes.' Emilie faked remembrance. 'I believe Monsieur Jonathan said he was your boyfriend.'

'Well, I wouldn't go that far,' chuckled Bella, 'but Seb and I have had one of those "things" for years. We met ages ago when he came to view my final show at St Martins. He stays with me when he's in town. It's very relaxed,' she added. 'More wine?'

'Why not?' Emilie watched as Bella poured a trickle into her glass and filled up her own.

'Between you and me,' Bella confided, 'he's recently married and I'd presumed our comfortable arrangement would be at an end. But it seems it isn't. Anyway, I'm digressing,' she said, taking another gulp of her wine.

'Do you not mind that he is married?' Emilie asked, feigning interest.

'To be honest, my motto is that life's too short to

chain one person to another. Seb and I have a relationship that works very well. It suits us both. He knows I have other lovers too.' She shrugged. 'And I'm not really the jealous type. Mind you, I am surprised he married. I haven't really asked him the details. I mean, I don't even know his wife's name, because that's not our style, but I gather she's quite wealthy. He turned up here a couple of weeks after he'd tied the knot with her and gave me a beautiful Cartier diamond necklace.' Bella's hand went instinctively to touch the exquisite solitaire placed around her swan-like neck. 'He also found a Matisse in his wife's house, for which he earned a serious commission when he sold it. He bought himself a new Porsche out of the proceeds, which he loves cruising around London in. Bless him.' Bella sighed. 'He's been in debt ever since I knew him. He's absolutely useless with money—whatever he has he spends—but he's always got by somehow.'

'So you're not dependent on him financially?'

'God, no—' Bella rolled her eyes—'now that *would* be a disaster! If anything, it's the other way round, actually. I'm lucky enough to have parents who are wealthy enough to support me and my ambition of becoming a successful artist. Which, as I'm sure you know, is bloody hard. However, just in the last few months I've been able to tell them that I'm making enough through my painting not to need their monthly cheque. That was a real moment of triumph, as you can imagine.' Bella smiled.

'I see.' Emilie knew she had reached her limit and could take no more. She needed to bring this cosy tête-à-tête to a conclusion. 'Then perhaps I

489

can help your journey towards independence. I would very much like to commission you, Bella. So you must put me in touch with Sebastian and we can arrange the price. Will you be seeing him soon?'

'He's got some meeting with a possible client early this evening, but he'll be home later tonight. If you write down your number, I'll tell him to give you a call. I know he's leaving tomorrow evening to go back to the ghastly pile he inherited in Yorkshire. And the wife.' Bella rolled her eyes conspiratorially. 'Anyway, it suits me—I get my weekends all to myself. I'll find you some paper so you can write down your number.'

'OK.'

'Would you mind if we kept Jonathan Maxwell and the gallery out of it? Technically, as he introduced us, he may well expect some commission,' Bella explained. 'I won't mention you turned up here if you don't, and it means we can offer you a better price.'

'Of course.' Emilie nodded as Bella went to the kitchen and rummaged for a piece of scrap paper in a drawer.

'Here.' Bella handed it to her.

Emilie paused then carefully wrote down her full name, number and address in France. She placed it on the table. Then she rose. 'It's been . . . interesting to meet you, Bella. I wish you good luck with your future. I'm sure you will be very successful. You are a talented woman.'

'Thank you,' said Bella as she accompanied Emilie to the door. 'It's been a pleasure to meet you too. I really hope we'll meet again soon.'

'Yes.' On a whim, she put her hand on Bella's

forearm. 'I think you are a good person, Bella. Take care.'

With that, Emilie turned away and walked out of the apartment.

32

It was almost midnight when Emilie arrived back at Blackmoor Hall. She'd taken a taxi from York station—the Land Rover was still at the airport and Sebastian could go and retrieve it if he wished. It was no longer her concern.

She was glad Alex's light was still shining from his corner of the building—she'd be leaving early the next morning and she wanted to say goodbye to him.

Walking through the house, she knocked on the door of his flat.

'Come in, Em,' he called. 'You're late home. Did you miss your flight?'

Alex was sitting on the sofa, reading a book.

'No. I've been to London.'

Alex took in Emilie's wide eyes and drawn features. 'What's happened?' he asked in concern.

'I came to tell you that I'm leaving for France tomorrow. Sebastian and I will be getting a divorce as soon as I can arrange it.'

'Right,' he said with a sigh. 'Any particular reason?'

'I visited his long-term lover in London today. And saw my husband's current sleeping arrangements for myself.'

'I see. Shall I get the brandy?' Alex asked.

'No, I will.'

Emilie marched into the kitchen and returned with the bottle and two glasses. 'Did you know of her?' she asked as she poured the brandy and handed him a glass.

'Yes.'

'And were you aware Sebastian was still carrying on his affair with her after he married me?'

'I suspected it when he started to disappear off to London so frequently and didn't take you with him, but I wasn't sure.'

'And you didn't think to tell me, Alex? I thought we were friends!' she cried.

'Emilie, please, that's unfair!' He was shaken at her vehemence. 'Sebastian was painting me as a total liability, who lied and cheated and would do anything to sully his name. Do you really think you'd have believed me if I had?'

'No.' Emilie took a large sip of the brandy. 'You're right, I wouldn't have done. Sorry.' She put her fingers to her forehead. 'It's been a stressful day.'

'The mistress of understatement.' Alex smiled wryly. 'Does Sebastian know that you've paid a call to his girlfriend?'

'I haven't switched on my mobile since I left London, so I have no idea.' She shrugged.

'Did you tell Bella who you are?'

Emilie stared at Alex. The fact that he knew Bella's name, that she'd obviously been such a big part of Sebastian's life, threatened to break her hard-won calm. 'No. I said I wanted to commission her, so she asked me to write down my full name, address and telephone number. So I did. She promised to give it to Sebastian when he arrived . . . home.'

Whatever reaction she had been expecting from Alex, it was not throwing back his head and roaring with laughter.

'Oh! Brilliant, Em! Just brilliant! Sorry,' he wiped the tears from his eyes—'inappropriate reaction. My God, that was a masterstroke. And so typically you: low-key, subtle, elegant . . . beautiful. Just beautiful,' he added admiringly. 'Can you imagine Seb's face when Bella hands him that piece of paper with your name and number on it?'

'Alex,' Emilie sighed, 'I don't care what he thinks. I simply want to leave this house as soon as I can and go home.'

Alex's expression changed. 'Yes, of course you do,' he said soberly. 'Look, can you understand that I've been between a rock and a hard place from the moment you arrived? I was obviously hoping that Seb really had found someone he loved.'

'Well, if he can love anybody other than himself, it's Bella. She's beautiful and very talented. If it wasn't for the fact that she was my husband's lover, I would seriously consider commissioning her.' Emilie managed her first, albeit grim, smile of the day. 'Have you met her?'

'Yes. Before you married him, she'd sometimes come here at weekends.' Alex studied her. 'My God, Em, you're amazing. How are you able to deal with this?'

'It's very simple.' She shrugged. 'Sebastian is not the person I fell in love with any longer. The feelings I originally had for him in France have died.'

'Then I salute you, even if I can't totally believe

493

you. You are . . . incredible. And I could happily strangle Seb with my own bare hands that he's let you go.'

'Thank you,' she said, not looking at him. 'I have one question to ask you before I leave.'

'And that is?'

'Why did your brother *marry* me? What is it, Alex, he wanted from me that he couldn't already get from Bella, who told me she is also from a wealthy family?' Emilie shook her head. 'I just can't understand.'

'Well, Em . . .' Alex sighed. 'The answer, as always in these dilemmas, is right under your nose. And you've already seen it.'

'Have I?'

'Yes, but you almost certainly wouldn't have noticed.'

'Just now—' Emilie squinted—'I can see my nose, but there's nothing beneath it except my knees.'

'Quite,' Alex agreed. 'The question is, do you really want me to tell you?'

'Of course! Tomorrow I leave for France. My marriage is over.'

'All right.' Alex nodded slowly. 'But it's "gloves off" from now on.'

'That's fine with me.' Emilie nodded in agreement.

'OK,' he said. 'Come with me and I'll show you.'

*   *   *

'Right.' Alex switched on the light to the small study where Sebastian worked when he was at home. He went to a bookcase, felt under a certain book and produced a key. He turned his wheelchair round and proceeded to unlock the drawer of the desk on which Sebastian's computer sat. He pulled out a file and handed it to Emilie.

'Exhibit A. Don't look at it until I've collected all the evidence.' Alex positioned himself behind Sebastian's computer and switched it on. He typed in a password and the computer gave him access.

'How can you know what his password is?' she asked.

'If you live with the fact that someone is intent on making your life as difficult as possible, you make it your job to know these things. Especially if you have as little to occupy you as I do,' he added as he continued to type. 'Besides, I can read my brother like a book. It didn't take a genius to work it out.'

'Is it "Matisse", by any chance?' guessed Emilie.

'No shit, Sherlock.' Alex grinned at her. 'The thing with Seb is that he makes little or no attempt to hide his tracks, believing so totally in his consummate skills as a liar if he has to explain himself. Now—' Alex reached down to pull some pages off the printer and handed them to her— 'Exhibit B. Just one more thing—' he pointed to an oil painting of his grandmother that hung on the wall—'could you remove that for me?'

Emilie did so, revealing a small safe behind it.

'Right, unless he's changed the combination, which I doubt, it's my grandmother's date of birth.' Alex stretched for the dial on the front of the safe and twisted it carefully. 'I just hope Seb hasn't removed what I want to show you since I last looked,' he said as he reached inside the safe. He ferreted around its interior, and then, with a sigh of relief, produced a padded envelope and a smaller plain white one. 'Exhibits C and D,' he stated as he closed the safe and motioned to Emilie to re-hang the picture. 'I suggest we return to my quarters, just in case the man himself is racing up the motorway from London as we speak to save his marriage, or rather, to save himself. It's also a damned sight warmer.'

Alex switched off the computer and the printer, and they left the study. Back in the flat, Alex asked Emilie to place the four exhibits he'd handed her in a line on the coffee table. 'OK, Em.' He glanced at her sympathetically, searching her face. 'This is likely to be upsetting, I'm afraid.'

'I am past being "upset", Alex. I simply want to know the reasons why.'

'Right then. Take a look at the first file.'

Emilie opened the file and saw her own face and that of her mother's staring out from the pages. They were photocopies of all the articles in various French newspapers detailing the death of her mother. And announcing that Emilie was the lone heiress.

'Next, open the envelope we took out of the safe and remove its contents. Be careful, it's very, very old.'

Emilie slid her hand inside the envelope and retrieved a book. She glanced at the title in awe. 'It's *The History of French Fruit*. I heard from Jacques yesterday that my father gave it to Constance as a keepsake when she left the château to return here. It's the book you said you couldn't find from the library here.'

'Yes,' said Alex. 'Now, very, very carefully open the cover and read what's on the first page.'

'Édouard de la Martinières,' she read, '1943. So?'

'Hang on a tick,' Alex said, 'I need to get something else to show you.' He wheeled himself out of the sitting room and returned shortly, handing her an envelope. 'Inside you'll find a letter written to me by my grandmother. She lodged it with her solicitor just before she died. I doubt she trusted Seb to hand it over to me. What's new?' He sighed.

Emilie began to read.

Blackmoor Hall, 20th March 1996

Dear Alex,

I am writing this in the hope that one day you will return home to Blackmoor Hall, although I accept now it may not be in my lifetime. My dearest grandson, I want you to know I now understand why you felt you had to go away, and firstly I want to offer my most heartfelt apologies for not seeing or reacting more to what was happening to you. I fear I let you down and didn't protect you when you needed me to. But it was hard to believe that your brother, whom I also love dearly, could be so methodical in his destruction of you.

I do hope, dear boy, that you can forgive me for ever doubting you. So many times I, too, was duped by your brother, whose intelligence was not in the same strata as yours, but whose quick wit and capacity for deception and lies equals it in its magnificence. And perhaps I, as your grandmother and then in the role of your

497

mother, felt guilty that from the first moment I set eyes on you, I loved you more than him. You, so adorable, angelic and loving, and your poor brother so much less appealing on every possible level.

There is a poem I read once—by Larkin—which talks of wishing his newborn godchild to be 'ordinary'—blessed with enough of each gift, but never too much or too little. I understand now exactly what he meant. For your gifts, Alex, have been your downfall. I digress, forgive me.

Now, Alex, I have obviously been praying that you will return before I die. Because I must decide what to do with my beloved Blackmoor Hall. As you know, it has been in your grandfather's family for over 150 years. As I'm unaware of your whereabouts, or how much money it will take to restore the house, I am uncertain of what to do. So, my dearest boy, I have decided that I must leave it jointly to the two of you, hoping that the mutual ownership will reunite you. I know it is the faint wish of a dying and optimistic old woman, and perhaps it will prove to have the opposite effect. I can only pray it won't prove a burden for either of you. If it does, please sell it with my blessing.

I am also leaving you a book—I know how you value old editions—which is of sentimental rather than monetary value to me. I was given this by a friend of mine a long time ago in war-time France. Also in this envelope is a book of poems written by his sister, Sophia, of whom I was extremely fond. If you wish to, the owner's name in the front of the book is enough to help you find out more about what happened to your grandmother in France during the war. I chose to keep it secret in my lifetime, but it's an interesting story, and perhaps it will make you think better of the woman who did all she could to care for you, but made some fatal mistakes. The book and the poems are where they've always been—on the third shelf to the left in the library. You can retrieve them if you wish.

Other than that, I am leaving you half of what I have left, the grand sum of £50,000. I can only pray that one day, dear Alex, you will return home and can forgive me. However flawed, I had to love Sebastian too. Do you see?

Your loving grandmother, Constance X

Emilie wiped her eyes, the stress of such a long and traumatic day finally getting the better of her. 'It's a beautiful letter.'

'Yes, it is,' said Alex. 'You know, Em, I did write at least three or four letters home when I was abroad, giving Granny my address in Italy. I can only believe that Sebastian got to the postman here first. He recognised my writing and snaffled the letters, which allowed Granny to think I hadn't bothered to let her know where I was. In other words—' Alex sighed—'that I didn't care about her.'

'That wouldn't surprise me at all now. He's an arch manipulator,' Emilie agreed. 'Thank you for letting me read the letter. But what relevance does this have to the other things you've shown me?'

'Please pick up the last file.'

Emilie did so, her eyes widening as she read the contents. She looked up at Alex for confirmation.

'You can see that Granny was certainly wrong in one respect: the book she left me was not just of "sentimental" value,' he commented as he watched her reading.

'Yes.' She nodded.

'Of course, when I eventually got her letter, then went to search for the book in the library when I came home from hospital after the accident, I made the fatal mistake of telling Seb what I was looking for and where to find it. I couldn't reach it, you see, it was on the third shelf up,' Alex said with a shrug. 'When Seb retrieved it for me, I showed the book to him willingly. At the time, I was eager to try and forge a relationship with him, so when he asked if he could borrow the book for a few days to read it, I agreed. After that, every time I asked him for it, he'd say he would return it, but of course he didn't. And knowing Seb as I do, I suspected something was up. I looked the book up on the Internet, like he obviously had, and knew that if he hadn't sold it already, it would be tucked away in his safe. And there it was.' Alex shook his head sadly.

'But why hasn't he sold it already?' asked Emilie. 'And if you knew it was so valuable, why haven't you reclaimed it?'

'Em, maybe you haven't glanced fully at the detail on the sheet I printed up. I was convinced that Seb wouldn't sell it,' Alex explained. 'The one thing I know about my brother is that he's greedy. He'd never be prepared to settle for what he had already when he knew the main prize was possibly on offer. Read out what it says to me. From the beginning.'

Emilie was beyond exhaustion, but she did her

best to concentrate on the words.

RARE BOOKS ARCHIVE

The History of French Fruit

By Christophe Pierre Beaumont. 1756. 2 Volumes. Arguably the finest and rarest book on fruit. With illustrations of fifteen different species of fruit trees. The work was inspired by an earlier Duchamel publication *Anatomie de la Poire* published in the 1730s. Illustrations by Guillaume Jean Gardinier and François Joseph Fortier. Beaumont's intention was to promote the virtue and nutritional value of fruit-bearing trees. Fifteen different genera of fruit and a number of their different species are described in the work: almonds, apricots, a barberry, cherries, quinces, figs, strawberries, gooseberries, apples, a mulberry, pears, peaches, plums, grapes and raspberries. Each coloured plate illustrates the plant's seed, foliage, blossom, fruit, and sometimes cross sections of the species.

Provenance: Both volumes believed to reside in a private collection in Gassin, France.

Value: Approximately £5 million.

Emilie finished reading and looked up at Alex. 'I still don't understand.'

'Right then, I'll spell it out for you,' Alex said. 'I contacted a rare bookseller of my acquaintance in London, as I presume Sebastian had already done.

He told me that, separately, the two volumes were probably worth around one million pounds each. But, together, five times that. Do you understand now, Emilie?'

Finally, the penny dropped.

'Sebastian was looking for the first volume in my father's library,' she stated flatly.

'Yes.'

Emilie was silent for a while, processing the information. 'Now, at last, it all makes sense. That was why Sebastian was in France a few weeks ago. My friend Jean, who runs the vineyard on the domaine, found him in the library searching through the shelves. No wonder he came back to Yorkshire in such a bad temper that weekend. He obviously hadn't found the first volume.'

'Well, at least that's something,' said Alex.

'I can understand everything,' said Emilie, 'except why he went as far as to marry me.'

'Well, maybe having failed to find the first volume up until the moment the château was about to go under renovation and the library was about to be packed away, Seb needed to have "access all areas",' mused Alex. 'As your husband, no one could deny his presence and he could continue to investigate. Your marriage allowed him free rein to keep looking.'

'Yes. You're right,' Emilie agreed. 'And I trusted him completely with it.'

'Em, are you up to opening the last envelope?' Alex indicated it lying on the table. 'I have a feeling this one might be very upsetting for you.'

'Yes, I'm fine,' Emilie replied stoically, grasping it and tearing it open. Inside was the new key to the front door of the château. Sebastian had asked for a copy at some point and she had handed it over to him without thinking about it. But also in the envelope was the original rusting key that had gone missing.

'Oh God,' she mouthed eventually, involuntary tears springing to her eyes. 'It was *him* who broke into the château that day! And then he had the gall to return almost straight afterwards . . . and *comfort* me! How could he, Alex, how could he?!'

'As I said, he needed access all areas,' Alex replied. 'God, Em, I'm sorry, so sorry. And to be completely fair to him, I do know he was very taken with you at the start,' he equivocated, seeing her pain and desperately wanting to make her feel better. 'He certainly waxed lyrical about you to me when he came back from France after he'd met you. Perhaps his intentions were not all bad. Maybe he thought he could make the marriage work. But then the honeytrap of Bella raised its ugly head and he couldn't resist. He's never been able to let her go completely over the past ten years.'

'Do *not* excuse him, Alex, please,' Emilie snapped. 'He doesn't deserve your sympathy on any level. Taking everything else he has done to me aside, in my book, if you love someone it's to the exclusion of all others,' she said vehemently, wiping her tears of shock roughly away with the back of her hand. She *would not* waste them on him.

'I can assure you, in my book too,' Alex agreed. 'So, there we are. God, Em, I hate that it's me who's had to tell you all this. It breaks my heart to upset you. Please don't hate me too, will you? I despise my brother for what he's done to you, I really do.'

'Of course I won't hate you,' she answered, exhausted now. 'I asked you to tell me.'

'Well, I really hope you won't,' Alex said with feeling. 'By the way, I think you should keep the book.' He indicated it lying innocently on the table. 'Take it with you to the château and put it back where it belongs.'

'But it was given to your grandmother by my father, and then to you by her. It's yours.'

'You're right, under normal circumstances,' Alex agreed. 'But perhaps it's best if it goes with you to France, out of harm's way,' he suggested. 'Just out of interest, do you know where the other volume is? Obviously not in your father's library.'

'You haven't seen the library,' said Emilie. 'It's vast—over twenty thousand books. I think it would have taken Sebastian longer than a couple of days to check it wasn't there.'

'Sorry, Emilie,' Alex looked pained, 'but he's had far longer than a couple of days, hasn't he? His recent journey to France was simply a last-ditch attempt to recheck that he hadn't missed it before the library went into storage. Sebastian had spent plenty of time in the château beforehand with you.'

'Yes,' Emilie agreed. Her thoughts moved back to when she'd first met Sebastian. And the random books on fruit trees which she'd noticed standing proud in the library after the suspected burglary. He'd been searching from the start.

'Anyway—' she shook her head, aghast at Sebastian's duplicity and her own naivety—'the good news is, as far as we know, he's failed to find it. I'll look for it when the library is back in place and finished after the renovations. And at least I know the truth, at last. Now I must move on.'

'Emilie, you're a seriously amazing woman,' Alex said with genuine admiration.

'No.' Emilie gave a sigh that turned into a yawn. 'I'm nothing of the sort. Just a pragmatist at heart, swept away by false love. I took the leap to trust for the first time in my life and it went wrong. Besides . . . there are things about me that Sebastian doesn't know.'

Alex watched her silently as Emilie decided whether to continue.

'For example,' she said, when she finally spoke, 'I didn't tell him before we married that we couldn't have children. Or, at least, *I* couldn't.'

'Right,' Alex replied calmly. 'Did Seb ever ask you whether you could?'

'No. But that doesn't mean to say that I shouldn't have told him, morally, does it? I knew I should tell him, but revisiting the time when it happened . . .' Emilie struggled to explain. 'I couldn't go there.'

'I see. Then do you mind me asking how you know this? Listen, if it's too painful to recount, please don't worry.'

Emilie poured herself another brandy to give her courage, knowing she *had* to let it out. 'When I was thirteen,' she began, feeling her heart rate increasing at the thought of speaking the words, 'I became very sick. My father was at the château and I was at home in Paris with my mother. She was very busy socialising and one of our maids told her how ill I seemed, and that she should call the doctor. She took a quick look at me in bed, pressed her hand to my forehead and said she was sure I would be fine in the morning. Then she left for a dinner. Anyway—' Emilie took a further sip of her brandy—'within the next few days I deteriorated. Finally, my mother did send for a doctor, an old friend of hers, who diagnosed food poisoning. He gave me some tablets and left. A day after that, I was unconscious. My mother was elsewhere, so it was the maid who called an ambulance to take me to hospital. I was diagnosed with pelvic inflammatory disease. To be fair, it was very rare for someone of my age to contract it, so I'm not surprised the doctor didn't pick it up. Sadly, it's easy to cure in the early stages of the illness, but fatally damaging to the area beyond a certain point. Subsequently,' Emilie sighed, 'I was told I was never able to have children.'

'Oh, Em, how awful for you.' Alex looked at her with sympathy in his eyes.

'Alex—' Emilie stared at him, shocked at her sudden honesty—'you're the first person I have ever told this to. I've never been able to speak the words out loud. I—' Her shoulders began to shake and she put her head into her hands and started to sob.

'Em, Emilie . . . Oh, sweetheart . . . I'm so, so sorry.'

An arm came around her on the sofa and pulled her to him. She settled into the warmth of Alex's chest and continued to cry. He said nothing, just stroked her hair gently as the sobs turned to hiccups and her nose streamed.

'Whatever was wrong with me, how could my mother have ignored how ill I was? Why didn't she see!'

'Em, I don't know, I really don't. I'm so sorry.'

A hanky was pressed silently into her hands.

'I'm sorry,' she snuffled, 'this isn't like me.'

'Of course it's *like* you,' he said softly. 'The pain is part of you, and it's OK to talk about it, it really is. It helps to let it out, honestly it does.'

'When I was younger and I was told I wouldn't have babies, I tried to think it wouldn't matter much. But it does, Alex!' she cried. 'It matters more as every year passes and I realise that the one thing I believe we're put on this earth for, that makes us humans have a point, I cannot fulfill!'

'Are you absolutely sure it's the case?' he asked gently.

'If you're asking me if the miracles that occur these days with infertile women are possible for me, then the answer is categorically no,' she said firmly. 'I can't produce eggs, nor do I have a womb that's healthy enough to carry another woman's eggs.'

'You could always adopt,' suggested Alex.

'Yes, I could.' Emilie blew her nose. 'You're right.'

'I only mention it as it's something that's crossed my mind. As it happens, I'm infertile too. I won't go into detail,' Alex added with a half smile, 'but although the "equipment" works perfectly well, due to the accident, the shots won't fire. I would have loved kids too. Honestly—' he gave an ironic chuckle—'we're a pair, aren't we?'

'Yes.' Emilie lay in his arms silently, feeling so comforted she didn't want to move. She sat up and turned to him. 'Before I go, which isn't long now, I want to apologise for ever doubting you. You're the best and bravest person I've ever met.'

'Please, my dearest Em,' Alex countered, 'I

507

think that's the brandy talking. I'm nothing of the sort.'

'Yes, you are.' She looked up at him suddenly. 'The only thing I'll be sorry to leave behind in England is you.'

'Goodness! Stop it. You'll have me blushing.' Alex smiled down at her and stroked her cheek. 'Well, if we're paying each other compliments, and as we're unlikely to see each other again, I want to tell you that if life had been different, well . . .' He gave a long sigh. 'I'll miss you, Em. I really will. Now, you'd better be off; it's almost three in the morning. Don't forget the book, and please let me know if you come across Volume One. I'll write down my email address for you. I'd like to keep in touch.'

'What will you say to Sebastian?' Emilie asked, now concerned for Alex.

'If he mentions the book—*my* book—has gone missing, it will only be the story he's told me for the past two years.' Alex shrugged and grinned. 'What can he say? His own lie has become the truth. The book *has* disappeared.'

'But what if he thinks you've taken it? And makes your life even more difficult?'

'Oh, Em, please don't worry about me. You have enough to think about at the moment. I can look after myself, promise.' Alex smiled at her. 'Now, off you go.'

She stood up and took the book, the file and the printed pages from the table. 'I can never thank you enough, Alex. Please take care.' She bent down to kiss him on both cheeks. On a whim, she wrapped her arms around his shoulders and hugged him tightly. *'Bonsoir, mon ami.'*

508

'Adieu, mon amour,' Alex whispered as he watched her leave.

33

When she entered her bedroom, Emilie did not bother trying to sleep; she'd only be on edge expecting Sebastian to arrive at any minute. So, calling a taxi as the dawn rose, she threw what she could into a suitcase then sat on the end of the bed debating whether to leave her husband a note. Deciding against it, she instead wrote one to Alex, included her email address in it and slipped it under his door.

As the taxi bore Emilie away from the house for the last time, her one regret and concern was for Alex; it was very likely that Sebastian would take his anger out yet again on his brother. But what could she do?

Later that morning, as the plane slipped smoothly up into the sky, carrying her away from the terrible mistake she had made, Emilie closed her eyes and blanked out her mind. When she arrived in Nice, she checked into a hotel near the airport, sank onto the bed and slept.

She awoke as dusk was falling, feeling dreadful—weak, shaky and with a thumping headache from too much brandy the night before. She ordered a hamburger from room service, realising she hadn't eaten since the croissant yesterday morning. Forcing the food down, Emilie lay back down on the bed, pondering the fact that she was currently homeless. Her flat in Paris was rented out until the end of June, and the château, undergoing renovation, was not an option.

Emilie decided she'd stay where she was for the night, then head down to Gassin in the morning. She was sure Jean wouldn't mind putting her up for another few days until she thought about where to go next. Perhaps she could rent a gîte nearby— at least then she'd be on-site to oversee the renovations.

Emilie stopped herself. It was too soon to think about future plans.

She wondered if Sebastian had arrived back in Yorkshire yet. She knew she must grit her teeth and make contact with Gerard as soon as possible and ask him for the name of a good divorce lawyer. At least she'd not been married long enough to begin to change any documentation and the two of them had shared nothing official between them. Emilie thought of the beautiful diamond Sebastian had bought Bella, just after she'd given him a cheque for £20,000, and the Porsche she'd never even seen, and felt physically sick.

She wished she could share Alex's calm and accepting attitude towards his brother, but as he'd said once, it was good to get angry, it helped you heal. And at least while she felt angry there was no hurt, although she realised that might come later. She was surprised she currently felt so little; after all, the passion she'd felt for Sebastian at the start of their relationship had been overwhelming. It had bowled her over. But perhaps it had never really been 'love', in the way that Constance had described to Sophia long ago in Paris. At least, not the enduring kind which was quieter, yet steadfast, and took you through the trials of life together.

Sebastian had arrived with the Mistral and swept her away. But had she ever been confident enough to truly be herself with him? She realised now that she'd spent the vast majority of the past year on edge, trying to do everything to please him, her gratefulness for his presence in her life overwhelming what was right. There were so many moments when she should have confronted him, been stronger, but Sebastian had held all the cards from the start. They'd always done as *he* wished, and she had followed, ready to bend, equivocate and believe anything he'd told her.

No, Emilie thought, that wasn't love.

Switching on the television to dull the silence of the room, Emilie wondered if it had been the brandy that had made her tell Alex what her mother had done—or not done—when she was younger.

It felt surreal now; all those years of burying the result of her mother's lack of interest and care. She had allowed the inner bitterness to grow and, like bindweed, strangle her good thoughts, her heart and her trust in other people. Yet, in the past few weeks, Alex had shown her there was no point in hating or looking back. The only person who suffered was yourself.

Dear Alex . . . how wise and kind he was. Emilie remembered the feeling of being in his arms as she'd wept. She'd felt comforted and comfortable. And why had she been able to tell *him*, when she'd never been able to say the words to her husband?

But, Emilie reprimanded herself before she went further, the English episode had closed. She must try to forgive, forget and move on.

'Emilie! Long time no see.' Jean smiled up at her sympathetically when she walked into the *cave*.

'I just couldn't keep away,' she replied with irony in her voice, then noticed that another pair of bright eyes was gazing at her from the bench where Jacques usually sat. 'Hello, Anton.' She smiled at the boy. 'You're helping out here, are you? Earning some extra centimes to buy books?'

'Anton is staying with us for the next few days, whilst his maman is in hospital,' Jean answered.

'Margaux? I didn't know she was sick. Is she all right?' Emilie frowned.

'Yes, we're sure she'll be fine.' Jean shot her a warning glance. 'But, in the meantime, I'm teaching Anton all about wine. Papa's sitting in the garden. Why don't you go out and see him? I'll join you in a while.'

Jacques was looking far less weary than he'd seemed two days ago. He smiled and reached out his gnarled hand to her. 'I thought you might be back quite soon. I won't ask why, Emilie, but I will always listen.'

'Thank you, Jacques.' She sat down at the small table next to him. 'Tell me, what's wrong with Margaux?'

Jacques looked nervous. 'Is the boy still in the *cave* with Jean?'

'Yes.'

'Then, Emilie, the truth is, she's very ill. It was only last week she complained of a pain in her stomach and back, although she has almost certainly known she was unwell for much longer.

512

She went to the doctor on the day you left and he sent her straight to hospital. The boy doesn't know, but they've discovered she has ovarian cancer and it's very advanced. They operate today, but—' Jacques shrugged—'the prognosis is not good.'

'No, Jacques!' Emilie cried in despair. 'Not Margaux! She was like a mother to me when I came down here after my father died.'

'Yes, she's a very good woman, and we must not give up hope yet.'

'I'll go and see her in hospital in the next few days,' she promised.

'Margaux would like that. So, what about you, Emilie?' Jacques eyed her. 'What are your plans?'

'Right at this moment, I have no idea,' said Emilie, shaking her head sadly.

*   *   *

In the next few days, Emilie slept, ate, went to see how the château was progressing and drove Anton to Nice to see his mother. The operation had not been a success and Margaux was very ill. As Emilie left Anton at her bedside, her heart went out to mother and child—both trying so hard to be brave for each other.

After Anton had gone to bed—he was sleeping temporarily on a mattress in the tiny downstairs study—the three of them talked of what would happen to Anton if his mother did not recover.

'His father is dead, so what about other relatives?' asked Jean.

'I think there's an aunt in Grasse,' said Jacques. 'Perhaps we should contact her.'

513

'Yes,' said Jean gravely, 'but I'm the boy's godfather. Perhaps we should think of offering him a home here with us?'

'We could, temporarily, but a young boy needs a woman,' said Jacques. 'It's a house full of men here.'

'Well, Anton is almost thirteen and I am sure he will have thoughts of his own,' replied Jean.

'Talking of our current household,' said Emilie, 'I've heard of a gîte which is available locally. It's in the vineyard of the Bournasse family. I'll go and see it tomorrow. From what Madame Bournasse said to me on the telephone, it sounds perfect.'

'You know there's no rush for you to leave,' impressed Jean.

'Yes, you're very kind, but I should start to make plans too.'

After Jacques had retired to bed, Jean and Emilie cleared up the supper dishes.

'Has your father said any more about whether he's prepared to reveal the identity of Sophia's baby?' she asked.

'No, and I haven't pushed him,' replied Jean firmly. 'He's so much better at the moment, and I don't want to upset him.'

'He's amazing,' agreed Emilie. 'It's ironic—at one point I thought it would be your father we would have to say goodbye to, but it seems as though it might be Margaux. She looked so terrible in the hospital this afternoon, Jean. And Anton is so brave.'

'He's a special young man,' Jean agreed. 'Sadly, having lost his father so young, he's very close to his mother. Tomorrow afternoon, Papa has asked to be driven to Nice to see Margaux alone. So if it's convenient, can Anton stay with you?'

'Of course. He can come with me to see the gîte. I didn't think it would be Jacques visiting a dying patient in Nice hospital.' She sighed.

'My father's a creaking gate, Emilie,' commented Jean. 'He'll probably outlive us all.'

*   *   *

It took Emilie and Anton less than a few seconds to decide that the gîte was the perfect temporary home for her to live in until the château was ready for occupation. Ten minutes' walk from the château, and set in the middle of glorious vines, it was prettily decorated in Provençal style, with a woodburner which would keep her warm when winter arrived in a few months' time.

'It has two spare bedrooms too,' exclaimed Anton as he wandered out of one of them. 'Perhaps, Emilie, I could come and stay with you sometimes if Maman is . . . away for a long time.'

'Of course you can.' She smiled. 'Whenever you wish. Now, are we agreed? Should I take it?'

'Yes! It even has an Internet connection here,' he replied eagerly.

After the price had been agreed with Madame Bournasse, Emilie took Anton for a celebration lunch at Le Pescadou in Gassin.

Anton sat with his head resting on his hand, staring out at the magnificent view from the hilltop setting. 'I hope I don't have to leave this village,' he said sadly. 'I've lived here all my life and I'm happy here.'

'Why should you?' Emilie asked as the waiter delivered freshly baked pizzas for both of them.

Anton turned his huge blue eyes to her. 'Because my mother is dying. And when she does, I might have to go and live with my aunt in Grasse.'

'Oh, Anton.' Emilie stretched out her hand and squeezed his forearm across the table. 'Don't give up hope, she may well get better.'

'No, she won't. I'm not stupid, Emilie. It's kind of you all to pretend, but I know the truth here.' Anton thumped his small chest. 'I don't really like my aunt or my cousins. They're only interested in football and tease me that I like to read and study.'

'Please, try not to think about those things yet. And if the worst does happen—' Emilie acknowledged it was a possibility in front of him for the first time—'I'm sure there are other solutions.'

'I hope so,' he replied quietly.

*　　　*　　　*

A few days later, Emilie left the cottage and moved into her new home. Anton assisted her willingly. He had become her shadow, especially as Margaux, who had deteriorated further and wished to spare her son the pain of seeing her so ill, had suggested he took a break from visiting her every day at the hospital. She was so full of morphine, she was hardly conscious. They all knew now that it was simply a matter of time.

'Would you mind if I sometimes cycled down to see you here?' he asked as Emilie plugged in her laptop to check the Internet worked.

'Of course not, Anton, you can visit me as often as you wish.' She smiled at him. 'Now, how about we make some tea?'

*   *   *

Later that evening, when Anton had been safely deposited back at the cottage with Jean and Jacques, Emilie sat down in front of her computer and read her emails. She was dreading one from Sebastian, but there were none. Instead, she saw Alex's name blinking in front of her.

To:edlmartinieres@orange.fr
From:aecarruthers@blackhall.co.uk

Dearest Em,

I hope this letter finds you well. And that France is proving a balm to your poor, battered soul. I hope you don't mind me writing, but I thought I would bring you up to date on what happened after you left. If nothing else, you might find it amusing.

Sebastian arrived back home a few hours after you'd fled the house, huffing and puffing about there being some terrible mistake. (I was tempted to mention not only his lover's verbal confession, and that the sight of his clothes strewn around the bedroom he shared with her may have had something to do with rousing your suspicions, but you'll be happy to hear I managed to restrain myself—just.) He asked me where you were. I, of course, feigned ignorance yet again, but mentioned I thought I'd heard you leave early that morning. He muttered something about being

517

sure you'd be back once you'd calmed down and then he left to go back into the main house. All was quiet for a few hours then suddenly I heard a yell and the sound of feet marching along the corridor towards me.

Mentally donning my bulletproof vest, as I guessed what was coming, my brother stormed in and demanded to know who had been into his safe and stolen his book.

'What book is that, brother dearest?' I ask.

'The one I asked you if I could borrow ages ago,' he replies.

'Oh,' say I, 'you mean, *my* book? But I thought you'd said that you'd mislaid it? To be truthful, Seb,' I continue, 'I'd forgotten all about it.' I frown at him. 'So, you did know where it was then, all this time?'

Oh, Emilie, the look on his face was priceless. He'd been caught out in one of his own lies!

He then began (I kid you not) to ransack my flat, accusing me of taking the book. Which, considering it was mine in the first place, I felt was a downright cheek. Then, after he'd searched through every single nook and cranny—poor Jo the cleaner was very upset about the mess he made—he tried another tack.

'Look, Alex,' he said, in that irritatingly earnest way he has when he's trying to pull a fast one. 'I was going to tell you as soon as I'd made absolutely certain, but I discovered recently that that book of yours is actually extremely valuable.'

'Really?' I say. 'Goodness, what a surprise!'

518

'*Yes*, in fact, it's extremely valuable indeed.'

'Well, aren't I the lucky one! How much?' I ask.

'Around half a million pounds,' he says. (HAH!) So, if I would happen to have it in my possession, could I keep it safe, because—and at this point he leans closer to appear more confidential—there's a chance that he might know how to turn that half a million into one million!!

'Goodness!' I say again. 'How could that be?'

He then goes on to explain that there's another volume of the book and he's been doing some research on its location. He's very close to tracking it down and, if he does, the two volumes together will be worth a lot of money. So if he can source the other volume, perhaps it's possible for both of us, as the good, honest, caring, sharing brothers we are, to put the two together and then split the winnings?

I do an awful lot of serious nodding and listening intently until I say: 'That all sounds wonderful, Seb. There's only one little problem. I don't have the book. I haven't stolen back my own property and I have absolutely no idea where it is. So,' I ask (goading him a little), '*who* could have taken it . . . ?'

We both sit and think deeply for a while. I watch him and, as the penny finally drops, I look at him as though I've reached the same sad conclusion.

'Emilie.'

'It must have been her,' I agree.

He then stands up and paces manically around the room, questioning how on earth she could have found out about it. And that, in fact, if she had 'stolen' it from us, then he— he corrected himself immediately— *I* should contact the police at once.

I then pointed out that if it *was* you, it would be pretty difficult to prove, considering the book bore your father's signature on the inside cover.

This really stymied him, until he turned suddenly with a look of relief on his face. 'But of course, Alex, you received a letter from our grandmother saying she was bequeathing it to you.'

Now, what's interesting about this, dearest Em, is that I, to my knowledge, have never shown my brother the letter my granny's solicitor handed to me after I returned home.

'What letter?' I ask him. 'I can't remember any letter.'

'The letter you told me said that Granny had left the book to you,' he says.

'Ah yes,' I say, scratching my head in vague remembrance, 'I think I remember tearing it up.'

At this point, the angst on my brother's face is almost comical. He shoots me a look—no, I would call it a death stare—and slams back out of my flat.

At this point I decide that a mad Seb is a dangerous Seb. Or even more dangerous than usual. I took steps, dearest Em, which sound vaguely disproportionate considering this email is regarding a lost book, and called a locksmith. That afternoon, he duly arrived and battened down my hatches. I'm now incarcerated in the kind of state-of-the-art security that would normally only be found surrounding the *Mona Lisa*. I have an intercom on both the external door and the internal one, plus a variety of locks and padlocks on the doors themselves. It sounds dramatic, but I at least want to be able to rest in my bed safely at night.

Interestingly, that afternoon, Seb left the house. This was good in one sense as it allowed the installation of my security systems to continue uninterrupted, but the bad news is (a) they haven't so far been tested and I'm feeling like a fool for wasting my money and (b) I'm concerned he will make his way across to you in France.

Dearest Em, I have no idea what your circumstances are or where you're living, and I'm probably over-exaggerating, due to my concern for you, but does he know where your library is stored? I wouldn't put it past him to try to search it again. And as I believe he organised the storage, and he's your husband, he would have full access to it if he so wished. Also, if he does turn up in France to see you, please don't see him alone, will you?

I'm probably being alarmist—we both know Sebastian's not violent, except in the days when he was, with *me*, that is—but I want to tell you to be on your guard. It's an awful lot of money we're talking about, after all.

And now . . . all this shenanigans with my

brother has caused me—especially imprisoned as I am at present—to think of the best way forward for myself. Perhaps it was hearing you re-read the letter from my grandmother that did it, but I've come to some important conclusions. At some point soon, I'd be happy to share those with you, but they are not for now. You have enough to be thinking about. By the way, I officially 'bequeath' in writing the book back to you—please, if you manage to find Volume One, do as you wish with both of them. I can assure you I don't need the money—luckily enough, the new 'children' I adopted are all behaving exceptionally well just now.

I'm hoping you'll respond to this email, firstly because I want to know you've received it and have been pre-warned about Seb, but secondly because I'd love to hear from you.

The house is very quiet without you.

With best regards and love,
Alex x

Having read the email, a horrified Emilie picked up her mobile and made two immediate calls. One to the storage company, leaving a message informing them she was getting divorced and under no circumstances was her husband to have access to any of the possessions from the château, especially not the library. And secondly to Jean, requesting that if Sebastian did turn up, he was to say he hadn't seen her.

'I think I knew that already, Emilie,' Jean had replied sagely.

Then Emilie began an email back to Alex. She thanked him profusely for his warning, apologised for her late reply and said there had been no sightings of Sebastian so far. She said she hoped to hear all about his plans for the future and signed off with a return kiss.

It was dark now. Emilie poured herself a glass of wine and paced around the gîte, feeling restless.

Alex might be worried about her, but in return, she was very concerned about him.

More than concerned . . .

Emilie retired to bed straight after supper. The new mattress, which was so much softer than the old horsehair ones she'd been used to sleeping on, did not help her to relax.

What if Sebastian had returned to Blackmoor Hall and managed to batter his way through the security and into Alex's flat?

No. She stopped herself. Alex was simply her ex-husband's brother and she was not responsible for him.

But . . . Emilie got up and paced around the small bedroom; it was more than that. She missed him. *And* was just as concerned about him as he seemed to be about her.

Emilie stopped pacing suddenly, remembering Jean's words.

'Looks like you picked the wrong brother. . .'

She was tired and over-emotional. And imagining feelings that weren't there.

Emilie took herself back to bed and determinedly closed her eyes.

34

Jean called her two days later.

'I'm afraid I have bad news. Margaux died in the early hours of this morning. I'm not sure what to say to Anton. He's been very brave, but . . .'

'I'll come immediately,' said Emilie.

*   *   *

'Anton has taken himself off for a walk alone in the vines,' said Jean, when Emilie arrived at the cottage.

'Did you tell him?'

'Yes, and he took the news calmly. I've called the aunt in Grasse, who has said she'll take him in, but Anton isn't happy at the thought.'

'No. We must all do what we can to help him.' She sighed.

'He's very attached to you, Emilie,' Jean said quietly.

'And I to him. Certainly for a time I could take him, but . . .'

'I understand.' Jean nodded.

Feeling uncomfortable, Emilie stood up. 'I'll go to him,' she said.

As she walked away from the cottage and towards the vineyards, Emilie asked herself what the 'but' had been when she'd spoken to Jean just now. She was a rich single woman, with an enormous house and, currently, the time to offer to a bereaved young boy. Not only that, but a boy she had become increasingly fond of in the past few weeks. It was unlikely now that she'd marry again. And, of course, she would never have children of her own.

Emilie realised then what the 'but' had been: she was frightened, scared of the responsibility of having a dependant, someone who would need her, whom she would have to put first at every turn. The polar opposite of how her mother had been with her.

Would she be the same kind of mother?

Emilie was terrified she would be.

'That boy needs me, he needs *me* . . .'

Was she up to the task?

Of course she was, she comforted herself. She was like her father—everyone said so. And Édouard had often told her the joy of being needed far outweighed needing.

Emilie realised suddenly that if Anton wanted to stay with her, it was *she* who would be honoured, not him.

She walked in amongst the vines, searching for him. Eventually she saw him, staring disconsolately at the château in the distance, his thin frame wracked with sorrow. A sudden wave of maternal love washed over her, and Emilie's decision was made. She went towards him, her arms outstretched.

He heard her footsteps and turned, trying to wipe away his tears.

'Anton, I'm so, so sorry.' She wrapped her arms around him and, after a few moments, he took courage and did the same to her. They stood together, holding each other as the tears fell down both their cheeks.

When his shoulders had stopped heaving, she

wiped both their faces with the edge of her cardigan.

'There's so little I can say to you, Anton. I know how much you loved her.'

'Jacques said to me this morning that death is a part of life. And I know that somehow I must try and accept it, but I'm not sure I can yet.'

'Jacques is very wise,' Emilie agreed. 'Anton, perhaps this isn't the time to talk of it, but if it would suit you, at least for a while, perhaps you could come and stay at my gîte and keep me company? It's quite lonely there. I could do with a man around the place.'

He looked up at her, amazement in his eyes. 'Are you sure?'

'Very sure. Will you think about it?'

'Emilie, I don't need to think about it! I promise I won't be a bother, and I can help you . . . do things,' Anton offered pathetically.

'Yes, you could. We're both orphans, aren't we?'

'Yes, but . . . I may like it too much, and never want to leave . . .'

'Well, the good news is—' Emilie smiled down at him, then pulled him to her again as she stroked his hair—'you might not have to.'

To:edlmartinieres@orange.fr
From:aecarruthers@blackhall.co.uk

Tuesday 5th

Dearest Em,

It was a relief to hear from you, not that I thought You Know Who would start charging over to France waving a pistol and demanding *my* treasured book back—part of his psyche is that he's a coward. And you might be glad to know he is still yet to return here, so I live in Mona Lisa Towers waiting for his old banger to charge up the drive. My bet is, he's cut his losses and has declared undying love to Bella. (Sorry.) Anyway, as you can imagine, it's pretty lonely here—it comes to something when you have to admit you're even missing the odd shower of abuse from your brother. And on that note, the tension of waiting for him to reappear has confirmed in my mind the plan I talked of in my last email. I mentioned 'my children' were flourishing—in fact, so much so that I sold them to the highest bidder for a dowry of some considerable size. (DON'T TELL YOUR ALMOST EX-HUSBAND THIS, OBVIOUSLY!) But 'tis a fair sum, enough to keep me in foie gras for the rest of my life. And also buy somewhere for myself that's a little less isolated and allows me to consort occasionally with my fellow human beings. I'm currently perusing some details of ground-floor flats in the centre of York, which is a very beautiful city with an awfully nice cathedral.

You might be surprised at this *volte face*, given that I told you I was so determined to stay here. Sadly, the joint ownership of the house has brought nothing but pain. And although a reconciliation between Seb and me was my grandmother's last wish, it hasn't materialised. And I know it never will. So, for both our sakes, I have decided to finally agree

527

to his demand that we sell Blackmoor Hall. One thing I may not have mentioned is the fact I know Seb has run up a huge overdraft secured against his share of the house. I presume the bank has been pressurising him to repay it, which is why he needs to sell so much. He will, of course, be delighted when I tell him and, all in all, I think it's time to sever past ties and move on.

Em, I should also say at this point (which I know may upset you, and is why I've said nothing so far) that I have paid for every penny of the renovations to my apartment in the east wing. *And* for the costs of all my general domestic needs. I received a large settlement through the courts from the insurance company of the driver who rendered me legless (HAH!). I say this because it's important to me you know I haven't been freeloading off my brother. You should also know I initially offered to use my settlement to renovate Blackmoor Hall. It was only when I discovered Seb had mortgaged it to the hilt that I backed off. Funnily enough, he hasn't been my friend ever since.

Anyway, what do you think of my plan to move on? I'm only 80 per cent decided, but I think it's the right thing to do.

To be honest, Em, since you left, I've been horribly lonely. And now I've sold my children too, at rather a loose end. Of course, I may well consider adopting some more . . .

If you have time, do reply with your

thoughts—I was very happy to hear from you.

I miss you.

Alex XX

Emilie had no time to reply as both she and Anton were getting ready to leave for Margaux's funeral. But even as she sat in the beautiful medieval church of Saint Laurent in Gassin, with her hand tightly holding Anton's, she thought of Alex's email.

I miss you.

After the service, many local residents came back to the cottage. The *cave*'s new vintage was tested and approved by the locals.

When the last mourner had left, she saw Anton standing alone, looking drained.

'Why not take yourself upstairs and start packing? We'll be going home soon,' Emilie said gently.

Anton's face brightened a little. 'All right, I will.'

As she watched him trudge disconsolately up the stairs, Emilie was comforted that the decision to let him move in with her after the funeral had taken place was the right one. At least he'd have the newness of beginning afresh after the terrible ending today.

Jean appeared in the kitchen. 'Emilie, my father's asked you if you would join us in the garden whilst Anton is upstairs.'

'Of course,' she agreed and followed Jean outside.

Jacques was in the chair he'd sat in all afternoon. He'd been very much the host, and Emilie had seen how he loved his local community.

'Sit down, Emilie,' he said gravely. 'I wish to speak to you. Jean, you stay too.'

There was a note in his voice that indicated he had something serious to discuss with her.

Jean poured them all a fresh glass of wine and then sat down next to Emilie.

'I have decided it's the moment to tell you who Sophia's child is. And when I tell you, I hope you will understand why I have waited until now to do so.' Jacques cleared his throat, which was tired and hoarse from all the talking he had done during the day.

'After Constance and I took Victoria to the convent orphanage and Constance left for England, I begged Édouard yet again to reconsider,' Jacques began. 'However, he would not hear of it and, a few days later, left the château to return to Paris. I, however, was wracked with guilt. I knew Sophia de la Martinières's child was lying, unloved and unwanted, only a few kilometres away.' Jacques shrugged his shoulders. 'Try as I did to rationalise the fact that war had left such terrible unwanted human detritus behind and that I was not responsible for Victoria, I could not forget her. I had grown to love her, you see. After two weeks of battling with myself, I decided to return to the orphanage to see if Victoria had already been adopted. If she had, then it was God's will and I would not search for her. But, of course, she hadn't been.' Jacques shook his head. 'By then, Victoria was over four months old. The moment I walked into the nursery, her eyes lit up and she recognised me. She smiled . . . Emilie, she smiled at me.' Jacques put his head in his hands. 'When she did that, I knew it was impossible for me to simply abandon her.'

Unable to continue, Jacques sat in silence as Jean put an arm around his father's shoulder, trying to comfort him.

'So—' Jacques looked up suddenly—'I returned home and tried to think what I could do. Adopting her myself was an option, but not one I felt was right for the child. Men in those days didn't have the first idea of how to care for a baby and Victoria needed the loving arms of a mother. I wracked my brains to try to think who would take her locally, so that at least, if I was unable to care for her, I could watch over her as she grew. Eventually, I came across such a woman. She had one child already—I knew her because, before the war, her husband had worked in the vineyard for me during the *vendange*. I went to visit her and discovered her husband had not yet returned home and she'd heard nothing from him. She and the child were desperate . . . starving, as so many were after the war,' Jacques explained. 'But she was a good woman and I could tell from the child she already had that she was a caring mother. I asked her whether she would be prepared to adopt another one. At first, of course, she refused, saying she could barely feed her own child's mouth, as I knew she would. So then I offered her a sum of money. A significant sum of money—' Jacques nodded—'and she accepted.'

'Papa, how could you offer this?' asked Jean. 'I know how poor you were after the war.'

'Yes, I was. But . . .' Jacques paused and gazed suddenly at Emilie, who could see he was agonising over telling her. 'Your father, Emilie, had given me something before he left for Paris, after Constance had returned to England. He'd pressed it into my hands, rather than using words. Perhaps it was his way of asking my forgiveness for refusing to accept Sophia's child and of making amends. So I contacted someone I knew who dealt in the black market, which thrived just after the war. I asked him to value what your father had given to me, to raise the money to pay for the kind woman I knew to adopt Victoria.'

'What was it my father gave you, Jacques?' asked Emilie softly.

'It was a book, a book he knew I'd loved. It was very old, and the plates in it were exquisite. I knew he'd managed to find the second volume to complete the set—you remember I told you, Emilie, that he sent it from Paris with Armand, the courier, to tell us of his safe escape? And that Édouard gave it to Constance to take to England?'

'Yes,' answered Emilie, with a glimmer of a smile on her face. 'I know the book. It's called *The History of French Fruit.*'

'You are correct,' said Jacques, 'and I discovered my copy, Volume One, was very rare and very old. I managed to sell it for enough to pay the woman to take Sophia's baby into her home. Forgive me for what I did, Emilie. I should not have sold your father's gift to me. But it bought his niece's safety and her future.'

Emilie's eyes were blurred with tears and she was almost too choked to speak. 'Jacques, believe me,' she said eventually, 'I think what you did with the book could not have been more perfect.'

'How much did the sale raise?' asked Jean.

'Ten thousand francs,' said Jacques. 'Which, in those days, when so many were starving, was a fortune. I paid the woman a thousand francs immediately, and told her she would receive another five hundred francs a year until the child reached sixteen. I couldn't risk giving her the money all at once; I wanted to make sure she would earn it by taking care of the baby. The woman knew nothing of the child's background. I made completely sure of that. She also asked me sif she could rename Victoria after her own mother.'

'And you said yes, of course?' said Jean.

'I did. And, thank God, my choice was a success,' breathed Jacques. 'In fact, when the girl was five, the woman refused to take money for her any longer. Her husband had returned and their circumstances had improved. She said she loved the child as her own and felt uncomfortable receiving recompense for her. I'm happy I chose the right woman. Emilie, your aunt's child could not have found a more loving or happier home.'

'Thank you, from the bottom of my heart, and on behalf of my aunt and my father, for doing what you did. Jacques—' the question was now burning on Emilie's tongue—'who is the child? What's her name?'

'Her name is—'

Jacques swallowed hard and tried again.

'Her name was Margaux.'

35

All three of them sat silently, working through the ramifications of what Jacques had just revealed.

'Do you understand, Emilie,' said Jacques eventually, 'why I was so concerned about revealing the baby's identity? If I had done, it would have thrown Margaux's life into disarray. She had worked as a housekeeper at the château for over fifteen years. After your father died, the old château housekeeper, whom you may remember, retired. Margaux's mother was by then a friend and I recommended her daughter to Valérie, your mother.'

'I now understand why you've felt you could say nothing, Papa,' Jean said softly. 'How would Margaux have reacted to knowing that she'd spent so long working for the de la Martinières, when in fact she was one of them?'

'Exactly,' agreed Jacques. 'But, of course, now Margaux has left us, and Anton, like a homing pigeon, has landed on our doorstep and a relationship has blossomed between the two of you ...' Jacques indicated Emilie. 'So I had to tell you. The boy who is at present packing to return to your home with you is in fact your first cousin once removed.'

Emilie listened as Jean, analytical as ever, probed for more details. She understood now ... understood why everything about Anton felt familiar ... they shared the de la Martinières blood. Seeing Anton sitting on the floor that day, reading in the library, with his fine features and dark hair—no wonder a shiver had passed through her. Ironically, it was not his grandmother he took after, but his great-uncle, Édouard.

'Emilie,' continued Jacques, 'I've decided I must pass the decision to you. It will be up to you whether you tell Anton of his heritage. Many would say it's now irrelevant and would perhaps burden him. But Anton Duvall is the only other surviving de la Martinières.'

In the ensuing silence, Emilie listened to the birds preparing for sunset.

'Whether Anton was the son of my housekeeper, or related to me by blood, the decision to offer him a home would have been one and the same,' she said eventually, leaning forward and patting the old man's knee. 'Jacques, I want to tell you two things. The first is that I can think of no better way of using my father's gift to you than to buy his niece's safety. And, secondly, I'm so very happy you have trusted me enough to tell me the truth. But you must also know that, to me, the fact that Anton is related to my family is merely an added bonus. It's felt natural from the first time I met him.' She smiled. 'Really, Jacques, you've made me very happy tonight. I hope at some point I can repay you.'

'Emilie, Emilie . . .' Jacques reached out his hands to her and she clasped them. 'Maybe it's fate, but undoubtedly Margaux's death provided a sad resolution to my dilemma. Anton has a home and you will make a compassionate mother to him. Édouard lost his compassion some time during the war, as many of my compatriots did. Don't lose yours, will you?'

'No, I won't. I swear,' Emilie said firmly.

'Life is too short for hatred and bigotry. When you find something good, seize it with both hands.' Jacques gave her a weak smile.

'I will,' said Emilie, 'I promise.'

'Are we ready to go?'

All three turned to see Anton standing there, a small suitcase in his hand. He looked bewildered as he registered the obvious emotion hanging in the air.

'It would be better if we arrived at our home before dark, Emilie,' he said quietly.

'Yes.' Emilie stood up and offered Anton her hand. 'We'll go before the light fades.'

*　　*　　*

Once Anton was settled in his new room and in bed, Emilie, rather than feeling exhausted, felt elated. She would decide another time whether and when she would tell Anton about his past. The most important thing for now was that he felt loved and wanted. There was a chance, because he was such a bright boy, that if she told him immediately that he was related to her, Anton might assume this was the only reason she was prepared to take him in. She wanted to let the bond and the trust grow stronger and deeper before she told him anything further.

Switching on her computer, she reread the email message from Alex. Then stood up, so full of nervous energy, she couldn't sit still.

'I miss you too,' she told her laptop as she paced around the sitting room. 'A lot,' she added, just for good measure. 'In fact, more than a lot.'

She stopped suddenly in her tracks; was she

being ridiculous?

Perhaps. Any relationship she'd so far forged with Alex had been under difficult circumstances, to say the least. But the odd feeling that entered her tummy when she thought of him—the one that had been there for so long now she couldn't remember it *not* being there—wasn't disappearing.

More pacing . . . of course, it might be a total disaster—but why not? Nothing was forever, as she had realised so painfully in the past few months. Life could turn on the switch of a coin. So what harm could it do? If she had learned one thing from both her past and her present, it was that life did not provide second chances. It asked you, *begged* you, to go out and grab what was on offer, to recognise the good and try to discard the bad. Just as Jacques had implored her to do earlier . . .

Emilie yawned suddenly then flopped onto the sofa like a rag doll. She would think about it tomorrow, and in the cold light of morning, if she still felt the same, then she would write the email. With that, she heaved herself from the sofa and went off to bed.

To:aecarruthers@blackhall.co.uk
From:edlmartinieres@orange.fr

Thursday

Dear Alex

Thank you for your email. I thought I would write firstly and tell you I know what happened to Volume One of the book. Suffice to say it's no longer in the de

537

la Martinières's possession, but it's a long story, which I would have to tell you in person. All I can say is that the book went to buy the safety of a member of my family and I can't think of a more fitting use of it and its worth. It also pleases me that Sebastian's search was pointless from the start, and that the money from the sale of the book went to a far higher cause than his greed.

Secondly, I seem to have adopted a child. He is a twelve-year-old boy called Anton and, again, it's another very long and complicated story. Thirdly, given your indecision over your future, I wondered whether it would be at all helpful for you to have some space and time to think about it. My gîte is small, but all on one floor and has a spare bedroom. And although there are not many human beings around us, only grapes, I hope that Anton and I might suffice for company.

Let me know if you can come. We can be three orphans together!

I miss you too.

E xxx

To:edlmartinieres@orange.fr
From:aecarruthers@blackhall.co.uk

Dearest Em,

Thanks for the invitation. Will arrive next Monday at Nice Airport at 13.40 hours. If it's not possible to collect me (and my wheelchair!), please let me know. Otherwise, looking forward to it immensely and, of course, meeting Anton.

A xxxx

PS Thank God I don't have to miss you any longer, just look forward to seeing you.

The Life Inside Me

Blindly striving to protect you,
Knowing that you live in me.
Forged from love, a soul so perfect.
You will be all you can be.

I must give my body to you,
New life grows and thrives inside.
One day we will live in freedom
Never more be forced to hide.

You must know the love that made
you
Shining like the brightest sun.
I will tell you of your father,
Don't be frightened, little one.

I can't see the force that made you,
Or the hearts that beat in time.
Yet I feel you, so I see you
Inside me now, oh child of mine.

Sophia de la Martinières
May 1944

541

Epilogue

One Year Later

Emilie unlocked the front door of the château and swung it wide open. Anton helped push Alex's wheelchair over the threshold and into an echoing entrance hall, empty apart from a ladder one of the decorators had left against a wall for applying the final coat.

'Wow,' said Anton, looking up above him to the ceiling, 'I think it's got bigger in here.'

'It's the fresh white colour after seeing weeks of plaster,' explained Emilie. She looked down at the floor and nodded in approval. 'They've done a very good job of restoring the marble. I would have hated to lose it.'

'Yes,' said Alex, following her eyeline. Then he glanced towards the stairs. 'I'm a little concerned that one of those ghastly chair systems to hoist me up there might not look quite in keeping with all this elegance.'

'That's why you're here.' Emilie winked at Anton. 'Shall we show him?'

'Yes!' Anton's eyes danced with excitement. 'Follow me.'

Leading Alex along the echoing corridors, the rooms still in a state of disarray—it would be another few months before the inside works were finally completed—Anton took them to the back of the house and into the lobby next to the kitchen. Angling Alex's chair in front of a door, he pressed a button on a panel, and the door slid open

542

smoothly.

Alex gazed inside. 'It's a lift.'

'Correct, Monsieur Detective.' Anton smiled. 'And it's my favourite new toy. Shall we take a ride?'

As they stepped inside and Anton pressed the button to reclose the door, Alex's eyes swept up towards Emilie's. They were misty with tears. 'Thank you,' he mouthed.

'Don't thank me, this has been put in for when *I'm* too old to climb the stairs.' She grinned. 'And just in case you want to stay for a while.'

The phrase had become their shared joke. Alex had arrived a year ago, and even though they hadn't made any plans for the future to be together, nor were either of them intending to ever be apart. They had taken each day as it had come, neither feeling they had to formalise the arrangement, yet knowing that as each month passed their bond grew deeper and stronger.

The mutual admiration society between Alex and Anton had been evident from the start. Anton's bright, enquiring mind soaked up Alex's intellect and Emilie knew the relationship was hugely beneficial for both of them. Their strange little family might look odd to outsiders, but the three of them had found happiness, contentment and peace together.

Anton still knew nothing of his true blood but, very soon, their relationship to each other would be formalised—Anton would be adopted to enable him to use his rightful surname and to one day inherit the château. Similarly, perhaps when that happened, she and Alex would legalise their own arrangements, but Emilie was in no hurry. Life was perfect the way it was.

She watched Anton's excited face as the doors opened and the three of them emerged onto the wide landing.

'Good God!' Alex commented. 'You could put a marquee and parking for two hundred people on this,' he joked as Emilie indicated Anton should turn to the left.

'I thought this could be ours,' Emilie said as Anton steered Alex through her parents' beautiful old bedroom and then into an anteroom. Once Valérie's dressing room, it was now fitted out as a disabled bathroom, with everything Alex would need to provide himself with the independence he craved.

'The builders haven't tiled it yet. I thought you might like to choose the colour and style,' Emilie commented.

'It's wonderful, my darling, thank you,' said Alex, moved almost beyond words at the effort Emilie had made for him.

'And no, we don't have to share the facilities.' She grinned. 'My dressing room and bathroom are over there.' She indicated as Alex wheeled himself back into the centre of the bedroom. 'Do you like the view?' she asked.

'It's simply stunning.' Alex looked through the long windows across the garden and the sweeping vineyards to the hill of Gassin in the distance. 'Long time since I've looked down on anything,' he muttered, his voice croaky with emotion.

'Alex, come and see my bedroom,' interrupted Anton. 'Emilie said I can choose the colours when it's ready to be painted, as long as it isn't black.'

Emilie smiled and watched them leave the

room. She stayed behind, still looking out of the window, watching the light pour in through it. Two years ago, her mother had died in here, and as she savoured the view she felt a mixture of conflicting emotions. She thought of her father, whose loss of those he loved had made him turn inwards on himself. He'd hidden away from the world here in the library for most of her childhood.

She'd also begun to feel an empathy for her mother; from reading the love letters she'd written to her husband, she'd realised how Valérie had adored him. She also must have struggled to gain love and attention from a man who was too damaged to give it freely. And, in retrospect, Emilie realised Valérie had spent much of her marriage in Paris, alone.

The fact that Sophia's grandson would be restored to his family, and that she had taken Anton in simply through compassion, at least righted some of the terrible wrongs of the past. The circle had been completed and it was a whole new dawn.

Emilie turned and walked slowly towards the door to find Alex and Anton. As she left the room, she realised that the lost, angry little girl, who'd screamed and wept over her mother's lifeless body two years ago, had finally grown up.

*   *   *

'I must admit, I'm eager to move in now that I've seen my new bathroom,' said Alex later as he lowered the sides of his chair and twisted first his torso and then his legs onto the bed, next to her.

'The foreman has told me no more than three

545

months, so we'll definitely be in for autumn and our first Christmas,' confirmed Emilie.

'By the way,' said Alex, 'I received an email earlier from my solicitors. Seb's found a buyer for Blackmoor Hall. I'm sure he's thrilled. And I'm equally sure that he'll try and fleece me of my share of what's left of the profits.' Alex raised his eyebrows. 'My lawyer said that the deeds of the house had a charge of over £350,000 on them, the exact size of Seb's current overdraft.' He shook his head. 'I'll guarantee any further money he gets from the sale will have disappeared within a year. I suppose that at least Bella knows him of old. She must love him to put up with him. By the way, heard anything more from the divorce lawyer?'

'No, only that Sebastian has come back with even more outrageous demands,' Emilie replied. 'Of course, he won't get what he wants, but I almost feel like paying him off now just to get rid of him. The lawyers' fees will end up costing more than the settlement.'

'I'm sure my presence in the mix hasn't exactly helped,' sighed Alex. 'It's meant that Sebastian's been able to assuage any guilt of his own by painting you as a hussy and me as a cad and a bounder, stealing his wife from right under his nose.'

'I'm sure.' Emilie paused before she said, 'Alex, there's something I haven't told you. I've invited someone to visit. And he arrives tomorrow. I was sure it was a good idea at the time, but now . . . now, I'm nervous,' she admitted.

'You'd better tell me, then,' Alex suggested.

*   *   *

Jacques was dozing by the fire as he heard a car pull up in front of the cottage. It had been a long, cold winter and once more he had succumbed to bronchitis. He'd wondered, as he did every year, whether he'd live to see another summer.

He heard the door to the kitchen open and remembered Emilie had arranged to bring a friend of hers round for lunch.

Jean appeared first in the sitting room. 'Papa, are you awake?'

'Yes.' Jacques opened his eyes as his son walked towards him.

'Papa—' Jean took hold of his hand—'Emilie has brought someone to see you.'

'Hello, Jacques,' Emilie said as she led her guest into the room with her.

Jacques stared at the guest. He was an old man, like him. Tall, straight-backed and elegant.

'Jacques,' the man spoke to him, 'do you remember me?'

His French had a strong accent. He was definitely familiar, but Jacques struggled to place his face.

'It is over fifty years since we last stood in this room together,' the man prompted.

Jacques stared at the faded, but still piercing blue eyes. And finally realised exactly who this man was.

'Frederik?'

'Yes, Jacques, it is I.'

'My God! I cannot believe it!'

Jacques dropped his son's arm and refused help as he hoisted himself to standing. The two men stared at each other for a few seconds, a multitude

547

of memories passing between them. Then Jacques held out his arms to the German, and the two men embraced.

*   *   *

Alex arrived with Anton at the cottage after lunch, as Emilie had requested. He'd recently bought himself a custom-made car, controlled with his arms, rather than his legs, which had revolutionised his life and given him some autonomy, albeit only reserved for short journeys and accompanied by Emilie or Anton.

Anton lifted the wheelchair out of the back of the car and brought it round to Alex's door. 'Who is it that Emilie wants me to meet?' he asked as he helped Alex from the car into his chair.

'I think I'll leave it to her to tell you that,' Alex replied.

As the two of them entered the kitchen, Anton saw Emilie, Jean and Jacques, and another old man, drinking coffee at the kitchen table.

'Hello,' Anton said awkwardly.

Immediately, Emilie stood up, came over to him and put an arm around Anton's shoulder.

'Anton,' she said as she watched Frederik's eyes fill with tears at the sight of the boy. 'This is your grandfather, Frederik. And, when you're ready, he has a story to tell you about your family . . .'

Acknowledgements

My very grateful thanks go to Jeremy Trevathan, Catherine Richards and the team at Pan Macmillan. Jonathan Lloyd, Lucia Rae and Melissa Pimentel at Curtis Brown. Olivia Riley, my PA, Jacquelyn Heslop, Susan Grix and Richard Jemmett. Susan Boyd, Sam Gurney, Helene Ruhn, Rita Kalagate, Almuth Andreae, Johanna Castillo and Judith Curr, each one a friend and a fount of invaluable advice, both personal and professional.

Damien and Anne Rey-Brot and their friends and family at Le Pescadou in Gassin, Tony Bourne, and Monsieur Chapelle of the Domaine du Bourriane, whose surname, château and *cave* was borrowed by Constance and her fellow characters before I knew such a family and their beautiful home actually existed in reality. I walked into my own fictional story last August and it was a humbling and magical experience. Thank you all for the detail you gave me. Any mistakes are certainly mine, not yours. Also Jan Goessing, who gave me a vivid potted history of pre-war Germany, and Marcus Tyers, Naomi Ritchie and Emily Jenkins at St Mary's Bookshop, Stamford, who kindly sourced two very old and valuable French volumes on which to base my fictional rare books.

To all my wonderful foreign publishers, who have invited me to their countries and welcomed me with open arms. The travel and culture feeds my imagination and provides me with fertile ground for future settings.

And of course, 'The Family', whose support and encouragement in this past, manic year has been invaluable. My children: Harry for the insightful editorial comments and the speeches; Bella for the initial plot discussions and naming two of the main characters; Leonora for the beautiful poem which she wrote for me as 'Sophia' at the same age; and Kit for being the household's no. 1 Amazon customer . . . in the sports section! My mother, Janet, 'Grandpa Johnson', my sister, Georgia, and my husband, Stephen, who has been simply amazing.

And, lastly, to every single reader across the world who has spent their hard-earned money on one of my books. Without each one of you, I'd be a very miserable writer without an audience and I'm honoured that you choose my stories to read. Thank you.

Lucinda Riley, May 2012